The
French
Wife

The
French
Wife

Diney
Costeloe

HEAD
ZEUS

9 7 5 3 1 2 4 6 8

A catalogue record for this book is available from
the British Library.

ISBN (HB): 9781789543292
ISBN (XTPB): 9781789543308
ISBN (E): 9781789543285

Typeset by Divaddict Publishing Solutions Ltd

Printed and bound in Great Britain by
CPI Group (UK) Ltd, Croydon CR0 4YY

Head of Zeus Ltd
First Floor East
5–8 Hardwick Street
London EC1R 4RG

WWW.HEADOFZEUS.COM

Prologue

It was almost dark and she was freezing. The floor and the walls of the cell were stone, damp and slippery. She sat on the small heap of straw piled into a corner, the only light illuminating her prison filtering through a barred window high above her. She curled into a ball, her arms wrapped round her body, trying to retain some warmth, but her clothes were torn and her body was bruised and she shook with cold and fear. Then she heard it, the key scraping in the lock, and when the door opened she saw his face, lit by the candle he carried. Flickering flame showed her the black beard, the scarred cheeks, the cruel eyes, now alight with lustful anticipation.

'On your feet!' he ordered. 'It's playtime!'

She screamed then, a shrill, penetrating scream of terror, a scream that woke her and left her shivering in the dark.

Chapter 1

Paris 1876

There was a silence about the house. The curtains were drawn across the windows and the old priest lay in bed in his room attended by his housekeeper, Madame Agathe Sauze, sitting at his bedside, keeping him company in his dying hours. Father Thomas, the curate who also lived in the St Jacques Clergy House, had administered the last rites earlier in the day and now it was simply a matter of time before the old priest slipped away to meet his maker.

Agathe had been Father Lenoir's housekeeper for nearly thirty years, and over that time their mutual regard had grown into a comfortable friendship. Well aware of her common sense and respecting her judgement, the priest occasionally asked her opinion on parish matters. Agathe always considered her answers carefully, and always spoke to him with the formality due to his cloth. In public Father Lenoir treated her with the same respect, but in private he had used her Christian name and there was a genuine affection between them.

Now he was dying, and as she kept watch at his bedside,

she considered her life without him. Father Thomas had been dismayed that Father Lenoir should confide parish affairs to his housekeeper and had long ago decided that when he had his own parish, there would be no such impropriety. Discussion of such business with a mere layperson – and a woman into the bargain – would never happen when he was in charge. He had been shocked that the old priest had allowed her to sit with him in his last hours, but when he, Father Thomas, had tried to dismiss her from the bedroom, the old man had opened his eyes and murmured, 'Leave us alone! She can stay. She's my friend.'

His friend indeed! She was his housekeeper, a paid employee! What right had she to be the one to see him into eternity? Father Thomas, now clearly excluded, withdrew from the room, every line of his body rigid with indignation.

Father Thomas will be an exacting man to work for, Agathe thought as she sat at the bedside and listened to the old man's ragged breathing. Perhaps it was time to leave the Clergy House, but, after so many years, where would she go? She had no home of her own, her only family an estranged sister, and very few friends.

Maybe, she thought suddenly, the bishop will send another priest to take over the church of St Jacques. After all, Father Thomas is still young; perhaps he'll be considered too inexperienced to take on the responsibility of such a large parish.

The thought raised her spirits a little. She closed her eyes for a moment or two, but jerked awake as there was a slight movement in the bed. She realised that Father Lenoir's eyes were open again, gazing unseeing into the air. Then his face relaxed in a smile and the rasp of his breath was silent.

Agathe leaned forward and gently closed his eyes. She tried

to pray for his departing soul, but somehow the words would not come and she simply sat in the silence of the empty room.

Once the funeral was over, Father Thomas took over the parish, the Clergy House and the lives of the two women who looked after him. Madame Sauze continued as housekeeper, assisted by Annette, the orphan she had rescued some years earlier, with Father Lenoir's blessing, from St Luke's orphanage to train as a housemaid. The young priest was determined to show his bishop that he was perfectly capable of running the parish, and the bishop, taking the easy route, made no move to appoint a new, more experienced parish priest. For a while Father Thomas's future hung in the air, but after several weeks he was summoned to the bishop's office and told that for the present, at least, he was responsible for the parish. He was no longer a curate, but a parish priest with responsibility for a church, a congregation and the souls of men. A person of importance.

Thus established in his position, the young priest called Agathe Sauze into his study and told her that he no longer needed her services.

'The girl, Annette, is perfectly able to look after me here. It doesn't take two women to look after the simple requirements of a priest.'

Simple requirements of a priest! Apart from the general keeping of a house, Agathe thought of the large meals Father Thomas consumed without comment; the spotless vestments she was expected to provide for the church services. With Father Lenoir that had been a privilege, her pride in his pristine appearance always appreciated with a smile of recognition or word of thanks. She received no such acknowledgement from Father Thomas. Would young Annette, aged only about eighteen, be able to cope with the demands of running the Clergy House and looking after the daily needs of its incumbent? It would not be easy.

Agathe looked him firmly in the eye. 'So, you're throwing me out into the street,' she said flatly.

'Certainly not,' snapped Father Thomas. 'You are getting old and I am releasing you so that you may retire.'

'But I don't want to retire.'

'That's your problem, madame, not mine. I no longer require your services. You must be out of this house in two weeks' time.'

'But I have nowhere to go.' Agathe heard the dismay in her voice and struggled to hide it.

'Which is why,' Father Thomas replied smugly, 'I am giving you two weeks to find somewhere. It's the Christian thing to do.'

Agathe returned to the kitchen to break the news to Annette. Over the years she had become fond of the girl. She had taught her to cook and clean properly and in the evenings she had taught her to read and write. At first Annette had dismissed 'book learning' as a waste of time, but Agathe had insisted, and as she came to grips with it Annette had realised that it wasn't that difficult and had discovered a whole new world in the few books Agathe had to offer her.

'You never know when such learning may come in useful,' Agathe had said, 'and in the meantime you can enjoy reading.' And Annette had found that she did.

Now, when Agathe told Annette what the priest had said, the girl turned pale.

'You can't leave me with him,' she cried. 'Madame, don't leave me with him.'

Agathe smiled ruefully. 'Annette, I can't take you with me, I've nowhere to go. At least you will have a roof over your head and food on the table.' It was the best she could offer. She was well aware that if she took Annette with her and both of them became vagrant, the girl could well end up on the streets, selling her body to keep herself alive. 'I looked after Father Lenoir for nearly thirty years, and in that time we learned to get along. You'll get used to Father Thomas's ways and find that you rub along together.'

Alone in her room she considered her options and found they were very few. She was only sixty but she knew it would be difficult to find another place. No one would want to employ an elderly woman who might become infirm, when they could get someone so much younger with years of work left in her. Who could she turn to? Briefly she thought of Madame Rosalie St Clair.

Agathe had taken care of Hélène St Clair, Madame Rosalie's daughter, when, at the age of eleven, she'd been lost and alone in the city during the Communard siege. When the fighting was over and Hélène had been reunited with her parents, Madame St Clair had come to visit Agathe at the Clergy House, bringing Hélène with her. She had wanted to thank Agathe and Father Lenoir for taking her daughter in off the streets. She had been deeply grateful and the two women had got on well, speaking as equals. Agathe had seen Hélène once or twice more when the family was in Paris, but that had been in the early days. Since then she had seen neither mother nor daughter for several years. Would the gratitude so sincerely expressed then still be as strong now? Could she approach them for help after all this time? Turn up out of the blue and expect their gratitude to become practical assistance? No. It would be asking for charity;

Agathe Sauze would ask that of no one and she dismissed the option from her mind.

Another possibility was to ask for work from the bishop. Not from the man himself, of course, he was far too exalted to deal with such mundane matters, but perhaps one of his chaplains would know of a parish priest who needed a housekeeper. It was something she had done all her life and there seemed little else she could do. Eventually, as the two weeks were closing in on her, she steeled herself and made the approach to the bishop's office.

She was greeted with a blank stare from the young priest who had been sent to find out what she wanted.

'Madame,' he said dismissively, 'if your own priest has dispensed with your services, he must have good reason. I'm afraid it is not something the bishop or this office can concern itself with. You must look for charity elsewhere.'

'I am not looking for charity, Monsieur l'Abbé,' she replied sharply, 'I am looking for work and was simply asking if you knew of a parish priest in need of a housekeeper. Clearly you do not!' As the young priest blinked in astonishment at her riposte, she turned on her heel and, with a ramrod straight back, walked to the door before saying, 'I'll bid you good afternoon... Father!'

With that avenue closed to her Agathe finally turned her thoughts to the only other possibility. She had told Father Thomas that she had nowhere to go, and in reality that was true, but her thoughts now turned unwillingly to her elder sister, Fleur. She and Fleur had never been close. As children they had continually quarrelled; as young women they had disagreed on almost everything; and when Fleur had decided to marry Yves Bastien, Agathe had disliked him on sight and had tried to make her change her mind. This was the final straw for Fleur. She was the elder and wasn't prepared to listen to any advice about her choice of husband from her younger sister.

'He's a bully,' Agathe warned her. 'Why would you marry him? Listen to the way he speaks to you, Fleur, ordering you about, even before you're married.'

'He's a man of means,' returned Fleur. 'He has a good business and he owns his apartment. I'll have a home of my own. This is the best chance in life that I'll get, Agathe, and I mean to grab it with both hands, so don't you dare tell me what I should or shouldn't do.'

Yves Bastien was a butcher whose family had owned their shop and the three apartments above it for generations. When his elderly sister who'd kept house for him died, it was clear to Agathe, if not to Fleur, that Yves was not looking for a wife but an unpaid servant to replace her.

'But,' Agathe said, 'you don't love him.'

'What has love to do with it?' demanded Fleur. 'If we marry it will suit us both. He's looking for a wife and I'm looking for the security that he can provide.'

'You will never be safe, married to a bully like him!' cried Agathe in a last bid to make her sister see sense. 'You've seen what he's like when he's drunk!'

'It's nothing to do with you,' snapped Fleur. 'Just mind your own business!'

Within the month Fleur and Yves were married and from then on the sisters had hardly spoken.

Agathe had been proved right, and though she never admitted it to her sister, Fleur found herself trapped in a loveless and abusive marriage, from which there was no escape. Yves dominated her in every respect, making her life a misery, until, that was, coming home one afternoon already reeling from midday drink, he staggered out in front of a coal merchant's waggon. The horses reared in fright, knocking him to the ground, and their hooves came plunging down on his head, killing him instantly. Her husband was dead, and when they came to tell her of this tragedy, Fleur's only emotion was profound relief. With no other family to lay claim to his possessions, everything he'd owned was now Fleur's, and she dealt with her new prosperity shrewdly. She rented the ground-floor shop to Yves's erstwhile apprentice and continued to live above in the apartment that had been her married home. The rents from the apartments on the two floors above provided further income. At last Fleur had the security she had so longed for; she had the apartment and enough money to live on, and with no children, she had only herself to please. Her relief at her new-found security she shared with no one, not even her estranged sister.

Now, reluctantly, Agathe set out to visit her, but before knocking at her door, stood outside in the street. She peered in through the window of the butcher's shop. The apprentice, now a master butcher himself, seemed to be doing a brisk trade. Chickens, their wrung necks dangling, hung above the counter; a butchered sheep swung from a hook on the ceiling and even as she watched, the man sharpened a large knife and sliced meat from the carcass for his waiting customer.

Agathe turned away from the shop and looked back along the cobbled street. It was narrow, lined with tall buildings similar to Fleur's; a street from an earlier age, it had a gully down the middle to carry away water and much else, but if it wasn't the best address in Paris, it wasn't the worst either.

Pull yourself together, she admonished herself. You've nowhere else to go and it'll only be for a very short time, just until you find yourself another position.

The door to the upper floors stood beside that of the shop, and when she pushed it open Agathe found herself in a narrow hallway from which a staircase ascended to the floors above. Slowly she made her way up the stairs and again paused outside the door with the single name beside it. Bastien. Hesitantly, she stepped forward and, grasping the knocker, let it fall.

When Fleur opened the door and found her sister on the threshold, she took an involuntary step backwards.

'Well,' she said acidly, 'and to what do I owe this honour?'

Not an auspicious opening, but she stood aside and let Agathe enter the apartment. She led her sister through an ill-lit hallway into a fair-sized room with long, narrow windows facing the street below. Dust motes danced in the shafts of afternoon sun playing on the old, heavy furniture that crowded the space and on the heavy curtains that attempted to conceal a small kitchen at the far end of the room.

Fleur did not sit down, nor did she offer her sister a seat; she simply stood with hands on hips and waited for Agathe to explain why she had come.

Uninvited, Agathe took a seat on a heavy sofa and then wished she hadn't as Fleur continued to tower over her.

Agathe gave herself a mental shake and, drawing a deep breath, said, 'I've come to ask if I can stay with you for a few days. Father Lenoir has died and Father Thomas no longer wishes me to be his housekeeper.'

Fleur remained silent, looking down at her, and so Agathe went on, 'It would only be for a few days until I find myself another job.'

'And where will you find one?' asked Fleur, scorn in her voice. 'Who's going to employ an old woman like you?'

It echoed her own question, but Agathe replied firmly, 'I don't know yet, but I intend to find someone. I have no wish to be a burden to you.'

Fleur looked at her, her brain whirling. She was now sixty-three. She was lonely and tired of managing for herself. Here was a chance to deal with both these problems. She could agree to let Agathe have the tiny room, meant for a maid and currently used for storage, but only on the understanding that she would play the part of that maid while she was there. Fleur had no intention of paying her, but she would shelter her and feed her as a sister should, which, she considered, would be more than enough recompense.

'I've a suggestion,' she said at last, and, sitting down, made her offer.

'Just until I find somewhere else,' stipulated Agathe.

'Of course,' agreed her sister, knowing there was little likelihood of that.

The next day Agathe Sauze left the Clergy House for the last time, carrying her few possessions in a small suitcase and her meagre savings in a purse tied round her waist, and moved in with her sister.

Chapter 2

It was some weeks after Agathe left the house that Annette began to discover Father Thomas's 'ways'.

At first he'd hardly spoken to her, just expected his food to be on the table, his clothes to be laundered and the house to be cleaned. Agathe had taught Annette well and she had no trouble performing these tasks. She kept the house clean and tidy and took messages for the priest when he was out of the house. The first time she had written down a message, Father Thomas had looked at her askance.

'Where did *you* learn to read and write?' he demanded.

'Please, Monsieur l'Abbé,' she replied, addressing him as he had stipulated that she should, 'Madame Sauze taught me.'

Father Thomas pursed his lips. That interfering old woman again, he thought, but he looked at Annette with new interest in his eyes. She was young, not more than eighteen, and had a certain awkward prettiness. She was, of course, a child of shame, dumped as a newborn bundle on the doorstep at St Luke's. As such, obviously conceived in sin, she was hardly worthy of thought, and provided with bed and board, she was paid a few sous a month, hardly more than a slave.

Over the next few weeks things began to change. To his

dismay Father Thomas found himself watching her. When she came into the dining room to serve his meals his eyes followed her, aware of the fluid movement of her maturing body unconfined beneath her shapeless, black uniform dress.

Child of the devil, he thought. Conceived in sin and now tempting him as Eve had tempted Adam. For several days he closed his mind to the way she 'flaunted' herself, provoking him to sin, but she was there, in the house, and he found it increasingly difficult to ignore her and his own response.

It was on a dark November evening, when she was in the kitchen clearing away the supper dishes before sitting down to her own evening meal, that she suddenly found him at the kitchen door.

'I am going to a meeting now,' he said. 'There is no need to wait up for me.'

This surprised Annette. If Father Thomas had no evening meetings he normally remained in his study, having curtly dismissed her after supper. If he was going out on parish business he expected her to remain downstairs and wait for his return, despite the fact that he always insisted he should lock up himself.

'Thank you, Monsieur l'Abbé.' She spoke with downcast eyes and waited until she heard the front door close behind him before she heaved a sigh of relief and went up to her attic bedroom, where she lit her candle and closed her door. It was cold in the room and she undressed quickly, putting on her nightgown and wrapping her blanket round her as she sat up in bed to read a news sheet she had picked up off the street on her way to the market. Sometime later she heard the front door bang and after a moment Father Thomas's heavy tread as he made his way upstairs. To her dismay he did not stop on the first floor, where he had taken over

Father Lenoir's bedroom, but continued up the steep stairs that led to the attics. Hurriedly Annette blew out her candle and, turning her back to the door, curled up in her blanket as if already asleep. She waited with bated breath as she heard the footsteps stop outside her door. There was a long pause and then she heard the handle turn and the door creak open. With thumping heart she tried to keep her breathing even, as if she were sleeping and had no idea that he was standing in the doorway. For a long moment he stood, and then, turning on his heel, he closed the door and went back down the stairs.

Annette found she was shaking and drew deep breaths to calm herself, but believing she had been reprieved, she felt her heartrate slacken and she closed her eyes and prepared to fall asleep.

It was as she dozed off that she heard the footsteps on the stairs again and this time they did not pause in the doorway, but with a lamp in his hand Father Thomas marched across the room and stripped back the covers. For a moment he stared down at her, his eyes lascivious as he saw the fear in hers. Without a word he set the lamp on the floor and reached for her nightgown. Instinctively she curled up, clinging to the nightdress, trying to retrieve the blanket, but he slapped her hard across the cheek. As he did so, the gown he was wearing fell open and Annette could see that he wore nothing beneath it. Annette cried out and was rewarded with a further slap before he flopped down on top of her and began to squirm across her body, grunting as he did so. Annette tried to push him off, but he was too heavy.

'Lie still, bitch,' he growled. 'You've had this coming for a long time!' But Annette did not lie still, she fought him every inch of the way. Her resistance seemed to inflame him more and he held her down as he forced himself inside her. His attack seemed to go on for ever, but when at last he had finished, he rolled off her and, wiping himself on her sheet, sat up on the edge of the bed, looking down at her.

'You are the product of sin,' he said. 'You should never have been born. God blesses no child that's born through sin.' When Annette simply stared up at him, hatred in her eyes, he went on, 'You are a child of the devil, sent to tempt good Christian men like me. You are a snare, sent to lure men away from the paths of righteousness. You deserve the treatment you receive and I am the instrument of God's punishment.' He got slowly to his feet and, picking up the lamp again, raised it high so that he could see her face clearly.

'Understand this, spawn of the devil: if you ever speak of what goes on between us, you will burn in the fires of hell for all eternity.' With that he retrieved the robe he'd discarded and turned to the door. As he reached it he turned once more and whispered, 'The fires of hell.'

And so it began. He did not come to her every night, but the fear was always there. In the daytime he continued to treat her as he always had, snapping out orders and expecting her to jump to his bidding. Most of the time she did so, but if she was too slow, or showed any sign of rebellion, he would grip her by the shoulder, his bony fingers biting into her flesh, and catching her by the hair, jerk it hard and painfully, his eyes promising further punishment... later. After that first night, he never slapped her round the face again. His attacks could be vicious, but nothing ever showed; there was never a visible mark on her. No caller at the house, or visitor come to discuss parish affairs with the priest, would ever suspect the cruelty that lived within it. And fearing the eternal fires of hell, Annette spoke to no one.

Once, when she was certain that Father Thomas would be safely saying Mass in the church, Agathe went back to the Clergy House to visit Annette. She was shocked at the sight of the girl she had lived with and come to love. She could see the pale face and drooping shoulders of a deeply unhappy child, for she still considered Annette a child despite her probable eighteen years.

'Annette!' she cried. 'Are you ill?'

Annette shook her head. 'No, madame,' she replied, mustering a weak smile and leading the way into the familiar kitchen. 'It's hard work on my own, but apart from that, everything is fine.' There was absolutely no question of Annette confiding her nightmare life to Madame Sauze. Father Thomas's threats of the fires of hell kept her silent, but Madame Sauze looked at her askance, not believing her.

'Annette,' she said, 'if there's something wrong, you can tell me.'

'No, madame,' Annette replied vehemently, before saying more quietly, 'no, madame, there is nothing wrong.' She started as she heard the grandfather clock in the hall begin to chime. 'Please, madame, please go, I need to start on the midday meal.'

'Of course,' Agathe said. She didn't want to be there when Father Thomas got home either. 'I just wanted to know that you were getting on all right with Father Thomas. He's lucky to have you. Perhaps I'll see you in the market one day. We could drink a cup of coffee together?'

'Yes,' agreed Annette as she hurried to open the front door. 'Yes, I'll look out for you.'

As the door closed behind her and Agathe walked away, she saw Father Thomas emerging from the church. She watched as he let himself into the Clergy House, and sighed.

As she had thought those months ago, Father Thomas must be an exacting man to work for. Clearly there was something the matter, but unless Annette trusted her enough to confide in her, there was nothing she could do.

Chapter 3

It was some weeks later that Annette made the fatal discovery. She had only started having an irregular monthly bleed nine months earlier and at first she had not missed it. Unaware of the symptoms, which certainly had never been discussed at the orphanage and had been unnecessary for mention at the Clergy House, Annette had no idea that she was expecting a baby until it began to show in her waistline. Father Thomas had continued to take his pleasure with her whenever he chose. She had long since ceased to fight him; indeed, she had realised that made him more brutal in his use of her. She now lay back and waited for him to stop grunting and for it all to be over. It was, she supposed, inevitable that she should have fallen pregnant at some time in her future, but in her innocence she had assumed that priests were not as other men and could not father a child.

Father Thomas had no such innocence and as Annette's breasts grew fuller and her stomach more rounded, he realised with disgust that she must be with child; another child of shame. His immediate thought was that he must hide the fact from the parish. He certainly would disclaim paternity; indeed he *did* disclaim it. The woman herself had been conceived out of wedlock and so it must be in her blood to be promiscuous.

Clearly, she must have been having an illicit liaison with some man, perhaps when he, Father Thomas, was out on parish business, or when she pretended to go to the market – some man of similar parentage, similar lack of morals, similarly promiscuous. Thus assuaging his own conscience, the priest absolved himself of all guilt and became convinced in this belief; the father was someone else. Whoever it was, Father Thomas realised that Annette had to go. No shadow of suspicion must fall upon him, and certainly, as the parish priest, he could not employ a woman carrying a bastard child as his housekeeper.

Having made this decision he acted upon it at once. That evening, when she was clearing away the supper, he cornered Annette in the kitchen, barring her way to the door. 'You are with child,' he stated coldly. 'You are carrying a bastard... spawn of the devil!'

By now Annette had realised that she was indeed pregnant but naively had not been prepared for the inevitable reaction of the priest, and she stared at him with frightened eyes.

'And who is the father of this abomination?' he demanded, leaning towards her, his face so close that she could feel his breath on her skin. 'Which man have you been creeping out to meet?'

'None. No one,' stammered Annette, shrinking away from him, her back against the dresser.

'Liar!' Father Thomas's face grew red with anger. 'Liar!' He was determined that she should admit she had been with some man, but although her fear was stark in her eyes, she remained silent and his anger boiled over. How dare she defy him – him, a man of the cloth? 'Well, it's out of the house with you! I'll keep no fallen women here.'

Annette stared at him and suddenly she realised that,

though she was afraid of him, at this moment she wasn't afraid of the hellfire he threatened. 'It's your child,' she said, 'and you know it. If you throw me out *everyone* will know it.'

In that moment he saw the depths of her hatred in her eyes, a hatred so intense that he took an involuntary step backwards. It was gone as quickly as it had come, but he had seen it and felt a sudden jolt of fear.

'Don't you dare to threaten me,' he blustered. 'If you try to spread malicious rumours about me, who do you think they'll believe? Me, the man of God, or you... the whore?' His lip curled as he asked the question, but expecting no answer, he went on, 'The only place for you is back in St Luke's, where women like you belong. That's where your bastard will be born.' Annette still made no reply and he said, 'Get up to your room! I shall go and see Reverend Mother in the morning.'

'I will never leave my child at St Luke's,' Annette said, far more bravely than she felt. 'I would rather kill it.'

'What? And add murder to your list of sins?' mocked the priest, quashing his fear and reasserting his authority. 'The sisters will take you in until the child is born and then you will return to the streets and it will be theirs. It will learn its place in the world... just as you should have done. Now get out of my sight. You disgust me.'

I may disgust you, thought Annette miserably as she heard him coming up the stairs yet again later that night, but it doesn't keep you away from me.

She was right. Despite his feigned disgust he couldn't resist the pleasure he would get from invading her body, from possessing her just once more. The feeling of power surged through him as he thrust and thrust again, his excitement building until he exploded in waves of ecstasy. But as the ecstasy ebbed away and the disgust flooded back through him, he never considered whether it was for her or for himself. Spent, he rolled away, pushing her from him, and looking down in revulsion at her swollen body, he thought, Tomorrow she will be gone and my temptation will be over.

When he left her, Annette lay on the bed amid the soiled sheets considering and discarding ideas of escape. Nothing in the world would make her return to St Luke's orphanage, where she had spent her first thirteen miserable years. She had been deposited on the doorstep as a baby, left to the mercy of the nuns. Nothing would induce her to let that happen to any child of hers. She had no idea of what to do or where to go, but she was determined it would not be back through those forbidding doors. Clearly Father Thomas was taking no responsibility for his child. He had too much to lose if his behaviour became known – his reputation, his authority as a priest, even his livelihood.

She still feared his threats of hellfire, but set against that fear was her instinct to protect her unborn child. She had never in her life had anyone to love, but now, growing inside her was a baby who would rely on her for everything. Hers and hers alone.

She lay awake throughout the night, but all she had decided as a pink-and-pearl dawn began to lighten the eastern sky was that when Father Thomas crossed the square to the church for early morning Mass, she would leave the house and take her chances in the world outside. The service would not be a long one and when Father Thomas returned from the church he would expect his breakfast to be waiting for him on the table.

Well, thought Annette. Let him wait!

Quietly she got up and gathered her few possessions together before emptying the sack that served as her pillow and packing them into it. From under a loose floorboard, she retrieved the few coins she had gleaned over the years, nearly six francs, and knotting them into her kerchief, thrust them into her bosom.

She crept out onto the landing and listened for the priest's departure. She could hear him moving about downstairs, going into his study and for some reason into the kitchen and then, finally, the sound of the front door shutting behind him.

For a long moment Annette waited, the silence of the house closing round her. Suppose he'd forgotten something and came back? She shuddered at the thought, but when the silence remained unbroken, she picked up her bag and tiptoed downstairs. She paused in the hall, wondering for one moment if she were being incredibly stupid, thrusting herself out into an unforgiving world. However, the thought of Father Thomas forcing her to go back to St Luke's was enough to stiffen her resolve, and she reached for the door handle. Turning it, she tried to pull the door open, but it wouldn't move. It wasn't bolted, but she realised with a jolt that it was locked. The key was not hanging on its daytime hook beside the door; Father Thomas had locked it from the outside and taken the key.

He's locked me in! she thought as she rattled the door handle in futile panic. He's locked me in! She put down her bundle and ran to the kitchen door, which opened out into the narrow lane that ran alongside the house. Again, the bolts were not drawn, but the door was locked and the key was missing. She was a prisoner in the house. Tears of frustration filled her eyes as she pulled at the handle in vain.

'Stop!' Annette was startled by the sound of her own voice. 'I *will* not cry! Calm down, stupid girl, and think!'

He's locked you in. The doors are locked and you're inside, but that doesn't mean you can't get out. Think!

She went into the sitting room and looked at the French windows that opened into the garden. But the garden was protected by a high wall with no gate to the road. She returned to the hall, which had a narrow window beside the front door. She could look out to the street but it was far too small for her to squeeze through. The only room with windows large enough was Father Thomas's study.

Dare she go in there? Of course. She had to.

Annette pushed at the study door, praying it wouldn't be locked. It was not. Father Thomas never dreamed that she would have the temerity to go into his room uninvited or in his absence.

The room had dual-aspect windows, one giving onto the street, the other opening to the back lane. Ignoring the front window, she crossed to the one on the side and peered out. It was a double casement, rising from a low sill almost to the ceiling. The window looked towards the blank wall of the building across the lane. As far as she could tell there was no one about to see her climb out, but that was a risk she'd have to take. She undid the catch and tried to pull the window open. It was old, heavy and stiff from lack of usage. Neither Father Lenoir nor Father Thomas had ever opened it, fearing contagion from the city air. Desperation gave her strength and Annette pulled with all her might. There was an ominous creaking until, with an unexpected release, the casements parted so suddenly that she staggered backwards. Her way out was before her. After one cautious look along the lane, mercifully empty, she picked up her bundle and slipped out. She did not turn into the main street but took to her heels, following the lane's twisting way between high walls until it emerged into the tangle of streets far beyond the Clergy House.

Annette had no idea of where she was going, but she knew she had to be well away before Father Thomas got home again and perhaps sent a hue and cry after her. She and her baby had escaped, but from now on it would be up to her to keep them both alive.

Father Thomas had not had his mind on the Mass that morning. He, too, had lain awake for some time the previous night, considering his options, and his thoughts continued to roam even as he recited the prayers and distributed the wafers among his tiny congregation of elderly men and black-clad widows. He was faced with a dilemma. Obviously no whiff of scandal must attach to him, so the girl had to go, but if he got rid of Annette immediately, it would leave him in the difficult position of having no one to look after him. He had been too hasty, he realised, threatening to send her to St Luke's straight away. He must pretend to have relented and keep Annette on while he found her replacement. Then, and with righteous indignation, he could 'discover' her situation and turn her out. Otherwise who would cook and clean for him? Wash his clothes? Starch his surplices? The answer came to him as he was giving communion to a grey-haired dame in her sixties, a woman who looked uncannily like his mother's importunate cousin, Lena.

Of course, Cousin Lena! Cousin Lena was a woman of no means who battened on his parents for support and she might make him an admirable housekeeper. Surely she would be pleased to have home and board and would know it was dependent on doing what she was told and keeping her mouth shut. Another week with Annette in the house would do no harm; just one more week with Annette looking after him in all the ways he demanded while he contacted Cousin Lena, the answer to his problem.

When Mass was finally over, Father Thomas bid his parishioners farewell before he stepped out into the street and hurried back to the Clergy House. He would say to Annette that after much prayer he had decided to allow her to stay, without mentioning St Luke's or her replacement.

When he reached the front door he unlocked it and went straight inside, not noticing immediately that the door to his private study was standing ajar.

He set his hat on the hatstand and called to Annette. When there was no reply he looked first into the dining room, where he found no sign of breakfast being laid, and then into the empty and silent kitchen.

'Annette!' he shouted up the stairs, but there was no answer. Where was the wretched girl? And more to the point, where was his breakfast? She couldn't have gone to the market, as she wouldn't have been able to leave the house. Sudden doubt came over him and he ran up the two flights of stairs to the attic bedroom. One glance told him she had gone. There was nothing in the room but the tumbled, malodorous bedsheets to show she had ever been there.

For a moment Father Thomas was at a loss. Annette had gone and it was clear that she was not coming back. Well, good riddance! But suppose the wretched girl tried to tell the world how he had used her! A shudder of fear ran through him before he pulled himself together. Of course she would do no such thing, she wouldn't dare... and if she did, who would believe her?

It was when he went back downstairs that he saw that the door to his study was open. For a moment he froze. Surely the girl had not ventured in there? He pushed it wide and stepped inside. The room was empty, but the windows to the lane stood wide open. Had the wretched girl stolen money from his desk before she climbed out of the window? Father Thomas pulled open a drawer of his desk and saw to his relief that his small leather purse was lying where it always did, hidden beneath his Bible. The girl might have gone, but at least his money had not gone with her.

Comforted by this thought, he went back into the hall, picked up his hat and set out for a rare visit to his parents. There was no point in writing to them now about Cousin Lena—he needed her at once, so he would have to go and fetch her. As he took the omnibus across the city, he considered what he would tell them. He decided to explain that the housekeeper he'd inherited from Father Lenoir, a flighty young girl far too inexperienced for the job, had run off and left him in the lurch. Did they think Cousin Lena could come and look after him until he was able to find a more permanent housekeeper? He was certain his parents would be delighted to be rid of Lena, and once she was installed he was sure there'd be no question of having to replace her for years to come. She would be a fixture.

Chapter 4

Agathe had not repeated her visit to the Clergy House. Once, she had met Annette in the market and treated her to a cup of coffee in a street café. Annette had been pale and withdrawn, unlike the girl Agathe had lived with for so long. She still refused to admit that there was anything wrong, but Agathe still didn't believe her. When she had suggested that she might visit the Clergy House again, Annette had begged her not to.

'I don't think Father Thomas would like it if he saw you there,' she said.

And he'd take it out on you! thought Agathe.

She had not seen Annette for several weeks, which, she decided, was strange. Surely she must come to the market to buy provisions for the house, as she herself did. Was Annette avoiding her? As the days passed Agathe became increasingly worried about her, and though Annette had asked her to stay away, she finally decided that she must return to the Clergy House. She would wait until she was sure Father Thomas was saying Mass in the church and there was no chance of meeting him and then call at the house.

Two days later Agathe made her way back to St Jacques church and watched as Father Thomas went in. Once the door had closed on the congregation, she walked briskly across the square and rang the Clergy House bell. She heard movement inside and was already smiling as the door opened. Her smile froze as she was greeted by an elderly woman, spherical in shape, her head perched on the end of a short neck, her face the colour of pastry, from which protruded two bulbous eyes that regarded her suspiciously.

'Who're you?' she demanded by way of greeting. 'Father Thomas isn't here. He's in the church.'

Agathe overcame her surprise at this reception and said, 'It isn't Father Thomas I've come to see, but his housekeeper, Annette. May I come in?'

'I'm Father Thomas's housekeeper,' said the woman, standing firmly in the doorway. 'And there's no one called Annette here.'

'She's gone? When did she leave? Where did she go?'

'If you mean the flighty bit who was looking after the father before I came, I don't know and I don't care. She was no better than she should be! Simply disappeared, she did, leaving poor Father Thomas in the lurch. If I hadn't come to help out, what sort of state would the poor man have been left in, I'd like to know? No one to look after him.'

Agathe looked at her for a moment and then said quietly, 'In that case, madame, I won't take up any more of your time.' She turned away, only to find a pudgy hand grabbing at her arm.

'Who shall I tell the father came to see him?'

Turning back, Agathe removed the hand from her sleeve and looked into the two piggy eyes. 'Just one of his parishioners,' she lied. 'I'll call again to see him.'

That evening, when she had cleared away the supper things and Fleur was doing her household accounts, she went to her room and considered what she had learned. Annette clearly wasn't at the Clergy House any more, but why had she left? Agreed, the work was hard and she had always been sure that Father Thomas would be an exacting man to work for, but at least Annette had had board and lodging.

I knew there was something wrong, Agathe thought, but what could it have been that was so awful that Annette ran away?

'No better than she should be,' that unpleasant woman had said. Surely Annette hadn't got herself into *that* sort of trouble, had she? Was that why she'd run away... or had Father Thomas thrown her out? That was more likely.

'Oh, why didn't the silly girl confide in me?' Agathe sighed. 'I might have been able to do something.'

Where could she have gone? Had she gone for help to St Luke's? She thought that most unlikely, but where else could she go?

Agathe considered returning to the Clergy House and asking Father Thomas herself, but eventually decided against it; he would tell her no more than she'd learned already from his new housekeeper. Perhaps she should go to St Luke's and ask after her there.

In the morning, on her way to the market, she paused outside St Luke's orphanage. It was a forbidding building, its entrance a pair of heavy wooden double doors set in the high encircling stone wall. Surely Annette would not have returned here, the place where she had spent her miserable childhood. But if she were desperate?

Agathe drew a deep breath and walked up to the front door and rang the brass bell that hung there. A grille in the door opened and a face peered out.

'Yes? Who is it?'

'Madame Sauze, to see Reverend Mother.' Agathe spoke with an authority she did not feel, but with which the portress was familiar. She opened the door at once.

'I am Sister Gabrielle,' said the nun. 'Is Mother expecting you?'

'No,' admitted Agathe, 'but I do need to speak to her.'

'Mother is in chapel,' said Sister Gabrielle. 'If you want to see her, you'll have to wait.'

'In that case, perhaps *you* can help me,' Agathe said, forcing a smile to her face. 'I wonder if you remember a girl who used to live here? Annette?'

Colour flooded the nun's face and she scowled. She certainly remembered Annette, and her expression made Agathe remember too. Sister Gabrielle! It was Sister Gabrielle whom Annette had tripped up when her friend Hélène was trying to escape from the convent all those years ago.

Sister Gabrielle continued to scowl. 'I remember her,' she said. 'An evil child! What about her?'

'I am looking for her,' replied Agathe. 'I wondered if she was here.'

'No,' replied the nun firmly, 'she is not. And were she to come here she would not be admitted.'

'I see.' Agathe forbore to add, 'How very Christian of you.' Instead she said, 'That's most helpful, Sister. If you are quite sure, I needn't trouble Reverend Mother.'

'I am quite sure, madame,' replied Sister Gabrielle, and then as her curiosity got the better of her, she asked, 'Why do you want her anyway? What's she done now?'

Madame Sauze did not answer her questions; she simply said, 'Thank you for your help, Sister.'

Agathe stepped out into the street again and the door was slammed shut behind her. Well, she thought, I have my answer without having to see Reverend Mother. And for that she was very grateful, even though she was no nearer to finding Annette.

When she reached the market she searched the busying crowds for a sight of her, but she saw no sign of the girl she was looking for. She would have to look for her every day until she found her.

Annette had seen her, however. Crouched in a doorway where she had passed the previous night, she watched Agathe move from stall to stall making her purchases. For a moment she was tempted to call out to her, but she stifled the urge. How could she ask Madame Sauze for help? Now that it was clear that she was with child? She shrank back into the doorway as her erstwhile friend passed by, so close that had she reached out she could have touched her.

Moments later the owner of the house came back and with a bellow hauled her to her feet and ejected her from his doorway. She screamed as he flung her onto the stone pavement.

'And don't let me find you here again, whore,' he cried as he tossed her bundle after her. Annette scrambled to her feet and made a grab for the bag, which contained everything she owned in the world. The man gave her another violent push and she crashed back to the ground, making her cry out again with pain and shout, 'Leave me alone, I ain't doing no harm!'

It was the voice! Agathe spun round and saw a man standing over a beggar on the ground. You could see violence like this to those on the street any day of the week, but it was the voice that had caught her attention. She stared at the woman, who was trying to stagger to her feet, and gasped as she realised who it was.

'Annette!' she cried, and rushed across the road towards her. 'Annette!'

The girl turned and stared at the woman coming to her aid. 'Madame...? Oh, madame!' Tears sprang from her eyes and she collapsed onto the ground once more.

Agathe knelt at her side and reached for her hands. 'Annette, come along, child, get up.' With the tears still coursing down her cheeks, Annette struggled to her feet, clutching her precious bundle.

'People like you deserve what you get,' growled the man as he watched the two women move away, one limping and leaning on the arm of the other, into the shelter of a side street away from curious eyes. Once they were a safe distance from the still-grumbling owner of the doorway, Agathe paused and turned Annette to look at her.

'Annette,' she exclaimed, 'what on earth has happened to you?' She was horrified to see the state of the girl. In grubby clothes, her pale face streaked with dirt, her hair straggling and unkempt, she had clearly been on the streets for a while and she was clearly pregnant. 'Come along, let's get you away from here.' She led the way to a nearby food stall and bought coffee for them both. Then they sat on a low stone wall to drink it. Annette gulped hers down at once, almost choking as the hot liquid hit her throat.

'Are you hungry?' asked Agathe. Annette nodded and Agathe went back to the stall and bought some bread, cold bacon and a wedge of cheese. Returning to the wall, she handed the food to Annette, who devoured it, stuffing it into her mouth as if it might be snatched away.

'When did you last eat?' demanded Agathe.

'The day before yesterday,' replied Annette, licking her fingers individually to be sure she had not missed a scrap.

Agathe stared at her in dismay. 'Annette, what on earth has happened? How do you come to be...' She gestured with her hand. '...as you are? You wouldn't tell me before, but you must do so now.'

Haltingly, the girl began to tell her what, since she, Madame Sauze, had left the Clergy House, She had been suffering at the hands of Father Thomas. 'And now I'm expecting his child he's thrown me out!'

'Thrown you out?' echoed Agathe fiercely. 'Yes, well, I suppose he would.'

'Well, no, not exactly,' admitted Annette. 'He refused to accept that it's his child. He insists I've been with other men and one of them is the father. He called it devil's spawn and threatened to make me go back to St Luke's.' She shuddered at the memory and added, 'I'd rather die first, so I ran away.'

'So you've been living on the streets?'

Annette nodded. 'Rather that than let a child of mine be brought up by those witches at St Luke's.'

'And have you been with any other men?' asked Agathe, as always getting straight to the heart of the matter.

'No, of course not,' snapped Annette, adding miserably, 'I *knew* you wouldn't believe me.'

'I had to ask you,' answered Agathe quietly, 'but I do believe you – that the child is his.'

Annette nodded again. 'Yes, poor little bastard.'

'Annette! Don't use such language.'

'Well,' Annette said philosophically, 'that's what it is, isn't it?'

'But you can't simply live on the streets,' said Agathe. 'What will you do when your time comes?'

'Die, probably,' replied Annette. 'Both of us. And Father Thomas will say it's God's punishment for my sin.'

'Enough of that,' Agathe chided her, trying to suppress her fury at what the priest had been doing. 'Just let me think what we can do for the best.'

'There's nothing you can do,' said Annette, 'but thank you for believing me.'

'When is the baby due?' asked Agathe.

'I don't know,' admitted Annette. 'I don't know how long. But I'm getting fatter, so it must be soon.'

Agathe sighed. What could she do? She had her room in Fleur's apartment, but it was tiny, and she could just imagine what Fleur would say if she brought home a girl from the streets, six or seven months pregnant. She and her sister had been rubbing along reasonably well over the past few months, but Agathe was still adamant that the arrangement was temporary. She was determined to find another position and move out by the end of the summer. In the meantime she didn't want to upset the status quo. Could she persuade Fleur to give the child houseroom, promising it would not be for long, just while they worked out a plan and decided what to do? Possibly, but unlikely. And what could they do? Where would Annette be safe? Where could she go to have her baby if it wasn't somewhere like St Luke's?

It was then that Agathe thought again of approaching Madame St Clair. She had not done so for her own benefit, but this was for someone else, a child whom over the past few years she had come to love and who now was in desperate need of help. Perhaps the St Clairs could find a place for Annette somewhere in their household. Not in Paris, but out at their country home in St Etienne. No one would know the girl there and she could be passed off as a very young widow, whose husband had fallen victim to the influenza that was rife in the city. Rosalie St Clair was a woman of the world. Her own daughter had once been subjected to abuse by a man, so surely she would have compassion on a girl of the same age, now in a dreadful situation, but not one of her own making.

She made a decision and rose to her feet. 'Come with me now,' she said, 'and let's see what we can do for you.'

'Where are we going?' Annette picked up her bag and together they walked back across the market square.

'I'm taking you back to where I'm staying,' Agathe explained as they threaded their way through the narrow streets. 'Just now I live with my sister, and I'm hoping she'll let you stay with us while I visit a friend and try to get you some help. When we get home I shall open the front door and you must go inside straight away. Go down the hallway and into my room... the door straight ahead of you. Stay there and stay quiet, while I talk to my sister and explain to her what I'm hoping to arrange.'

'But what if she won't let me in?' muttered Annette.

'She won't know you're there if you stay in my room,' Agathe said reassuringly. 'She seldom comes out of the salon except to her own bedroom. I will go in and talk to her, and once she understands the situation, I'm sure she'll let you stay for a short while.' Agathe was sure of no such thing, but she was determined to do her best for the child, and would stand up to Fleur if necessary.

'I shall tell her you are the daughter of an old friend and as she is now no longer with us, you've come to me in your hour of need. We shall say that you were married last year and your husband has recently died in the flu epidemic, leaving you expecting his child with nowhere to go. There is no reason to doubt such a story – lots of people have died of this dreadful flu, and there must be other women truly in the situation I'm describing. Why should my sister not believe us?'

Annette still looked at her anxiously and Agathe gave her a shake. 'It's the best we can do for now, Annette. That's the story we'll stick to and my sister will hear nothing of Father Thomas or the Clergy House. Now, give a name to your dead husband, because he has to seem real for you to be able to pull this off!'

'Marc,' replied Annette after a moment's thought. 'Marc Dubois.'

'Good. A very common name,' said Agathe. 'Marc Dubois it is – which makes you Annette Dubois, so remember it if someone asks.'

When they reached Fleur's apartment and Agathe opened its front door, she gave Annette a silent push down the corridor towards her own room before going to find Fleur in her salon.

As soon as the bedroom door closed behind her, Annette crossed to the narrow bed in the tiny box room where Agathe slept. She had scrounged food, drunk from fountains and slept in doorways and under waggons for the past three weeks, flotsam in the bustle of the city, invisible, tossed aside and disregarded. The quiet of this room, where the noise of the streets outside was only a distant hum, claimed her, and the moment she lay down on Agathe's bed, she descended into a deep and dreamless slumber. She was still fast asleep when, hours later, Agathe finally came to the room at the end of her working day. She had changed her mind about explaining Annette's presence to her sister. So far she had not told Fleur that she had an extra lodger in her apartment; time enough for that in the morning when she had worked out her plan in detail.

Annette slept until morning and by the time she awoke, Agathe, who had slept only fitfully in her armchair, had finalised her plan. She would go to see Madame St Clair in Avenue Ste Anne, the St Clairs' Paris home, and ask her for help. After all, Agathe thought, it's worth a try, and she can only say no. Neither way would Annette be any the worse off.

She explained her idea to Annette as the girl ate the food Agathe had purloined from the kitchen.

'Hélène's mother? Why should she help?'

'Why should she not?' replied Agathe. 'They have first-hand evidence of what can happen to a young girl forced to live on the streets. Hélène is safe now, but you are in need of help.'

Annette shook her head. 'They'll say it's my fault,' she said, 'call me a slut and turn me away.'

'We don't know that,' said Agathe firmly, though she knew in her heart that it could well be the case. 'Indeed, we shan't know unless we ask, so it's worth asking.'

Reluctantly Annette had agreed, and leaving her still hidden in her bedroom, that afternoon Agathe had sallied forth to the Avenue Ste Anne to renew her acquaintance with Rosalie St Clair.

Chapter 5

Rupert Chalfont, younger son of Sir Philip Chalfont, baronet, took the train to Dover and then the steam packet across the English Channel to Calais. He had been advised by his twin brother, Justin, that he should beat a hasty retreat from his father's London house in Eaton Place and for once he'd taken Justin's advice.

Justin had travelled up especially from Pilgrim's Oak, the family home in Somerset, to warn Rupert of the scandal of Mary Dawson, the gamekeeper's daughter.

'The governor's absolutely furious with you,' Justin warned him. 'Dawson says you've put young Mary in the family way and he's kicking up one hell of a stink about it.' He looked quizzically at his younger brother. 'Did you?'

'I might have,' Rupert admitted cautiously, 'but so might have plenty of others! Puts herself about a bit, does young Mary.'

'Well, Dawson has sworn to the governor that Mary was white as the driven snow until you had your wicked way with her!'

Rupert laughed. 'The driven snow must be pretty grey round the Dawsons' cottage then!' he said.

'No laughing matter, Rupe,' Justin said with mock severity. 'Dawson is saying that she should be paid off.'

'Can't see the governor wearing that one,' scoffed Rupert.

'No more can I,' agreed Justin. 'Even so, it wouldn't hurt to make yourself scarce till it all blows over.'

Rupert nodded. 'Probably a good idea,' he said. 'I was thinking of going over to France anyway. Met a chap from somewhere outside Paris at Maud Berrow's coming-out last month. Handsome in a sort of French way, all bowing and kissing hands. The mamas were *enchanté*' – Rupert kissed his own hand with an exaggerated flourish – 'and enquiring as to his heritage, but turned out he was already spoken for, back home in France. Invited me to his wedding.'

'He what?' Justin sounded incredulous. 'Why would he do that?'

Rupert shrugged. 'Took to me, I suppose,' he replied before adding with a grin, 'People do, you know.'

Justin knew that this was no idle boast. Rupert, with an easy charm, had the knack of making himself agreeable to all sorts of unlikely people, dowagers to scullery maids, grooms to girls still in the schoolroom. The dark good looks he'd inherited from his grandmother were just the sort that appealed to those with a romantic mind: dark hair worn a little too long, deep-set dark brown eyes above an aquiline nose, a wide mouth and determined chin. It was only because he was a younger son that the mamas with eligible daughters did not flock about him. Charming and good-looking he might be, but with no title and no fortune he was not on the list of suitable husbands.

'Well,' remarked Justin, 'I suggest you take him up on his offer. The governor's coming up to town at the beginning of next week and I wouldn't want to be in your shoes when he does.'

Justin had taken the train back to the West Country, feeling he had done all he could for the moment to rescue Rupert.

He was the elder of the twins by two hours, but those two hours were the difference between him being his father's heir, the future Sir Justin Chalfont, and Rupert being a younger son with a mere competence and his way to make in the world. Far from being identical, the brothers couldn't have been more different, both in looks and character, but they had always been close and watched each other's backs as they had grown up on the family estate, Pilgrim's Oak. Justin had warned Rupert of his father's wrath and in doing so had probably brought it down on his own head.

Rupert, grateful for the warning, had treated himself to one more night of gaming at Brooks's in St James's Street before he left. It had been more successful than his last few evenings at the tables, and when he set off the next morning he was considerably better off than he had been for some time. It seemed as if the gods were smiling on him, and Rupert crossed over to France with a high heart. He decided that he would spend a week or so in Paris enjoying himself – perhaps renewing old acquaintances to be found in the gaming clubs and certain ladies' boudoirs – before heading to this place, Montmichel at St Etienne, where his acquaintance, Lucas Barrineau, had invited him to stay and attend his wedding.

When he arrived at the Gare du Nord, he took a cab from the rank outside and had himself driven to the Hotel Montreux in a side street off the Boulevard St Germain. It was not a large hotel, but it was comfortable and convenient for the centre of the city. He had stayed there before and it would welcome him back without too much strain on his pocket. The proprietor, Jacques Rocher, recognised him at once and greeted him with a welcoming smile and an outstretched hand.

'Ah, Monsieur Chalfont, it is a pleasure to see you back in

Paris. Welcome to the Hotel Montreux. Will you be making a lengthy stay?'

'No, Monsieur Rocher, only a week or so and then I shall be moving out into the country.'

'Indeed, monsieur,' agreed Rocher with a sigh, 'I think you will find many people are leaving early this year for the cooler air of the countryside, it has been so hot these past weeks.' He summoned a lad to carry Rupert's travelling trunk and led the way upstairs.

'For you, Monsieur Chalfont, the best room, in the hotel.' He waved a hand expansively at the room, which was indeed large and looked down on the narrow street below. 'I will leave you to unpack, monsieur,' he said. 'No doubt your man will be following with the rest of your luggage.'

'Probably,' Rupert replied vaguely. 'I will send for him in due course. In the meantime, Monsieur Rocher, no doubt your man Robert will be able to look after me when I require him.'

'Of course, monsieur, you have only to ring.'

'Thank you. I think that is all for now.'

'Of course, monsieur.' Rocher took the hint and, shooing the lad out of the room, followed him downstairs.

Once Rupert had settled into his room, he decided to take a stroll along the river, enjoying the warmth of the late spring evening and feeling content with the world. He took his dinner in a cheerful brasserie, enjoying the hubbub around him as he ate a dish of bouillabaisse followed by a filet de boeuf washed down with a bottle of Burgundy. Paris, he decided, as he walked back through the still-busy streets to the hotel, was definitely a more welcoming city than the grey London he'd left behind.

He slept particularly well that night and after breakfast he went to nearest telegraph office to send a wire to Lucas

Barrineau, announcing his arrival in Paris and accepting the invitation to his wedding.

The telegram caused some consternation at the Barrineau home, Montmichel.

'But who is this man, Lucas?' demanded his mother, Suzanne. 'Why is he coming to your wedding? I have never heard of him!' At that moment her husband came into the room and immediately Suzanne turned to him. 'Louis,' she cried in agitation, 'Lucas has invited some complete stranger to stay here at Montmichel for his wedding and the man has not only accepted but has already arrived in Paris from London. What are we going to do?'

'We are going to tell the St Clairs that we've had a late acceptance,' replied Louis calmly, 'and ask them to lay another place on the family table.'

'But he's not family!' wailed his wife.

'No, chérie, but if Lucas has invited him, we must make him welcome. He won't know anyone else, so he must sit with us. I am sure Madame Rosalie will understand when you explain the situation to her.'

'I believe she has taken her daughters to Paris,' protested Suzanne. 'She is not at home.'

'She will be back well before the wedding, Maman,' remarked Lucas. 'I'm sure it will not be a problem. Rupert Chalfont is charming, I know you will all like him as much as I do.' He gave his mother his most dazzling smile. 'Surely you're able to do this for me. We cannot retract the invitation now, and indeed I have no wish to do so.'

Suzanne was less than pleased with him, but she did as her son asked and promised that when Rosalie St Clair was back from Paris she would pay her a visit and explain.

Chapter 6

'What do you mean, Rupert's gone to a wedding in France?' demanded Sir Philip Chalfont. 'I thought he was in London.'

'He was, sir,' replied Justin. 'I saw him two days ago, and that's when he told me he'd been invited to a wedding in France and that he'd decided to go.'

'A wedding in France? Whose wedding?'

'I don't know, sir, someone he met at Maud Berrow's come-out recently.'

'Very sudden decision,' said Sir Philip suspiciously. 'He hasn't even taken Parker with him.' He gave Justin a wry smile. 'You mentioned young Mary's situation, I suppose.' It wasn't a question and Justin didn't treat it as such.

'Yes, sir, I thought he should be given a chance to defend himself.'

'And did he?'

'Not exactly, sir.' Justin hesitated.

'Well, come on, spit it out,' said his father irritably. 'What did he say?'

'He said he wasn't really surprised to hear of her present condition, and as far as he knew there could be several possible fathers.'

'Did he indeed?' grunted Sir Philip. 'What were his exact words?'

'His exact words? I think he said something like, "puts herself about a bit, does young Mary".'

Sir Philip grimaced at the vulgarity. 'I see. Better not to pursue that any further, I think. I just wanted to know when he might be back here at home. At present neither your mother nor your sister knows anything about Dawson's accusations about Rupert, and I would prefer it stayed that way, but it won't be long before Mary's situation becomes obvious, and I may have to deal with Dawson if he becomes difficult.'

'Surely, sir,' Justin said, 'it is not in his own interest to maintain this story.'

He looked across the desk at his father seated behind it and suddenly thought, The old man is getting older.

Though never a large man, Philip Chalfont had a certain presence that made one prefer to remain on the right side of him. He still had a full head of hair, though there were definite strands of silver in its darkness, and his eyes, deep-set and dark as those he had passed on to his younger son, had always been compelling. They narrowed now as he considered the question of Mary Dawson.

'It certainly won't be if he does,' he agreed. Then, changing the subject, he said, 'Enough of all that. What about you, Justin? Isn't it time you engaged yourself to marry Katharine Blake?'

Justin's expression hardened. 'I know that is what you and my mother wish,' he began.

'And Katharine herself, I would think,' put in his father.

'Kitty and I are extremely good friends, sir, but that is very different from being married.'

'There'd be nothing wrong with being married to that girl,' said Sir Philip briskly. 'It would be a perfect match for both

45

of you and friendship is the ideal basis for marriage – not to mention that as her father has no male heir, the estate will come to Katharine on his death. Much of it marches with our own land and will make a great inheritance for your son.'

'I understand what you are thinking, sir,' replied Justin evenly, 'but I do think an inheritance for any children I might have is a long way into the future.'

'Well, in such matters one must think ahead,' said his father. 'One can never tell what fate has waiting for us around the corner.' He got to his feet. 'It isn't as if you've got anyone else in mind, is it?' It was a rhetorical question and he didn't wait for an answer but went on, 'Now I must go to the estate office and have a word with Foxton before I join you all for luncheon.' With that he went out of the room, leaving his son and heir to follow him outside.

There was still another half hour before the midday bell would summon them to luncheon, and Justin decided to take a turn in the rose garden and give serious consideration to his father's question. When, if ever, was he going to propose to Kitty Blake?

Justin knew that both sets of parents wanted him and Kitty to get married and, he supposed, they probably would. There would be small chance of escape. It wasn't that he didn't like Kitty, he did and always had, but marrying her would feel a bit like marrying his sister, Frances.

All right for Rupert to sow his oats and then walk away, he thought bitterly as he felt a stab of envy. As the younger son he's got no responsibilities. It's not up to him to increase the family estates, nor to provide an heir to inherit them! Lucky Rupert – within reason he can marry whom he likes, when he likes, and live where he likes. This last thought brought a smile to Justin's face as he tried to imagine his brother ever settling down with a wife. Rupert had always enjoyed the company of women, but had always worked on the principle that there was safety in numbers. Rupert, Justin had long ago decided, would end up a crusty old bachelor, perhaps an indulgent uncle to his brother and sister's children, but never marry and have any of his own – or none, Justin thought wryly, that he could bring home to Pilgrim's Oak. Whereas Justin had always known that he was to become the next Chalfont baronet. He'd been brought up as the heir and certain things were expected of him, like producing an heir himself. When his father died he would be Sir Justin Chalfont, and with this in prospect, he was extremely eligible in the marriage market. Well and good in some ways, he thought wryly, but it limited his own choice of bride, and though several hopeful mamas had edged their daughters in his direction, none of them had taken his fancy. He knew he would have to propose to Kitty soon, or make it abundantly clear that he had no intention of doing so. After such a long 'family understanding', quite apart from being a huge blow to her pride, it would hurt Kitty deeply, and that he had no wish to do.

He turned back towards the house and paused to look at it, sleeping in the midday sun. Built by his great-great-grandfather, it was an elegant stone house, three storeys high with tall chimneys, pointed gables and mullioned windows.

Seeing its dusky mellow stonework, its windows glinting in the summer sunshine, it struck Justin just how beautiful the house was, and he realised that he didn't envy Rupert all his freedoms at all, because Pilgrim's Oak would never be his. It had been their family's home for five generations and Justin suddenly knew he could never be happy living anywhere else.

He squared his shoulders and went back indoors. The old man was right. Procrastination must end; it was time to act.

He would ride over to Marwick House after luncheon and call on Kitty. He already had his grandmother's engagement ring, designed to be given to his future bride. Perhaps, if things went well, today he would give it to Kitty.

Unless there were guests, the midday meal at Pilgrim's Oak was taken informally. Often it was little more than a bowl of soup, a plate of cold meats with vegetables from the kitchen garden, and a dish of summer fruits with a jug of cream.

'Shall we go for a ride this afternoon?' Frances suggested as they sat down at the table. 'It's a beautiful day and we could ride up over the hill and look at the view. On a day like today we should be able to see the sea.'

Justin almost accepted her suggestion. After all, it wouldn't matter if he didn't go to see Kitty this very afternoon. He could go another time, another day soon. However, his mother spoke before he could and said, 'I plan to call on Lady Charteris this afternoon, my love, and she particularly asked me to bring you with me. She has someone she would like you to meet.'

'Oh, Mama.' Frances gave a theatrical sigh. 'Not another suitable young man!'

Amabel Chalfont smiled indulgently. 'I know how you feel about her efforts, Frances, but we have to remember she's an old lady and enjoys the company of young people like you. Anyway, when she sent her groom over with an invitation to call and take tea with her this afternoon, I accepted.'

Frances knew there was no point arguing with her mother. Amabel, though an amiable and generally indulgent mother, could be decidedly obstinate. Once she had made up her mind to something, all her children knew there was little point in trying to change it. Arguments, pleas, tears and tantrums were greeted with the same indifference and so Frances sighed and, turning back to her brother and speaking with great formality, said, 'Well, Justin, I should like to make an appointment to ride with you tomorrow… if the weather is clement.'

'Certainly, Frances,' he replied with equal formality. 'We shall ride together tomorrow… if the weather is clement.' At which they both broke out laughing.

'What are your plans for this afternoon, Justin?' enquired his mother. 'I know Lady Charteris would be delighted to see you as well. She is sadly short of company these days.'

'I would have been delighted to escort you and Fran to visit her,' Justin said, 'but unfortunately I am engaged to call at Marwick House this afternoon.'

Frances flashed a look of interested enquiry to him but he simply smiled back at her enigmatically, giving her no idea of his inner thoughts. He would give no hint to anyone of what he had finally decided to do; he would ask Kitty and then spring it on them all!

At the end of the meal Sir Philip got to his feet. 'If you'll excuse me, my dear, I am meeting with Dawson this afternoon. Just a few decisions to be made.'

If his wife was surprised at his explanation of his doings that afternoon, when normally he told almost nothing of his business, she gave no sign. Despite her husband's careful discretion about Mary Dawson, Amabel already knew the situation from her maid, Bessie. News like that spread through the servants from house to house like wildfire. In a village the size of Pilgrim St Leonard, nothing remained secret for very long. She also knew that Rupert was considered to be one of the putative fathers, and though she hoped he was no such thing, one had to bear in mind that young men did occasionally get themselves and young maids into scrapes. As long as there was no scandal it could be ignored, and she was certain that Sir Philip would allow no breath of scandal to touch his family. Somehow the problem, if there really was one, would go away. She was glad that Rupert had gone to London and was thus out of the way. Until the talk this lunchtime she had had no idea that he had gone to a wedding in France.

So like him, she thought as she sat at her dressing table preparing to visit Lady Charteris, to vanish into thin air without a word to anyone. Well, Justin knew he'd gone, but he had no idea of his whereabouts in France. Still, he'd disappeared before for weeks at a time and always come home again with stories of the places he'd been and the people he'd met.

She was surprised that Parker, his man, had not accompanied him when he left London, but she did not know that Rupert had sent Parker home to bury his father. It was none of her business to know such things.

'Take a couple of weeks,' Rupert had said to Parker. 'I shan't need you, and I'm sure your mother will be glad of your support. I'll send for you if I want you.'

Justin heard his mother and sister being driven away in the chaise and went out to the stables. Jack the stable lad saddled up his horse, Rufus, and having checked that he had the ring box in his pocket, Justin set off to Marwick House to propose to Kitty. As he rode he wondered exactly what he would say, but decided to wait until the moment arose.

How ironic it would be, he thought suddenly, if she tells me that I've kept her waiting too long and turns me down, saying she's going to marry someone else.

The thought suddenly seemed totally unacceptable and he kicked Rufus into a canter.

Kitty Blake was sitting in the garden reading when

Campbell came out to ask if she were at home to Mr Justin Chalfont.

'Of course, Campbell,' she replied, setting aside her book. 'Bring him out here. We'll take tea under the oak.'

'Very good, Miss Kitty,' answered the butler, and he disappeared into the house. Moments later Justin appeared and Kitty rose to her feet to greet him. He took her outstretched hands, bowing over them.

'Kitty,' he said, 'I trust you're keeping well?'

'Very well, thank you, Justin. As you see, I have been enjoying the afternoon sun. Have you come to see my father?'

'No,' Justin replied, though he realised at that moment that he ought to have done so before speaking to Kitty. Everyone assumed he and Kitty would ultimately make a match of it, but he had never actually asked her father's permission to pay his addresses.

'I've asked Campbell to bring tea out here,' Kitty said, waving Justin to another chair as she sat down again. 'I thought it would be most pleasant.'

'It certainly would.' Justin sat down and then immediately got up again. 'But before he returns, Kitty, there's something I want to ask you.' Now the moment of asking had arrived, Justin found himself at a loss for words. He looked down at her sitting peacefully in her chair, looking up at him enquiringly, waiting for him to speak.

'Kitty...' he began and then stopped.

'Kitty,' he started again, 'we've known each other from childhood...'

'Indeed we have,' Kitty said encouragingly.

'We've always been good friends, have we not?'

'Yes,' Kitty agreed affably.

'Do you think we could be more to each other? I mean,

well, Kitty, would you consider being my wife? Marrying me and becoming my wife?'

'I might,' she replied, 'if you got on and asked me.'

Justin could hear the laughter in her voice and he dropped to one knee beside her chair. 'Will you, Kitty?'

'Will I what, Justin?'

'Oh, Kitty, you know what I'm asking. Will you marry me?'

'Yes, Justin, thank you.'

He grasped her hands again and said, 'Do you mean it?'

'If you do,' she replied with a smile.

'Of course I do,' cried Justin, pulling the jeweller's box out of his pocket. 'And here is my grandmother's ring to prove it.' He opened the box and took out the emerald ring it contained, slipping it on the third finger of her left hand. Then he raised her hand to his lips and kissed it.

Campbell, emerging into the garden with the tea tray, saw Mr Justin on one knee beside Miss Kitty and, thinking, About time too, retreated into the house unseen.

'Perhaps we should go and find your parents now,' Justin said, 'and tell them the good news.'

'Of course.' Kitty stood up and found herself gathered into Justin's arms. He kissed her cheek and then, when she made no move to pull away, kissed her on the lips. Her first real kiss.

It was not the one she had been hoping for. Kitty knew that she must marry and she was fond of Justin, but she knew he would always be second best and could only hope that he did not. It was Rupert, so charming and carefree, so different from his more conventional older brother, who had long ago captured her heart, but he had always treated her like Fran, as another sister. And even if he had returned her devotion, she knew that as the younger son, not heir to the baronetcy and its estate, her father would never have countenanced such an alliance.

If I put away all thoughts of Rupert, she thought as she and Justin walked hand in hand back to the house, if I forget all about him, I can be happy with Justin and I hope I can make him happy too.

Chapter 7

Rosalie St Clair dropped into an armchair in the drawing room of the house in the Avenue Ste Anne and sighed. It was good to be home again after such a long day and she felt unexpectedly tired.

What is the matter with me? she wondered as she rang for Didier the butler to bring her some cake and a glass of wine. I feel every day of my age.

At just forty-eight Rosalie was not old. Heavier than she had been in her youth, following the birth of her five children, she carried her age well. Generous of figure, she was still a good-looking woman. Her dark eyes, deep-set behind thick, dark lashes, could still sparkle with pleasure, her generous mouth curved readily into a smile that lit her face, but her once-glossy dark hair was now laced with threads of grey and there were times, as now, when she found her energy seemed to have seeped out through the soles of her feet.

She had brought her three daughters, Clarice, Hélène and Louise, up from the country to their house in Paris four days ago, and since their arrival every day had been crowded with a round of engagements; drives in the Bois, dinner parties, soirées and evenings at the theatre. Today, however, had been their most important appointment of all, an appointment at the House of Worth for the final fitting of Clarice's wedding dress. She, the eldest of Rosalie and Emile St Clair's three daughters, was to be married to Lucas Barrineau of Montmichel in just three weeks' time and today had been the final fitting of her specially designed dress. Her younger sisters were to be bridesmaids, but their dresses were already hanging in the wardrobe back at Belair, their country home. They had been made locally, but Clarice's dress had not been entrusted to a provincial dressmaker. Clarice was the centre of attention wherever she went; she had left her rounded, childish figure behind and grown into a beautiful young woman. Her thick, curling fair hair was a legacy from her maternal grandmother, as were the speedwell-blue eyes that danced with the happiness of a bride-to-be.

The St Clairs at Belair and the Barrineau family at Montmichel had moved in the same social circle near the village of St Etienne for more than a generation. Clarice had known Lucas all her life, but the gap of four years between them had made Clarice a child when Lucas left home to study at the Sorbonne and then make the grand tour of Europe. On his occasional visits home their paths had not crossed, but when he'd finally come back to St Etienne three months ago, he had met her again at a dinner party given at Gavrineau, the home of friends of his parents, Elisabeth and Raoul Barnier, and discovered not only that Clarice had grown up while he was away but that she was the toast of the neighbourhood. He'd watched her across the dinner table, the candlelight gleaming on her shining hair, her wide blue eyes sparkling as she conversed with the man on her right, the son of the house, Simon Barnier. Though Lucas had known Simon from childhood, he had not seen him for some years, as Simon had been living abroad. Now he was back. Lucas had never particularly liked him but suddenly, watching his easy discourse with Clarice, he realised he *dis*liked him excessively.

It was only a matter of days before Lucas visited Emile St Clair to ask permission to address Clarice, a matter of weeks before he proposed, and a matter of moments before she accepted him. It was a splendid match for Clarice and her delighted parents were determined that everything should be perfect for their daughter's wedding day.

Emile St Clair, a professional man, a successful architect, had picked up the pieces of his architectural business after the civil war that had raged through Paris had nearly bankrupted him six years earlier. With hard work and determination he had repaired the family finances and, recognised by his colleagues as a shrewd businessman, he had prospered. Now his favourite daughter was about to marry into the landowning Barrineau family. Emile was particularly pleased with the match, recognising it as a step up in society for Clarice. Though the St Clairs' country home – bought by Emile's father when he married some sixty years ago – was a substantial house gracious in design and set in delightful gardens, it was completely eclipsed by the grandeur of Montmichel, which had been in the Barrineau family for several generations. Proud of his Clarice, when it came to her wedding, Emile was determined no expense should be spared. When Rosalie had suggested to him that Clarice should be dressed by the finest designer in Paris, he had not demurred, simply saying, 'Certainly, if Monsieur Worth is truly the best.'

'He has even dressed the Empress Eugénie,' Rosalie replied.

Emile had no time for the erstwhile empress who had fled to exile in England at the end of the Prussian war, but accepted that if this man commanded royal clientele he must be the best, and only the best was good enough for his beloved daughter. So Rosalie had taken Clarice to 7 Rue de la Paix, and with the attention of Monsieur Worth himself, they had chosen the fabric and the design of the dress and it had been created exclusively for Clarice.

Wedding arrangements were now well advanced, but it seemed to Rosalie that every minute of her day had been taken over by the preparations. Today had been particularly long and it was not yet over. She only had two hours before she would be leaving the house again to chaperone Clarice to a performance of *The Pearl Fishers* at the new opera house. She had already sent Clarice upstairs to rest and intended to lie down for an hour herself before dressing; thus she was not pleased when Didier came quietly to the drawing room.

'Excuse me, madame,' he said, 'but there is a person at the door asking to speak with you.'

Rosalie raised tired eyes and said, 'A person, Didier? What sort of person?'

'A woman of the lower classes, madame,' replied the butler.

'Then send her away,' said Rosalie, wearily. 'I don't want to see anyone just now.'

'Very good, madame.' Didier left the room to deal with the unwelcome woman caller. Not wanting to leave her standing on their doorstep for all the neighbours to see, he had brought her indoors, but then told her to wait while he would discover if Madame St Clair was at home. When he returned, she was standing exactly where he had left her, and on hearing his tread she looked up expectantly.

'Madame St Clair is not at home to visitors,' he said stiffly, and moved to open the front door.

The woman stood her ground and said, 'Please will you tell her my name? It's Agathe—'

At that moment Hélène came down the stairs and saw Didier about to eject someone from the house. As she reached the hallway she paused, staring in confusion at the woman who seemed so familiar. Then, with a cry of delight, she recognised her. Madame Sauze, who had taken her in when, as a child, she'd been lost and alone on the streets in Paris.

'Madame Sauze! Is that you? Is it really you? Didier, it's Madame Sauze! Why are you showing her out? Have you been visiting Maman, madame? Why didn't she call me?'

'Madame St Clair is not receiving visitors this afternoon, Miss Hélène,' Didier said repressively.

'But did she know it was Madame Sauze?' demanded Hélène. She turned back to Agathe. 'Did you want to see my mother, madame?'

'I was hoping for the favour of a word with her, but if it's inconvenient I can come again another time.'

'Of course it's not inconvenient, madame. Did you send in your name?'

'Miss Hélène,' Didier tried again. 'Madame is not receiving guests this afternoon.'

'I'm sure she will receive Madame Sauze,' Hélène replied firmly. She reached out and took Agathe's hand. 'Stay where you are, madame, and I'll tell Maman that it's you.'

Ignoring the butler's outraged look, Hélène went straight to the drawing room and, opening the door, said, 'Maman, Madame Sauze is here. Shall I bring her in?'

Rosalie, having already placed her feet on a footstool, had been drifting into a doze, and when Hélène burst into the room she awoke with a start.

'Hélène? What's the matter? What did you say?'

'I said Madame Sauze is here, Maman. She's come to see you.'

'Madame Sauze? Here?'

'Yes, Maman, and she's asking to speak to you. I said I was sure you'd like to see her. Shall I bring her in?'

Rosalie was not best pleased to be placed in this position by her younger daughter, but her good manners came to her aid and she said, 'Of course. Do ask her to come in.'

'Yes, Maman.' Hélène hurried back to the hall where Madame Sauze stood waiting uncomfortably, under the eye of the butler. 'Madame, Maman says please do come into the drawing room.' And then turning to Didier, she added, 'Thank you, Didier, that will be all.' Didier looked less than pleased at this dismissal, but he simply said, 'Yes, Miss Hélène,' and retreated to his own domain.

'Do come with me, madame,' said Hélène, extending her hand again. 'Maman's in here.'

Madame Sauze followed her into the drawing room, and immediately Rosalie St Clair got up to greet her.

'Madame Sauze,' she said, 'I didn't realise it was you. What a pleasure to see you. Please do take a seat.' She waved her guest to a chair and then sat down opposite her. 'May I offer you some refreshment?'

'No, madame, I thank you, but' – she glanced across at Hélène, who had moved to take a seat beside her mother – 'if I might have a word with you in private?'

'Of course,' replied Rosalie. 'Please leave us, Hélène.'

'But Maman,' protested Hélène, 'I wanted to talk to Madame Sauze. We haven't seen her for ages.'

'Maybe you can speak later, but not until we have finished our conversation. Now, please, go and leave us in peace.'

Reluctantly Hélène got to her feet and, with one disgruntled backward glance, left the room, closing the door behind her.

'Now, madame,' said Rosalie, 'you have my ear.'

'I am very sorry to have to come to you, madame,' began Agathe, 'but I don't know where else to turn. It's not for myself that I've come, but for the girl Annette. You may remember she was with Hélène in St Luke's orphanage.'

Rosalie nodded. She did remember; Hélène used to refer to her as the bread thief, and it was Annette who had helped her slip away from the nuns. 'I see; well, what about her? Did she not come to work at the Clergy House with you?'

'Yes, she did, but I don't work there any more. Father Lenoir died and young Father Thomas no longer required my services.'

Rosalie looked surprised. 'But surely he still needed a housekeeper?'

'He did, but over the years I have trained Annette well and he decided that she could do the job as well as I.' Agathe faltered as she wondered how best to explain what had happened to the girl since she herself had been dismissed. She had sallied forth to the Avenue Ste Anne to renew her acquaintance with Rosalie St Clair. Now here she was, seated opposite that lady, and she had to introduce a subject so distasteful that it could well get her thrown out of the house. A friend, Agathe had described her to Annette, but as she looked across at Rosalie now she knew that they were not friends, simply two women who had met in the most peculiar circumstances some years ago, and had made some sort of connection.

'I'm sorry, madame,' she said. 'But may I speak directly to you?'

'I think you should,' replied Rosalie. She wondered if Madame Sauze had come looking for a position as she no longer kept house for the priest at St Jacques. Briefly she reviewed her household, here in Paris and in St Etienne. She liked the woman, respected her and had seen that she was a good housekeeper when she had visited the Clergy House all those years ago. Perhaps she could find something, an under-housekeeper at Belair? That might be a possibility. Old Madame Choux the housekeeper was getting on and would have to retire soon. As these thoughts flitted through her mind she began to give proper attention to what Madame Sauze was saying and, appalled, realised what she was actually asking for. Would she take an expectant, unmarried woman into her household?

'It's a great deal that you ask, madame,' she said when Agathe finally fell silent.

'I don't ask it for myself,' Agathe replied quietly, 'I ask for a child who has been abused and is now in a cruel situation that is none of her making.' She did not remind Rosalie that her own daughter could have been in just such a situation some years ago if Agathe had not stepped in to keep her safe; she didn't have to. The words lay between them, unspoken.

At last Rosalie said, 'So, madame, tell me again what you want of me.'

Agathe outlined her plan, that Annette should be introduced to the house at St Etienne as *her* niece, recently widowed by *la grippe*, currently rife in Paris, and allowed to work for the family there until her time should come.

Rosalie listened in silence, considering the possibilities of the plan. She knew Emile would be against such an idea, even if he believed the tale of the dead husband. He knew a little of what had befallen Hélène when she was lost during the siege, but his wife had not gone into any details and it appeared that Hélène herself had been able to block the memory entirely from her mind. She never referred to it, and she seemed to be a normal, untroubled girl on the brink of womanhood. Could she expose her to Annette in her condition without awkward explanations? How could she explain the sudden arrival of such a girl to the rest of the household, who, deliberately, had been told nothing of Hélène's experiences? Hélène would recognise her, of course she would, but would meeting her again trigger memories better left undisturbed? And yet, Rosalie knew, she owed it to Madame Sauze to agree to help.

'I understand that you wish to protect this woman,' she began and was surprised when Agathe put in gently, 'She's still a child, madame, little older than Hélène.'

'I understand what you're saying, madame,' Rosalie continued briskly, 'and I promise you I will consider what you're asking of me. My mind is full of family affairs at present – my eldest daughter, Clarice, is getting married in less than a month and she is my priority just now. However' – she held up a hand as she saw Agathe was about to speak – 'I will give the situation serious thought and see if there is any way I can help you and the girl. Let me sleep on it. Come back and see me again tomorrow and I'll give you my decision then.' She got to her feet to indicate that the interview was now over. 'I'd be grateful, madame, if this remained a private matter between us. It would distress me greatly if Hélène came to hear of the situation.'

'Certainly, madame,' Agathe agreed. 'I would never speak of this matter to Hélène.'

Rosalie nodded. 'Then, until tomorrow. Please call at the same time and I will instruct Didier to bring you straight to me.'

'She didn't say no,' Agathe told Annette when she got back to the apartment. 'She said she'd think it over and give me her answer tomorrow.'

'That means she'll say no,' sighed Annette.

'Not necessarily,' said Agathe firmly. 'It means she's giving the idea consideration.'

Chapter 8

Rosalie St Clair was indeed giving the idea consideration, but so far she was coming down on the side of refusal. How could she introduce an expectant mother into the Belair household? At this moment of all times? Hélène would know that Annette was not Madame Sauze's niece. The whole project would be built on lies and deception and would, inevitably, come out in the end. Perhaps it was not the girl's fault that she found herself pregnant and unmarried, but few people would see it like that. Maybe she could be placed with one of the village families until the baby was born. It could be brought up there and Annette could get work elsewhere to provide for it. Well, that was a possibility, she supposed. One heard of such arrangements.

Her thoughts were interrupted by Hélène's return to the room. 'Maman,' she cried, 'Didier told me Madame Sauze has gone. What did she want? Why didn't she stay and talk to me? I so wanted to hear how she is. And Annette.'

'She had something she wanted to discuss with me,' returned her mother easily. 'It took longer than we thought and she had to go back to where she's working now.'

'But isn't she still looking after the fathers at St Jacques?'

'No. I believe she keeps house for her sister.'

'For her sister? I didn't know she had a sister.'

'Really, Hélène, why should you? You actually know very little about her.'

'I know she's kind and looked after me,' replied Hélène.

'Indeed she did,' agreed Rosalie carefully. 'Now, chérie,' she went on, anxious to change the subject, 'have you done your piano practice today?'

'No,' Hélène admitted, and finding herself dismissed to the music room, she left her mother deep in thought in the drawing room.

Rosalie's thoughts were interrupted again when the door opened and Emile walked in. She knew a moment's surprise. With everything that had been happening, including Madame Sauze's unexpected visit, she had forgotten he was arriving in Paris today. She stood up to greet him and for the moment the question of Madame Sauze and Annette was pushed to the back of her mind.

'Emile,' she said, presenting her cheek for the touch of his lips. 'I hope you had an easy journey.'

'Easy enough,' replied her husband as he flung himself down into his armchair. 'Ring for Didier, will you?'

Rosalie did as she was asked and then said, 'Madame Choux looked after you well?'

'Well enough, I suppose,' grunted Emile. 'But she's getting very forgetful. Forgot to have my dinner served in the morning room as I'd asked. Laid us up in the dining room.'

'Yes, I've been thinking about Madame Choux,' Rosalie said. 'I think that after Clarice's wedding, we must suggest she retires. Find someone experienced but younger. There is always a great deal to do in a house such as ours and I think she's struggling.'

'Whatever you decide, my dear,' Emile replied dismissively,

and picking up the paper Didier had laid out on the side table, he began to read.

'Will you be joining us at the opera tonight?' Rosalie asked him.

'I beg your pardon?' Emile looked up from the paper. 'The opera?'

'Yes, we've been invited into Madame Descamps' box to see *The Pearl Fishers*.'

Emile shook his head. 'No, I don't think so, my dear. I shall probably go to my club.'

Rosalie was not surprised at his refusal. Over the last few years she and Emile had drifted apart, the first coolness between them occurring when eleven-year-old Hélène had been missing in Paris during the siege of the Communards. Rosalie had blamed Emile for not bringing Hélène to safety when he had had the chance, and if he were honest, he knew she was right, but could not admit the fact.

Outwardly they continued to live together as they always had, but the rift had gradually increased between them. Emile, always rather a distant father, had little to do with the day-to-day upbringing of his daughters. All such matters he left to Rosalie, and the atmosphere in the house was one of detached civility. Rosalie transferred all the love she had once had for him to her daughters and her son Georges and his children, her beloved grandchildren.

Now, as she watched him sipping his cognac, reading his paper, entirely unaware of her scrutiny, she thought, How he's aged over these last years!

Stooped where once he had been so erect, his hair receding to a fringe around his bald pate and the muscles of his face drooping to soft, fleshy pouches, she realised with a pang of regret that he looked older than his fifty-four years. Where, she wondered, had her Emile gone? The handsome young man who had swept her off her feet and married her when she was just eighteen? Only the ghost of him remained.

'I must go up and change,' she said with a sigh and she got to her feet. Her remark was greeted by a grunt and she added quietly, 'So you'll go to your club for your dinner?'

Emile glanced up and answered, 'I just said so, didn't I?' before returning to his paper.

Rosalie saw little of *The Pearl Fishers* that evening, as Madame Sauze's request filled her mind. Emile was not yet home when they returned from the opera and it was with relief that she went immediately to her bed. Despite her fatigue she still couldn't sleep. Lying in the darkness, Rosalie went through all the possibilities. She knew, even against her better judgement, that she was going to take in the girl, Annette, but there had to be definite conditions, and working these out kept her awake until the small hours. She realised that the story of Annette's 'husband' was thin, but the girl would be entirely unknown in St Etienne and it couldn't be disproved. If Madame Sauze accepted her offer, Rosalie would be the one to tell Hélène, to ensure that she had no doubt about the veracity of the story. She would have to speak to Emile about it in the morning, but the story she would tell him would be of the death of a young man, leaving a young widow expecting his child.

When Agathe arrived back at the Avenue Ste Anne the following afternoon, she was immediately shown up to Rosalie's private sitting room. Rosalie was sitting at a desk in the bay window with papers spread out before her.

'Madame Sauze, madame.' Didier's voice conveyed his distaste that this person should be received twice in as many days.

'Thank you, Didier.' Rosalie got up from her chair and, having greeted Agathe, invited her to sit in one of the armchairs and took the one opposite.

'Madame,' she said, leaning forward and coming straight to the point. 'I have been giving your request a great deal of thought and I think I may be able to help you and the young person concerned. However, I have to insist on several strict and unalterable conditions.' She paused, but Agathe made no reply, simply waited to hear what the conditions were.

Rosalie gave a nod of appreciation. 'Firstly, the fiction of her being recently widowed must be upheld. She must speak to no one at all of the Clergy House or what has happened there. Secondly, you will have to accompany her.'

'Oh, but, madame—'

Rosalie raised her hand. 'Hear me out, madame,' she said. 'Very soon I shall be looking for a new housekeeper at Belair. Madame Choux, my present housekeeper, is old and tired. She has served the family well for many years, but the work is getting too much for her. Before long she will be pensioned off in one of the cottages in the village. You and the girl—'

'Annette,' put in Agathe, determined that Annette should be a real person rather than a nobody without a name.

'Annette,' conceded Rosalie. 'For now, you and Annette will both work for me, until the baby is born. You will have to share a room on the servants' landing, but that can easily be explained as you are aunt and niece. After the birth, Annette will have to move out of the house. We cannot keep the child there, but it may be possible to find a family in the village who, for a little extra cash, would be happy to take them in, and it will be up to the two of you to find that money.' Rosalie glanced at Agathe for her reaction when she said this. Agathe, thinking of her few savings, gave a slight nod, and Rosalie went

on, 'Depending on circumstances I may be able to employ...
Annette... in the house again, once the child is of an age to
be left while she is working. In the meantime, you will work
with my housekeeper, Madame Choux, easing her load until
Clarice's wedding, after which she will be retired. I am hoping
that you and I will find we suit each other very well, in which
case I shall offer you her position as the Belair housekeeper.'

Agathe's eyes widened at this. She had never considered
that she might find a permanent place at Belair, and she was
about to speak when Rosalie continued, saying, 'However,
there is one further proviso. Hélène will undoubtedly
recognise Annette, and it is she who must be protected from
the unsavoury truth of the matter. She will know that Annette
is *not* your niece but I will tell her that when you were
working together over the last few years, you became fond
of each other and you adopted her as such. It is I who will
explain this and the circumstances of Annette's widowhood
to Hélène. I intend to preserve her innocence in the matter. I
shall say that Annette was married to... Have you decided on
a name?'

'Marc Dubois,' replied Agathe.

'A good name,' agreed Rosalie. 'There must be hundreds
of those in Paris, so no one can query which one she was
married to. Marc Dubois will have died in the flu epidemic,
and Annette came to you, as she was left with nowhere to
go. There must be no suggestion of anything else. You and
Annette must concoct the details of the story and you must
both stick to it rigidly. Annette must not share confidences
with Hélène, and should I find that she has even hinted that
her marriage and widowhood are not the truth, she – and
you – will be out of the house within the hour, and so you
may tell her.'

Rosalie sat back in her chair and, looking across at the other woman, said, 'That, madame, is what I have to offer, no more, no less.'

It was an offer that had been difficult to achieve. Emile had not returned home until the small hours and she'd had to wait until he awoke to discuss things with him. She had found him in the morning room partaking of a late breakfast, and pouring another cup of hot chocolate for herself, she sat down with him and told him what she had in mind. Despite her presenting him with the fictitious version of the matter, his reaction had been predictable.

'Taking in a pregnant girl who's probably no better than she should be?' He had been incredulous. 'What are you thinking of, my dear? Whatever made this woman think she could come to you in the first place? The answer is definitely no.'

'That of course was my initial reaction,' agreed Rosalie, 'but then I remembered how Madame Sauze had looked after Hélène when she was lost during the siege, and I felt we owed her something. The poor woman is desperately worried about her niece. The unhappy girl is left widowed, with a baby on the way and no visible means of support.'

'Indeed,' replied Emile drily, 'and this woman, Madame Saude...?'

'Madame Sauze...'

'Well, whatever she's called... is expecting *us* to provide one?'

'Madame Sauze is an extremely capable housekeeper,' remarked Rosalie.

'Is she now?' Emile was surprised at the apparent change of subject. 'And what has that to say to anything?'

'Emile, we have already agreed that Madame Choux will

have to be pensioned off after the wedding,' Rosalie said. 'And it seems to me that Madame Sauze would make an admirable replacement.'

'But you hardly know the woman!' scoffed Emile. 'How do you know she's any good? Have you seen references?'

'No, but I have seen how she keeps a house,' replied Rosalie. 'You may remember I visited her at the Clergy House to thank her for her care of Hélène when she was in trouble.'

It was clear from Emile's expression that he remembered no such thing, but undeterred, Rosalie went on. 'She had been there for years and only left recently when Father Lenoir died. She is now looking for another position and I thought she might suit us.'

'Bringing a pregnant niece with her!'

'She's her only relative, and no doubt the girl will work as well.'

'Hhhmm,' grunted Emile, already tired of the subject. 'I suppose you'll do as you choose. You know I leave the management of the servants entirely to you, but I hope you will give the matter great consideration before you introduce some pregnant drab into the household. Now,' he said, reaching for the bell, 'I need a fresh coffee.' Didier appeared in answer to his ring and the matter was closed.

So, Rosalie had made her offer, and silence lapsed round them as Agathe Sauze considered it. It was indeed a generous one for both of them. Annette would be away and out of Paris, beyond the clutches of Father Thomas and St Luke's orphanage. Difficult though it still might be, she would have the chance of a new life. As for Agathe herself, she too would be able to leave Paris, leave her sister, with the prospect of a real job in the country. She could hardly believe it. The idea of working in the country home of a family like the St Clairs was such a wonderful opportunity – like a dream. She longed to leap at the offer for both of them, but what about the deception required to carry it through? Suppose it were exposed? It would reflect badly on them, but far worse on the St Clairs for having colluded with it. They had a reputation to lose.

'Madame,' she said at last, 'I'm overwhelmed with your generosity. But I am concerned about the lies and deceit necessary for it to be successful. Your husband, what will he think?'

'I have of course discussed the idea with my husband,' Rosalie told her, 'but,' she admitted, 'I told him the story of your niece and the loss of her husband, and he left the matter entirely with me. The decision is mine.'

'Then, madame, with great gratitude, I accept your offer for both of us.'

'Good,' said Rosalie briskly and got to her feet. 'I will send a message down to Belair and tell them to expect you both the day after tomorrow. You can take the train. Once you arrive, you will find the household very busy and you will take up your duties immediately... working under Madame Choux's direction, of course.'

Agathe also stood up. 'Certainly, madame. I quite understand.' There had been no mention of wages, but Agathe knew that whatever Rosalie decided would be fair. In this she was immediately confirmed as Rosalie went to her desk drawer and drew out a purse. Handing Agathe some money, she said, 'For your train fare, madame. I'll see you next week, when we shall be returning to St Etienne ourselves.' Surprising Agathe, she held out her hand. 'I'm trusting you, both of you, to keep your side of the bargain,' she said.

Agathe took the proffered hand and said, 'I promise you, madame, your trust is not misplaced.'

When Agathe Sauze had left the house, Rosalie sat down at her desk and, having written a brief note to her housekeeper, summoned Pierre the coachman.

'I need you to return to Belair,' she told him. 'You will take the train tomorrow and give this letter to Madame Choux. Then the next day you're to meet the Paris train to collect two new servants I've employed to help over the wedding, a Madame Sauze and her niece, Annette Dubois. Take them to Belair and introduce them to Madame Choux.'

'Yes, madame,' said Pierre. 'And shall I then return here? In case Monsieur needs me?'

'No,' Rosalie replied. 'Stay and help at Belair. We shall all be coming back after the weekend. There is much to do before the wedding.'

Chapter 9

When Agathe got back to the apartment, she found Annette sitting on the landing outside the front door.

'Annette? What on earth are you doing?'

'She threw me out, your sister. Told me to get lost.'

'Did she now? And how did she know you were there?'

'She came to your room. She knew you weren't there and she simply walked in. At first she didn't see me, I was lying on the bed, but she went straight to the wardrobe and opened it. She was peering inside when she caught sight of me in the mirror.' Annette gave a throaty laugh. 'Gave her a shock, it did, seeing me tucked up in your bed. She shrieked! I said it was all right because I was a friend of yours but she didn't believe me. At least she said she didn't. She accused me of being a burglar and then was furious because I laughed and said "What burglar goes to bed in the house he's robbing?" She didn't laugh.'

'No, she wouldn't,' said Agathe. 'What was she doing in my room, I wonder?'

'Snooping,' replied Annette. 'Anyway, she told me to get out, so I grabbed my things and waited for you out here.' Suddenly she was serious. 'What did Madame St Clair say?'

Agathe smiled and, reaching down, pulled the girl to her

feet. 'She said yes! She said that you and I are both to go to this place Belair in St Etienne and work for her there. There is more to it than that, but we're not going to discuss it here. Let's get indoors and I'll tell you all about it – and I need to tell Fleur that I'm moving out.' She went across to the front door of the apartment and put her key in the lock. Before she could turn it the door was flung open and Fleur stood in the doorway, blocking her entrance. She stared at Agathe with angry eyes.

'So you do know this vagabond who was sleeping in your bed.'

'Yes,' replied Agathe mildly. 'She's the daughter of an old friend of mine. She's fallen on hard times and I—'

'She's certainly fallen,' retorted Fleur, pointing an accusing finger at Annette's rounded stomach, 'and I won't have her here in my home.'

'You won't have to after tomorrow,' Agathe said, 'but perhaps we should discuss this inside. Better than on the doorstep, don't you think?'

'There's nothing to discuss,' Fleur snapped. 'She's not coming in!'

'In that case,' said Agathe, 'I'm sure she won't mind standing out here for ten more minutes, just while I pack my things.'

'Pack your things? Why, where are you going? You can't just walk out after all I've done for you.'

'I hadn't planned to,' agreed Agathe, reasonably. 'I have come home with some excellent news, but as I said, I'm not going to discuss it standing on the landing. You either let us both in, or I shall simply pack up and leave.'

Fleur flushed red, but faced with this ultimatum, she stood aside and allowed both Annette and Agathe into the apartment.

'Why don't we go into the salon and I'll make some coffee,' suggested Agathe. 'Then I can tell you all about it.'

While Agathe boiled water for the coffee, Fleur sat rigidly silent in one of her armchairs. She made no effort to speak to Annette, nor did she offer a chair, so that when Agathe appeared with the tray, she found Annette still standing by the window looking down into the street.

'Come and sit down, Annette,' Agathe said, 'and have some coffee.'

Rather unwillingly Annette sat down, perching on the edge of the chair as if about to take flight. Agathe poured coffee for them all and then sat down herself.

'Well?' demanded Fleur.

'Well,' replied Agathe placidly. 'As I said outside, poor Annette is the daughter of an old friend of mine and she has fallen on hard times. She was married last year and is, as you see, expecting her first child, but sadly her husband Marc died in the recent flu epidemic, so she's been left a widow. Their room went with his job and she's been turned out by her landlord as she can't pay the rent. What would you like me to do' – Agathe's voice grew harsher – 'leave her in the gutter to die?'

'No, of course not,' muttered Fleur, 'but I think you might have told me she was here. She gave me the fright of my life, rearing up from the bed like that.'

Agathe didn't bother to ask what Fleur had been doing in her bedroom, poking through her things. She had a fair idea it wasn't the first time, but she didn't want to provoke another quarrel. Indeed, she was simply relieved that Fleur seemed to have accepted the fiction of Annette's marriage without demur, so she said, 'Drink your coffee, Fleur, and let me explain.'

Briefly she told her sister of her visit to the Avenue Ste Anne and Rosalie's offer of employment for them both.

'But why?' demanded Fleur. 'Why did you go to this Madame St Clair? How did you know she would help you?'

'I knew her some years ago when I looked after her daughter for a while. She remembered and offered to help us now.'

'But why do *you* have to go?' protested Fleur, suddenly realising how much she would miss Agathe if she moved away. She had become used to the company. Loneliness loomed and she spoke sharply. 'I can see Annette needs work and a place to live, but your place is here... with me.'

'No, Fleur, it isn't,' Agathe replied gently. 'You have been more than kind and generous in giving me a place to live while I was out of work, but I always told you it was only until I found another job, and now I've found one, and it's time for me to move out.'

'Huh!' exclaimed Fleur. 'You batten on me when you want to and then you're up and off with no warning at all.' Her face flushed a dull crimson as her anger took hold. 'You've used me, Agathe—'

'No more than you've used me, Fleur,' Agathe answered mildly.

'—and now you're casting me off!' Fleur cried, ignoring Agathe's comment entirely.

'You used me as an unpaid servant,' Agathe reminded her, 'but the arrangement suited both of us. I agree, we have made use of each other!'

Annette listened as the argument escalated, and then very quietly got to her feet and left the room, knowing that she was the cause of the row.

'You certainly are not,' Agathe told her when she came

back to her room. 'Fleur and I always have argued. We shall both get over it.' She smiled reassuringly at Annette. 'Now, tomorrow we have to get ready to leave.'

Two days later they bought their tickets and were on their way to St Etienne. As they left the apartment they said goodbye to Fleur, who was surprisingly tearful.

'When am I going to see you again, Agathe?' she wailed as they carried their bags to the front door. 'I need you. I'm not well!'

'Soon,' soothed Agathe, used to her sister's hypochondria. 'As soon as we're settled and my work allows, I'll come up and see you.'

As they left the building, she glanced up at the window that overlooked the street and saw her sister standing, pale-faced, watching them leave. Agathe lifted a hand in farewell and turned away, not knowing that her sister had spoken the truth, that she had consumption and that within months she would be dead. Agathe would never see her again.

Neither Agathe nor Annette had ever been on a train before. Annette spent the journey with her nose pressed against the window, watching sunlit countryside such as she had never seen nor been able to imagine, slip past her as the train chugged its way south from the city. Agathe was watching as well, but she was looking anxiously for the names of the stations they passed, afraid that they might miss theirs. Other passengers in the compartment came and went, and once Agathe plucked up the courage to ask one elderly woman how much further to St Etienne.

'I leave the train at the station before,' the woman replied, and with a sigh of relief Agathe knew she could relax until then.

When the train finally steamed into St Etienne she quickly

got to her feet, saying to Annette, 'Come along, hurry and pick up your bag, this is where we get off.'

They clambered down onto the platform, each of them carrying a small case containing her worldly goods. When they had passed through the ticket barrier, they stepped outside into the summer sunshine and looked about them.

'Madame St Clair said someone would meet us,' Agathe said anxiously.

Annette, looking about her, saw a man of about thirty standing beside a pony and trap, his eyes searching the few passengers who had alighted. 'Perhaps that's him,' she said.

The man spotted them at the same moment and came across. 'Madame Sauze? I am Pierre, sent by Madame St Clair to fetch you.' He added anxiously, 'You are Madame Sauze?'

'Yes, monsieur, thank you, and this is my niece, Madame Dubois.'

The man looked surprised. He had been assuming that the niece he'd been told to meet was a *Mademoiselle* Dubois, but in that instant he saw that she was expecting a child and quickly averted his eyes, saying, 'I have the trap over here. Come this way, please.'

As they drove away from the station, Annette stared wide-eyed at the scattered houses of St Etienne. Some lined the main street, hidden by high protecting walls; other, smaller houses opened directly onto the roadway; and yet more scrambled, higgledy-piggledy, up narrow lanes that branched off on either side to the rising ground beyond. The thoroughfare bisecting the village opened out into a stone-paved square, the Place, and clearly this was the heart of St Etienne. It was bounded by shops on two sides, and a busy coaching inn, a silver cockerel above its door proclaiming it Le Coq d'Argent, lay across a third. The fourth side was dominated by the Mairie, the town hall, by far the most important building in the square. In the centre of the Place, market stalls, some shaded by colourful awnings, offered fruit, vegetables and other produce from the surrounding countryside. It was a gathering place where people met to do business, to catch up on news, to share a glass of wine. Several elderly men were sitting out in the sunshine, glasses in hand, smoking pipes and chatting as they watched the progress of a game of boules; women, carrying baskets, paused to share gossip before returning home with their purchases. There was a lazy bustle about the place as it lay in the warm summer sunshine.

Pierre drove down one side, past the Mairie, and at the far end turned out of the Place towards the village church, standing atop a rise. With grey stone-flinted walls and a slender tower topped with a steeple looking out across the countryside, the church seemed to grow up out of the hill on which it stood, its encircling walled graveyard gathered protectively around it. Annette stared up at it as they drove past; it was nothing like the cheerless churches that had dominated the streets and squares of Paris, but she was done with churches and determined that she would not set foot in another unless she were forced to do so.

When Pierre turned the pony in through the gates of Belair and they were driven up the drive, they had their first sight of the house that was to be their home for at least the next few weeks.

It stood as if dreaming in the midday sunshine, symmetrical and well proportioned, with two wings extending forward a little from the main part of the house, which stood three storeys high. The walls, cream-painted stucco, were punctuated by tall windows that flashed gleams of sunlight across the drive, three to each wing and two on either side of the arched portico above the front door.

What a beautiful house! Agathe thought as, ignoring the carriage sweep at the front of the building, Pierre drove the pony and trap past the door and on round to the stable yard at the back before pulling up to allow his passengers to alight.

Could this really be the place where she might find a permanent position?

Annette had stared up at it and, assailed by an increasing fear, wished she were back in Paris. She had looked at the emptiness of the countryside from the windows of the train and longed for the close-lived bustle of the city streets she knew. And now the house. How would she ever find her way about such a large house?

Pierre got down and called to a stable lad who had appeared from the stables, 'See to the pony, Henri, I'll take these indoors to meet Madame Choux,' adding as he turned back to the two women in the trap, 'She's the housekeeper.'

He did not hand them down as he would have one of the family, but as Annette stepped down her foot slipped on the cobbles and she would have fallen had he not put out his hand to steady her. For a moment he gripped her arm and then she pulled free, colour flooding her face as she whispered her thanks.

'This way,' he said, and with that they picked up their bags and followed him through a side door into the house.

Madame Choux was in the kitchen and it was clear when she received them that they were not welcome. She looked them over for a few moments, taking in Annette's pregnancy with a pursing of her lips. She already knew that Agathe Sauze's niece was expecting a baby, that had been explained in Madame's letter, but she resented the fact that these two women had been engaged at all and without any reference to her.

'I am Madame Choux, the housekeeper, and you answer to me,' she announced by way of greeting. 'Madame said to expect you. Your uniforms are in your room. Lizette will show you where to go. Once you have changed come straight back down and I will explain your duties.' She turned away, calling over her shoulder, 'Lizette, take these two upstairs and show them where they will be sleeping.'

A small, dark-haired girl with wide, frightened eyes emerged from the scullery and, edging round the table, murmured, 'It's this way.'

They followed her up two flights of twisting stairs onto a landing that ran the length of the house. Halfway along she opened a door and said, 'In here, but you'd better be quick, Madame Choux don't like to be kept waiting.'

'Thank you, Lizette,' Agathe said with a smile. 'You go back downstairs, we can find our own way down.'

'Yes, miss,' whispered the girl, recognising that the older of the newcomers was of higher status than she, and with that she scurried off down the stairs.

Annette and Agathe looked round the room that was to be their refuge for the next few weeks. It was small, with two metal bedsteads crammed in, side by side. A chest of drawers stood in a corner and there were hooks on the back of the door on which to hang clothes. In a pile on the single chair that stood in the other corner was a plain black dress, a starched apron and a white cap, clearly meant for Annette, and on one of the beds was another apron and a black lace cap. Both clearly denoted the standing of the wearer in the household.

Agathe took off her travelling cloak and, putting her bag on the bed where the apron lay, said, 'Well, we're at close quarters, Annette, but at least we have beds to sleep in and work to do to earn our bread.' She reached for the apron and put it on over the plain stuff dress she was wearing, the one she'd always worn when keeping house for Father Lenoir. She glanced across at Annette, who remained standing pale-faced by the door, and said briskly, 'Come along, Annette, change into your uniform. You're lucky you have one provided and don't have to buy your own, as many maids must do.'

For a moment Annette didn't move and then – it was almost as if she had given herself a shake – she took off her outdoor shawl and hung it on the back of the door. Removing her skirt and bodice, she reached for the dress on the chair and struggled into it. At first she doubted she could do it up, but with help from Agathe and careful adjustment she managed to ease it over her stomach before tying the apron around her waist to disguise the bulge of her baby. It was a very snug fit, but it would have to do until she could loosen it further.

Agathe surveyed her and then said with a smile, 'You'll do.' Then, with a more serious expression, she went on, 'Remember, Annette, that Madame St Clair has put her trust in us, taking us on here. I can see that Madame Choux is not pleased with our arrival, but whatever happens, we must not cause any disharmony below stairs. She may well find fault with you, whatever she gives you to do, but if she does, simply duck your head and accept her comments without fuss. If we lose our jobs here, there will be nowhere else to go.'

'I know,' returned Annette tightly.

'I know you know,' said Agathe soothingly, 'but it may not be easy, that's all. There's sure to be speculation about you and the baby, so we have to be certain to stick to our story.'

She reached forward and took the girl's hand. 'Come on then, let's go and face Madame Cabbage.' That elicited a smile from Annette and together they went down to the kitchen.

Although Madame Choux slept on the servants' landing, not two doors away from Agathe and Annette, she also had her own tiny parlour off the kitchen and it was there that she waited for them.

'You took your time,' she snapped. 'You can leave the door.' They did as she said, even though it meant that everything she said to them could be overheard by those working – or simply listening – in the kitchen.

'Madame St Clair has written a letter,' she began, 'and tells me I am to use you wherever I need you as we prepare for the wedding. I do not know why she has employed you at all. I have no need of anyone else; the servants we have here are more than able to cope with such preparations.' There was an edge of anger in her voice, but she continued. 'However, I will of course follow Madame's orders.' She pointed to Annette. 'You, girl, are a maid-of-all-work. You will work in the laundry, the kitchen or as a chambermaid, wherever I tell you.' She glowered at Annette. 'You understand?'

Remembering Agathe's admonition, Annette ducked her head and murmured, 'Yes, madame.'

For a moment the housekeeper eyed her suspiciously and then gave a brief nod and said, 'Into the kitchen with you and find Cook. She'll have plenty of work for you.' She did not ask either of the newcomers if she had eaten, simply waved her hand at the door and turned her attention back to Agathe. Taking this dismissal, Annette went out into the kitchen where she was greeted by the cook who gave her a far warmer welcome.

'Annette, is it? I'm Madame Paquet; I'm the cook and' – her

eyes flicked to the parlour door – 'it's my kitchen. I'm pleased to see you. We can do with another pair of hands in here.' She glanced down at the roundness of Annette's stomach and went on. 'I see you're in trouble—' she began, but Annette interrupted her.

'No, madame, I am not. It's true I'm expecting a child, but it will not be born a bastard.'

'Oh ho!' laughed the cook. 'He's going to marry you then, is he?'

'No, madame,' replied Annette, looking her firmly in the eye, 'I am already married, but my beloved husband died a month ago of the flu. I am now a widow and it is his child!'

The cook looked taken aback at this outburst, but she was not unsympathetic. She turned to the other maid, the pale-faced Lizette, who stood open-mouthed at the scullery door, and Henri, who'd just come in from the stables to have his dinner, and said, 'There you are, now you know all about poor Annette. She and her aunt, Madame Sauze' – she nodded towards the open door to Madame Choux's parlour – 'are with us at least until after Miss Clarice's wedding, so let's make the most of the extra help, shall we?' She turned back to Annette. 'Have you eaten?' she asked.

'No, madame.'

'Well, sit up to the table, you can eat with the others. Lizette!'

The little maid hurried to the range and began to ladle broth from a cauldron into waiting bowls. As instructed, Annette took a chair at the big wooden table, and Lizette placed a bowl of steaming chicken broth, thick with vegetables, in front of her. There was already bread and cheese on the table and after a muttered grace from the cook, Lizette and Henri helped themselves and began to eat. Annette watched for a moment and then took some bread and a piece of cheese and picked up her spoon.

At that moment Pierre came into the kitchen. Coming along the outside passage he had overheard the interchange between the cook and the new maid.

So, he thought, that's what's happened to the girl... if you can believe it. Very sad if it's true. But is it? He gave a wry smile. He hadn't come down with the morning dew. He had seen her rounded figure, had assumed her unmarried and had been surprised when Madame Sauze had named her as *Madame* Dubois.

He walked in and sat down at the table and tucked into the broth that the cook set before him. As he mopped his bread round his bowl and licked the last drops from his fingers he considered what the girl had said. She had spoken up bravely in answer to Madame Paquet, and he admired her for it. She was able to stand up for herself, not like the other maid, Lizette. She was timid as a mouse, scared of her own shadow and thus bullied by Madame Choux. If this Annette girl and her aunt were here, it should certainly help relieve the pressure in the wedding preparations. The household managed with fewer servants these days.

Agathe had heard the raised voices as well, and seen Madame Choux's expression darken as she heard Annette's defence of her situation. However, she had told the prepared story and the way she had spoken was, Agathe decided, convincing enough. She turned her attention back to the housekeeper, who was speaking quite candidly.

'I don't know why Madame has engaged you,' she said. 'Of course, another maid is always helpful' – she gave a sniff – 'despite the state she finds herself in.'

'A widow with a baby on the way,' Agathe said, wilfully

misunderstanding her and nodding. 'Very difficult for the poor girl, I do agree.'

'But you?' Madame Choux looked at Agathe through mistrustful eyes. 'You're too old. What use will you be to me?'

Agathe, remembering her own warning to Annette, bit back a retort at such rudeness, simply saying, 'Madame St Clair knows how much extra work there will be preparing for Miss Clarice's wedding. I think she thought you might welcome another pair of hands to lighten the load.'

Madame Choux looked at her suspiciously. 'Did she now? She must know I'm well able to prepare the house for both the wedding and the house guests who will be staying over.'

'She certainly does,' Agathe agreed quietly, 'and of course it's you she's relying on, but she suggested that you might have a use for me with so much happening just now.' When Madame Choux didn't answer, Agathe said, 'I am at your bidding, madame.'

Reluctantly the housekeeper told her she was to sort and check through the linen cupboard, looking for anything that might need laundering or mending before it could be used in the guests' bedchambers. It was a job she had been putting off. It had been a long time since she had performed this particular task, one she disliked, and she was afraid there might be much in need of repair; the part-time seamstress they normally used for such work was ill and would not be able to take on the job. 'I assume you are able with your needle.'

'Indeed, madame,' replied Agathe.

'But first,' the housekeeper said with an exaggerated sigh, 'you had better have your midday meal.' And with that she led the way back into the kitchen and sat down at the table, waving Agathe to a vacant chair beside Annette. At once

Lizette leaped to her feet and served them each with a bowl of broth.

It was extremely good, and as Agathe ate she looked round the well-ordered kitchen and thought, Well, we're here, though unwelcome, and despite Fleur being so cross with me for leaving, Annette and I are well out of Paris, and thanks to Madame St Clair we both have the chance of a new life.

Chapter 10

Rosalie and the girls returned from Paris amid a flurry of excitement. The final purchases had been made; the wedding dress that had been packed in tissue paper and boxed for the journey was now hanging in the wardrobe in Clarice's bedroom. Rosalie sighed when Didier, who had returned with them, came quietly into her parlour to tell her that Madame Barrineau had called and was asking the favour of a few moments' conversation with her. Suzanne Barrineau was the last person she wanted to see just now but, as Clarice's future mother-in-law, she was due every courtesy, and when Suzanne was announced, as always she stood to greet her visitor with a smile and ordered some refreshment.

When she heard the purpose of Suzanne's visit, she smiled wearily and replied, 'Of course it will be no problem, Suzanne. Any friend of Lucas's is welcome at the wedding and of course he'll be seated with your family.'

Suzanne went on to explain at some length the unexpected arrival of Rupert Chalfont, the son of an English 'milor', now in Paris and on his way to visit them.

Rosalie hardly heard what she was saying. Suzanne was always a rattle, and Rosalie had other things on her mind.

She had recognised from the resentful expression on her housekeeper's face when she'd got home earlier that Madame Choux was not best pleased with the arrival of Agathe and Annette, but though she knew she needed to smooth her housekeeper's ruffled feathers, so far she'd had no chance to do so. Neither had she seen the newcomers – she would send for them in due course but had not yet had time. She also needed to speak with Hélène in private to tell her of the new arrivals and explain their presence.

'So, my dear Rosalie, you see how difficult it would be for the poor man, knowing no one but Lucas...'

Rosalie returned her attention to Suzanne, saying as she poured more coffee and offered the plate of Cook's ratafia biscuits, 'Please don't concern yourself, Suzanne. There will be no problem with the arrangements, I assure you.'

It was a relief when Suzanne rose to go, pleading, 'So much to do, my dear Rosalie,' adding as a decided afterthought, 'as you must have yourself!'

Rosalie agreed that indeed she did, and rang for Didier to show Suzanne out.

While their mother had been engaged with Madame Barrineau, the three girls had been happily settling back into their country home. Though they all enjoyed the occasional visit to Paris, they had always preferred living at Belair, where they were allowed far more freedom. Clarice went upstairs to rest before yet another evening engagement, Louise made herself scarce before her governess, Mademoiselle Corbine, could summon her to the schoolroom, and Hélène decided to go into the drawing room and play the piano. It was as she was crossing the hall that she saw Annette, the bread thief. She stopped in her tracks as Annette emerged from behind the heavy door that separated the kitchen and servants' area from the main part of the house. She was carrying a pile of ironed sheets that Madame Sauze needed upstairs. She, too, stopped short, almost dropping her load of linen.

'Annette?' Hélène stared at her. 'Is it you?'

'Yes, Miss Hélène,' answered Annette carefully.

'It is, isn't it?' Hélène looked perplexed. 'But what are you doing here?'

'Taking these sheets upstairs to Madame Sauze to be—'

'Madame Sauze! Is she here too? What's going on?'

'Your mother has employed us both to help out over the busy period of Miss Clarice's wedding, miss. She said it was going to be a very busy time.'

'I see,' said Hélène, but she didn't. She didn't see at all. Why hadn't Maman told her what she'd done? Then she remembered the visit Madame Sauze had made to the Avenue Ste Anne the previous week. Had she come there looking for work? Hélène was at a loss and said lamely, 'How long have you been here, Annette?'

'Just five days, miss,' came the reply.

'Five days?' Only a week since Madame Sauze had come to see Maman. This was all very sudden.

'Excuse me, miss, but I have to take these up to Madame Sauze. She's waiting for them.'

'Of course, Annette, sorry.' Hélène stood aside, and as the other girl stepped onto the stairs she added, 'But I don't think you need to call me "miss", Annette. You never did before.'

'Yes I must, miss,' came the firm reply. 'I'm a housemaid and you're family. If you'll excuse me, miss?' She turned and went up the stairs, watched for a moment by Hélène, left standing in the hall. As Annette reached the top Hélène called up to her, 'In that case, you should be using the back stairs.'

'Yes, miss,' said the bread thief quietly. 'Thank you. I'll

remember in future.' And with that she disappeared along the landing.

Not like the bread thief of old, thought Hélène. Not at all like the girl who had stolen her bread and then, later, taken a beating for tripping up Sister Gabrielle, allowing Hélène to make her escape from St Luke's orphanage all those years ago. That girl wasn't meek and mild – she'd been rebellious and full of spunk. So what, Hélène wondered, had happened to her to account for the change?

At that moment Didier appeared in the hall and said, 'Miss Hélène, your mother would like to speak to you in her sitting room.'

And I'd like to speak to her, too, thought Hélène as she replied, 'Thank you, Didier, I'll go and see her now.'

Rosalie was pouring herself yet more coffee when Hélène knocked and went into her mother's private sitting room. It wasn't a large room, but prettily furnished, with tall windows looking out over the garden, and it was entirely her mother's domain. No one went into it except by invitation, and Rosalie guarded, jealously, the peace that she found there.

'You wanted me, Maman?'

'Yes, sit down, chérie, we need to have a quiet talk. Would you like some coffee?'

Rosalie rang the bell for another cup and a second pot of coffee and waited until they had been brought before she said, 'I've a surprise for you, Hélène.'

'A surprise? What sort of surprise?'

'While we were in Paris, you may remember Madame Sauze came to visit me. Well, she was looking for a job. She no longer works at the Clergy House, and nor does her niece.'

'Her niece?' echoed Hélène. 'Who's that?' But even as she

asked the question she knew the answer. 'You mean Annette? But she's not her niece!'

'No,' agreed her mother, 'I know that and so do you, but since they have been working together over the last few years they have become close and Madame Sauze now introduces Annette as her niece; it gives them both a feeling of family. Anyway,' she went on, 'the old priest died and the young curate gave them notice. Annette was going to be married anyway, so she was happy enough to leave the house.'

'Annette's married?' asked Hélène, startled.

'Yes, or at least she was, but her husband died in the flu epidemic soon after, so now she's a widow.'

'Oh, poor Annette,' cried Hélène. 'How awful!'

'Yes, it's very sad for her. Still, what I was going to tell you is that after Madame Sauze came to see me, I decided to employ them both, just over the wedding period to begin with, so you mustn't be surprised to see them about the house. Agathe Sauze is helping Madame Choux, taking on some of the more mundane housekeeping jobs, and Annette is a general maid-of-all-work.'

'That explains it,' exclaimed Hélène. 'I saw Annette just now and—'

'You've seen her?' interrupted Rosalie. 'And did you speak with her?'

'Yes, of course,' answered Hélène. 'Why?'

'And what did she say?'

'Nothing much. I was surprised to see her and asked why she was here. She told me you'd just hired her and Madame Sauze to work here over the wedding.' Hélène gave a slight smile and added, 'She called me "miss".'

'As indeed she should,' said Rosalie. 'I know you knew each other as children, but that was long ago. Now the situation is quite different.' She paused and, looking speculatively at her daughter, said, 'How did you think she looked?'

Hélène frowned. 'What do you mean, Maman? How did she look?'

'I just wondered if you recognised her easily.'

'Well, yes, she hadn't changed much. A bit older, of course, and a bit fatter than I remembered, but she looked much as she did before. Why?'

Rosalie shrugged. 'No reason. You've changed as you've grown up and I wondered if she'd done the same – if she was different, you know, having been married.'

'She seemed sad, somehow, but if her husband has died recently that's to be expected, isn't it?'

'Of course,' agreed her mother, and she got to her feet. 'Now I must go and get changed for this evening.' She smiled across at her daughter. 'After the wedding, when you're really out, it'll be your turn to find a husband!'

In her boudoir Rosalie prepared to change into evening dress. She was content with her conversation with Hélène. Clearly Annette had not mentioned her pregnancy, and Hélène had not recognised it for what it was. She would have to know in the end of course, when the baby was born, but the less she knew in the meantime, the better.

It was the next day before Rosalie was able to send for her housekeeper. Madame Choux joined her in the morning room once the breakfast had been cleared away and stood waiting, her face stony, her hands folded across her stomach.

'Good morning, Madame Choux,' Rosalie said, looking up from the page she had been writing on. 'How has everything been since I was away?'

'Fair to middling, madame,' replied Madame Choux. 'We've all been preparing for the arrival of Mr Georges and his family. I believe the nursemaid is coming with them. I've put a truckle bed into the night nursery so that she will be close to the children.'

'Good, that's as it should be. And how have the new servants settled in?'

'The girl, she's a good worker, been turning her hand to anything I ask her. Pity she'll be leaving us so soon, but that baby must be due at any time. Her aunt, that Madame Sauze, has been to the village and arranged with Widow Leclerc for her to live there when her time comes.'

'That seems a good arrangement,' said Rosalie. 'It's best to be prepared. I knew I could rely on Madame Sauze to organise things.'

'That's as may be,' said Madame Choux darkly, 'but I won't need her once Miss Clarice is married.' She looked Rosalie in the eye and added, 'I don't rightly need her now, madame, if you don't mind me saying.'

'I do mind,' said Rosalie briskly. 'Whom I choose to employ is none of your business, and' – her lips tightened – 'I choose to employ Madame Sauze.' There was a moment's silence as Madame Choux realised she had gone too far and then Rosalie said, 'I'm glad everything is under control, madame. Please ask Madame Sauze to come and see me straight away.' She picked up the notebook in which she'd been writing and Madame Choux bobbed a curtsy and left the room.

A few minutes later there was a knock at the door and Agathe came in. Rosalie set aside her writing and said, 'Good morning, Madame Sauze. How have you settled in?'

'Well, thank you, madame. Annette and I are very comfortable, and there has been plenty to keep us busy.'

'I'm sure there has,' agreed Rosalie. 'I hear from Madame

Choux that you have managed to make arrangements for Annette when her time comes.'

'Yes, madame. I spoke to Father Bernard at the church and he suggested that Madame Leclerc, who was recently widowed, might be pleased of the company and the extra money.'

Rosalie nodded. 'I have heard of her,' she said. 'I believe she is well known in the village both as a midwife and for laying out the dead.'

'Indeed, madame. I went to see her and for a small recompense, she is happy to give Annette and the baby a home. We have agreed that the baby should be born in her house, where she would be on hand to help deliver the child. If you agree, madame, I think she should move there immediately after Miss Clarice's wedding. She can still come to work from there if that's acceptable to you, until the baby is born.'

'That sounds a good arrangement,' Rosalie said, and with that decided, she glanced down at the list in her notebook and asked, 'And how are the preparations going in the house?'

'Well, madame. I know you'll be pleased how much we've achieved. The windows still need to be cleaned, but better just before the day. Everything else has been prepared, and with Monsieur Didier back with us to supervise in the butler's pantry, you can rest assured nothing will be overlooked.'

'Good.' Rosalie got to her feet and picked up her notebook. 'I'm glad you're here, Agathe; we need someone with sound common sense. I will see Annette later. I believe she and Hélène have already spoken, and I have explained to Hélène about Annette's husband. She quite understands and, having every sympathy for Annette, will ask her no questions. I want to ensure that there are no upsets before Clarice's big day.'

Chapter 11

Rosalie was not the only one who was determined that nothing should spoil the special event. The day before the wedding, Suzanne Barrineau sat alone in the drawing room of Montmichel, waiting to receive their unexpected guest from London, her mind seething with resentment. How could Lucas have invited someone he hardly knew, foisting some unknown Englishman onto them like this? They had received a second telegram last evening announcing the time of his arrival in St Etienne today and clearly expecting someone to be at the station to meet him. How inconsiderate of this young man simply to assume he was welcome to stay at Montmichel as if he were one of the family, or even an old friend.

'But I invited him to,' Lucas had pointed out patiently when Suzanne again confronted him with this. 'He's a great fellow. You'll like him. He's good-looking, charming and, Mother, very well bred!' It was the well bred part that Lucas emphasised. To his mother, breeding was everything.

'You will be here to greet him,' she said.

'No, I'm afraid not, Mother. You know I am to lunch at Belair tomorrow, but he won't mind, he's a capital fellow. You know lunch tomorrow will be the last time I shall see Clarice before we meet at the Mairie. Don't worry. I will be back in plenty of time for dinner, and you will be here to make him welcome, won't you?'

Suzanne reluctantly agreed she would, but with a mutinous expression on her face. Lucas leaned forward and kissed her powdered cheek. 'Knew I could rely on you, Maman,' he said.

Rupert was met at the station by Lucien, the Barrineaux' taciturn groom, who, having greeted him politely, drove all the way to Montmichel in complete silence. Rupert, unperturbed by the quiet, looked with interest at the village as they passed through its centre. The place was not large but had some interesting buildings. The town hall was the most imposing, complete with arched windows, a clock tower and a fluttering flag. However, Rupert was more interested in the inn, Le Coq d'Argent. Rupert always liked to discover the local watering holes wherever he went, and Le Coq looked a decent sort of place. Perhaps there would be time for a glass of wine with Lucas before the big event. Lucien drove them out of the square and past the church, set upon its knoll. That must be where the wedding would take place tomorrow, Rupert thought. A pretty enough church if one had to get married, and with a slightly guilty smile he thought of Mary Dawson back at Pilgrim's Oak and was glad he did not.

About a mile beyond the village, they came to two huge stone gateposts, topped with stone eagles. Lucien turned the chaise in through wrought-iron gates and along a winding drive that opened into a turning circle in front of an imposing chateau – for, thought Rupert, who was impressed despite himself, it could hardly be regarded as anything else. His friend Lucas had let it be known while he was staying in London that his family were landowners, but Rupert had had no inkling of quite how impressive Montmichel would be. Built in mellow golden stone, with a slate mansard roof, its façade stood three storeys high, above which, set in the steepness of the roof, were the tiny windows of the servants' quarters. Tall casement windows topped with decorated pediments opened off the ground floor, and above, a similar row of windows, each flanked with painted wooden shutters, looked out across the garden to the orchards and vineyards of the estate. It was a house that demanded attention, built to display its owners' wealth and position in society. As he looked at its magnificence Rupert wondered, with a grin, if Lucas had any sisters. He got down from the chaise and waited for Lucien to bring his valise before approaching the imposing front door.

As he raised his hand to sound the brass bell, the door swung open and he was greeted by an unsmiling butler who said, 'Good afternoon, Monsieur Chalfont, I am Gaspard. Welcome to Montmichel.' He stood aside to let Rupert into a wide expanse of marble-floored hall. Doors opened in several directions and a graceful staircase with a carved banister curved up to the first floor.

'Aristide will take your luggage, monsieur,' said Gaspard as a footman appeared from a passageway. 'Will your man be arriving later?'

'I'm afraid not, Gaspard,' Rupert answered in fluent French. 'My man Parker has been detained in England.'

'I see, sir.' Gaspard's tone was studiously neutral. 'But that is of no consequence. If it is convenient, Aristide will take care of all your requirements while you are staying with us.'

'Thank you, Gaspard.' Rupert suppressed a smile. 'That would be most convenient.'

Aristide disappeared to collect Rupert's luggage from the chaise and the butler said, 'Please come this way, Monsieur Chalfont; Madame Barrineau is expecting you.'

Rupert followed Gaspard into a large, sunlit drawing room, where Suzanne Barrineau was seated in an armchair by the window, an embroidery frame in her hand. As Gaspard announced Rupert, she laid aside her stitchery and, getting to her feet, held out her hand.

'Monsieur Chalfont, we are very pleased that you found yourself able to come to Lucas's wedding,' she said, 'even at such short notice.'

'You are more than kind to invite me, madame,' he replied, raising her extended hand to his lips and thinking... even if you didn't.

'Any friend of Lucas's is, of course, a welcome guest. I regret that he is at Belair, the home of his bride, just now, but he will be back for dinner, when the rest of our family will have the pleasure of meeting you.' She glanced out of the window and added as she waved her hand vaguely in the direction of the garden, 'I'm afraid I have duties that require my attention now, but Lucas will be home well before dinner to greet you.' She turned back to him and went on, 'I'm sure you are tired after your journey, monsieur, so should you require any refreshment in the meantime, please don't hesitate to ring and Gaspard will bring it to your room.'

Where you, unwanted guest, should stay until Lucas gets home, thought Rupert cynically. But he showed no sign of his thoughts in the smile with which he greeted this suggestion, simply saying, 'Thank you, madame.'

Suzanne reached for the bell cord beside her and Aristide appeared at the door.

'Ah, Aristide, please show Monsieur Chalfont to his room, and show every attention to our honoured guest.'

Rupert had to smile at her obvious lack of sincerity, but he thanked her again and followed the footman out of the room.

Suzanne sank back down in her chair with relief. She had not wanted this supposed friend of Lucas's to intrude on the wedding, but at least he seemed presentable enough. Good-looking in an English sort of way, with deep-set dark brown eyes, determined chin and a lazy smile. She had been relieved when he had answered her in perfect French – at least there would be no difficulty in communication. She had to admit Lucas had been right, Rupert Chalfont did have a certain charm, which brought her thoughts at once to her younger daughter. The elder, Diane, was already safely married to Baptiste Marelle and would be in no danger from the English guest's easy manner, but Lucie, at only sixteen, was of an impressionable age. She must ensure that Lucie did not have her head turned by this unknown Englishman with the good looks and the lazy smile. Immediately her mind turned to her dinner table for that night and she began rearranging the seating plan so that Rupert Chalfont would be seated well away from Lucie.

Had he known of them, Rupert might have smiled at his hostess's worries after his earlier thoughts about Lucas having a sister, but he did not. He followed Aristide up the gracefully curving staircase to the floor above, then along a landing to another corridor that intersected it. A second flight of stairs led them upward to the next storey; not the servants' floor, but not the main guestroom floor either. Here, the footman opened a door and stood aside for Rupert to pass into a guest bedroom, where his trunk was already waiting for him. It was not a large room, but well furnished with all that he could need for a short stay.

'Monsieur will find the bathroom at the far end of the corridor,' intoned Aristide. He clearly knew the status of this unexpected guest and though Gaspard had assigned him to look after him, he had little hope of a gratuity. In this, however, he was wrong.

'Aristide, is it?' Rupert asked in fluent French. He reached into the pocket of his coat and extracted a guinea. 'English money, I'm afraid,' he said, 'but I'm sure you'll be able to find a use for it?' He gave the footman a quizzical smile and saw the young man's eyes gleam.

'Fair enough, Aristide, but I shall expect something in return. I don't know anyone in the family except for Monsieur Lucas, so perhaps you can enlighten me?'

'Certainly, monsieur,' replied Aristide. 'There is, of course, Monsieur and Madame Barrineau; Monsieur Lucas, his sister Madame Diane Marelle and her husband Colonel Marelle, and his other sister, Mademoiselle Lucie, not yet out of the schoolroom. Monsieur Barrineau's mother also lives in the house, but she seldom leaves her room these days.'

'But she will attend the wedding?'

Aristide shrugged. 'Who can tell, monsieur? She is very old.'

'I see.' Rupert made a mental note of all the names so far. 'And are there any other guests staying at the house?'

'Madame's sister and her husband,' replied Aristide, 'that's Monsieur and Madame Beaumont, and some cousins of Monsieur Barrineau, Mademoiselle Pauline Roubert and her sister Mademoiselle Mia, two unmarried ladies of a certain age. You will meet them all at dinner.'

Feeling he now had a better knowledge of the household, Rupert dismissed Aristide, clutching his guinea, and began to unpack his bag. Though he had no valet with him, he was travelling light and he was well used to looking after himself. He had all the clothes required for a gentleman staying at a country house for a few days. He would not disgrace Lucas, nor make him regret his impulsive invitation. Perhaps if he decided to stay away for more than another week or so, he would send home and ask his man Parker to bring him more clothes.

The view from his window, when he crossed to look out, was wide and far reaching. Montmichel boasted beautiful gardens and an extensive park. Had he known it, Suzanne Barrineau had wanted to hold the wedding breakfast and reception here at Montmichel. 'So much more suitable,' she had murmured to her husband, but Emile and Rosalie were determined to host their daughter's wedding at their own home, and eventually, encouraged by both her son and her husband, Suzanne had acquiesced.

'There is absolutely nothing wrong with Belair,' Lucas had said. 'It's where Clarice wants our wedding celebrations to be.' And if that was what Clarice wanted, as far as Lucas was concerned, there would be no question of anything else. However, after further discussion it was decided that a ball should be given in honour of the young couple at Montmichel the day after the wedding, and Suzanne had thrown herself into the preparations for that. She was determined that the Barrineaux' contribution to the festivities would not be second best.

Rupert decided now, as he looked out into the beautiful summer's day beyond his window, that he would go outside and explore the garden. He had no wish to remain cooped up in his room until Lucas's return. Thus it was that Suzanne saw him wandering through her rose garden sometime before her son came home and another black mark was chalked up against him.

That evening the dinner party was a convivial affair. Rupert found himself seated by Lucas's sister Diane Marelle and found her extremely good company. On his other side was

Madame Beaumont, his hostess's sister. These two women he set out to charm, knowing that to Suzanne he was already persona non grata. The other ladies at the table, the Roubert cousins, remained almost silent, only answering in soft voices if someone addressed them directly, and at the far end, sitting between her father and Lucas, was the daughter of the house, Lucie. Pretty enough, Rupert thought wickedly, worth a moment's dalliance perhaps, enough to worry Madame Barrineau. He treated Lucie to a smile, which she returned shyly before lowering her eyes as a young girl should.

Later, when the ladies had withdrawn to the drawing room, Madame Beaumont said, 'Your English guest seems a very pleasant person, Suzanne.'

Her sister turned on her at once. 'Isabelle, how can you say so? He wheedled an invitation from Lucas when he was in London, and we know nothing about him. He will leave as soon as the wedding is over and Lucas has left on his honeymoon. There will be no excuse to trespass on our hospitality after that.'

Surprised at her antagonism, Isabelle replied mildly, 'He's the son of an English baronet, I believe, Suzanne, and thus entirely unexceptionable.'

'I have to say, Maman, that I also found him quite charming,' said Diane. 'I liked him very much.' She turned to her cousin, Mademoiselle Roubert. 'Did you not think him so, Cousin Pauline?'

Pauline Roubert coloured. 'I'm sure any friend of Lucas's will be charming,' she replied softly, and Mia, as always taking her lead from her sister, murmured, 'Charming.'

'I don't intend to discuss him any more,' snapped Suzanne, murmuring sotto voce, 'I don't want Lucie to get any stupid ideas about him.'

Lucie, overhearing this conversation, said pettishly, 'What ideas, Maman? How can I have any ideas? I haven't even spoken to him yet.' But, she thought privately, he did smile at me and he has a lovely smile.

As the ladies discussed him in the drawing room, Rupert was enjoying a cigar and cognac in the dining room with the gentlemen, the conversation flowing easily as he was accepted as Lucas's English friend. At one point there was some discussion about the following day and Rupert was surprised to learn that the actual marriage would take place at the Mairie, the town hall he had seen as Lucien had driven him through the village.

'In France one cannot be married in a church only,' Lucas explained. 'First is the civil ceremony to make us man and wife in the eyes of the law, and then the church service to marry us in the eyes of God. We will drive to the Place for the first part and then as husband and wife we will walk together to the church. Most of our guests will await us there. You will see us as we walk down the aisle together.'

It was delicately done, Rupert thought as he lay in bed later that night. He was to wait in the church with the less important guests.

Well, he didn't mind. He knew that Madame Barrineau would prefer he wasn't there at all, but he'd enjoyed meeting Lucas's family that evening. He had also learned that there was to be a ball on the second evening. They certainly know how to celebrate a wedding, he thought, and he wondered if Lucie would be there. She was very young, too young really, but she would probably be allowed to dance at her brother's wedding.

I'll ask her for a dance, Rupert thought with a grin, if only to tease her mother. He realised, as he drifted off into an easy sleep, that he was looking forward to the following day.

Chapter 12

The day of Clarice's wedding dawned bright and clear. When Hélène threw back her bedroom curtains and opened the window, the sun streamed in and the dawn chorus was filling the garden with birdsong. She sat on her window seat and looked at the beautifully tended garden, the flowerbeds a riot of colour. Seen from above, the parterre that lay just below her window was a waggon wheel with a fountain at its hub. Hélène had always loved it, the immaculately clipped box hedges, the smooth gravel of its pathways. She found such order soothing; she often sat at her window looking out into the cool of the early morning garden, watching the sun rise over the orchard to begin its journey to evening, when it would sink at last behind the distant hills, no more than smudges in the west.

Today there was already activity in the garden as Patrice and his assistant walked the pathways, deadheading any plant that had dared to fade before Miss Clarice's special day. The gardeners were not the only ones abroad. From round the stable block beyond the corner of the house came the laughter of children, and as Hélène watched she saw her brother Georges's offspring, five-year-old Monique and three-year-old Clément, appear with their nursemaid, Delphine.

They were to carry their Aunt Clarice's train as she walked down the aisle and had been bursting with pride the previous evening when they had finally been allowed to try on their wedding clothes. Now they were running ahead of Delphine, shrieking with laughter as two of the dogs gallivanted about them, tails wagging furiously and barking. When they looked up and saw her at her window, Hélène waved to the delighted children and felt her heart lift at their excitement. Today was going to be special, she just knew it. A perfect day. She loved Clarice dearly and wished her every happiness on this her wedding day.

In the last few days the whole house had been buzzing with preparation and there had been no rest for anyone. With Rosalie's consent, Madame Sauze had gradually taken over duties as the housekeeper when Madame Choux, beginning to founder with all the extra organisation and work to be done, withdrew to the sanctuary of her parlour with a fit of the megrims. The rest of the servants, including Yvette, Madame St Clair's maid, and Pierre the coachman, had accepted their arrival readily enough, and once Annette had made clear her pregnancy would not affect her work, it was never mentioned again. Even the dignified Didier relaxed a little, particularly towards Agathe, treating her almost as an equal. It was clear that below stairs everyone was determined that Miss Clarice's day should be perfect, that nothing should go awry.

With so much to do, Annette and Agathe had seen little of each other during the days. It was only as they crawled wearily into their beds at the end of each evening that they saw each other alone and had the chance to speak.

'You're looking washed out, Annette,' Agathe said one night. 'As soon as this wedding is over I think you should move in with Madame Leclerc. You can still come daily into Belair until your time, but you need to rest a little.'

'I will, after the wedding,' agreed Annette, for indeed she was feeling inordinately tired, 'but I'll be fine until then and you'll need me here.'

She'd been right. The Belair kitchens had been busy for the previous week as pies and patties were made, meat marinated ready for the ovens, and syllabubs and creations built of spun sugar created by a master chef, Antoine, specifically employed to prepare the feast for the wedding breakfast. Adèle Paquet, the St Clairs' cook, had been angry that preparation of the food had not been left to her, but as Monsieur Antoine took over her kitchen, she had become more and more relieved that such a banquet for more than sixty people had not been her responsibility. The kitchen servants had peeled vegetables brought in from the kitchen garden; had chopped and mixed and stirred all that Antoine needed for his exotic dishes and his delicate sauces.

The preparations had risen almost to fever pitch, with the arrival two days ago of Captain Georges St Clair and his family and Madame's sister Madame Clémentine Gilbert and her husband Edouard adding to the excitement.

Rosalie and Emile's son Georges and his family occupied their usual three rooms on the first floor: one as a night nursery for the children and their nursery maid; one as a day nursery; and the last, a large apartment with a view out over the drive, as a bedchamber for Georges and his wife, Sylvie. Despite having been wounded in the civil war some years earlier, Georges was still a serving officer in the army, and though he now had a wooden leg and walked with a stick, that did not stop him from keeping his men up to scratch. Most of the time he was stationed near Versailles, and though he and his family had lodgings in a small village outside, he was often away from home. He had received special leave to be away for a week to attend his sister's wedding, and as always he and his family were warmly welcomed by those below stairs.

Monsieur and Madame Gilbert, bringing a maid and valet, were another matter altogether and their arrival was greeted with far less enthusiasm. Clémentine Gilbert was nothing like her sister but fussy and demanding, her bell was forever jangling in the kitchen. Her husband, a small, petulant man, was never quite satisfied with anything and continually found fault where there was none.

'And that,' Madame Sauze confided to Annette as the bell rang yet again and Madame Gilbert's maid, Claudy, scurried upstairs to answer it, 'we can well do without.'

The only person missing, Rosalie had thought sadly as the family had gathered the previous evening, was Marcel. Marcel, her younger son, killed during the civil war in Paris six years ago. Georges and Marcel had found themselves on opposite sides, but they had joined forces to keep Hélène safe throughout the strife. Rosalie loved both her sons and thought of Marcel with great sadness on family occasions, but Emile, horrified that Marcel had been a Communard, never spoke of him, allowing the general assumption that he had died fighting with the French army.

Now at last the wedding day had arrived. Annette had been hard at work in the house since cockcrow. Once she had rekindled the kitchen stove and set water to heat, she and Lizette laid the large table in the dining room. The company in the house were too many for them all to eat their breakfast as the family usually did, informally in the sunny cheerfulness of the morning room.

Almost at once the household was astir; on such a special occasion everyone was awake early, in eager anticipation of the day ahead. Bells began to ring below stairs with demands for hot water. Annette answered these calls, carrying buckets up to fill washing bowls, and in Monsieur St Clair's case the bathtub he had had installed in his dressing room. She found carrying so many extra buckets extremely tiring. She knew everyone was under pressure and made no complaint, but more than once she had to pause on the stairs, resting the bucket on the floor to ease an increasing ache in her back.

Gradually the family came downstairs and Madame and Monsieur Gilbert emerged from the blue guest room just as Rosalie St Clair appeared on the landing.

'Good morning, Clémentine,' she said. 'I trust you slept well.'

'As well as can be expected,' sighed Clémentine. 'It's never the same in a strange bed, is it? I feel distinctly unrested, but I make no complaint, my dear Rosalie. None at all.'

'Well, it's going to be a wonderful day,' Rosalie said brightly. 'Look at that sunshine!'

Her sister looked out of the window and replied with a shake of her head, 'It's going to be very hot,' adding almost as an afterthought, 'And how is dearest Clarice this morning?'

'Breakfasting in bed,' replied Rosalie. 'None of you will see her before she arrives at the Mairie.'

'Indeed, I should have asked Claudy to bring me a tray upstairs,' Clémentine bemoaned, 'but I wouldn't want to be any trouble on such a busy day.'

'Of course not,' Rosalie agreed, wishing her sister had asked and had stayed out of the way. 'Shall we go down?' And together they descended the stairs in search of breakfast.

At that moment the door to the kitchen passage opened and Annette, carrying a heavy tray, crossed the hall into the dining room. She eased the door open and entered the room with baskets of freshly made croissants, strawberries from the garden and tall jugs of coffee and hot chocolate.

'Have you taken up Miss Clarice's tray, Annette?' asked Rosalie.

'Not yet, madame,' Annette replied.

'Then leave all that on the sideboard,' Rosalie told her, 'and take her tray straight up. You have a great deal to do and we can serve ourselves.'

Annette bobbed a curtsy and, having unloaded her tray, quietly left the room and returned to the kitchen.

'I'm surprised you employ a maid so obviously in the family way,' remarked Clémentine as she accepted the cup of coffee Rosalie had poured for her. 'I would turn off any maid who has got herself into such an embarrassing predicament.'

'Ah, but Annette's case is a little different, Clémentine,' Rosalie replied easily. 'The poor girl's husband has recently died, leaving her carrying a posthumous child.'

'Even so...' Clémentine sniffed and left the rest of her sentence unfinished.

Hélène opened her mouth to speak, but at a frown from her mother she closed it again. There was no need, her mother's frown said, to discuss the matter further with Aunt Clémentine.

Once she had delivered Clarice's breakfast tray to her room, and while the rest of the family were still at breakfast, Annette quickly made beds and aired bedrooms before returning to the turmoil of the kitchen, where Antoine issued instructions, insisted on immediate obedience and snapped at those who were careless or inattentive. It was a relief that hardly had she been there for half an hour before she was summoned to her mistress's boudoir.

'Annette, I need you to go up to Miss Hélène's room and help her to dress. Go along to her now, she's expecting you.'

Annette bobbed a curtsy and was about to leave the room when Rosalie said, 'One moment. How do you like working here? Have you settled in well?'

'Yes, madame, I like it very much.'

Rosalie nodded satisfaction at her answer. 'Good,' she said. 'Perhaps something can be arranged in due course, after...' She paused, interrupting herself, and said, 'You're keeping well? It can't be long now, can it?'

'I am well, madame, thank you.'

'Well, run along now, Hélène is waiting for you.'

'Yes, madame, thank you, madame.' Annette bobbed another curtsy and hurried along the landing to Hélène's room. Her heart was singing. Madame seemed pleased with her and was hinting that she might be allowed back to work at Belair... after. Over the last few weeks she had tried to put 'after' out of her mind. When the baby was born she would be living with the Widow Leclerc in the village, cut off from Madame Sauze, Aunt Agathe, at Belair. Somehow she would have to look after her child and earn their living, but she had no real idea of how she would manage. Now it seemed Madame St Clair had given her hope for the future, hers and her baby's.

She tapped on the door, and when Hélène called her in, she was greeted with a smile.

'Isn't this fun?' Hélène said. 'I asked Maman if you could come and help me dress. She's helping Louise herself, but I know she really wants to be with Clarice.'

She looked across at Annette and asked almost the same question as her mother. 'Are you happy here, Annette?'

'Oh yes, Miss Hélène,' Annette replied. 'It's a lovely place to work.'

With an abrupt change of subject Hélène asked, 'When is your baby coming?'

'Very soon, miss,' replied Annette, laying a hand on her stomach. 'I can feel it kicking.'

Hélène stared at her in amazement. 'Kicking? Really? Can you?'

Annette nodded. 'You could...' she began, but her voice tailed away as she realised what she had been about to say.

Hélène stared at her for a moment and then said, 'You are saying I could too?'

Annette nodded again. 'Yes, miss, if you wanted... if you put your hand...'

Hélène stepped forward and, holding out her hand, said, 'Show me.'

Annette hesitated and Hélène said, 'Take my hand and show me where.'

Annette did as she was asked and Hélène rested her hand against the bulge beneath Annette's apron. For a moment she felt nothing, and then there was a definite movement under her palm and then another. She glanced up into Annette's face. 'I felt it,' she said in wonder. 'I felt him move! Fancy being able to feel him move before he's even born! He's alive inside you, Annette. Waiting to be born.'

Annette, who had already experienced this wonder, knew it again. Her baby was alive... and kicking. 'It may be a girl,' she murmured.

'What? Oh, yes, I know, but when he kicked I thought, it's a boy!'

At that moment they heard Rosalie's voice in the corridor and Hélène moved quickly away. 'I must get ready,' she said. 'Maman will be in to see how we are getting on in a minute.'

At once Annette moved to the bed where Hélène's undergarments, chemise and stockings had been laid out ready by Rosalie's maid, Yvette. The pale yellow silk gown was hanging in the wardrobe and once Hélène was ready, Annette lifted it over her head. Its graceful folds slipped over her hooped petticoat, the square neckline emphasising the delicacy of her shoulders. Hélène stood facing the mirror staring at her reflection as Annette adjusted the back and straightened the neckline.

'I don't look like me,' she said.

'You look beautiful, Hélène,' replied Annette, in that moment quite forgetting to address her as 'miss'. 'Come to the dressing table and let me arrange your hair.'

When Rosalie finally came into the room she found Hélène standing by the window, ready dressed, a circlet of fresh flowers resting on her hair.

'My darling girl,' she whispered, 'you're all grown up!' She turned to Annette. 'Doesn't she look beautiful? I was going to send Yvette in to do her hair, but there is no need. Well done, Annette. Now,' she carried on briskly, 'you and Louise are both ready, Hélène, so go downstairs and wait for me there. Pierre will take the three of us to the village first and then come back for Clarice and Papa.' She bustled out of the room and returned to where Yvette was arranging Clarice's veil.

The two girls looked at each other and there was a moment's return to the bond of friendship they had known as children, then Annette said, 'You're quite ready now, Miss Hélène, so I must go down to help in the kitchen. There're so many last-minute things to be seen to.' She bobbed a curtsy and went down the back stairs, leaving Hélène alone in her room with the memory of the baby, kicking her hand. She knew nothing about babies, had no idea how they were conceived. She knew it took a man and a woman to produce a child, but how that was achieved she had no idea. When they kissed, perhaps? Ladies and gentlemen did not kiss each other until they were married, so perhaps a kiss between husband and wife was what started the growth of the baby. Her mother had never even mentioned the subject and Hélène knew she could not ask for enlightenment there, but Annette? Annette knew – she must do because she was having a baby. When next they had any time together, Hélène decided she would ask Annette; then she would know. She thought again of the baby's feet kicking against her hand. When he's born, she thought, I shall see those little feet.

Chapter 13

Earlier that morning Rosalie had watched as Yvette had slipped Clarice's wedding dress over her head and fastened the row of tiny pearl buttons up the back. As she returned to her bedroom now her eyes filled with tears at the sight of her eldest daughter, ethereal in the beautiful milk-white gown, embroidered with silver flowers, made specially for her by Monsieur Worth. Yvette had dressed her hair, leaving it tumbling to her shoulders as became a maid, with a silver circlet holding the lace veil that would cover her face. She had attached the embroidered train that the children would carry and was standing back to survey her handiwork critically.

'My darling, you look radiant,' Rosalie murmured. 'Lucas is a lucky man. Come, let's go downstairs to your papa.'

Emile was waiting in the hallway and looked up as Clarice paused at the top of the staircase. Normally an undemonstrative man, he found he had tears in his eyes, and pretending to sneeze, he drew a handkerchief from his pocket to wipe them away.

'Come, girls,' Rosalie said to Hélène and Louise, and she shepherded them out to where Pierre was waiting to take them to the Place.

When he returned, Emile handed his daughter up into the barouche, and sitting proudly side by side in the June sunshine, they were driven to the Mairie. As they drove into the Place they were greeted with applause from the crowd who had gathered there to cheer the arrival of the bride. When Emile handed Clarice down from the carriage, she paused for a moment looking up at him, her face misty behind the lace of her veil.

'Ready, chérie?' he asked softly.

'Yes, Papa,' she replied, 'quite ready.'

She placed her hand on her father's arm and took her bouquet from Hélène and then, followed by their close family, they walked up the steps of the Mairie and through the arched doorway into the vestibule, where Lucas was waiting for her.

When they re-emerged some twenty-five minutes later, Clarice's veil had been thrown back and her face was alight with the joy that filled her, joy that was reflected on her new husband's face as they paused for a moment on the steps, surrounded by their families. They were welcomed with more cheers and applause from those of the village who had waited patiently in the Place to greet the young couple.

With Clarice's hand tucked under Lucas's arm, they descended the steps, and with Hélène close behind to lift the lace train clear of the road, they led the way out of the Place and along the lane that led to the church. More villagers were standing outside it, and it was here that little Monique and Clément waited, ready to carry Aunt Clarice's train. Delphine held Clément firmly by the hand as he jiggled from foot to foot with excitement, Monique standing solemn and silent, ready for the important part she was about to play.

The newly married couple waited for their families to move into the church and take their places before Lucas led his bride, attended by her bridesmaids, into the coolness of the church and up the aisle to where Father Bernard was waiting for them.

Rupert, sitting in the row behind the Barrineau family, saw Clarice in all her happiness for the first time and thought he'd never seen such a beautiful girl, but that was until he saw the bridesmaids. As Hélène turned to pass Clarice's two small attendants back to their mother on the other side of the church, he saw her face and changed his mind. Clarice was a woman who had the radiance of a bride who knew she was beautiful; the elder of the two bridesmaids who followed her seemed entirely unaware of her own dark beauty. Despite the fact that the bride was fair-haired and the bridesmaid was dark, there was a definite family likeness, enough for Rupert to be almost certain that they were sisters. Indeed, the third bridesmaid, though much younger, also had the family resemblance, though she still retained the chubbiness of face and form of a younger girl.

Rupert watched the proceedings with interest. He had never been inside a Catholic church before, let alone attended a service, and he was anxious not to remind his hosts that he was not a Catholic and probably should not have been allowed into the church at all. As he watched he thought about this. He had attended the village church with his family as a child, but since he had left home he had given very little thought to religion or God. He supposed that if he were anything, he was Church of England, but, he decided, mostly he wasn't anything. He was relieved when only the bride and groom took Communion at the nuptial Mass.

When at last it was over and they had been blessed as man and wife in the eyes of God, the newly married couple left the church, Clarice proudly on Lucas's arm. Standing aside in the porch, Rupert watched the bridesmaids gather round them in the churchyard. The elder of the two, dressed in the palest of yellow silk, was standing in a shaft of sunshine, and it seemed to Rupert that she stood in a halo of light. She was smiling as she remained with the excited children until their nursemaid stepped forward and led them away from the wedding party.

'Who is she?' he longed to ask another guest, but he knew no one well enough to pose the question. He continued to watch her until she was handed into a barouche by the bride's father, also clearly her own.

Led by the bride and groom in the Barrineau landau, a procession of carriages passed back through the village, to the cheers of those watching. Hélène and Louise travelled to the house with their parents in the barouche.

'Didn't she look beautiful?' Emile said. 'Today I'm a very proud father.'

'Only today, Papa?' ventured Hélène.

'Of course not!' Emile exclaimed. 'I'm always proud of her!'

'He's proud of all of you,' Rosalie said, trying to smooth the thoughtlessness of his words, 'and the children did very well, don't you think?'

Hélène, well aware of her father's bias towards Clarice and used to it, didn't answer but turned away, her gaze drifting over the villagers lining the streets, and it was then that she saw him. Jeannot. At first she thought her eyes must be deceiving her, but as he caught her eye he raised his hand in salute, and seeing his familiar grin she had no doubt that it was indeed Jeannot. She felt a flush of pleasure flood her cheeks and hurriedly she turned her face forward again, having no wish to alert either of her parents to his presence.

Not that they'd recognise him after all this time, she thought, but you never know. Hélène knew they would want no reminder of the time she and Jeannot had survived together in the besieged city of Paris. For the rest of the short journey back to the house she wondered what he was doing in St Etienne and whether she'd be able to see him. She looked up at Pierre's straight back on the box in front and wondered if he had seen Jeannot as well. He had always had a soft spot for the street urchin – had he perhaps known that he was going to come?

When they arrived back at the house, they all alighted from the barouche and Pierre quickly led the horses away to make room for the carriage following. There had been no chance for Hélène to speak to him, nor would there be for the rest of the day, but she was determined to ask him about Jeannot as soon as she could.

The promise of the early morning had not failed; it was a perfect June day, and once they had been formally received in the house, the guests walked out into the garden, where hired waiters offered glasses of wine and lemonade. Hélène had slipped upstairs to her own room, and from her usual perch on the window seat, she watched as more guests emerged through the drawing room doors to stand in the sunshine awaiting the call to the wedding breakfast, to be served in the large pavilion that had been erected on the lower lawn. Hélène knew that very soon she must make her own appearance but for a moment she leaned out of the window a little and looked across at the stables. She could see Pierre and Henri rubbing down the horses in the yard. Was Jeannot there too? She couldn't see him.

At that moment her door opened and Louise appeared.

'Maman says where are you? She says you're to come down at once.'

'I'm coming,' Hélène replied, and having tucked an escaped tendril of hair behind her ear, she glanced in the mirror to ensure she was tidy before following her sister down the stairs.

Rupert had been driven to Belair in one of the Barrineau carriages. He lingered outside the front door, allowing other guests to overtake him, and thus it was that Hélène was coming down the stairs in answer to her mother's summons as he came into the hall. As she saw him walk through the door she paused on the staircase, wondering who he was. She didn't think she'd ever seen him before and decided he must be one of Lucas's cousins.

For a moment Rupert was at a loss, his normal self-confidence deserting him as, almost ethereal in her pale silk, a wreath of flowers on her dark hair, she stood looking down at him.

Hélène's well-bred manners came to their aid and she descended the last few stairs, saying, 'How do you do? I don't think we've been introduced. Are you a cousin of Lucas's?'

Rupert pulled himself together and said, 'No, a friend, from London.'

Hélène's eyes widened. 'You're English?'

Rupert, suddenly returning to himself, gave her a lopsided grin. 'Afraid so. Rupert Chalfont, at your service.' He held out his hand, and when Hélène took it in hers and replied, 'I'm Clarice's sister, Hélène St Clair,' he raised it to his lips and murmured, 'Enchanté, mademoiselle.'

At that moment Didier came through the hall and stopped abruptly when he saw Hélène, her hand being kissed by one of the gentleman guests, whom he did not recognise and to whom she clearly had not been properly introduced. With disapproval in every line of his body, he said, 'Miss Hélène, your mother is looking for you in the garden.'

'Yes, I know, Didier, I'm just coming. Please excuse me, monsieur.' And leaving Rupert standing in the hall, she hurried out into the garden.

'Allow me to announce you to your hostess,' Didier said stiffly. 'She is in the garden now that she has already received her guests.' He gave Rupert a chilly look, clearly wondering if this stranger was indeed one of the invited guests or some interloper who should be shown the door immediately.

'Thank you, Didier.' Rupert spoke loftily, very much the aristocrat. 'I fear I was detained and have yet to meet my hostess.'

'What name shall I announce... sir?'

'Rupert Chalfont, the guest of Monsieur Lucas Barrineau.'

When they had reached the garden and the introduction had been made, Rosalie said, 'It's a pleasure to welcome you here, monsieur, on such a happy occasion. I understand that you have few acquaintances here, but I hope you will make yourself known to some of our other guests.'

Rupert smiled, his handsome face alight with pleasure. 'Thank you, madame, you're very kind.'

I don't know what Suzanne was worried about, Rosalie thought as she watched him walk among her other guests, accepting a glass of wine from a waiter as he did so. He seems utterly charming.

When the guests were summoned into the pavilion for the wedding breakfast, Rupert found himself again seated with members of the Barrineau family. As before, he had Madame Beaumont on his left, but today on his right was an elderly lady who had been brought to the table in a bath chair. Suzanne accompanied her and said, 'Monsieur Chalfont, allow me to introduce my mother-in-law, Madame Barrineau. Madame, this is Monsieur Rupert Chalfont, Lucas's English friend.'

Once the old lady was settled in her seat, she raised her lorgnettes and, peering at Rupert with shrewd blue eyes, said rather disconcertingly, 'Come looking for a French bride, have you?'

Rupert smiled. 'That wasn't my intention, but now I am surrounded by so many beautiful ladies, perhaps I shall find myself a wife.' Taking a risk, he added, 'Are you available, madame?'

For a moment he thought he'd made a mistake, but then the blue eyes crinkled into a smile and she said, 'Yes, but be sure you want to ask me, for I might accept and then where would you be, eh?'

'The happiest man alive,' Rupert replied at once, his own eyes twinkling in return.

The old lady gave a cackle of laughter. 'You must be the despair of your mother,' she remarked.

And Rupert, shaking his head sadly, answered, 'Yes, madame, I think you're probably right.'

The bridal pair were seated at a flower-bedecked table on a raised dais with their parents and attendants. From her seat beside Emile St Clair, Suzanne looked across at Louis's mother, now chatting easily with the Englishman, and sighed. The old lady, usually so difficult to please, seemed to be charmed by the young man next to her. He was charming – even she, Suzanne, could see that – and it made her even more determined to keep Lucie away from him. She needn't have worried, however, for Rupert had completely forgotten Lucas's young sister. He was only interested in one woman in the room, in the world, he might have said, and she was sitting with the bride and groom and their parents. Once he saw her look across to his table and meet his eyes with the flicker of a smile, but most of the time her attention was given to her family, and he, knowing that he'd discovered some sort of ally in the Barrineau household, gave his to the elderly lady on his right.

Chapter 14

The banquet was lavish, with many courses brought out in regular procession by the waiters. It wasn't long before the old lady seated at Rupert's side was beginning to doze. She had been determined to attend her grandson's wedding celebrations. She had not been at the Mairie or the church, but she had always loved a party and decided to save her strength for the wedding breakfast, when she could raise her glass to the bride and groom. That done, she gave her attention once again to the man seated next to her. She had understood very quickly that for some reason her daughter-in-law did not like him, and that in itself was interesting and inclined her to think well of him. She did not dislike her daughter-in-law – indeed, she really had no feelings for her either way – but she considered that Suzanne always seemed to put a damper on proceedings. She had never understood what Louis had seen in her, but it had been a respectable match, the bride bringing with her a substantial dowry, and they had seemed happy enough. She loved her grandchildren, particularly Lucas. It's funny, she thought as she looked across the pavilion to where he was seated beside his new wife, but I always seem to get on better with boys than girls. She gave a sniff of laughter and murmured, 'And with men!'

'I beg your pardon?' The young Englishman had thought she was asleep and was watching Hélène, learning the turn of her head, the tilt of her chin, the way her smile lit her face, but hearing the old lady speak, he immediately returned his attention to her.

'We had nothing like this when I was married,' she remarked, looking up at him with gleaming eyes. 'All a bit vulgar, do you think?'

Rupert considered. 'I hadn't thought about it,' he said at last. 'Surely as long as everyone is enjoying themselves. The bride and groom look happy enough.'

'So they should.' The old lady sat back in her chair. 'But I'm getting tired. I shall go home now.'

'Shall I call for your maid, madame?' suggested Rupert, beginning to get to his feet.

'No,' replied Madame Barrineau firmly. 'You can push me. We can call my carriage when we get back into the house.'

Rupert looked surprised at this suggestion, but immediately stood and reached for the handles of her chair, which was a simple armchair that had been attached to a set of wheels. The wheels were small, made of wood and shod with iron, and once he had turned her away from the table he found it quite a struggle to push her across the compressed lawn on which the pavilion had been erected. As they made slow progress towards the entrance, Louis Barrineau suddenly realised what was happening and hurried over to them.

'My dear fellow,' he cried, laying a hand on Rupert's arm. 'There's no need for you to be pushing my mother, no need at all. I'll call a servant.'

'Don't fuss, Louis,' his mother replied briskly. 'Monsieur Chalfont has no objection to pushing me out of the tent in this damnable contraption.'

'Mother! Please!' Louis Barrineau hissed. 'Your language!'

'It's what it is,' she insisted, 'but since I have to sit in it, I prefer to be pushed by a handsome young man.'

Rupert made no contribution to this conversation, deeming it to be a family matter, but he smiled inwardly as the old lady took her fussing son to task. His attention was reclaimed when Madame Barrineau said, 'You don't mind, do you, Monsieur Chalfont?'

Rupert had no idea if she were referring to her language or to using him as a servant, but he inclined his head and murmured, 'Not at all, madame.'

For a moment Louis looked perplexed, then he shrugged and said, 'Very good of you, Chalfont. Grateful. I can see my mother is very tired. If you can get her into the house there'll be plenty of servants there to help her to her carriage.' He glanced round the pavilion, where some waiters were clearing plates from tables while others appeared with yet more trays of food. 'These chaps are no good, they're simply men hired for the day.'

'Certainly, sir,' Rupert replied. 'I'm happy to help.'

He heard a chuckle as they moved out of the pavilion and followed the path into the house. 'You really are a charmer, aren't you?' she said.

Rupert grinned down at her. 'I try to be, madame.'

Once they were inside the house there were, indeed, plenty of the Barrineau servants ready to help, and Rupert handed his charge over to a strapping young man, who pushed the chair out of the front door to where a carriage awaited them in the gathering summer twilight. Rupert followed and waited as Madame Barrineau was lifted into the carriage and had a rug tucked securely around her knees.

'Goodnight, madame,' he said as the footman closed the door.

'And goodnight to you, too,' said the old lady. 'I like you, Rupert Chalfont. I don't always like Lucas's friends.'

Rupert swept her a bow and, smiling, said, 'I'm honoured, madame.'

'So you should be. Come and see me tomorrow, or the next day, after the ball.' She looked up suddenly and added, 'You will be going to the ball?'

'For certain, madame,' he replied. 'I'm looking forward to it.'

'Well, make sure you behave yourself. Too many silly girls here, ready to have their heads turned.'

'They are in no danger, I do assure you, madame,' Rupert said gravely. 'I'm afraid my heart is already taken.'

She looked up at him sharply and saw in his face that he was speaking the truth. 'Someone back in England, I suppose,' she said. 'Lucky girl! But that doesn't mean you won't turn heads here, whether you intend to or not.' And with that she tapped her cane on the door of the carriage. The coachman flicked his whip and the carriage drew away, its lights disappearing into the gathering dusk.

Rupert, standing and watching it as it disappeared round a bend in the drive, realised with sudden certainty that he had spoken the truth. With a wry grin he turned back towards the house. Typical of me, he thought as he entered the hall and paused where he had seen Hélène St Clair come down the stairs. So beautiful but almost certainly unattainable; his status as a younger son would ensure that, but, he decided, he wasn't going to let that deter him. He walked back through the house to the garden and the pavilion, where many of the guests were still seated at the tables, some still eating or drinking coffee, some just chatting. Others had drifted out into the lantern-lit garden, seeking fresh air after the hot atmosphere within the pavilion. As soon as he came in through the door, Rupert's eyes sought out Hélène. Could she be persuaded to take a turn in the garden? Would her parents allow her such a freedom?

He saw the bridal pair at the far end of the room, Clarice's hand still delicately resting on Lucas's arm as he showed off his bride to all their guests. Monsieur St Clair had left the bridal table and was standing with a group of gentlemen, chatting, but Rosalie St Clair remained at the table, seated with the bridesmaids and Lucas's young sister Lucie. She was almost holding court, Rupert thought as various other women came over to her and congratulated her on the marriage of her daughter. Even as he watched, Rupert saw Lucie Barrineau murmur something to the younger bridesmaid, who turned to her mother, and having received a nod in reply, the two young girls slipped away from the table.

Hélène watched them go and felt herself very much alone. I'm neither fish nor fowl, she thought. Not quite a child to be let away from the table to amuse myself somewhere else, not quite an adult, allowed to mingle in the room and admitted to the general adult conversation. She didn't actually mind that; most of what they all talked about she found dull. She looked round the room and saw that though there was no withdrawing room for the ladies, most of the men seemed to have withdrawn themselves to the far end of the pavilion, their laughter loud, their talk unheard by the women who remained seated at the tables.

Then she saw someone standing just inside the entrance from the garden, watching her. It was his stillness and solitude amidst the hum that had attracted her attention, and she realised that it was the man she'd met in the hallway before the meal, Lucas's English friend. What was his name? Rupert Chalfont? Yes, that was it, and his eyes were fixed on her. She felt the colour rise in her cheeks and glanced away, leaning towards the lady on her left, apparently exhibiting great interest in what she was saying.

Rupert had seen her blush. He had also seen the two younger girls leave the table. Perhaps she might be allowed to do so too.

Well, Rupert thought, nothing ventured! As he began to cross the room he saw Suzanne Barrineau return to the table and wished he had approached before she had come back. Still, he could hardly turn away again now; Madame St Clair had seen him walking towards them and there was nothing to do but brazen it out. He was surprised therefore when Suzanne said, 'My dear Rosalie, I don't think you've met Lucas's English friend, and I am sure he hasn't been introduced to Hélène.'

Rosalie looked up and, seeing Rupert at her side, said, 'Of course we have met, Suzanne. I welcomed Monsieur Chalfont on our return from church. However, I don't think you have been introduced to my daughter, Hélène.'

Rupert executed a small bow and, raised Hélène's extended hand to his lips as he had earlier.

'Enchanté, mademoiselle,' he said, the ghost of a twinkle in his eye.

'How do you do, monsieur,' Hélène responded, lowering her eyes with becoming modesty and with no hint that this was not their first encounter.

Rupert smiled as he released her hand, knowing this small secret was something they shared.

'It was kind of you to take my mother-in-law out to her carriage,' Suzanne was saying. 'I'm sure she was exhausted with the excitement of the day. I hope she was not a difficult dinner partner.' She added with a gay little laugh as she turned to Rosalie, 'So difficult for Monsieur Chalfont, knowing no one but Lucas!'

'Certainly not, madame,' replied Rupert, thinking how uncharitable his hostess was about her mother-in-law. 'She was most entertaining.'

Rosalie gave him a quick smile of appreciation and then said, 'Hélène, chérie, you're looking hot, why don't you take a turn outside in the garden? I'm sure Monsieur Chalfont will be happy to escort you. I believe that Georges and Sylvie have already gone out to take the air. You may introduce Monsieur Chalfont to them.'

Hélène felt her cheeks grow red. She could hardly believe her mother was encouraging her to go into the garden with a man she'd only just met. Still, there could be no impropriety in it if she took him out to meet her brother and sister-in-law. She got up from her chair and accepted the arm that Rupert offered. Together they walked away and out into the garden.

Suzanne watched them go with satisfaction. At least he was nowhere near her beloved Lucie, and very soon, after the ball tomorrow night, he would depart and the danger would be over.

Rosalie also watched them leave the pavilion. 'He seems a charming young man,' she remarked. 'Has Lucas known him long?'

'He met him on a recent visit to London,' replied Suzanne. 'He's the son of a baronet.' However, she didn't feel it was necessary to mention that he was only a younger son. After all, as he would be gone in a couple of days, that was of no consequence.

When they emerged from the pavilion into the cool of the evening, Hélène saw Georges and his wife, sitting in an arbour that overlooked the rose garden.

'I must introduce you to my brother,' Hélène said. It was

the first time she had spoken since they had left her mother and Madame Barrineau at the table.

Must you? Must you really? Rupert didn't speak the words, though they were fighting to be said; he simply allowed her to lead him over to the couple seated in the arbour. He had seen them in the church and had seen the two small attendants being passed back to them once their train-carrying duties were over. He had noticed outside the church that the man had a decided limp and walked with a cane.

As they approached, Georges stood up to greet them and Hélène made the introductions. Rupert smiled and very soon they were all four seated in the arbour, the conversation flowing easily enough.

Better to have them here too, Rupert thought. It saves any embarrassment, and they'll have to get used to me!

As dusk turned to darkness, a small breeze blew up and Sylvie shivered. 'I think I'd like to go back into the pavilion now, Georges,' she said. 'It won't be long before Clarice and Lucas leave, will it?'

'Well, at least they haven't far to go,' Georges reminded her.

'They're moving into the west wing of Montmichel until they find a suitable house of their own,' Sylvie told Rupert.

Rupert already knew this, but he said, 'How convenient it must be that the family has enough space to accommodate them.'

'Yes, for a short while,' Sylvie agreed cautiously. 'But there's nothing like your own home, is there, Georges?'

'Even if it is officers' quarters?' teased her husband.

'Even if,' Sylvie responded firmly as together they made their way across the lawn to the lights of the pavilion.

Hélène watched them go before she said, 'We should go too, monsieur.'

'Are you cold as well?' Rupert asked, longing to put a protective arm about her shoulders, but knowing it was far too soon.

'I think I'd like to fetch a shawl,' Hélène replied. 'It will be cold when we see Clarice and Lucas into their carriage.' There was still a scattering of people in the garden, but everyone knew that the day was drawing to a close.

They walked into the house and Rupert waited in the candlelit hallway while Hélène ran up the stairs to find a wrap. When she came back downstairs, they were about to return to the pavilion when the door from the servants' quarters opened and an elderly woman hurried through. She came to an abrupt halt as she saw the couple standing in the hall.

'Madame Sauze?' Hélène looked at her in surprise. 'Is there anything wrong?'

'No, no, Miss Hélène, but I need to speak with your mother.'

'She's in the pavilion,' replied Hélène. 'Can I give her a message?'

'No, no, it's not that important. I will speak with her later, when her guests have gone.' And with that she hurriedly withdrew through the door, which closed softly behind her.

'Who was that?' Rupert asked.

'It's Madame Sauze, the housekeeper.' She paused and then added, 'She seemed worried, didn't she?'

'A little agitated,' agreed Rupert.

'Yes, that's what I thought. It's probably nothing, but we should return to the pavilion and I'll mention it to Maman.'

As they turned to go through to the garden, she rested her hand on his sleeve, smiling up at him confidingly, and Rupert had to catch his breath and fight the urge to pull her into his arms.

Chapter 15

It was the end of a long day and in the Belair kitchen there was a general feeling of relief; at last they could begin to relax. Miss Clarice's wedding day was almost over and all had been well.

There had been a hectic two hours while the meal was being served, when everyone in the kitchen was at full stretch, but there had been no hitches. Clarice and Lucas's wedding feast had proceeded exactly according to plan. Didier, dignified as always, had presided in the pavilion and had no problem instructing the waiters hired in for the day. In the kitchen Monsieur Antoine had worked his magic and the exceptional dishes prepared under his eagle eye had been sent out to the guests with smooth efficiency.

Now the tables had been cleared, the remnants of the food were in the cool of the pantry and the piles of dirty plates were stacked up in the scullery to be washed later. Food had been sent out to the visiting coachmen, who waited patiently for the carriages they drove to be summoned, but the household staff were called to eat in the kitchen and there was a welcome respite as everyone sat down at the table.

Leaving nothing to chance, Didier was still busy within the pavilion, making sure that the gentlemen were not short of wine, or following the meal, a cognac or a glass of port; that the ladies, still seated, were supplied with dishes of sweetmeats and their glasses were topped up with cordial or sweet wine.

Madame Sauze took her place at the foot of the kitchen table and began to serve out the food. She sat in Madame Choux's habitual chair, leaving Didier's, at the head of the table, ready for his return. She looked round the gathered servants, and having said a brief grace, she began ladling chicken onto a plate.

'Lizette, child, take this to Madame Choux in her parlour.'

Lizette paled at the idea of going into Madame Choux's private room, and taking pity on her, Annette got to her feet.

'I'll take it, madame,' she said, and as she picked up the tray she was rewarded by a look of profound relief on Lizette's face. The young maid, unused to kindness, was finding life more comfortable since Madame Choux had taken to her parlour.

It was as Annette came back to the table that it happened. Her back had been aching most of the day, but now she suffered a sudden stab of pain, so sharp and unexpected that she had to catch hold of the table to steady herself; for a long moment she couldn't move as she fought the pain and then it was gone, leaving her breathless.

Agathe looked anxiously across at her. 'Annette! Are you all right?'

'Yes, aunt,' she replied shakily. 'Just a little pain in my back.' She sank down onto her chair and then realised in horror that her skirt was soaking as water was seeping out between her legs. Colour flooded her cheeks in humiliation. Surely she had not wet herself, here in front of everyone! Those about the table suddenly fell silent as, with a low moan, Annette grabbed her damp skirts and fled from the room.

Ella, a girl who'd come in from the village, giggled, breaking the silence. 'Annette's pissed herself, she has! There's a puddle on the floor!'

Agathe turned on the girl, furious, and snapped, 'Don't be ridiculous! She's expecting a baby. That's a sign it's about to be born.' She got to her feet. 'I'm going to find her; and you, Ella,' she retorted, 'can mop the floor. Now!'

As she followed Annette out into the passageway, she heard an excited burst of conversation in the room behind her.

It's the worst possible time for this to happen, she thought as she took the back stairs up to their bedroom. On Clarice's wedding day of all days, when the house is full of strangers and everyone's at full stretch.

Due to Father Thomas's systematic abuse, they did not know exactly when the baby was due, but judging from Annette's size Agathe had guessed there were a few more weeks to go. She had thought there would be plenty of warning when Annette went into labour and they had planned she should be safely in the home of the Madame Leclerc for her lying-in and the birth. But now Agathe was at a loss. Now her waters had broken the birth seemed imminent. Poor child! They should get her conveyed to Madame Leclerc's at once, but how?

She hurried up the stairs and, on opening the bedroom door, found Annette sitting, pale-faced but dry-eyed, on the side of the bed.

'Annette!' she cried. 'Are you all right?'

'I've wet myself,' Annette replied bleakly. 'In front of the whole room!'

'No, you haven't,' said Agathe, going over to sit beside her and taking her hands. 'Your waters have broken. It's a sign that the baby is coming. Are you having pains?'

'No. Yes. Well, some backache, it comes and goes, but that's from carrying those heavy buckets this morning.'

'No, Annette, it's not. I think you're in labour.'

As she spoke Annette was gripped by a sudden pain, making her gasp and grip Agathe's hands so tightly that it hurt. After a few moments she relaxed again.

'Your baby is on its way,' Agathe said gently. 'Very soon you will be a mother... something I've never been.'

'You've been like a mother to me,' responded Annette softly.

Agathe knew a moment's warmth at the girl's words, and then she was all practicalities.

'We should prepare for the little one's arrival,' she said. 'I think it's too late and too difficult to get you to Madame Leclerc's now. Lie back on your bed while I send Pierre to fetch her here.'

As she got downstairs Adèle Paquet came out of the kitchen. The cook caught her hand and asked, 'Annette! What's happening? Is she going to be all right?'

'She's gone into labour,' replied Agathe. 'We need to send for Madame Leclerc.'

'But will she come?'

'She has to.' There was panic in Agathe's voice. 'Who else can deliver the baby? I'm going to find Madame and ask if Pierre may fetch her from the village. Will you go and sit with Annette, Adèle? Tell her I'll be back in just a minute.'

The cook immediately started up the stairs and Agathe hurried out into the hallway in search of Madame St Clair, and there she found Hélène, standing talking to a gentleman she didn't recognise. Even as she explained that she needed to speak to her mistress, Agathe realised what she was doing. How on earth could she interrupt Madame at her daughter's wedding? She, Agathe, was in charge of the household servants. It was up to her to decide what they should do.

Leaving Hélène and the young man staring after her, she hurried back to the kitchen, where most of the servants were still gathered, and an expectant silence fell as she appeared.

'Annette's baby's about to be born,' she told them. 'I'm sending Pierre for the midwife.'

She hurried out into the yard, where she found Pierre sitting on a bench outside the stables, having a last smoke before he turned in for the night.

'Pierre,' she cried when she saw him, 'I need your help. Annette's gone into labour. I need you to go to the village and fetch the midwife. Madame Leclerc.'

'Madame Leclerc? Where will I find her?'

'She lives in the lane behind Le Coq d'Argent. Anyone will direct you. Hurry, Pierre, before it's too late.'

'Too late? Can't you—' began Pierre.

'I can't deliver a baby, Pierre,' Agathe said, a break in her voice. 'We have to get help... now. Please, there's no time to waste.'

Pierre got to his feet. 'All right,' he said. 'I'll take Magic and cut across the fields. He's quite strong enough to carry both of us back. Tell Annette I've gone for help.'

Agathe clasped his hand. 'Thank you, Pierre.'

'Though what the master will say when he hears I've been gallivanting off into the night on one of his horses without a word or a by-your-leave, I don't know.' He grinned down at her. 'Still,' he said, 'we'll worry about that when the time comes.'

Moments later he was clattering out of the yard on Magic, heading into the night in search of the midwife. He didn't mind going. He'd quite taken to Annette. She was a pretty little thing, and though he didn't for one moment believe the story of the dead husband, he thought her brave the way she coped with her situation, for whichever way you looked at it the baby had no father and she was going to have to manage on her own.

Agathe returned indoors knowing she had done all she could with regard to the midwife. She hurried up the stairs to the bedroom, where she found the cook had managed to get Annette into her nightdress and into her bed.

The look of relief on Annette's face when she came in through the door was heart-rending.

She's relying on us to see her through, Agathe thought in panic. How are we going to cope if Madame Leclerc doesn't get here in time?

She pasted a smile onto her face and said, 'How are you feeling, Annette? Pierre's on his way to fetch Madame Leclerc. He's taken a horse and they'll be back as soon as they can.'

At that moment Annette was overtaken by another sharp contraction and couldn't suppress a cry of pain. Agathe was at her side at once, grasping her hand as she fought the griping in her belly.

When the contraction had passed, Annette collapsed back onto the bed, breathing heavily. Agathe turned to Adele and said, 'We'll need some clean towels. Will you wait with her while I go and find some? Then perhaps you could go down to the kitchen and set some water to boil.'

It was as she gathered towels from the linen cupboard that Rosalie appeared at the head of the stairs.

'Madame Sauze,' she said, 'Hélène said there was some kind of trouble, some problem?'

'Oh. Madame, I didn't want her to trouble you. I should not have spoken to her.'

'Well, you did,' replied Rosalie briskly. 'So, what is the problem?'

'It's Annette, madame. She has gone into labour and…"

Rosalie closed her eyes. Today of all days! Still, there was nothing they could do about that now. 'Where is she?'

'In our room, madame.' Agathe drew a deep breath and added, 'I took the liberty of sending Pierre for the midwife.'

'Did you now?' If Rosalie was surprised at her housekeeper sending the coachman on errands on behalf of a maid, she didn't say so. 'Let's hope she gets here in time. Bring those towels and let's have a look at her.'

'Oh, madame, it's not appropriate for you to—' Agathe began.

'And it's not for you to tell me what's appropriate!' interrupted Rosalie. 'Come along.' And with that she turned on her heel and set off along the landing, followed by Agathe, still clutching the pile of clean towels.

When they reached the bedroom they found Annette sitting up in her bed, with Adèle sitting beside her, admiring the small clothes Annette had made in readiness for her baby.

'Now then, Annette,' Rosalie said when the girl stared at her in horror at having been found in her bed by her mistress and tried to get up. 'No, no, stay where you are.' Rosalie waved a staying hand. 'I hear your baby is on the way. Pierre has gone to fetch Madame Leclerc, and as soon as she arrives she'll be up here to help you. I'm sure she won't be long.'

Even as she spoke Annette was gripped by another contraction, making her cry out in pain. Agathe was immediately at her side.

Rosalie turned to Adèle Paquet. 'How long since the last one?' she asked.

'Not long, madame,' replied the cook. 'Maybe fifteen minutes.'

'Then you'd better go downstairs and as soon as the midwife arrives bring her straight up. Make sure there is plenty of boiled water ready when needed.'

As the cook scurried out, Rosalie said, 'We'd better spread the towels, I fear the birth is very close.' But there were no more contractions before the door opened and Madame Leclerc stepped into the room.

Rosalie greeted her with relief and said, 'I'll leave you to it, madame, I have matters to attend to downstairs.' As she reached the door she said, 'Madame Sauze, I will expect to hear from you as soon as the child is born.'

Madame Leclerc moved quickly to the bedside. 'How long has she been like this?' she asked.

'For over an hour,' replied Agathe. 'At first her contractions were coming regularly, but they aren't any more.'

'This is serious,' said the midwife as she began her examination. The waters staining the bed ran dark, which she knew was a bad sign. When she had finished her examination she turned to Agathe and said, 'The baby is lying crosswise. The only chance of saving it – and the mother – is for me to try to turn it so that its head is able to engage.' She looked at Agathe and went on, 'It is all I can do.'

At that moment Annette gave another cry as a further contraction gripped her, her face now the colour of putty and covered in sweat.

'Do what you can,' Agathe said, and standing aside she watched as the midwife struggled to turn the baby.

Annette's son was born several hours later. With difficulty and skill Madame Leclerc had managed to turn him, but still he was taking his time to arrive and the mother was getting weaker. Agathe sat beside her, holding her hand as Madame Leclerc encouraged her to bear down and push. At last, with a groan from his mother, the baby's head emerged and with one further push he slithered into the arms of the waiting midwife. Swiftly she cut the cord that was twisted round his neck and gathered him into a towel. She took one look at him and turned away, keeping her back to the mother, who now lay, eyes closed, exhausted on the bed. He was small, too small, and his skin was pale and blotchy and he made no sound. She rubbed him gently in the towel, wiping his face, clearing mucus from around his nose and mouth, but he remained unmoving in her hands. She turned him over and gave him a sharp slap across his tiny bottom, but still there was nothing, no catch of breath, no cry and gulp of air. She had seen this once before, when the baby, a girl that time, had never drawn breath. She felt for a pulse, holding the baby against her face in search of a heartbeat, but there was none.

Chapter 16

Hélène lay in bed, her eyes wide open in the darkness. She had left her curtains slightly apart so that she could see the full moon hanging in the sky – the moon under which she had walked with Rupert Chalfont. She had no wish to go to sleep; she didn't feel in the least tired, and she didn't want the day to end. Clarice's wedding day, the day when she, Hélène, had first seen Rupert Chalfont, looking up at her as she stood on the stairs. He was different from every other man she had known. Handsome, charming, well-bred, yes, indeed, but as she'd been growing up she'd known plenty of men who were all of those things, but they were nothing like Rupert. She had no idea what *made* him different, all she was certain of was that he was.

After their return to the pavilion, they had parted company, Hélène to tell her mother of her encounter with Madame Sauze in the hall, Rupert to join with a group of men gathered at the far end. Louis Barrineau introduced him to Simon Barnier, another neighbour. Simon made a polite bow but soon drifted away, uninterested in a stray Englishman with whom he had nothing in common.

'Had his eye on young Clarice,' Louis Barrineau murmured, 'until our Lucas cut him out. Still, if he's looking for a pretty girl with a decent portion, there's always her sister!'

'Miss Hélène?' Rupert kept his tone one of casual interest. 'I was introduced to her earlier by your wife, sir.'

'Well, between you and me I wouldn't be surprised if they made a match of it. She and Barnier have known each other from childhood, of course, and it would be a good bargain. She would marry into a distinguished local family and he would have a much-needed injection of cash.' Louis glanced up at Rupert. 'All the St Clair girls bring a sizeable dowry, you know. Comes from their maternal grandmother, theirs entirely on the day they get married.' As if suddenly recognising the freedom with which he was mentioning his neighbours' financial affairs to a relatively unknown young Englishman, he tapped the side of his nose and said, 'Nothing said, you know. Common knowledge, of course, but it's not discussed. Lucas gave that no consideration when he proposed to Clarice. Head over ears in love with her, he is, and I'm not surprised, eh?' Obviously feeling that the wine had led his tongue astray, Monsieur Barrineau changed the subject and continued, 'Very good of you to look after my mother earlier, sir. Very thoughtful. Much appreciated.'

'It was a pleasure, sir,' Rupert replied. 'And indeed she's invited me to visit her in her rooms after the ball. I rather think she wants me to tell all that goes on there.'

Louis Barrineau gave a laugh. 'I'm sure she does and that you'll be more than welcome,' he said. 'My mother was determined to be at Lucas's wedding, she hates to be left out, but I think the ball will be beyond her strength.'

At that moment there was a general movement from the pavilion as the bridal couple went out to their waiting carriage. Their departure was soon followed by the last of the guests, and Rupert had to take his place in one of the Barrineau carriages to return to Montmichel. He watched as Hélène turned to go back into the house. He'd had no opportunity to speak with her again before he took his leave of her parents, but as she reached the door she glanced back. For a moment their eyes met and he saw the colour flood her cheeks and couldn't repress a smile. Tomorrow night they would meet at the ball and he would hold her in his arms as they danced.

As Hélène relived the evening from the moment she had seen him, she gave herself a mental shake. His manners were easy and engaging and must make him agreeable to any woman; there was no reason to think that he had treated her differently from anyone else, that he thought of her differently, or at all. But she thought of him and it was he who filled her mind as she finally drifted off to sleep.

Many in the household slept late the next morning, but despite only a few hours' sleep Hélène was awake early. As she did so often, she went to her window seat and looked out over the parterre. Although it was early, the sun was up, flooding the garden with sunshine. She looked down at the arbour by the rose garden where she had sat with her brother and sister-in-law last evening... and with Rupert Chalfont. Her reverie was broken by a clattering in the stable yard and, turning, she saw that Henri, the stable boy, was hitching one of the farm horses to a waggon. It seemed to be a strange activity for so early in the morning and even as she watched, a woman she didn't know emerged into the yard carrying a bundle, followed by Madame Sauze with her arm round Annette, almost as if she were supporting her. Then Pierre appeared, and to Hélène's surprise, he gathered Annette into his arms and lifted her onto the waggon, setting her down gently on a pile of sacks. The strange woman got in beside her, and with that Henri climbed up on the seat and with a click of his teeth and a shake of the reins drove the waggon slowly out of the yard.

What is going on? wondered Hélène. There was only one way to find out; she must ask Madame Sauze. Dressing quickly, she went out onto the landing. The house was still quiet, and though she could hear voices from the nursery, it appeared that no one else was awake. Quietly Hélène went downstairs and made her way to the kitchen. There she found Lizette stoking the stove into life, but there was no sign of Agathe Sauze.

As Hélène came in, Lizette looked up, startled, dropping the poker with a clatter. 'Lizette,' Hélène said. 'Where is Madame Sauze?'

Colour and confusion flooded the maid's face and she said, 'I think she's upstairs, Miss Hélène. Sorting things out.'

'Sorting things out?' repeated Hélène. 'What sort of things?'

The girl looked near to tears as she replied, 'I don't know, miss. I don't know.'

Realising that she was going to get nothing more from the maid, Hélène said, 'Then I'll go and find her.' She left the kitchen and climbed the back stairs to the servants' quarters. As she neared the top she could hear someone moving about, and as she reached the landing Madame Sauze emerged from one of the rooms. She stopped abruptly when she saw Hélène.

'Miss Hélène,' she exclaimed. 'You shouldn't be up here!'

'I came to find you,' replied Hélène. 'I came to ask you why Annette's been taken away in the waggon. Where's she gone?

Who was that woman with her? She looked ill. Has she gone to have her baby?'

Agathe drew a deep breath. 'All these questions, Miss Hélène,' she said as her brain raced to provide answers she could give. Madame St Clair had already been apprised of the events of last night, and it was she who had insisted that Annette should be removed as soon as possible to Madame Leclerc's house. Agathe had no idea of the explanations her mistress would give to Hélène, but she did know that she would want to be the one breaking the news to her daughter. She wouldn't thank her housekeeper for taking that duty. Agathe was well aware of Madame St Clair being particularly protective of her daughter and, understanding why, had no wish to interfere.

'When you have a baby, it is best to have a midwife with you,' she said cautiously. 'Madame Leclerc, the woman who went with her, is the midwife from the village. She's going to take care of her.'

'I see.' Hélène looked relieved. 'That's all right then.'

Later, when Hélène had a chance to speak with her mother about Annette, Rosalie had already decided that she was not going to tell the family of the happenings in the night. The baby's death was sad, but really nothing to do with her or her family, and she was determined that nothing should spoil the further celebrations of Clarice's wedding. Hélène would be going to her first society ball, and she was determined that nothing should tarnish that special moment for her. Louise was angry that she was considered too young to be allowed to attend. She had been thrilled to be a bridesmaid, making her an important participant at the wedding, and thought she should have been invited to the ball at Montmichel.

'I'm the only one of the family not going!' she fumed. 'It's not fair!' But her mother had remained adamant. 'You're too young, chérie,' she'd said. 'Even Hélène isn't formally out yet and you certainly are not.'

When Hélène mentioned having seen Annette leaving in the waggon, Rosalie asked guardedly what she had seen. On hearing it was all from her bedroom window, she said, 'She has gone to the house of the midwife,' and was surprised when Hélène said, 'Yes, Madame Sauze told me that.'

'Did she?' Rosalie asked sharply. 'And what else did she say?'

'Nothing, Maman,' Hélène said. 'Just that it was important for her to be with the midwife at a time like this.'

Rosalie gave an inward sigh of relief. Madame Sauze had stuck to her word and said nothing to alert Hélène to the reason she and Annette were at Belair, particularly at such a sensitive time. It might all come out later, of course, but at present there was nothing to spoil the day ahead, and that was as it should be. Later she called Agathe to see her in her parlour.

'I am sure you want to know how Annette is getting on, and once luncheon has been served please feel free to go into the village and find out.'

'Thank you, madame,' Agathe replied. 'I will go and visit her.'

'And please let it be known only that she was in labour and has been taken to Madame Leclerc's for her lying-in. I wish there to be no loose talk among the servants, no gossip to attach to the family. You understand?'

'Yes, madame, but I have to say that there is already talk in the kitchen – speculation as to what has happened. They were all at table when...' She paused to choose her words carefully. 'When it was obvious that the baby was on its way.'

'There is no need to tell them the sad news yet, however,' replied her mistress. 'Let them think she was taken to Madame Leclerc's early this morning and will be delivered there. Tomorrow will be time enough to tell them that the child was stillborn.'

'If that is what you wish, madame, but I'm certain Pierre at least knows what has happened.'

'You need not worry about Pierre. I shall speak to him.'

When Agathe had left the room Rosalie sat and considered what was to be done. No scandal must attach to the family, but there need be none provided those in the know stuck to the agreed story. Annette was a widow carrying a posthumous child and unfortunately, this morning at the home of the midwife, the baby had been stillborn. As far as Rosalie was concerned it must be a blessing in disguise, for how would a girl like Annette have managed to bring up a child on her own, with no money and no prospects of a job, as she had to nurse the child?

Maybe, she thought, the girl herself will greet the news with relief. She'll be able to put it all behind her and live the rest of her life free of the shame.

Well, Rosalie decided with a mental shake, she would give it no further thought today. There were the family staying in the house to consider, and she had no wish for them to hear what had happened. She would play with the children in the afternoon and then they all had to prepare to attend the ball this evening. Agathe Sauze could deal with Annette. She had proved herself a trustworthy servant, able to keep a still tongue, and she would be rewarded with the position of housekeeper now that Madame Choux seemed to have retired herself. And the girl? Well, she could come back to work in a week or so, once she had got over the birth. After all, she was a good worker and would be in need of a job. All in all, things had worked out for the best.

Later that afternoon Agathe walked across the fields to the little house in the lane behind Le Coq d'Argent. Madame Leclerc opened the door and led her inside.

'How is she?' Agathe asked.

'Exhausted,' replied the midwife. 'And I'm not surprised. We were lucky not to lose her as well as the child.'

'Thank God for that,' Agathe said. 'And thanks to you. You are a very skilful woman, madame.'

'I have seen most things,' sighed Madame Leclerc. 'But she's taken it hard, as you'd imagine – the last part of her husband gone for ever.'

Agathe was faced at that moment with an almost overwhelming temptation to tell this compassionate woman the truth, but realising that to do so would put both her and Annette's futures in jeopardy, she stifled the impulse and said, 'You are very understanding, madame. May I see my niece now?'

'Of course,' came the reply. 'I'll take you up. She may be asleep; she was earlier, and if so, let us not wake her. Sleep is the great healer and is what she needs. We have to make sure she has plenty of rest and there is no chance of infection.'

Agathe followed her up the stairs to a bedroom at the back. The thin curtains were drawn against the sun, leaving the room in a pale twilight. Annette was awake, lying in bed, her face pale, dark circles under eyes that were red with weeping. Agathe hurried to her bedside and took her hand in her own.

'My dearest girl,' murmured Agathe, 'I'm so sorry.'

'Léon,' she whispered. 'His name was Léon.'

Chapter 17

The ballroom at Montmichel was flooded with light, its mirrored walls reflecting the brilliance of the four large chandeliers that hung from its lofty ceiling. Monsieur and Madame Barrineau were standing at the double doors, opened wide to welcome their guests, and beside them stood the newly married couple. Clarice wore a ballgown of cream silk embroidered with gold thread, its scooped neckline edged with tiny rosebuds, leaving her shoulders bare, her arms in opera-length gloves. She radiated happiness as she stood beautiful and proud at her husband's side, her fingers resting lightly on his arm.

Rupert, having come down from his second-storey bedroom early at Lucas's request, was standing half concealed by one of the marble pillars that lined the room. Behind him on a raised dais, a string quartet was playing softly as a gentle background to the increasing flow of conversation. He watched each arrival, waiting for the moment when Hélène St Clair would enter the room with her mother and father. He had thought as the parents of the bride they might also be in the receiving line, but clearly Suzanne Barrineau, having been denied hosting the wedding breakfast, had no intention of sharing the celebration ball. Having understood this, Emile and Rosalie did not arrive promptly; rather they entered the ballroom among the last of the guests, making an entrance of which an earlier arrival would have deprived them. In their wake came their son Georges and his wife Sylvie, Rosalie's sister and husband, and Hélène. Hélène, a girl recently freed from the schoolroom, at her first ball, her eyes glowing with excitement. She was dressed in a simple white gown, the square cut of the neck showing off her delicate shoulders to perfection. A narrow gold belt defined her slim waist, and the fullness of the skirt was gathered behind into a modest bustle. As decorum in a young girl required, the gown had little cap sleeves, and Hélène's slender arms were encased in mid-length white gloves. Her hair had been dressed high on her head with ringlets allowed to escape about her ears to frame the oval of her face. She stood poised in the doorway, on the brink of entering adult society, waiting to be received by her hostess, and for a moment Rupert's heart seemed to stop. She was so beautiful, but she was so young, too young by far to be interested in an old man of almost thirty. Old man of thirty! He gave a sardonic smile: this old man of thirty was behaving like a lovesick schoolboy! He feasted his eyes on her as she made her courtesies to the Barrineaux. He ached to take her in his arms, feel her heart beating in time with his own. He longed to release her beautiful dark hair from its confining pins and let it tumble about her shoulders so he could bury his face in its shining softness.

Now you really are behaving like a lovesick booby, he told himself. How was he, Rupert Chalfont, a man well practised in amorous flirtation, a connoisseur of feminine beauty while remaining carefully unentangled, how could he be struck dumb by a girl of seventeen attending her first ball?

The St Clair party moved easily into the body of the room,

greeting friends and acquaintances with nods and smiles, moving to a furnished alcove between pillars on the far side. There they took their seats and watched as their eldest daughter and her new husband stepped onto the floor to open the ball.

From her place in the alcove, Hélène scanned the ballroom in search of Lucas's English friend. Surely he must still be here. She had just seen him standing across the room and speaking with Lucie Barrineau, her heart plummeting as she did so, when Simon Barnier appeared in their alcove and made his compliments to her mother.

'Madame,' he said, bowing, 'may I have the honour of asking Miss Hélène for a dance?'

Rosalie greeted him with a smile. The Barniers, like the Barrineaux, were local landowners and she had known them all her married life. She did not know Simon well, but he came of an impeccable family and there had been a time when she'd thought he might ask for Clarice. Lucas Barrineau had put paid to that idea, but she would not object if he transferred his affections to Hélène. Not immediately, of course – she was still too young to become engaged – but maybe, in a year or so, Emile might consider his suit and there could be an understanding. After all, *she* had become engaged to Emile at eighteen and married as she turned nineteen.

'Of course,' she replied. 'I'm sure her card is not yet full.'

Other couples had now entered the dance floor and when Simon made his bow to Hélène, she took his extended hand and was led out among those already dancing. The band was playing a waltz and she was soon whirled away, Simon's arm encircling her waist.

Rupert, who had decided to wait a little before presenting himself to Madame St Clair, saw her held in Simon's arms as they waltzed past him. He could have kicked himself for letting one of the local beaux steal a march on him and get to her first. Immediately he made his way across to where Rosalie, sitting with her family, was talking with her sister. Determined not to miss another opportunity, he reintroduced himself and engaged both ladies in conversation until Simon returned Hélène to her mother's side.

'Monsieur Chalfont,' Rosalie said, 'I don't know if you have met Monsieur Barnier, another friend of my son-in-law's?'

Rupert bowed in the direction of Simon Barnier, who still had Hélène's hand on his arm. 'I believe I had the honour of being introduced to Monsieur Barnier yesterday, madame,' he replied, adding with a smile, 'and to Miss St Clair, of course.'

Hélène, feeling the colour rising in her cheeks, kept her eyes demurely downcast, but her heart skipped a beat when he went on, 'Indeed, madame, I came to ask your permission to invite Miss St Clair to dance, if she still has a dance left on her card.'

Rosalie returned his smile. 'I'm sure she has, monsieur. Please feel free to ask.'

Simon, having danced with her once, would now have to wait. It would be considered improper to ask Hélène to dance again until, perhaps, much later in the evening.

'Perhaps I might ask for the supper dance, Miss St Clair,' Rupert said, 'and then take you in to supper?'

'Thank you, sir,' Hélène whispered. 'I should be delighted.'

'Thank you, mademoiselle,' he replied, and taking her dance card, he wrote his name.

At that moment Lucas appeared at her side and said, 'I hope you've saved me at least one dance, Hélène. I have to have a dance with my sister-in-law.'

From then on Hélène's card filled up rapidly. Young men

she had known as children came to demand dances, and she discovered how much she enjoyed dancing with someone other than her sisters or the dancing master.

Hélène was not the only one enjoying her first ball. Despite her youth, Lucie Barrineau's parents had allowed her presence at the ball celebrating her brother's marriage, and her dance card filled remarkably quickly. Young as she was, she was an heiress, and as such she would be courted by many hopeful suitors. Rupert claimed his dance, and was amused to see the look of anxiety on her mother's face. It was the look he had seen on the faces of other mamas over the years as he paid attention to their daughters. As he and Lucie danced an energetic polka they were watched by two sets of anxious eyes: Suzanne Barrincau's and Hélène's. He was enjoying the dance and saw neither.

Later, Rupert invited Sylvie St Clair to dance, but she refused him with a gentle smile.

'You're very kind, sir, but I do not dance these days.' Her eyes flicked sideways to her husband, seated across the alcove talking to his aunt, and Rupert remembered that he had lost part of his leg during the siege of Paris. Dancing must be impossible for him.

'Of course, madame, but perhaps I may sit with you for a while. I have danced with all the ladies with whom I am acquainted, except for Miss Hélène, but she has promised me the supper dance.'

Sylvie gestured to the chair beside her. 'Please, monsieur, do sit down.' She glanced round the room, which had become increasingly hot from the hundreds of candles and the press of people. 'It is a delightful evening, is it not? Such a wonderful celebration of Clarice's marriage.'

'An extremely good match, I must say,' put in her husband

as he turned back to his wife. He reached forward, extending his hand to Rupert. 'Good to see you, sir.'

They passed a comfortable quarter of an hour until it was time for Rupert to claim Hélène for himself, to dance and to escort her to the supper table. As they moved out onto the dance floor, Sylvie smiled.

'I'm glad she's not going in to supper with that Simon Barnier,' she said. 'I don't warm to the man, do you?'

'Hardly know the fellow,' replied Georges. 'Knew him as a child, but he's younger than I am and we were never friends.'

'I could see he was disappointed that Monsieur Chalfont had taken the supper dance.'

'You're probably right, my dear,' returned her husband. 'Makes no difference really – Chalfont will be gone tomorrow. Lucas's mother was telling me that he'll be leaving Montmichel in the morning.'

Rupert and Hélène did not speak for the first few moments of their first dance together, Rupert because he was enjoying the feel of Hélène light as thistledown in his arms, and Hélène because she did not know what to say. With her previous partners, including Simon Barnier, the conversation had flowed once the man had instigated it with a compliment or some innocuous comment about the evening, the ballroom or the band. She had been able to look up into their faces and answers came easily enough, but when Rupert remained silent, Hélène found that all genteel conversation deserted her.

After a moment or two, Rupert said, 'What a lovely evening. A wonderful celebration for your sister's marriage.'

'Yes, monsieur,' was all Hélène found she could manage in reply, but it made Rupert smile and he tried another tack.

'You're looking very beautiful tonight, mademoiselle, definitely the belle of the ball.' Even as spoke he thought how trite the compliment sounded and wished he hadn't said it. However, he was rewarded with a shy smile as Hélène replied, 'Oh no, monsieur, that accolade must be reserved for my sister. She is the true beauty.'

Rupert did not agree. He had thought Clarice beautiful as she had walked down the aisle, but the more he saw of her the more insipid he found her. She was like a beautiful doll, whereas his love, his Hélène, had a dark beauty that must draw the eye of any man. A man like Simon Barnier, perhaps.

'Have you know Monsieur Barnier for a long time?' he asked.

Hélène gave a small shrug. 'All my life, I suppose, though he is older than I am so we had little to do with each other as children.'

'He has been watching you all evening,' Rupert couldn't resist saying. 'I can see he admires you.'

Hélène looked a little flustered and she missed her step in the dance, almost treading on Rupert's toe. For a second he held her more firmly to steady her, but then she pulled away and said, 'I don't think that is the kind of thing you should be saying to me, monsieur.'

Rupert knew she was right, but he laughed. 'I'm sure you're right, but you must have noticed it yourself. Whenever you see him, he's looking at you.' Why don't I keep my mouth shut? Rupert thought even as the words escaped. But it was like touching a sore tooth with the tip of his tongue and he could not. However, Hélène's answer surprised him.

'Then I wish he would not,' she said fiercely. 'I don't like to be looked at!'

'And you don't like Simon,' Rupert said, not knowing why it was true, but knowing it was so.

'I hardly know him,' came the reply. 'He dangled after Clarice for a while, but luckily Lucas came home in time to save her.'

'Save her!' Rupert was startled. 'Save her from what?'

'Well, from Simon, of course. Anyway, she's always loved Lucas. One should always marry for love, don't you think?'

Rupert, who had never thought so in the past, said fervently, 'Yes, I do. It's what I intend to do.'

'I don't think it's seemly to be talking like this,' Hélène said suddenly. 'I know my mother wouldn't approve. Perhaps we should go in to supper now.'

Though the music was still playing, they broke apart, and Rupert led her, her fingers resting on his arm, into the supper room. From the corner of his eye he saw Simon Barnier watching them and knew a stab of guilty pleasure at his sour expression.

When they were seated at a table in the supper room, Rupert said casually, 'I'm leaving Montmichel tomorrow.' Hélène looked up, suddenly stricken, and he went on, 'I mustn't outstay my welcome. The Barrineaux have been very hospitable, but it's time I moved on.'

'Oh.' Hélène's voice was hardly more than a whisper.

'I think Madame Barrineau is afraid I will try to make Lucie have a *tendre* for me. She need not worry, of course; I have no intention of trying to do such a thing, for my heart is already given.'

'I see.' Hélène raised her chin. 'How delightful. And will you be married soon?'

'I don't know,' Rupert replied quite truthfully. 'I don't know if my feelings are reciprocated, and if by any lucky chance they are, I still have to convince her father to allow me to pay my addresses.'

'So' – Hélène worked hard at keeping her voice steady – 'you'll be leaving us to return to England.'

'Oh no, not yet,' Rupert said cheerfully. 'I've taken rooms at Le Coq d'Argent. I shall send for my man to come to me and pass some time in this beautiful part of the country.'

Hélène felt the colour rise in her cheeks as she took in the import of his words. 'So, you aren't going far after all.' She gave a sudden laugh. 'Poor Madame Barrineau will think you're staying to pay court to Lucie.'

Rupert grinned at this and said, 'Well, she'll discover that I am not. Though before I go tomorrow I'm invited to take coffee with her mother-in-law. She wants to hear all about the ball.'

'Surely Lucie will tell her,' Hélène said.

'I'm sure she will,' Rupert agreed, 'but perhaps from a slightly different perspective.'

After supper, Rupert returned Hélène to her parents; he knew that he would not dance with her again, though he longed to do so.

'Monsieur Chalfont.' Rosalie greeted their return with a smile. 'I hear from Suzanne that you're leaving tomorrow. It has been such a pleasure to meet you.'

'Indeed, madame, I am leaving Montmichel tomorrow, but I'm not going far. I've taken rooms at Le Coq d'Argent and plan to make an extended stay in the area.'

'Indeed?' Rosalie raised a polite eyebrow. 'How delightful!' And how Suzanne will hate it! 'You must come to dine with us when we've got over all the excitement of Clarice's wedding. I will send you a card.'

'How kind of you,' Rupert said with a smile. 'I shall await the invitation with anticipation.'

Chapter 18

The morning after the ball Rupert asked Aristide to pack his valise and arrange to have it conveyed to Le Coq d'Argent.

'I have taken a room there,' he said to the footman, who had been acting as his valet during his stay at Montmichel. 'They are expecting me.'

Aristide, now well aware of the Englishman's generosity, said, 'Would you like me to unpack it when I get there for you, sir?'

Rupert smiled. He didn't blame him. If he had to rely on the generosity of someone like himself, he would offer any assistance which might tap into that generosity.

'Provided Madame Barrineau can spare you,' he said. 'I've trespassed on her hospitality long enough. In the meantime,' he went on, 'I have been invited to drink a cup of coffee with Madame Barrineau, Monsieur's mother.'

He went downstairs and, finding Gaspard in his pantry, asked him to take his card up to Madame Barrineau senior and enquire if she was receiving visitors. Aristide wasn't the only one who had been charmed by Rupert's engaging manner – even Gaspard unbent enough to say, 'Certainly, Monsieur Chalfont. I know Madame is expecting you.'

Sure enough, within minutes the butler returned to say

that Madame would be delighted to receive him. 'If you would follow me, monsieur,' Gaspard said, 'I will show you to Madame's apartments.' He led the way into another wing of the house, where Monsieur Barrineau's mother lived separately with her own household.

Opening the outer door, Gaspard led Rupert into a lofty hall and, having knocked on one of the panelled doors that led off it, announced Rupert, standing aside to let him into the room beyond. It was a spacious apartment with cream-painted walls and a gilded ceiling. Wide windows gave out onto the rose garden immediately below with a more distant prospect across parklands and a vineyard, all resting peacefully in the morning sun.

Madame Barrineau was seated in a gilded armchair upholstered in deep red silk. She made no effort to stand, nor did Rupert expect her to, but she smiled at him and extended her hand in greeting.

'Monsieur Chalfont.'

'Madame Barrineau.' Rupert crossed the room to her and took the hand, lifting it to his lips. 'I hope I find you well this morning and not too fatigued after the wedding.'

'Well, I have to admit I am a trifle tired, even though I didn't go to the ball.' She waved him to another chair set at an angle to her own so that she could both see and hear him. 'You danced the night away, I suppose.'

'Much of it, madame,' he agreed with a smile. 'I knew so few ladies that I must admit I did not stand up for every dance, but it was an extremely pleasant evening.'

'And did you dance with my granddaughter?' she demanded with a sly twinkle.

'Yes, indeed,' he replied with an answering grin. 'A very beautiful young lady, if I may say so.'

Madame Barrineau gave a chuckle. 'My daughter-in-law must have known a few moments' worry,' she said. 'She wishes a brilliant match for Lucie, as indeed we all do, and you, I believe, are a younger son.'

Rupert inclined his head. 'Only by two hours, madame.'

'Might as well be two years,' pointed out the old lady.

'So it might,' Rupert said cheerfully, 'but I don't let that fact spoil my life. Indeed, I am extremely fond of my brother Justin and I'm sure that having spent an extra two hours in the world makes him a much wiser man than I.'

Madame Barrineau laughed. 'You'll do, monsieur, you'll do!' She turned to the table beside her chair where there was a tray with delicate china cups and a pot of coffee waiting to be poured. 'Perhaps you would pour the coffee for us,' she said. 'I find the pot too heavy to lift these days. Usually my maid Véronique pours for me, but I sent her away.' Her eyes twinkled. 'I didn't think I'd need a chaperone this morning.'

Rupert moved to the table and filled the coffee cups, adding, at her request, cream and sugar to hers. He carried his back to his chair. 'Perhaps not, madame, but maybe *I* do.'

'You are disgraceful, young man,' she said with a smile. 'Charmingly disgraceful!'

'You must allay your daughter-in-law's fears for Mademoiselle Lucie, madame,' Rupert said with a smile. 'I promise you I have no designs on her, and I am far too old!' And for Hélène too, he thought, but did not say. 'And as I think I told you the other night, my heart is already engaged elsewhere.'

They passed the next half hour in comfortable conversation, and when Rupert saw that the old lady was flagging a little, he rose to his feet.

'If you'll excuse me, madame, I must leave you now. I am removing to Le Coq d'Argent today.'

'Not, I trust, because Suzanne has made you unwelcome at Montmichel,' said the old lady.

'No, indeed, madame, Madame Barrineau has been most hospitable. It was an honour to be included in Lucas's wedding celebrations, but I would not wish to presume upon her hospitality any further.'

'Le Coq d'Argent, is it? How long do you plan to stay?'

'That I have not yet decided, madame,' Rupert replied. 'But this is an attractive part of the country and I thought I would take the opportunity to explore it a little.'

'Then we may still have the pleasure of your company from time to time,' she said as she pulled the bell ribbon that hung at her side. 'I hope you will find time to visit me again.'

Rupert bowed to her. 'Without a doubt, madame.'

A footman answered her call. 'Monsieur Chalfont is leaving, Albert,' she said. 'Please show him out.'

When the door had closed behind him, Madame Barrineau sat back in her chair and closed her eyes. She liked Monsieur Chalfont, she liked him very much. He was charming, yes, but something more. Something in the way he jousted with words reminded her of her own beloved Xavier, dead and gone these twenty years. Too long ago – his voice had already deserted her and now, unless she looked at the miniature she'd always had at her bedside, his face was also slipping away. Was Rupert Chalfont really like Xavier, or was she confusing the two?

'I've lived for too long,' she said to the empty room. 'Far too long.'

★

Rupert made his farewells to his host and hostess and left Montmichel as he had arrived, in the chaise driven by the taciturn Lucien. Rupert had been going to walk into the village, little more than two miles away, but Suzanne Barrineau had been horrified at the idea.

'Certainly not, Monsieur Chalfont. I will not hear of it.' She immediately rang for Aristide to order the chaise to be brought to the door. Rupert grinned inwardly as he considered the possible reasons for this rush of enthusiasm to get rid of him. Perhaps she wanted to be sure he was off the premises and not coming back. If that were the case she was out of luck, as her mother-in-law had already invited him to call again. Or maybe it was the relief of knowing he was no longer under the same roof as Lucie, or maybe she had already counted the spoons!

'Do you plan to remain in the area for long, Monsieur Chalfont?' Louis had asked him as they walked out to the waiting chaise.

'For some time yet, I think,' Rupert answered. 'I have telegraphed my man, Parker, who is at home on a family matter, and he will come to meet me at St Etienne before I travel further afield.'

'Capital,' cried Louis. 'You must come to dinner again before you leave. I know Lucas and Clarice will be away on their wedding journey for several weeks, but Suzanne and Lucie and I will look forward to welcoming you back.'

'Thank you, sir,' Rupert said with a smile as he wondered what Suzanne would think of the invitation, 'you're all more than kind.'

The room at Le Coq d'Argent was large and pleasantly appointed, with a dressing room off it and an indoor bathroom a little further down the corridor. It boasted a comfortable saloon downstairs as well as a dining room and a taproom for the local men. Rupert found that Aristide had been as good as his word and had unpacked and hung up most of Rupert's clothes. A few, needing the attentions of a laundress, he had set aside to be brushed or washed and then returned.

Rupert crossed to the window that looked out over the lane at the back of the inn. It was a narrow street, bounded by the high walls of the inn's yard below him and a line of cottages along the far side. Not a particularly interesting view, he thought, but perhaps quieter than one of the front rooms that looked out onto the bustle of the village square.

He was about to turn away when a movement below caught his eye. Someone was entering the lane, moving furtively along the wall beneath his window. It was a woman with a cloak thrown over her shoulders, its hood shading her hair and face. He stared down, intrigued, and watched as she edged along the lane. Why on earth was she wearing such a heavy cloak on such a hot day? It was only just after noon and the sun was splitting stones. Whoever it was must have been trying to hide her identity.

And yet, Rupert thought, by wearing such unusual clothes on this hot summer's day she was more likely to draw attention to herself.

Halfway along the lane she paused and looked at one of the cottages. It was in better condition than most of the others, its windows clean and glinting in the sun, its front door freshly painted green. The woman glanced about her and then moved swiftly to the green door and knocked. As she waited to be admitted, she glanced round again and her hood slipped sideways, revealing her face. It was then that Rupert recognised her, and he could hardly believe his eyes as he watched the front door open and Hélène St Clair be admitted to the house.

Hélène? What was she doing, creeping down a back lane to visit a house on her own? Surely her mother did not allow her to visit the village alone, with no maid to attend her. No, he thought. She's not supposed to be there, in that house in that backstreet. She had been trying to conceal her face with the hood of her cloak, and it was only when the hood had fallen back from her hair that he'd been able to recognise her. He decided to wait for her to come out again, and settled down on a chair by his window to keep watch. Then, he thought, when she reappears I shall run downstairs and meet her casually in the street. Would she be pleased to see him? Did he mind the fact that she was out and about on her own? He thought about his sister Fran. She was allowed some licence at home, allowed to ride out over the hills with just a groom for company, a precaution in case she fell. However, she sometimes walked unaccompanied, so perhaps Hélène was allowed to as well. He didn't know what was customary for young ladies of good families here in France. But Hélène hadn't simply been walking to take the air; she had come to visit someone in a slightly shabby house in a back lane and she was clearly anxious not to be recognised.

Rupert waited for what seemed an age and was actually considering whether he should go down and knock on the door of the cottage when it was opened by a middle-aged woman who looked quickly up and down the lane before standing aside to let Hélène slip out. Rupert was immediately on his feet, down the stairs and out into the street. Even so, Hélène had disappeared. She was not in the square, and when he followed the lane that led to the church, she wasn't there either. Where on earth had she gone? Rupert looked round him, bewildered. Where could she be? He'd only taken half a minute to get downstairs and yet he'd missed her. He walked up through the churchyard, wondering if she had gone into the church for some reason, and it was as he reached the hillock on which the church stood that he caught sight of her. She taken the footpath across the fields and was even now hurrying along the line of the hedge as if she did not wish to be seen. Rupert hurried after her, half running, half walking in his effort to catch up with her before she reached the field gate that led into the garden of Belair.

When he was only about fifty yards behind her, he called out, 'Hélène! Hélène! Wait! Wait for me!'

At first he thought she was ignoring him, or that she couldn't hear him for some reason, but after a moment or two she looked back over her shoulder and paused, still edging along the path like an animal about to take flight. He slowed his steps and, speaking more quietly, said, 'Hélène, don't run away, it's me, Rupert.'

It was the first time he had used her unadorned Christian name, the first time he had named himself to her. Carefully, as if approaching a spooked horse, he walked towards her, his hands at his side, unthreatening.

'Hélène, don't run, it's only me. I thought we could walk together, if you would care to?'

The girl didn't move, but as he came up beside her and he could see her face, Rupert realised that she had been crying. Her cheeks were tear-streaked, her eyes bright with unshed tears.

'What is it?' he whispered as he saw another tear course down her cheek. 'What is it, my darling girl? Why are you crying? What can I do to help?'

Hélène shook her head wordlessly, and so Rupert simply pulled a linen handkerchief from his pocket and handed it to her to wipe her eyes.

'My dearest girl,' he began again, 'what is the matter? Why are you so distressed? Who has upset you?' He held out his hand to her, and after a moment's hesitation she took it and he led her to a grassy knoll beside the hedge where they would not be easily seen. Taking her heavy cloak from her shoulders, he spread it on the ground and gently eased her down to sit upon it. Not wanting to tower over her, he sat down beside her.

'Now tell me,' he said gently.

For a moment Hélène seemed unable to form words, her throat constricted with the effort of controlling her tears, and then she managed, 'The baby is dead.'

Rupert stared at her. 'The baby? What baby?'

Gradually Hélène explained how she had known Annette when they were children, that they had met again when her mother had employed Annette and her aunt to help over the wedding. 'Her husband died in the flu epidemic in Paris before her baby was born and she came to work for us until then.' She lapsed into silence and sat twisting the now-damp handkerchief round and round her fingers. 'The night... the night of Clarice's wedding the baby started to be born, but there... there was something wrong with him. He was upside down or something. I don't know.' Her voice broke on a sob. 'The midwife was there, but she couldn't do anything. He was born dead. Poor Annette has no husband and no baby and is like to die herself.' She scrubbed her eyes again. 'My mother knew... about the baby being born that night and made Annette move to the midwife's house. I saw them take her in a cart, but I thought she was going there to have the baby. I thought she'd be happy. Maman did not tell anyone about the baby being born dead on Clarice's wedding night. She didn't tell us the next day either. She still hasn't told anyone what has happened. I asked Henri the stable lad where he had taken Annette. I wanted to see the baby. I've never seen a newborn baby, so when Maman was having her afternoon rest, I slipped out and went to the house. The woman who lives there is called Madame Leclerc and she is the midwife. She couldn't save the baby, but now she's trying to save Annette. I think she's dying. She's lying in bed. Just lying there, her eyes all blank as if she's gone blind, only I don't think she has because she knew who I was all right. But she didn't speak and her baby's dead. He's dead. He was never alive except inside her. I felt him kicking inside her. She let me put my hand on her… on her stomach and through her clothes I felt him kicking. He was alive then, but he came out dead. And Maman knew and she didn't tell me. Annette's my friend and Maman didn't tell me.'

'She probably didn't want to upset you,' suggested Rupert gently when she finally came to a stop. 'She probably wanted to give your friend Annette time to recover from what sounds like a difficult birth before anyone went to see her.'

'Madame Sauze went,' Hélène said bitterly, 'and she didn't tell me either.'

'Who is Madame Sauze?'

'She is Annette's aunt. She has come to work at Belair as well. She must know that the baby is dead.'

'Perhaps your mother asked her not to tell you.'

'Well, she shouldn't have!'

Rupert looked at her, the girl he'd fallen in love with, and felt completely at a loss. Even in her distress she was beautiful and he longed to gather her into his arms, to comfort her and kiss away her tears, but there could be no possibility of that. Just sitting here with her in a field could compromise her reputation, and they were discussing things that no gentleman should discuss with an innocent young lady. No one should be talking of babies inside their mothers, or the way you could feel them kick before they were born. Even after marriage, if discussed at all, such matters were kept strictly to the bedchamber.

'What will you do now?' Rupert asked.

Hélène sighed. 'Go home again, I suppose. Pretend that I was sitting in the garden and fell asleep in the sun. But when I get the chance I shall ask Madame Sauze about Annette and what she will do now.'

'Why this Madame Sauze? Why not your mother?'

'Madame Sauze looked after me for a while when I was a child. That's how I know Annette.'

'I see,' replied Rupert. But he didn't. He didn't see at all. All he knew was that Hélène was extremely upset that this Annette had lost her baby, and that she should not be wandering through the fields on her own.

He got to his feet and held out his hand. 'Come,' he said. 'If you're to have been asleep in the garden, we'd better get you back there before they start looking for you.' He reached into his pocket and brought out a second handkerchief and, silently blessing his mother for always insisting that a man should carry two, he handed it to her.

'Dry your eyes,' he said gently, 'and blow your nose. Then remember, chins are being worn very high this year!'

This brought a weak smile to her lips and she did as he told her, including, as she turned to face him, raising her chin.

Together they continued along the footpath towards the

gate in the wall that led back into the garden. As they opened it and entered, the first person they saw was Simon Barnier. He stared at them in amazement.

'Good afternoon, monsieur,' Rupert said smoothly. 'I hope I see you well.'

'Where have you been?' Barnier demanded, ignoring the greeting.

'I beg your pardon, sir,' replied Rupert, 'but if it's any business of yours, Miss Hélène has kindly been pointing out the convenient shortcut across the fields to the village.'

'They said she was in the garden,' snapped Barnier. 'I came to find her.'

'As did I, monsieur,' answered Rupert.

'Why was she?'

'Why was she what, monsieur?'

'Showing you the footpath to the village?'

'Because that is where I am staying.' Rupert smiled, but his smile did not reach his eyes. Nor did he offer any further explanation.

'Are you all right?' Barnier said, noticing for the first time Hélène's tear-stained cheeks. 'Has this man been pestering you?' He took a step towards Rupert, who stood his ground, his whole stance a challenge.

'No, of course not,' she snapped. 'I was simply showing him the footpath to the village. What do you want?'

'Your mother wants you,' Simon told her. 'I said I would look for you in the garden.'

'Then I shall go and find her.' Hélène spoke briskly. 'Good afternoon, gentlemen.' With that, she turned on her heel and, raising her chin, marched off towards the house.

Rupert watched her go, smiling slightly at the tilt of her head.

'As for you, Chalfont,' Simon said, turning on Rupert, 'you can stay away from my fiancée.'

Rupert turned his head and, lifting one eyebrow, remarked, 'I was not aware that you were engaged to Miss St Clair.'

Simon reddened. 'There is an understanding between us,' he said stiffly.

'I see,' Rupert said lightly. 'Thank you for telling me. Have you told Miss Hélène yet?'

When Simon made no answer, Rupert said, 'I see. Well, I'll bid you good afternoon, monsieur.' And with a languid lift of his hand in farewell, he set off along the footpath to the village.

Simon Barnier watched him go, anger burning inside him – anger that Hélène, whom he already regarded as his future wife, had been alone with the upstart Englishman, a nobody who had invaded their local society, and more at the invidious thought that somehow the Englishman had just bested him in their exchange.

Chapter 19

When Hélène reached the house she went straight to her mother's private parlour, rapped on the door and without waiting for an answer walked in. Rosalie was sitting at her little writing desk in the window, and she looked up, startled.

'Hélène!' she exclaimed. 'Whatever is the matter?' Seeing at once from her daughter's tear-streaked cheeks and reddened eyes that she had been crying, she got to her feet and reached for her hand, repeating more gently, 'Hélène, whatever is the matter? What has happened?'

'Annette's baby is dead,' she cried. 'Her baby is dead. He was born dead, but you didn't tell me.'

'Darling girl,' began her mother, 'there was nothing you could do. There was nothing any of us could do. It is very sad, of course, but really Annette's baby is nothing to do with us.'

'Of course it's to do with us,' snapped Hélène. 'She works for us. She had her baby in this house and it died.'

Rosalie stared at her. 'Who told you that?' she demanded. 'Who says the baby was born here at Belair?'

'Never mind how I know, Maman,' Hélène almost shouted, 'I know.'

She was not yet ready to admit that she had been to the

village alone to see Annette. If she hoped to do it again it was better that no one knew about that.

Still, the angry words poured out of her. 'She was my friend. She's lost her husband and now she's lost her baby, and you sent her away. You didn't even let her stay here with Madame Sauze. She needed our help, but you sent her away, and now she might die too, and it's all your fault!'

Rosalie's face hardened. 'I won't be spoken to like that, miss,' she said harshly. 'You may go to your room and stay there until I come to speak to you. Do you understand?'

The habit of obedience made Hélène turn to the door, but she paused with her hand on the handle and said, 'I understand, Mother. You've made yourself very clear!' Then she raised her chin and left the room, closing the door gently behind her.

For a moment Rosalie stared at the closed door and then she sank down onto a chair, suddenly exhausted. How could Hélène have discovered that the baby had been born here, upstairs? Only one person could have told her, and with sudden anger Rosalie got to her feet and rang the bell for Madame Sauze.

When the housekeeper came in answer to its summons, her mistress was standing in the middle of the room, her face a mask of anger.

'You rang, madame?'

'Give me one good reason why I shouldn't send you packing,' came the ice-cold reply. 'How dare you speak to my daughter about that cheap maid, Annette? I told you right from the outset that if ever you broke your word to me, your given word, you would be out of the house within the hour. So, Madame Agathe Sauze, what have you to say for yourself, eh? Why should I not dismiss you here and now?'

Agathe, surprised at this sudden and unjustified onslaught, spoke calmly. 'Because I have not broken my word, madame.'

'You must have done. Hélène knows not only that the baby was born here, but that it was stillborn. Only you could have told her.'

'But I did not,' Agathe said steadily. 'Miss Hélène saw Annette being taken to the village in the waggon early next morning, and when she came to ask me what was happening I referred her to you.'

Rosalie coloured. For the moment she had forgotten the conversation she had had with her daughter the morning of the ball. She had answered that Annette was being moved to the home of the midwife. But she had given no indication that the child had been stillborn, or that it had been born at all. She had been determined that the celebrations of Clarice's wedding should not be overshadowed by the private tragedy of one of her servants.

'As you instructed, madame,' went on Agathe, 'every care was taken that no one should suspect that the child had already been born when Annette left the house. The only other person who knew apart from the midwife was Madame Paquet, who, understanding your wishes in the matter, I am certain will not have spoken of it to Miss Hélène.'

For a moment Rosalie did not respond; she stood, her expression fixed, her hands clasped together in front of her, gripping each other as if she were trying to control them.

The silence extended between them and eventually Agathe broke it, saying, 'However, madame, if you no longer accept my word, I shall pack my things and leave your employ today.'

'No, no,' Rosalie said testily. 'There is no need for that. But how did she find out, Agathe? Who knows, and who told Hélène?'

Accepting that this was as near to an apology as she was going to get, Agathe shook her head. 'I don't know, madame. You will have to ask her.'

'I shall,' said Rosalie. 'She is in her room, where she will remain for the rest of the day. Perhaps you could arrange for a tray to be taken up to her later.'

'Yes, madame.' Agathe's voice was that of the perfect servant. 'If that is all?'

'It is for now,' Rosalie replied, and then almost as an afterthought she asked, 'How is Annette?'

'Very weak, madame, and very low in spirits. Madame Leclerc fears for her sanity, if not her life.'

'I see. I am sorry to hear it. Please feel free to go and visit her when your work allows and let me know how she goes on.'

'Thank you, madame. I will.' With that, Madame Sauze went back to the kitchen, leaving Rosalie with the unpleasant feeling that somehow she herself had been found wanting.

Alone again, Rosalie sat for a long time considering what she should do next. Clarice's wedding was over; the risk of blighting it with the death of a baby was past. The newly married couple had now departed on their wedding trip to Venice, and life should be returning to normal. But before that could happen she needed to speak to her daughter. Though Hélène had had peculiar freedoms as a child caught up in the siege, she was no longer a child and must learn her place in society, and that place did not include friendship with a girl of the streets brought up in an orphanage.

Half an hour later Rosalie tapped on Hélène's door, the first sign that she was treating her as an adult; until now she would have entered her daughter's room unannounced. When there was no reply she knocked again and then tried the door handle. To her astonishment she found the door was locked. Rosalie knocked a third time, calling out as she did so, 'Hélène, are you there? Open the door.' For a moment there was still no response; then she heard the scrape of the key turning in the lock and the door opened a crack.

'What d'you want?' Hélène's voice was stony.

'Hélène? Don't be silly. Let me in. We need to talk.'

'What about?'

Rosalie had never heard her daughter use that tone of voice and she took a deep breath before, keeping her own voice calm, she said, 'About Annette and what we can do to help her.'

The door swung open and Hélène moved away towards the window, leaving her mother to enter if she chose.

Rosalie saw her standing, watching, and noticed at once that she had washed her tear-stained face and bathed her reddened eyes. She still looked pale, but she seemed entirely in command of herself.

'Let's sit down,' Rosalie said and, pulling out a chair, did so. With a sigh, Hélène sat down on her window seat, her back to the light, her face partially shadowed.

'Hélène, darling, I realise you're very upset about Annette,' Rosalie began, 'but sometimes babies do die before they're born.'

'You didn't tell me,' Hélène said mutinously. 'You told me she was going to have the baby at the midwife's.'

'I didn't want to upset you,' replied her mother. 'It was a special day, a special day for all of us, but most of all Clarice. It was *her* special day. Can't you see that?'

Hélène relaxed a little and sighed. 'Maybe,' she conceded. 'But you could have told me afterwards.'

'This is afterwards,' said Rosalie. 'I'm telling you now.' She fixed her eyes on Hélène's face and added, 'Who did tell you, anyway?'

'Annette.'

'Annette?' echoed Rosalie. 'When? I mean, how could she have?'

'I went to see her,' answered Hélène. 'I wanted to see the baby.'

'You went to see her? In the village? How did you...? I mean, where did you...?'

'Everyone in the village knows where Madame Leclerc lives,' Hélène said truculently. 'She isn't hard to find. You said that was where Annette had gone, so I went to see her.'

Rosalie could hardly believe what she was hearing. 'You just went there and knocked on the door?'

'Of course,' said Hélène. 'Madame Leclerc was very pleased to see me. She said Annette was feeling very low and needed to see a friendly face. I went up to her room. She was still in bed, just lying there. She hardly knew I was there. Madame Leclerc says she's been like that ever since she realised Léon was dead. She's afraid that Annette will die too.'

'Léon?'

'The baby, Maman. The baby was called Léon.'

'Hmm.' Rosalie couldn't see the point of giving a name to a stillborn baby. She certainly had not done so to the one she'd lost between her second son, Marcel, and Clarice. She had mourned him privately but had never mentioned him again. 'Well, you should have asked me if you might go and see her,' Rosalie said, 'instead of just taking yourself off without a word to anyone.'

'You'd have said no,' Hélène answered.

'And I shall say no again,' said her mother.

'Well, I shall visit her again.' Hélène spoke without emphasis, simply stating a fact. 'I promised her I would.'

'But Hélène, darling, it's not fitting for you to go into the village entirely on your own, without a maid or someone to attend you. I don't know what your father would say.'

'I'm sure Madame Sauze will be going,' replied Hélène. 'I shall go with her. Or Pierre can drive me in the chaise, that would be perfectly proper.'

Her mother sighed. 'You can be very obstinate at times,' she said.

For the first time there was the trace of a smile on Hélène's face and she said, 'I think I take after Papa.'

'Hélène!' exclaimed her mother. 'You should not say such things!'

But it was true, Rosalie acknowledged to herself when she thought back on the conversation later that evening. Emile had a very stubborn streak.

In an effort to change the subject, Rosalie said, 'Georges and Sylvie have to return to Versailles in a few days' time. I thought perhaps we might have a small farewell dinner for them before they go. Just the family and a few good friends.' She looked enquiringly at Hélène, hoping to give her thoughts a more cheerful turn. 'What about Simon Barnier? Shall I ask him? He would like to be included, don't you think? And Lucie, if her parents will allow? And what about Lucas's English friend, Monsieur Chalfont? He seems a charming young man; I know Georges thinks well of him. We could ask him too, as he's alone in the area.'

Hélène had been about to admit that she did not particularly like Simon Barnier and would prefer he was not invited, but when she heard Rupert Chalfont's name added to the list, she said, 'That sounds a lovely party, Maman.'

'Good, I will send them all cards. And tomorrow, if Madame Sauze is going to visit Annette at a suitable time, you may go with her.'

Reconciliation made, Rosalie kissed her daughter on the cheek and went to change for dinner.

Hélène sat back onto the window seat. From the pocket of her dress she pulled out two damp linen handkerchiefs. They would need to be laundered, she supposed, and returned to their owner.

Their owner had walked back to Le Coq d'Argent, his mind busy with all he had heard that afternoon. Rupert had been alone with Hélène for only twenty minutes and yet that twenty minutes had changed everything. He had seen her in tears and listened as she poured out her heart to him, seemingly unaware of the impropriety of the situation, and in that time, sitting together on her cloak on the grass, they had become closer than several weeks of normal courtship could have brought them. She had spoken to him with no self-consciousness or artifice; she had simply said what was in her heart at the time and so had, unconsciously, revealed herself to him.

There was also the meeting with Simon Barnier. This was far more worrying. He had already heard from Louis Barrineau that Simon had wanted Clarice St Clair as his wife and was likely to transfer his attentions to Hélène, but he had not believed that Simon had any real claims upon her. Now, however, he might have to think again. Did Simon simply want her for the dowry that came with her? That might be another problem for Rupert himself – people could well believe that he was a fortune hunter, courting Hélène for her money.

By the time he had reached the inn, he had come to a decision. If he received the promised invitation to dine at Belair he would accept it, and after that, as someone who had been a guest in his house, he would go to Emile St Clair and ask permission to address his daughter. It would all be out in the open. There would be no secret assignations, no secret letters or messages, all of which had tended to be part of his flirtations up until now, because, he was clear in his own head, this would be no flirtation, it would be a serious proposal of marriage. Yes, he was a younger son, there would be no title, no large estate, but Rupert wasn't entirely without money, and the name he would be offering was that of a landed family of ancient lineage. Surely, a professional man such as Emile St Clair would consider that heritage acceptable, particularly if Hélène clearly wanted the match herself – but therein lay the question: would she? It was up to him to ensure that she did.

Rupert realised that he must move swiftly to make his claim, for if he were Simon Barnier, he would be losing no time in approaching Hélène's father. He wished there were some way that he could reach Hélène's heart, but until they could meet socially there would be little he could do.

When he reached his chamber he crossed to the window again and looked down into the lane. The sun was lower in the sky now and much of the street was in shadow, but a single shaft of sunlight probed between the tall chimneys of Le Coq d'Argent and directed itself onto the green-painted door of the house Hélène had visited. As he stared at it, it seemed to shine like a beacon in the shadowy lane, pointing the way forward.

Could he go there? he wondered. Could he, a complete stranger, simply knock on the front door and ask how the poor distressed mother did? What was her name? Annette, that was it, Annette. What reason could he give to the woman who lived there? Could he say he came from Annette's friend to ask how she did, or if she were in need of anything? Medicine? Special foods to tempt an invalid? Surely they would send him packing. No gentleman would even consider visiting a woman he had never met as she languished in her bed. Perhaps he could keep watch for when Hélène made a return visit and meet her once again quite casually in the village. No! He had already decided that there must be no deception in his suit. If her family thought he had been lying in wait to catch her on her own, that would be the end of any chance for him. He must, as his old nanny used to say, possess his soul in patience.

Chapter 20

The next afternoon Pierre the coachman drove Hélène and Agathe into the village so that they could visit Annette. The lane was too narrow for the chaise, so he left it in the inn yard and accompanied the two ladies on foot to the house with the green door, carrying the small bag of Annette's clothes and other necessaries Madame Sauze had brought with her. Madame Leclerc opened the door and, taking the bag, Madame Sauze stepped forward to enter. On the threshold Hélène turned back and said, 'Just wait for us at the inn, Pierre. We'll come and find you when we're ready to go home.'

'Yes, Miss Hélène,' replied Pierre, thinking as he did so how much she had changed in the last few days. Gone was the girl he had known nearly all her life, always getting in and out of scrapes but daring and brave, and in her place was a young woman, giving orders with the calm confidence of her mother.

A far cry from the little girl who had thrown cabbages at the Prussian soldiers when they had paraded through the streets of Paris, he thought now. It won't be long before she's married and running her own household, and what will happen to poor Annette then?

In the few weeks that she had been at Belair, Pierre had grown fond of the new maid, the strange girl who had arrived so unexpectedly. He didn't know if she was actually a widow, but he didn't really mind one way or the other. What he did know was that she was a woman adrift, having to make her own way in the world, and he had come to admire her courage.

When she had been brought downstairs on that dreadful morning, he had put his arms round her and lifted her gently onto the waggon. He had felt the warmth of her body against his. She felt small and frail in his arms. He suddenly felt protective and found himself reluctant to set her down. He had looked into her face and seen it white with pain and exhaustion and he'd wanted to hold her to him, to comfort her and say everything would be all right.

It wasn't all right, of course, but at the time Pierre had not known that it was all too late. The midwife had clambered up beside her, and she had been carrying a small bundle in her arms. At the time he had assumed it was necessaries belonging to Annette, but he was sure now that it must have been the tiny body of the baby. He had heard nothing since, except that the baby had been stillborn. Since then, for the first time in his thirty-five years, he'd begun wondering if it was time to think of getting married and settling down. He longed to know how Annette was, wished he could go to see her, but knew that was impossible. The intrusion of a man into her sorrow was the last thing she would want. However, he decided he could ask Miss Hélène how she was faring on the way home today; nothing could be more natural.

As Pierre was waiting with the chaise, Hélène and Agathe were taken upstairs to Annette's room. She was out of bed now, sitting in a chair, wrapped in a blanket. She looked up as the door opened, expecting it to be Estelle Leclerc. When she saw the two women she gave the ghost of a smile.

Agathe stepped forward and, setting aside the bag of clothes, grasped Annette's hands. 'Are you feeling a little better, child?' she asked gently. 'Here's Miss Hélène come to see you again as well.'

Estelle had followed them into the room, but knowing they would want to be left alone, she said, 'I made some fresh lemonade this morning, Annette. Shall I go and fetch it? I'm sure your friends would like some refreshment on such a hot day.'

'That would be most welcome,' Agathe agreed. 'Perhaps I could come and help you with the tray.' So saying, she followed Estelle out of the room, leaving Annette and Hélène alone together.

'They've put my Léon in the ground,' Annette said bleakly. 'They wouldn't let me see him. They took him away and put him in the ground.'

Hélène reached for her friend's hands and, when she found that despite the heat of the day they were icy cold, gently chafed them between her own. She had not given any thought to what must have become of the infant corpse, but now she realised he must have had to be buried, and quickly, due to the summer heat.

'They couldn't not,' she said softly. 'Your Léon had to be laid to rest.'

'The priest came and took him.' Annette spoke with chilling anger.

'He will have said prayers for him,' Hélène said comfortingly. 'He will have prayed for his soul, and your little Léon is now with his father, in heaven. They will both be looking down on you.'

'His father!' Annette gave a harsh laugh. 'His father isn't in heaven and never will be! If there is a God and he is just, Léon's father will burn in hell for all eternity!'

Hélène let go of her hands and stared at her in astonishment. 'But your husband...?' she faltered.

'Husband?' cried Annette bitterly. 'What husband? I never had a husband!'

'But the baby's father...'

'I was raped,' said Annette flatly. 'A man forced himself on me. That's rape and you know the man who did it.'

'*I* do?' Hélène was horrified. 'I don't know any men that you know.'

'Father Thomas,' stated Annette.

'Father Thomas?' echoed Hélène, incredulous. 'You mean Father Thomas at the Clergy House?'

'Where else?'

'But he's a priest!'

'Doesn't stop him raping young girls.'

'But Father Lenoir? Madame Sauze?'

'Father Lenoir died last year. Father Thomas stayed. He sent Madame Sauze away. When I was left alone in the house with him, he took me by force, coming to me in my bed at night. He could do as he chose... and he did.'

'I don't understand,' Hélène said. 'You're telling me that you had no husband and that Father Thomas is the father of the baby?'

'Yes.'

'But how? I mean he's a priest.'

'He's also a man; it takes a man and a woman to make a baby.'

Hélène knew that; she didn't know the mechanics of exactly how, she had wondered about kissing, but she had always assumed that the couple must be married to achieve this miracle.

'And Father Thomas made the baby... with you?'

'Yes.'

The single word sat between them for several moments and then Hélène asked, 'Does he know – about the baby, I mean?'

'Of course! That's why he was going to send me back to St Luke's.'

'St Luke's?' Hélène stared at her in horror.

'You remember that at St Luke's the nuns used to call us children of shame. That was because our parents, whoever they were, weren't married, didn't want us and dumped us on the orphanage doorstep. That's what he was going to do to me. Tell them that I had been with some man and was now having a child of shame myself.'

'But back to St Luke's?' gasped Hélène. 'Oh, Annette, no!'

'No,' Annette said. 'So I ran away. He called the baby spawn of the devil and said I would burn in hellfire.'

'You would burn in hellfire,' Hélène echoed incredulously. 'But wasn't it his fault? He *was* the father?'

'Who else? I've never been with another man.' Annette gave a bitter laugh. 'He's right, in a way – *he's* Léon's father and he is the devil incarnate. That made Léon spawn of the devil.' She closed her eyes and murmured, 'Perhaps that's why he died.'

Hélène looked at her friend in despair. How could all these dreadful things happen to anyone?

'What are you going to do?'

'I don't know,' Annette replied. 'Your mother will not take me back now I have told you the truth.'

'My mother...? She knows the truth?'

'Yes, she knows. Madame Sauze found me on the streets and took me in. She went to your mother to ask for help.'

'And Maman took you both in?'

'Yes, but with certain conditions. No mention of Father Thomas. We had to make up the story of my being a widow. She said if anyone learned the truth we would be dismissed at once.'

'She won't mind you telling me,' averred Hélène. 'And I won't tell anyone else. Your secret will be safe.'

'It was you in particular who wasn't to know,' Annette said. 'And now I've told you we can't go back to Belair. Oh, poor Madame Sauze,' she cried as she realised the consequences of speaking the truth to Hélène. 'I shouldn't have said anything!'

'But my mother won't know you've told me,' pointed out Hélène. 'I won't tell her and you won't tell her, and Madame Sauze won't know either. It'll be our secret, Annette. I promise you. When you're well again you can come back to Belair, you and Madame Sauze.'

She reached for Annette's hand again and saw that tears were pouring down her cheeks. 'Oh, don't,' she exclaimed in dismay. 'Don't cry. I'm your friend.'

'But why?' Annette sobbed. 'Why are you my friend? I'm a servant in your home.'

'You know why,' answered Hélène. 'When I needed a friend, you helped me. When I was running away from St Luke's, you stopped Sister Gabrielle from catching me... and took a beating for doing it.'

For a moment both the girls thought back to that time over six years ago when they had both been in the care of the nuns at St Luke's orphanage. Hélène had made a break for freedom during Mass at the parish church, and when Sister Gabrielle had tried to catch her, Annette had collapsed into the aisle in front of her, blocking her way for the precious moments that allowed Hélène to reach the church door and disappear into the myriad of streets outside.

'My whole life would have been different if I hadn't got away that day,' Hélène said. 'If I'd been taken back to St Luke's I might never have found my family again. My mother knows that too, and I'm sure she will continue to help you in her own way. So,' she went on, 'we must decide what we're going to do now.'

While the girls were beginning to make plans upstairs, Estelle Leclerc and Agathe Sauze were discussing the situation downstairs in the kitchen.

'Annette can stay here as long as is necessary. Madame St Clair has already paid me to look after her until she is well enough to return to Belair.'

Agathe stared at her in surprise. 'Madame St Clair has?'

'Yes, she sent a groom here yesterday with a letter and some money.' Estelle shook her head sadly. 'It's a dreadful thing to say, but in the circumstances it is, perhaps, a blessing that the baby did not survive. Your niece is young. She may marry again, and a woman alone with a child could find it more difficult to attract a man who would take on a child that was not his.'

For a moment Agathe had thought that Estelle, mentioning Annette's situation, had been told the truth, but her comments about 'marrying again' assured her that she still believed Annette to be a widow giving birth to a posthumous child.

'That's very generous of Madame St Clair,' she said carefully. 'It will certainly be better for my niece if she is able to come back to Belair soon. Work is one way to cope with grief.'

'I agree,' said Estelle, 'and sadly I speak from experience.' She went into the cool of her tiny pantry and picked up the pitcher of lemonade. As she did so, she went on. 'Father Bernard came to visit her, but she wouldn't see him. When she refused I told him she was asleep and should not be disturbed. The baby has been buried just outside the churchyard. He wasn't baptised, of course, which meant he could not be buried in hallowed ground, but there is a corner beyond the eastern wall where they bury those like him.'

Those like him, thought Agathe – someone of no consequence, unbaptised, a non-Christian... as if he'd had a choice in the matter! Encouraged by some of the priests, this was how many people thought, so she made no comment, simply nodded. She knew how Annette felt about priests, however, and she wasn't surprised that the girl had refused to see him, though she herself had met Father Bernard, an elderly priest, and had thought him a gentle and sympathetic man.

To change the subject, she asked, 'How long do you think Annette will be here with you?'

'It's hard to say,' Estelle replied. 'Physically she is beginning to recover; she has started to take a little food and her strength will return. Her mind is a different matter. She makes no effort to do anything. Your visits will help, but it's hard to lose a husband and a child in such a short time.'

'I'll tell her that Madame St Clair says her job is waiting for her as soon as she can return,' Agathe said.

When they went back upstairs, Estelle and Agathe found two very different girls in the bedroom. Annette was out of the chair, the bag was open on the bed and Hélène was helping her to get dressed. It was such a reversal of their normal relationship that Agathe paused in the doorway, staring in amazement.

'I want to visit my baby,' Annette announced without preamble. 'Miss Hélène and I are going to the churchyard.'

'Annette,' said Estelle calmly, 'you must certainly visit your baby's grave, but not today. You're not strong enough yet.'

'Today.' Annette spoke firmly. 'While Miss Hélène is here.' But when she bent down to put on her shoes, her head began to spin and she sat up again quickly, her face ashen.

'Annette, my dear girl,' Agathe stepped in to prevent an argument, 'I'll come and visit you again tomorrow and together we will go to the churchyard. Madame Leclerc is right, today is too soon. You have to rebuild your strength. Tomorrow or the next day.'

Although the wheels in her head were spinning more slowly, Annette knew that she was right, but she said belligerently, 'All right. Tomorrow.'

'I'll come too,' Hélène said. 'We can all go together.'

Good as their word, the next afternoon Agathe and Hélène returned to Madame Leclerc's and found Annette waiting for them, dressed and ready to go out. Pierre had again brought them into the village in the chaise.

'I want you to come with us today,' Agathe had told him. 'We're going to the churchyard with Annette, but in case she finds it too far to walk, or too...' She didn't explain, but she didn't have to. Pierre agreed at once, and leaving the carriage in the inn yard, they collected Annette and took the lane to the church.

The tiny grave, no more than a broken patch of earth in the shade of the eastern wall, had nothing to mark it as a place of burial, or to name the child who lay beneath the ground. Annette stared down at it, silent tears on her cheeks. In her hands was a posy of flowers that Hélène had brought from the garden at Belair.

Agathe and Hélène stood back as Annette moved forward with the flowers in her hands. Both Hélène and Agathe found tears in their own eyes as they watched her bend and lay the nosegay on the tiny grave, and Pierre, watching from a discreet distance, once again admired her courage.

At that moment Father Bernard emerged from the church and, seeing the little group beyond the wall, walked over to speak to them. He paused as Annette stood in silence at the graveside of her son, the flowers at her feet, but as at length she turned away he stepped forward.

'God bless you, my child,' he said softly. 'Your baby is with God in heaven now.'

Annette stared at him for a moment, her eyes filled with an emotion so violent that the old man took a step backwards.

'God?' she said, her voice full of contempt. 'God doesn't exist, and even if he does, I don't believe in him!' She turned her back on the priest and moved away.

'I can see you don't,' replied Father Bernard, 'but that doesn't matter. He believes in you.'

'And I am *not* your child!' She threw the comment over her shoulder and set off unsteadily down the hill towards the lane below.

Pierre went after her to steady her, but she threw off his proffered hand and continued alone.

Agathe and Hélène watched her progress for a moment and then turned back to the old priest, who stood beside the grave, his eyes closed and his lips moving in prayer.

How strange, Agathe thought as she watched him, that two supposed men of God could be so different – the arrogant, bullying Father Thomas full of hellfire and the kindly Father Bernard, understanding and filled with compassion.

As far as I'm concerned, thought Agathe, only one of them is a man of God.

They were turning to follow Annette and Pierre down to the village when Father Bernard opened his eyes and smiled at them. He didn't speak, merely raised his hand in what could have been a blessing or simply a wave, and returned to his church.

'Come along,' Agathe said to Hélène. 'We'd better go and find her.'

They set off back down the hill and found Annette and Pierre waiting for them in the lane behind Le Coq d'Argent. As they approached, Annette said, 'You told me yesterday that Madame St Clair said I could come back to work as soon as I was ready.'

Agathe nodded. 'Yes,' she said. 'When you are.'

'I'm ready now.'

'Perhaps you should wait a few more days…' began Agathe.

'No!' came the fierce reply. 'I'm ready now.'

The three women walked over to the house with the green door to collect Annette's few belongings and to explain to Madame Leclerc, and Pierre returned to the inn yard to put the horse to the chaise.

It was ten minutes later that Rupert saw them getting into the carriage as he was returning to the inn. He stepped forward and, raising his hat, said, 'Good afternoon, mademoiselle, I trust I see you well?'

Hélène turned her head at the sound of his voice and a faint pink coloured her cheeks.

'Quite well, I thank you, monsieur,' she said and then somehow feeling that further explanation was required of the company on the chaise, she added, 'We are just returning to Belair. I believe we shall have the pleasure of your company this evening, monsieur.' Even to her own ears the words seemed stilted and formal, but Rupert didn't seem to notice, in fact answering in the same vein.

'Indeed, I'm greatly looking forward to it.' He smiled up at her and then stepped back so that Pierre could drive out into the street and had the pleasure of seeing Hélène cast a glance back over her shoulder as the chaise rounded the corner and took the road to Belair.

They travelled in silence, each deep in thought, Madame Sauze deciding that she must speak to Madame St Clair about the money she had already disbursed on Annette's behalf; Annette vowing in her own mind that she would never again allow herself the self-indulgence of tears; Pierre glad that Annette was returning to Belair so soon, where he could keep watch over her; and Hélène thinking of Rupert Chalfont and the smile that lit his face and warmed her heart. She was amazed that with everything that had happened so far that day she had entirely forgotten that Rupert Chalfont was coming to dinner that evening. How could that have slipped her mind? Since the wedding and the ball, he had seldom been far from her thoughts, but until he had spoken to her just now, she realised, she had been so concerned with Annette she had not allowed him to intrude upon her mind. Now, however, with them all safely on their way back home, she found a bubble of excitement was growing inside her at the thought of his company that evening.

Chapter 21

When they arrived back at Belair, Pierre handed each of them down from the carriage. If he held Annette's hand a moment longer than was necessary, she was not aware of it. All she wanted to do was get into the house and lie down. The exertions of the day were beginning to catch up with her. Agathe insisted that she go straight up to their room, and having helped her up the stairs, she came down again and went in search of Madame St Clair. She found her in her private parlour.

'We have brought Annette home again, madame,' she said. 'She is much better and would like to return to work, if that is agreeable to you.'

'Is she fit to work?' asked Rosalie. 'I understood that she was very weak after such a difficult birth.'

She remembered that when each of her children had been born, she had been expected to remain in bed for at least two weeks to recover her strength, and had been glad to do so. She knew the servant classes, being less gently brought up, were up and about more quickly, but even so, the five days since Annette's baby had been born seemed a very short time to recuperate before coming back to work.

'She's not quite herself yet,' admitted Agathe, 'but Madame

Leclerc and I both feel it is better for her to return to her normal life as soon as possible.'

In truth Estelle Leclerc had not thought Annette fit to return to Belair and had suggested at least another week of recuperation before she considered taking up her household duties again, but Agathe had a sneaking suspicion this opinion had something to do with the generous payment Madame St Clair was making for her services as a nurse.

'I thought perhaps, with your consent, madame, that we could put Annette on light duties for a few days... ease her back into the household.'

Rosalie nodded. She was more than happy to have Annette back among the servants. Madame Choux had left that very morning, going to live in retirement with her sister in Orléans, and Rosalie was relieved that she had already had Madame Sauze waiting as her replacement.

'You must do as you think fit, Madame Sauze,' she said. 'As soon as the rooms have been cleaned, you must move into those previously occupied by Madame Choux. As my housekeeper you're entitled to your own bedroom and parlour.'

'Thank you, madame.' Agathe knew that Madame Choux had left, but she had not been at all sure if her own place as housekeeper had been confirmed, and it was with pleasurable anticipation that she looked forward to her new responsibilities.

'But I have decided to keep Ella on as extra help in the kitchen,' Rosalie continued. 'She'll be coming in daily from the village and can take care of some of the rough work. How do you find Lizette?'

'Hard working, madame, but in need of guidance.'

Rosalie nodded. 'Then train her up for work in the house.'

She picked up a paper from her desk as if to indicate that the interview was over.

'Thank you, madame,' Agathe said. 'However, there is one other matter I would like to mention.'

Rosalie put the paper down again and inclined her head. 'Well?'

'It is the matter of payment to Madame Leclerc. I believe you have been generous enough to pay her for her services, but when we made our original agreement, madame, it was I who would pay for any expenses and care Annette incurred at the time of her confinement.'

'Perhaps,' replied Rosalie, 'but what is done is done. Annette was, and is, in our employ. Please consider this the end of the matter.' She spoke with a finality that brooked no argument and Agathe recognised it as such. She bobbed a curtsy and simply said, 'Thank you, madame.'

While her mother and Agathe had been in the parlour, Hélène had gone up to her own room. Maman had said that Yvette would come up and help her dress for the evening. It was this small service that made Hélène realise for the first time that, as the eldest daughter living at home, she was now treated as such... a daughter needing to be presented to the world and in search of a suitable husband. Her mother had also suggested that she wear the gown made for her earlier in the year. Made of leaf-green silk swathed in delicate lace, it set off her pale skin, dark hair and dark eyes to perfection.

'But, Maman,' Hélène had said in dismay, 'that is so old! May I not wear my new white gown?'

'Certainly not,' replied her mother briskly. 'Of course you will have to wear that again, one cannot have something new to wear at every party, but never at two consecutive gatherings. This evening's dinner is a very informal affair, really only family, and so your green will do very well.'

Hélène still looked mutinous. She had seen the effect her appearance in white had had on several gentlemen at the ball, and two of them would be there again tonight.

'But Simon Barnier will be there, Maman, and Monsieur Chalfont.'

'And neither of them has seen you in your green lace,' replied her mother. 'You know that Madame Fosch has altered the neckline and adjusted the skirt. One would hardly recognise it as the same gown. You will wear your green.' The subject was closed.

As Hélène looked at it now, she had to admit the alterations had made it fit for a young lady, rather than a girl from the schoolroom. Will Rupert Chalfont like it? she wondered.

Meeting him unexpectedly in the village this afternoon had made her a little breathless, her heart beating faster than normal. When she had looked back at him from the chaise, he had been standing where they had left him, his hat in one hand and the other raised in farewell. Seeing him thus for the moment had pushed Annette's problems to the back of her mind. Though Annette had brought her loss with her, at least she was back at Belair with Madame Sauze as they had planned, and now Hélène was looking forward to the evening ahead.

When she came downstairs to the drawing room, the rest of the family was already assembled. The altered gown fitted her like a glove, emphasising her small waist and delicate shoulders, and there was no suggestion that it had ever been any different. Its colour suited her, and when Yvette had dressed her hair high on her head, held in place by two mother-of-pearl combs, allowing soft ringlets to fall about her ears and neck, Hélène had been amazed at how different she looked... and felt.

Because it was a family party, Louise had been included and was standing with her brother and sister-in-law in one of the bay windows. Yvette had also dressed Louise's hair, and though she still wore it down, it was threaded through with pink ribbons to match her dress. Her eyes were bright and her cheeks flushed with excitement, and she was talking to Georges with great animation.

Georges and Sylvie were prepared for their departure the following day, and though she had enjoyed the festivities of the wedding, Sylvie in particular looked forward to the return to her own home. She smiled at Hélène as she crossed the room to speak with them and murmured, 'You look beautiful, chérie. That colour is perfect for you.'

When Didier announced their guests, Hélène waited in the curve of the bay window while they greeted her parents. Lucie Barrineau, accompanied by her own parents, was dressed in the height of elegance in a dusky blue gown with tiny flowers dotting the skirt and outlining the neck. In age she came between the two St Clair girls, and when Louise saw her she suddenly felt childish in her pink dress and ribbons and greeted the Barrineau party with ill-concealed discontent. However, her mood improved as the other guests arrived. Simon Barnier, announced in sonorous tones by Didier, moved to greet his host and hostess. Even as he made his courtesies, his eyes roved the room until they rested on Hélène, and she saw from the rather intense look in his eyes that he appreciated how she looked. The moments ticked by and the conversation in the room became general, but Hélène felt as if she were an observer, looking at a play on a stage in a theatre. She had seen Simon moving in her direction, but he had been waylaid by Suzanne; he was an extremely eligible bachelor and there was Lucie to consider. As she watched, it was almost as if Hélène were holding her breath as she waited for Rupert Chalfont to appear.

The clock was striking the hour as Didier announced his name and he strode into the room, confident and charming, an outstretched hand and a smile for his hostess, his whole attention given to her. His dark hair was smoothed from curls to ripples, and thanks to the valet services at Le Coq d'Argent his evening dress was immaculate. He was careful to include all the St Clairs before greeting the Barrineau family. He spoke politely to the parents and made his bow to Lucie before returning to speak to Louise. Suzanne Barrineau felt confused. She didn't want him to pay marked attention to her daughter or to make any move to capture her affection, and yet now he had only given her the briefest of greetings Suzanne felt that Lucie had been slighted.

It was not long before Didier announced dinner and Rosalie led them all to the table. She had spent some time arranging it. The uneven number meant that the conventional seating must be a trifle disturbed. Emile, of course, sat at the head, flanked by Suzanne and Sylvie, and she at the foot, with Louis on her right and Simon on her left. Rupert was placed between Sylvie and Hélène opposite Georges, Lucie and Louise between Suzanne and Simon. It was not perfect but it was only an informal party and was the best she could do.

Rupert was delighted with his two dinner companions and he had inward satisfaction to see that Simon was trapped across the table between Louise, a child, and Rosalie, his hostess.

When the first course was brought in, both Rosalie and

Hélène were amazed to see that the guests were being served not only by Lizette, newly promoted to the dining room and supervised by a dignified Didier, but by Annette. Neither commented, but Rosalie exchanged glances with Agathe Sauze, who had appeared in the doorway. Annette moved round the table, offering the bowls of soup that Rosalie was dispensing from a silver tureen. There was no sign of weakness, nothing to indicate, except for a certain pallidity of complexion, that two days earlier she had been prostrate in her bed. Rosalie could only applaud her courage and determination.

When everyone had been served, the servants withdrew, leaving the family to their dinner and conversation. When they had met in St Etienne, Rupert had quickly assessed the group getting into the chaise. Clearly the wan-faced young woman must have been the maid who had lost her baby. Hélène had said they were returning to Belair, so the girl must be recovered, but of course there was no mention of that in their conversation now.

A little later on, Emile came to his feet and raised his glass. 'It is a pleasure to see you all here this evening,' he began. 'Our whole family, apart, of course, from our newly-weds, and some of our closest friends. It is also a pleasure to receive Monsieur Chalfont from England, a welcome guest at our daughter's wedding and at our table tonight. I give you, "family and friends".'

Not all here, Hélène thought with a pang of sadness. Papa never seems to remember Marcel, but perhaps he thinks it's too happy an occasion to mention his loss. She glanced across at her mother, but Rosalie was smiling at Georges and raising her glass.

The toast was echoed round the table, and then once again

the conversation became general until the ladies withdrew to the drawing room, leaving the men to their brandy and cigars.

'Are you planning a long stay in the area, Chalfont?' Simon Barnier asked. The abrupt and unadorned use of his surname, which at home in England would have been an indication of friendship between equals, made Rupert bristle, but he showed no sign of his anger, simply smiled and said, 'My man will be arriving with my traps any day, monsieur, and when he is with me I shall decide where to go from here.'

'I trust you'll visit us again before you go,' remarked Louis Barrineau, adding with a wry grin, 'I know my mother would be delighted to entertain you to coffee again.'

'It'll be my pleasure, sir,' Rupert replied, and found he meant it.

'No doubt you have business elsewhere, which will claim your attention,' suggested Emile, 'but I hope you will call upon us again before you depart.'

'Thank you, monsieur, I shall certainly do so.' Inwardly he smiled. Barnier's rudeness had awarded him two invitations, which he was only too pleased to accept.

When the gentlemen returned to the drawing room, Rupert, seeing that Hélène was engaged in speaking with Suzanne Barrineau, crossed the room to the window where Georges and Sylvie were sitting.

'I hope you will come and visit us at Versailles if you are passing that way, Monsieur Chalfont,' Sylvie said. 'Georges and I would be delighted to see you.'

'That would give me great pleasure, madame,' Rupert replied with a smile.

'Then we shall expect you. My mother-in-law will give you our direction.'

It was Simon who suggested that Hélène might play for them, and it was he who followed her to the piano to turn the pages of her music. He glanced back at Rupert, who seemed to be paying little attention to Hélène. Perhaps the Englishman was no threat at all. Surely, from what he'd said, he would soon be gone and as quickly forgotten.

Shortly afterwards the Barrineaux got up to take their leave. Sylvie and Georges went across to make their farewells, and Rupert, thus released, made his way over to where Hélène still stood by the piano.

'Mademoiselle Hélène,' he said softly. 'How charmingly you play.'

'Thank you, monsieur, I always get pleasure from music.'

'And I,' he said. Glancing across to make sure they were not overheard, he went on, 'I assume that was your maid with you in the village this afternoon.'

'Yes,' replied Hélène, 'Annette. We were bringing her home, but,' she confided, 'I didn't expect to see her waiting at table tonight. She's very brave.'

'She has your friendship to rely on,' Rupert said. 'That must be a great comfort to her.'

'She has been a good friend to me in the past,' answered Hélène.

Rupert realised that he might be intruding into something very private and so changed the subject. Across the room he could see that Simon had been captured by Lucie in conversation as he had bid the Barrineaux goodnight, so he said, 'Your father has invited me to call again at Belair. Would it please you if I did so?'

He was rewarded with the faint blush that warmed Hélène's cheeks. 'Yes, monsieur, I know we should all be pleased to see you.'

Rupert inclined his head and gave her his lopsided smile. 'Thank you,' he said, 'but you? I was asking about you.'

Hélène's colour deepened, but she gave him a shy smile in return and replied, 'It would please me if you visited us again, monsieur. You have been very kind.'

'Then I will certainly do so. But,' he said, extending his hand, 'now I must wish you goodnight. I look forward to our next meeting.' As he took her hand he looked into her face and, with words he had not planned, said softly, 'You are very beautiful, Hélène.'

Hélène's eyes widened and she murmured, 'I'm sure you shouldn't say such things, monsieur.'

Rupert held her gaze and, answering softly, said, 'Why not? If they are true?' He raised her hand to his lips and went on in a more normal voice, 'Goodnight, mademoiselle. A delightful evening.' As he turned away he almost collided with Simon Barnier, now free of Lucie Barrineau. He made a slight bow, acknowledged with the faintest inclination of Simon's head, and with a polite 'Goodnight, Monsieur Barnier,' Rupert went to make his farewells to Rosalie and Emile.

Simon's earlier optimism might have left him had he heard the brief conversation Rupert had with his host as he bid him goodnight. 'I wondered, monsieur, if I might call upon you tomorrow? I have something particular I would like to discuss with you.'

Emile looked surprised, but answered, 'By all means. I shall be at home at noon.'

Chapter 22

Peter Parker had been pleased to receive the telegram from Mr Rupert instructing him to return to Pilgrim's Oak, pack a trunk for him – enough for an extended stay abroad – and bring it to him in France. Parker and his master had travelled extensively together and there was an easiness between them that other men failed to achieve with those who served them. It was due to this that Parker had been able to return to the family home when his father had died, being struck down unexpectedly by a seizure. Rupert had sent him home to be with his mother and sister, to help arrange the funeral and to settle, such as they were, his father's affairs. He had done his best, but it was not long before he felt claustrophobic in the small house of his childhood. He longed to escape from its confines and, if he were honest, from his mother's misery. His sister, married to a clerk in a lawyer's office in Taunton, had returned to her husband, and when he left to return to Mr Rupert, his mother would be marooned in the house that had been her marital home, empty now of all that had given it life. She was lonely and sad and begged Peter to stay a little longer. As he had heard nothing from Rupert, he agreed, but it was with guilty relief that he was able to show his mother the telegram that summoned him. He packed his bag and with a kiss on her cheek he bade her goodbye, promising to come back and visit her as soon as Mr Rupert's business allowed.

On his arrival at Pilgrim's Oak, he was greeted by Mr Justin Chalfont.

'Parker, you're back!' he exclaimed. 'Is my brother with you?'

'No, sir. He has sent me to collect some things he requires.'

'Has he? Where is he, then?'

'He's in France, sir,' Parker replied. 'Someplace outside Paris called St Etienne.'

'Is he indeed? Well, you know more about him than any of us. Why didn't you go with him?'

'My father died, sir. Mr Rupert sent me home for his funeral.'

'Oh, sorry to hear that, Parker. Still, you're here now... and going to France?'

'Yes, sir. I'm to pack a trunk and take it to him at this place, St Etienne. He's staying at an inn called Le Coq d'Argent.'

'I see,' said Justin. 'Well, you can take a letter for me when you go. I've got news for him that may bring him home.' Justin looked at Rupert's man and said, 'You may as well know, as everyone else does – I'm to be married. Miss Kitty Blake has done me the honour of engaging herself to me. We're planning an autumn wedding.'

If Parker was surprised at this news, he didn't show it – he had always thought it was Rupert who had captured Miss Kitty's heart – but he simply gave a half bow and said, 'Allow me to congratulate you, sir.'

'Thank you,' said Justin. 'Now, before you get to work on your packing for Rupert, I think it would be a good idea if you went in to see my father. I'll tell him you're here and he'll ring when he's ready. I'm sure he'll want to have news of Mr Rupert and may well have messages for you to take. Probably my mother too.'

Parker repaired to the servants' quarters, where he found Mitchell, the butler, drinking a cup of tea with the cook, Mrs Darwin.

'Well, well,' said Mitchell when he walked in. 'Look who's turned up. Proverbial bad penny.'

'Cup of tea, Mr Parker?' suggested Mrs Darwin. 'There's plenty in the pot.'

Parker accepted the offer and sat down at the table with them while she stirred the tea and poured him a cup.

'Everything all right with your mother?' she asked. The servants knew why he'd been away, even if the family did not. 'Poor dear, she must be very sad.'

'She is,' agreed Parker, 'and thank you for asking. I was sorry to leave her, but Mr Rupert's sent me a telegram to collect his things and meet him in France. Still,' he went on with the air of someone happy enough to shift responsibility elsewhere, 'my sister Eliza's not far away, she can look in to Mother from time to time.'

At that moment a bell jangled. Mitchell looked up at the row and, seeing it was the library bell, said, 'That's Sir Philip. 'I'd better go, unless… I expect it's you he wants to see, Parker.'

Parker got to his feet. 'Yes, I'll go,' he said. 'I saw Mr Justin as I arrived, he said he'd tell the master I was here.'

He found Sir Philip sitting in his usual chair in the library bay window, looking out over the garden. The room was dual aspect, facing south and west, and at this time of day the sunlight streamed through the mullions of the window, casting patterns on the polished oak floor. He looked up as Parker knocked and came in, and for a moment his face was turned to the sun that poured into the room, bright and unforgiving, lighting his features with stark reality.

How he has aged! Parker thought suddenly. He's become an old man. How did that happen so fast? I've been away less than a month.

'Ah, Parker,' said Sir Philip, and Parker noticed that even his voice had aged, not querulous, but softer and less acerbic. 'Just the man. Now, tell me what news you have of Mr Rupert.'

Parker repeated all he had said to Justin and then waited for Sir Philip to comment.

'So you haven't been with him, or seen him since he went up to London?'

'No, sir, nothing until I received his wire. I shall get packed up today and set out first thing in the morning.'

'And how do you propose to travel?'

'I'll take the train to Dover, sir, and then packet. I've had a look at Bradshaw and there's trains all the way to this St Etienne place. I'm instructed to bring his large valise and trunk, so if I may ask Fortune to drive me to the station in the trap, that will set me on my way. With luck it should only take me two or three days to get there.'

'I see.' Sir Philip, though used to trains, had been born into an age where there was no network of railways and still felt more comfortable in a coach. 'Only three days. Well, if you're setting out tomorrow, Parker, make sure you come and collect a letter for Mr Rupert before you go.'

Parker promised he would and went up to Rupert's rooms to gather together the clothes he knew his master would want. Since Rupert had gone, Tess the laundry maid who came in from the village had washed and brushed all the clothes he had left behind and they were all clean, pressed and ready for Parker to fold into the trunk. The various sundries, boots, hats and gloves were packed into the valise. That evening he was summoned to Lady Chalfont's parlour, where she demanded that he repeat yet again the information he had about Rupert.

'And before you leave in the morning I shall have a letter for you to deliver to Mr Rupert.'

At supper that evening, served in the kitchen once the family had been fed, Parker heard all about Mary Dawson and her expected baby.

'Such a furore it caused when Dawson found out,' Mitchell said. 'Insisted that Mr Rupert was the father, but finally had to admit that he didn't know who it was.'

'If that baby is due when they say,' put in Mrs Darwin, 'it couldn't have been Mr Rupert what fathered it. He was staying up in Leicestershire somewhere hunting foxes last autumn.'

'Well, you women are the ones what keeps track of those sorts of things,' Mitchell said dismissively. 'All I know is, Dawson's had to back down. Could have lost his place if he kept on saying it was Mr Rupert.'

'Well, now she's marrying Fred Brooks from over Heathfield way,' said Mrs Darwin. 'Silly girl should have said straight out it were him, 'stead of pretending. He's been sweet on her since she were nobbut a girl. Reckon he wants to marry her, whether 'tis his babby or no; and a good thing too, if you asks me, before she gets herself into more trouble.'

Gradually Parker caught up with all the gossip he'd missed since his father died. Mr Rupert would want to know all that had been going on while he was away, not just what his pa and ma decided to tell him. Even Mr Justin might not tell all, though, thought Parker; Mr Rupert'll be more than interested that Mr Justin has finally offered for Miss Kitty. Once they started a family, that would be an end to any thoughts Mr Rupert might have had about inheriting his pa's title. He'd always said he didn't want it, that his brother was welcome to it, but Parker wasn't so sure. When it came down to it, Mr Rupert might regret its loss.

By the time he and Fortune lifted the trunk and the valise into the trap, Parker was carrying three letters to his master. All, he thought, probably telling him the same news, but all with a different slant on things. As they were about to leave, Miss Frances came running out of the house and waved at Fortune to wait.

'Thank goodness I caught you, Parker. Please will you take this letter to my brother? Tell him all is well here and give him my love.'

'Of course, Miss Frances,' he replied, and taking the letter, he stowed it with the others in the wallet he carried strapped to his waist. 'I'll give it to him as soon as I get there. I know he'll be eager for news from home.' It took Parker longer than he had anticipated to travel from the West Country to the port of Dover, and after a rather bumpy crossing to Calais, where he spent a night at an inn, he caught the train to Paris. He reached St Etienne in the early evening and found a carrier to transport the luggage to its destination at Le Coq d'Argent. When he reached the inn he discovered that Rupert was out, but he took another room and had the trunk and valise carried up there. Then he walked out into the Place, found himself a cheap café and had something to eat. It was a warm summer evening and he lingered over an extra glass of wine before turning his steps back to Le Coq d'Argent. As he walked towards the front door, a chaise drew up outside and

Parker saw the familiar figure of Rupert Chalfont step down into the street.

Rupert caught sight of him and paused on the threshold.

'Parker!' he cried. 'You're here. Have you brought my traps? We may be here for a longish stay.'

'Yes, sir. As you weren't here, Mr Rupert, I took the liberty of taking another room here at the inn and had your luggage placed safely in there while I went out to get something to eat.'

'Good man,' replied Rupert. 'Let's get it moved to my rooms and see what you've brought.'

A porter was called and within minutes the heavy cases were brought down from the room on the third floor that had been assigned to the gentleman's gentleman and carried into the suite hired by the gentleman himself.

Rupert flung himself down onto an armchair and watched as Parker opened the trunk and began to unpack the clothes he'd brought, hanging them in the ornate armoire in the corner of the room.

'So, Parker, tell all! What news from the old homestead?'

'I've brought you letters, sir,' Parker replied. 'From Sir Philip, Lady Chalfont and Mr Justin. Oh, and Miss Frances.'

'I'm sure you have, Parker, and I'll read them in a while, but you can tell me the news, the real news seen through the eyes of the kitchen!'

'What do you want to know, sir?'

'Well, let me see.' Rupert gazed up at the ceiling as if in search of inspiration, then turning again to Parker asked, his expression serious, 'How's Mary Dawson these days?'

For a moment Parker stared at him in horror and then, catching the flicker of a grin in Rupert's eyes, relaxed to answer calmly.

'I believe she's getting married, sir.'

'That's good to hear,' Rupert said cheerfully. 'I'm all in favour of marriage!'

'In that case, sir, I think you'd better read your letters before I pass on news that isn't mine to share.'

The laughter left Rupert's eyes, and holding out his hand, he said, 'Hand them over then and let me know the worst.'

He opened Justin's letter first, scanning it quickly and then going back to read it more carefully.

My dear Rupert

So you got to France, and I imagine, since you have sent for Parker, that you are having an enjoyable time with your friends there and are planning a lengthy stay. However, I have news that I hope will bring you home again before very long. Kitty and I are to be married in the early autumn and of course I need you here with me to stand as my best man. We have set the date for Friday 21st September, so we shall expect you back well before that date to join in the celebrations of our happiness.

Mother is now all of a fluster making wedding plans with the Blakes. We're to be married in the village church, of course, and then the Blakes are giving the wedding breakfast at Marwick House. It looks as if they're inviting half the county!

Otherwise, things go on here much as usual. The question of Mary Dawson and the baby has been resolved. She is to be married after the banns have been called to Fred Brooks. He's the blacksmith over at Heathfield and has accepted paternity for the child. Goodness knows if it is truly his, but both he and Mary seem happy enough with the plan and it saves face for everyone... you included?

The fishing looks good this year, there are plenty of trout about and even some salmon coming up river, so you're missing a treat. Dawson says it's the best year for some time, so I'm hoping for some big fish!

We all miss you here and look forward to your home-coming, especially now that you have something special to come home for.

Wish me joy, Rupert,

Your affectionate brother

Justin

'So,' Rupert said, looking up from the letter at last, 'my brother is to be married. I'm glad. I'd given up hope of him ever asking poor Kitty. I think they'll do very well together.'

There was no sign of sadness or disappointment at the news, so Parker thought that perhaps Miss Kitty's affection for Mr Rupert had been one-sided after all.

Rupert opened the other letters and read them through. They told him little more of what was going on at home, though Fran's comments about Kitty and the wedding shed a bit more light on the matter.

Kitty seems happy enough with the arrangement and clearly it is a very suitable marriage. I'm to be bridesmaid!

Can you imagine me in a new silk gown and an elegant hat?

Mama has sent for a dressmaker from Bristol to fabricate the frills and furbelows, so she and I shall be the height of fashion. What will you wear as best man, I wonder? No doubt Mama will decide for you when you get home.

We miss you, Rupert. Well, I do, anyway. It's no fun getting into scrapes without you.

Papa has not been well lately and Mama is relying on me more and more about household matters. They're suddenly older, Rupert. Don't leave it too long before you come home again.

Your loving sister, Fran

Rupert turned to Parker. 'How were my parents, Parker? Did you find them well?'

'Well enough, sir, though I thought Sir Philip a little aged since I saw him last. Your mother seemed much as always, but that is how she presents herself to the world.'

'You mean you never know quite what is in her mind? Well, neither do I.'

Rupert folded the letters back into their envelopes. 'It's time we were in bed,' he said. 'You must be tired after your journey and I shall do very well by myself tonight, but I shall want you first thing in the morning.'

Later, as he lay in bed, Rupert considered the news Parker had brought with him. Justin marrying Kitty at last. Well, that was good, wasn't it? There had been a time when he and

Kitty had wanted their friendship to progress further, but they both knew that Sir James would want a better match for his only child. The younger son of a baronet, however well-bred, would not do, especially as there was an extremely eligible elder son in the same family, the son who would inherit the estate which marched with his own. Rupert had remained fond of Kitty, but he had walked away from Pilgrim's Oak to travel the world, leaving Kitty behind in Somerset.

Now, with Hélène filling his mind, he knew that what he had felt for Kitty was a pale shadow of his feelings for Hélène. It had happened so quickly, completely out of the blue, but despite the speed of his headlong fall into love, he had never felt more sure of anything in his life. Tomorrow he would go to Emile St Clair and ask for permission to address her. He longed to claim her before the world, but he also recognised that she hardly knew him and was very young to be committing herself to any man, let alone one so recently encountered. He remembered how she had confided in him, how she had responded to his kindness, how she had blushed when he paid her a compliment, most of all how she had felt in his arms as they had danced. None of these things necessarily indicated that she felt anything out of the ordinary for him, but he could always hope that, in time, she might come to feel about him as he felt about her – that they should spend the rest of their lives together.

Rupert, being Rupert, did not consider what he would do if Emile St Clair refused his permission.

Chapter 23

R upert presented himself at Belair at exactly twelve noon
and was greeted by Didier, who said, 'Monsieur St Clair
is expecting you, sir,' took his hat and gloves and escorted
him to Emile's private study.

He knocked and opened the door, announcing, 'Monsieur
Chalfont.'

Emile, who had been standing beside a large flat-topped
desk studying the papers spread out upon it, turned and
greeted Rupert with a smile and an extended hand.

'Good day, m'sieur, I trust I see you well.'

'Very well, thank you, sir,' Rupert replied.

'May I offer you a glass of something? Wine? Brandy?'

'No, I thank you, sir.'

Emile nodded to Didier, who had been hovering in the
doorway. 'That'll be all, Didier.'

As the door closed behind the butler, Emile took a seat on
a chair by the open window and indicated another to Rupert.

Rupert sat down and Emile said, 'Well, Monsieur Chalfont,
how may I help you?'

Rupert had tried out several openings in his room that
morning, but now he was sitting opposite Emile, somehow
the prepared words deserted him. He stood up again and took

a couple of paces across the room before turning back and saying, 'I know we are only recently acquainted, m'sieur, but I have come to ask if I may pay my addresses to Mademoiselle Hélène.' There! It was said.

Emile looked startled. 'Hélène?' he said. 'But she's only a child. Only just out of the schoolroom.'

'Only just out of the schoolroom,' agreed Rupert, 'but surely no longer a child.'

'Perhaps.' Emile was getting over his immediate surprise. 'But she is still very young, scarcely ready for marriage – and I'm sure I don't have to remind you that, with respect, we know nothing of you or your family. You are a foreigner, an Englishman, unknown to us all.'

'I admit to all of those things,' Rupert said, a touch ruefully, 'but surely they can all be addressed. I can answer any questions you would like to ask. May I tell you straight away that my father, Sir Philip Chalfont, is a baronet. The title is hereditary and one day—'

'You will inherit it?' interrupted Emile.

'No, sir. My brother Justin will inherit; I am the younger by two hours. But one day I shall come into an inheritance on my mother's side. In the meantime I am well enough supplied to support a wife and an establishment of my own. If your daughter accepted my suit, she would be well provided for.'

Emile looked at Rupert with great suspicion. 'No doubt somebody has told you that on her marriage Hélène will inherit an annuity from her maternal grandmother. Perhaps it is this that has made you dare to ask for her hand.'

Rupert looked Emile firmly in the eye and said, 'It has been mentioned to me, and I am sure that it is common knowledge hereabouts, but at present I am not asking for your daughter's hand. I am only asking your permission to address her, so that we may become properly acquainted, and I hope eventually come to an understanding. Should that happen and we became engaged to be married, I should have no interest in Hélène's money. I give you my word, it will be hers and hers alone to do with as she wishes.'

'So you say now,' remarked Emile.

'So I say now, and so I shall say then.'

Having his given word doubted gave Rupert's tone a coolness that was not lost on Emile, who took a metaphorical step back, saying, 'I don't doubt your intention, sir, but this is all too quick.'

'Which is why I am asking you if I may come and visit Hélène, become her friend, let her get to know me before I ask for her hand. I would not want an unwilling bride.'

'And you will not have one,' Emile said sharply. Then he sighed and said, 'Do sit down again, m'sieur, and let us speak man to man.'

Rupert did as he was asked, sitting back into the chair opposite Emile.

'You must look at things from a father's point of view,' Emile said. 'You are a man of the world, you must be at least thirty and my daughter is only seventeen. What does she know of men and marriage? She is hardly out into society, has had little chance of meeting other gentlemen. She will remain here at Belair in the care of her family, and when a suitable man asks for her, then I shall consider my answer.'

'And you do not consider me suitable?' Rupert was not prepared to give up.

'I do not know you well enough to say,' replied Emile. 'Perhaps you are, perhaps you are not, but either way she is too young and too inexperienced in the world for a commitment now.'

'Then I am prepared to wait for her,' said Rupert, 'for as long as it takes. All I am asking you for is that she have a chance to get to know me.'

Emile shook his head as if confused. 'It is not something I can decide on the spur of the moment,' he said. 'I will give it some thought and I will tell you my decision when I have made it. Call on me again tomorrow. But before you go I will ask just one further question of you, Monsieur Chalfont. If you are not interested in her money and you are in a position to marry and provide for a wife, why have you not already done so?'

Rupert gave a wry smile. 'Because, m'sieur, I have never fallen in love before.'

When Rupert had gone, Emile went in search of Rosalie. She was in her parlour writing letters, but when he came into the room she put down her pen and said, 'Was that Monsieur Chalfont I saw leaving just now? Would he not stay for luncheon?'

'I did not ask him,' replied her husband. 'He came to discuss something with me and now he has gone.'

Rosalie had learned from long experience that if she wanted Emile to tell her something, she should not actually ask him. Now she wanted to know why Rupert Chalfont had called and why he had left without speaking to anyone other than Emile.

She said, 'He's a charming young man, don't you think? So unassuming and with such good manners.'

'Well, I agree he seems that way, but appearances can be deceptive, can't they? We don't know the man, after all. Indeed, I don't think the Barrineaux do either. He was invited to the wedding by young Lucas, and you may remember Suzanne wasn't best pleased. For all we know he's an adventurer out for what he can get.'

'Out for what he can get?' echoed Rosalie. 'A harsh judgement, Emile. What makes you say so? You hardly know the man.'

'Exactly,' said Emile. 'We hardly know him and here he is coming to ask for Hélène.'

'Ask for Hélène?' Rosalie looked startled.

'Ask my permission to address her.'

'And did you give it?'

'No,' snapped her husband.

'Why not?'

'Why not? Because as you so rightly said, we hardly know the man. How do we know he's not after her inheritance? How do we know he can provide for her as she should be? He's a younger son...'

'Yes, I know.'

'You know? How do you know?'

'Somebody told me; Suzanne Barrineau, probably. Does it really matter if he isn't going to inherit a title? You haven't got a title!'

'That's neither here nor there,' retorted Emile.

'So, what did you say?'

'I said I'd think about it and tell him tomorrow. He maintains he's not asking for an engagement, not yet, but that's what he has in mind. He actually told me he'd fallen in love with her. Ridiculous! He's only seen the girl about twice!'

Rosalie looked across at her husband and gently shook her head. 'Oh, Emile,' she sighed. 'Are we getting old? It only took me one dance with you.'

Emile stared at her. 'What d'you mean?' he said.

'I only danced with you once before I knew you were the man I wanted. Remember the evening of Madame d'Aramitz's Christmas ball?'

Emile coughed, trying to hide his emotion. He remembered the Christmas ball only too well. Rosalie had come escorted by her mother, young, only eighteen, in a white ballgown with pearls threaded through her hair. It had only taken him one look before he too was lost.

'My mother didn't approve of you because you weren't from a landed family. You had to make your own living. It didn't stop us, though, did it?' She reached for his hand and held it against her cheek. It was longer than she could remember since they had been as close as this and she didn't want the moment to pass.

Emile looked at her as if seeing her again for the first time in years. 'You're still beautiful,' he murmured before pulling his hand away.

'So,' Rosalie continued as if there had been no emotional interlude between them, 'what are you going to say when he comes again tomorrow?'

'I don't know,' he admitted. 'He's English!'

'He is, and we can't change that, though if they married they might choose to live here in France.'

'Married! You run ahead of yourself, madame.'

'You're right, I do,' admitted Rosalie. 'Perhaps we should speak to Hélène.'

'Hélène? Why? It's not her decision to make.'

'No,' agreed Rosalie, 'but if she dislikes the idea, then that makes the decision for you.'

'And what if she wants to encourage him? What then?'

'Then perhaps we let them have the chance to get to know each other. Make it clear there is no commitment on either side, but let them meet, walk and talk. She can always take Annette with her for propriety. You never know, either one might change their mind. If you forbid it, then perhaps all will be driven underground. They may meet secretly, and if that were discovered Hélène's reputation would be ruined.'

'Perhaps,' sighed Emile.

'If Hélène wants to get to know him, better to let it run its course. Throw them together and they may tire of each other, or find they don't suit.'

Rosalie could see that she had won her argument, and it was one she really believed worth winning. Apart from the fact that she had taken a liking to Rupert Chalfont, she knew that the more such a friendship was opposed, the more likely it was to survive in spite of the opposition. She had been lucky; she had met Emile at the age of eighteen and had never wanted to look at another man. They had married on her nineteenth birthday. Hélène might only be seventeen, but youth wasn't a true reason to refuse an engagement, for youth would cease to be an issue if the couple were prepared to wait.

'If you say so,' Emile conceded with a sigh. 'Where is she?'

'In the garden, I believe. Shall I ring and ask Didier to send her in to us?'

'Now?' Emile was always uncomfortable with emotional situations and was tempted to put it off.

'We should see her together, talk to her and then make our decision.'

'If you think that's best,' Emile replied reluctantly.

Rosalie smiled at him affectionately. 'I do,' she said, and she rang the bell for the butler.

Five minutes later there was a tap on the door and Hélène came into the room. She was surprised to see both her parents sitting waiting for her. Her mind raced as she wondered what she had done to cause them to send for her like this. Had they discovered somehow that she knew Annette's secret? She certainly hadn't spoken of it to anyone else, and surely Annette had not. She'd only been back in the house for a day.

'You wanted me, Maman? Papa?'

'Come and sit down, chérie,' said her mother, patting the seat beside her. 'Papa and I want to tell you something.'

Hélène sat down as directed, wondering as she did so if they were going to tell her about Annette themselves. She must pretend amazement if they did. She arranged her expression into one of interest, ready to hear whatever it was and react accordingly. When her mother actually spoke, Hélène couldn't have been more surprised.

'Your papa had a visitor this morning,' Rosalie said. 'Can you guess who it was?'

'Simon Barnier?' hazarded Hélène.

'No, not him,' said Rosalie, surprised that he should have been the one Hélène had first thought of. Then she saw the look of relief on her daughter's face and realised that she had been suggesting the person she least wanted to see.

'It was Monsieur Chalfont,' said her father.

Rosalie saw the tide of pink spread across Hélène's cheeks and gave an inward smile. So, Monsieur Chalfont had already made an impression.

'I find him charming, don't you?' asked Rosalie.

'Yes, indeed,' whispered Hélène.

Emile, who had not noticed Hélène's blush, said, 'Has he always behaved with propriety, Hélène?'

'Propriety?' echoed Hélène. 'How could he not?'

'But he has been attentive to you?'

'No more than anyone else. I danced with him at the ball

and you saw me sitting next to him at dinner last night.' She turned to her mother. 'And that was because you put me there, Maman!'

'Please don't speak to your mother in that tone of voice, Hélène,' snapped her father.

'Sorry, Maman,' she muttered, and Rosalie smiled to show that this time it didn't matter. After all, it was a fair comment.

'The thing is, chérie,' Rosalie said, taking the initiative and turning the conversation back in the direction she wanted, 'Monsieur Chalfont has visited your father this morning to ask if he may pay his addresses to you. Not to become engaged or anything like that, simply to have the chance to build a friendship. All good marriages are founded on friendship.'

'Though there is no question of marriage at this time,' stated her father. 'You're far too young to be thinking that far ahead.'

'Of course your father is quite right,' Rosalie put in quickly, 'but should you object to him coming to visit you, perhaps taking a walk or carriage ride? With Annette as well, of course. The proprieties must be observed.'

'No, Maman, I should not object. I should like to get to know him better.' Hélène spoke calmly, but inside her heart was racing. Rupert had come to Papa to ask for her. She understood that they must move slowly to please her parents, for the sake of decorum, but she also knew that if he asked her, she would go with him tomorrow.

She caught her father looking at her and hoped that he couldn't see into her heart and know the jolt of joy that had set it thudding so fast and so loudly that she was surprised neither of her parents seemed to hear it.

'If you are alone with him beyond the walls of this house,

you must take that girl with you,' said her father. 'I will not have your reputation compromised.'

'I understand, Papa,' Hélène replied demurely.

'Then if you will excuse me, my dear,' he said to Rosalie, 'I will leave you to it. I shall see you both at dinner.'

When he had left the room, Rosalie smiled at her daughter. 'Well,' she said, 'I told you that we should be looking for a husband for you next, and now you already have a beau. But you do understand, don't you, that when you are out anywhere with him you must have Annette in attendance.'

Hélène was very happy to comply with this dictum. It accorded very well with the plan she and Annette had in mind for the future. Indeed, this might be the right moment to make the suggestion to her mother.

She drew a deep breath and said, 'I was wondering, Maman, if Yvette might train Annette as a lady's maid – then when I get married, I shall be able to take her with me into my new home,' adding as an afterthought, 'wherever that happens to be.'

'Maybe,' replied her mother. 'I'll think about it. It would mean employing another housemaid in her place. Your sister didn't have a maid until she was married. And you know,' she went on, 'Annette might not want to become a lady's maid.'

'No, maybe not,' Hélène said, 'but we could ask her, couldn't we?'

'I'll think about it,' repeated her mother.

And think about it she did. When she had left home to marry Emile she had brought her beloved Marie-Jeanne with her and knew how much she had helped her in the transition from young, blushing bride to mistress of a household. Even now, after nearly seven years, the thought of Marie-Jeanne could bring tears to her eyes, her brave and loyal nurse who had been killed trying to protect Hélène during the war in Paris. She had no idea if Hélène was going to marry this charming Englishman, but if she did, how much easier it would be to have an old friend and companion with her, particularly if Rupert decided that they should live across the Channel.

Rupert did not sleep well that night. He kept going over and over his interview with Emile St Clair, wondering if there had been anything further he could have said or done to tip the balance in his favour. For he realised that Emile's answer was, indeed, very much in the balance. What was he going to do if his suit was turned down and he was not allowed to see Hélène? It didn't bear thinking about and yet he could think of nothing else. As the dawn light crept between the curtains, he finally drifted off into an uneasy doze, only to wake an hour or so later with the same question terrorising his mind. He had breakfast sent up to his room and then he allowed Parker to shave him, afraid his own hand might shake. He dressed with care and in a hired chaise had himself driven out to Belair.

This time he was shown into the drawing room, where he found both Hélène's parents waiting for him. Rosalie greeted him with a smile, and when he had shaken her hand, he turned to her husband.

'Good day, m'sieur,' he said.

Emile returned his greeting and then wasted no time in coming to the point. 'Monsieur Chalfont,' he said, 'I have given great thought to what you proposed to me yesterday, and with certain caveats, I am prepared to allow you to visit my daughter as a suitor, but I must emphasise that this will not lead to a formal engagement for some time.'

Rupert, filled with elation, wondered if his happiness showed on his face. Hélène was going to be his. He forced his attention back to Emile St Clair, who was still speaking.

'Hélène is very young,' he was saying, 'and though she is happy to receive your visits, we want no pressure put upon her to further your friendship, unless and until she is certain of her own mind. Whenever you meet, decorum must be preserved; I will not have her reputation put at risk by any dishonourable behaviour.'

'Thank you, sir,' Rupert answered. 'I thank you for your trust and I can make a solemn promise to you that I will do nothing that could be regarded as a slur on her honour... or my own.' He could feel the smile spreading across his face as he added, 'I swear I shall do everything within my power to make her happy.'

Chapter 24

Justin Chalfont collected his fly rod from the fishing closet and picked up his waders. He had been confined to the house all morning by thunder and lightning, but now the storm had passed and the persistent rain of the last few days had finally stopped, the air was less humid and he couldn't wait to get out of the house. A couple of hours on the river bank was exactly what he needed to relax and calm his mind.

Since Kitty had accepted his proposal there had been talk of little but the wedding and their future together. One important question had been where the newly-weds should live. It had been suggested that they might move into a wing of Marwick House, but to Justin's relief, Kitty had been as much against the idea as he had, and gracefully they had turned it down. There was no separate wing at Pilgrim's Oak, but after much discussion, it had been decided that Sir Philip and Lady Chalfont must remain in their home and Justin and Kitty should move into the Dower House where his grandmother had ended her days. Together he and Kitty had inspected the house, which had been left empty since his grandmother's death. It required some refurbishment and modernisation, and work had already begun so that they would be able to move in when they returned from an extended honeymoon. Justin had spent a great deal of time with the architect discussing the plans and making regular visits to the house to be sure that the work was progressing as it should. He didn't mind, he wanted everything to be just so, but it was yet one more thing requiring his attention.

The day of his wedding was only four weeks away, and though he found he was looking forward to being married to Kitty, he was becoming fed up with all the palaver of the preparations. It would have suited him, and possibly Kitty too, to have had a simple ceremony in the church and a family gathering afterwards before they set off on their planned wedding journey. But his mother and Lady Blake had had their heads together for weeks, and there seemed always something to be considered.

He said as much to his father, who laughed and said, 'It's always the way with the women. They want to make a splash of everything. Just let them get on with it, my boy, that's what I do.'

So, this afternoon Justin was doing exactly that. His mother had said she wanted to discuss the wine with him and he had replied, 'I'm afraid I have an appointment, Mama,' not bothering to explain that it was an appointment with the river. 'Surely the wine is the province of Sir James. I wouldn't dream of interfering.' He added gently, 'And nor should you.'

His mother's lips had tightened at the reprimand, but she had said no more, simply sighed and returned to her parlour to look over her lists.

As he crossed the yard, fishing gear in hand, Fran emerged from the house.

'You're escaping!' she accused when she saw what he was carrying.

Justin grinned. 'Afraid so,' he admitted. 'Why don't you come too... provided you don't mention the word "wedding".'

'I can't,' answered Fran ruefully. 'I've got another fitting for my bridesmaid's dress. The dressmaker is coming to fit both Mama and me. I daren't miss that appointment.'

'Well, come and find me afterwards,' suggested Justin. 'I shall be tired of my own company by then, and who knows, I might even have caught a fish.'

Fran promised to join him as soon as she was released by the dressmaker and went indoors to await her arrival.

Justin left the garden and took the footpath across the fields to where the River Chubb ran through their land, gliding between its banks into sleepy pools before chuckling over the stones in the shallows and on towards the weir. He stepped down from the bank onto a tiny pebble beach from which he could wade into the water and cast his line. The sun had come out and he knew it was really too bright for serious fishing, but he cast anyway. He felt himself relax as he stared down into the water. The river was running a little faster than normal after the last few days of rain and the water was not as clear as usual, but he could see the occasional quicksilver flash of a fish amid the weed.

Dawson had said he'd seen salmon recently and Justin hoped he was right. He had seen them leaping up the weir a little way downstream before now, struggling upriver to spawn, but not so far this year. It was a long time since he had landed a salmon from the Chubb, but he knew they made delicious eating and was ever optimistic.

It was peaceful, standing in the water, casting a fly in the hope of tempting a hungry fish, but on this beautiful summer's afternoon it didn't really matter whether he caught anything or not. He glanced back along the footpath to see if

Fran had escaped and was on her way to join him, but there was no sign of her yet. The meadows shone green after the rain, poppies gleaming like rubies amid the grass, and beyond them, sheltered by the stand of the oaks that gave the house its name, the house itself drowsed in the afternoon sun – the house where he, Rupert and Fran had been born and which would one day belong to him.

Life was good, he thought as he sat down on the bank to change his fly for another, and when he and Kitty were married it would be even better. He thought of Rupert and wondered where he was now. He had answered Justin's letter with a brief note saying that for the present he was putting up at Le Coq d'Argent in St Etienne, but promised to come home in plenty of time to take up his best man duties. His parents and Fran had each had a letter from him, but none of those told them anything further.

'Why does he stay in this St Etienne place, do you think?' asked his mother. 'Why doesn't he come home? Mary Dawson is married now, there would be no scandal.'

'I doubt if it is Mary Dawson keeping him away, Mama,' Fran had laughed. 'But it's probably some other lady, don't you think?'

'No, Frances, I do not,' her mother had replied firmly and the matter received no further discussion, but Justin agreed with Fran that there must be a woman involved somehow – there always was with Rupert.

Just then he saw something that made him leap to his feet: a splash as a fish jumped before falling back into the river in the midst of ever-widening ripples. It was big. Though he hadn't actually seen the fish, the disturbance in the water told him that. Justin was at the water's lip at once, edging out into the river again. He cast his fly, but nothing moved. Reeling in, he cast again, the line flying out from his rod, the fly settling gently on the water close to where the ripples had been. If the fish had been there it would have darted away again by now. Slowly Justin waded through the water, pausing from time to time to cast again. He reached a pool a little further downstream, no more than a bend in the river where the water slowed on one side but flooded past on the other, running fast and strong towards the weir. A flash of silver caught his eye and he stepped forward to cast again, and as he did so there was suddenly nothing beneath his feet. He had stepped off a ledge and was pitched forward into the water. For a moment he floundered, letting go of his rod in his efforts to right himself, but his feet gained no purchase, and water poured inside his waders, weighing him down. He could feel himself being dragged through the water, and the river in spate from a day of heavy rain carried him inexorably in its flood. As it narrowed between rocky banks, Justin made a grab for the trailing branches of an overhanging willow tree, but they came away in his hand and the river pulled him under, the water closing over his head. He struggled to keep afloat, forcing his head upwards to gulp air. Justin could swim, but his clothes and waterlogged waders tugged him down and then, suddenly, he was at the weir. Here the water tumbled across shelves of rock, breaking into spray flung high in the air before pouring over the next ledge. Justin felt himself tumbling too, unable to pull himself clear, and then, as his head was pounded against a jutting rock, he knew no more.

It was Fran who found him. She came from the house carrying a basket containing a bottle of cold tea and some of the scones Mrs Darwin had made that morning.

'You and Mr Justin can have a lovely picnic by the river,' the cook had said with a smile. 'It's a beautiful afternoon now the rain's stopped. Shall you take a blanket to sit on, Miss Fran? Just in case the ground's still damp?'

Fran thought this was a good idea and went back upstairs to find one. Carrying the basket, she draped the blanket round her shoulders and set off along the footpath. When she reached the river, she soon saw where Justin had been fishing. His fishing box containing reels, flies and extra line was on the bank, his landing net lying on the shingle beach, but there was no sign of Justin.

He must have moved along the river, she thought, but he can't have gone far without all his fishing kit. At first she walked a little way upstream to where the river straightened out, running through the water meadows. From this vantage point she could see for two or three hundred yards, but the banks were deserted, with no sign of a fisherman. She turned back, and leaving the picnic basket and the blanket beside Justin's things, she began to walk the other way. It was only a couple of hundred yards before she heard the sound of the water plunging over the weir. Suddenly alarmed, she hurried forwards, calling Justin's name as she went. Beyond the pool, she realised there was nowhere he could stand and fish. With dread in her heart she hurried along the bank until she was standing on a little promontory above the weir. For a moment she watched the relentless flow of the river, seeing nothing but the swirl of the water as it flung itself in a cloud of spray over the ledges. She was about to turn back, thinking he must have gone the other way after all, when she caught sight of something, floating in a pool of calmer water beyond the weir, beneath the branches of a weeping willow.

With a cry of anguish, she jumped down and followed the bank round to the tree.

Surely, she thought, it must be some sort of debris brought down by the storm, but as she approached the edge of the pool she saw that her worst fears had been realised.

Justin lay face down in the water, out of the current now, bobbing gently against the bank.

'Justin! No! Oh, no!' Frances's frantic cries echoed into the empty air. There was no one to hear, no one to help. No one to pull him out just in case he might still be alive. With no thought for her own safety, Fran scrambled down the sloping river bank and lowered herself into the water. She found she could stand, though her feet sank into the mud on the river bed. She ignored her sinking feet and moved forward to catch hold of Justin and pull him towards her. He was incredibly heavy, she could hardly move him, though he was still floating, half-submerged. With superhuman effort she managed to drag him towards the bank, but as she pulled, his face turned in the water, pale with eyes that stared and hair that drifted like water weed about his head. It was then that she knew for certain that she was too late – that there was nothing she, or anyone else, could do for him. Her beloved brother was dead. For a moment she stood waist deep in the muddy water, sobbing, with no idea of what to do. It was, she knew, impossible for her to pull Justin completely clear of the river, but she felt she must get him out of the water. Suppose he drifted away while she went for help? But waterlogged as he was, he was too heavy. She even had difficulty getting back onto dry land herself. For a long moment she scrabbled with her feet against the river bank, but at last she managed to grasp hold of a small bush and pull herself free of the muddy water. As she crawled up the bank, she looked back at Justin's body bobbing gently again at the edge of the pool and felt herself in the grip of despair. Then at last she had an idea. The dress she was wearing was an old one, a cotton dress for summer... with a belt tied loosely about her waist. Quickly she untied it and pulled it free. Making a slip knot, she lay down on her stomach and reached for Justin's hand, which was floating, strangely pale, almost disembodied, close to the bank. Looping the belt over fingers that moved with the movement of the water, she pulled the slip knot tight about his wrist. It was still no use trying to pull him from the water, but she tied the other end of the belt round the bush on the bank, knotting it firmly so it wouldn't pull free. Now at least when she fetched help, they would know where to find him.

Dripping wet and covered in mud, Fran scrambled along the river bank until she came to the footpath that would take her home. She was exhausted, unable to run, but she stumbled along as fast as she could. The first person she saw as she entered the yard was Fortune, her father's coachman.

'Why, Miss Frances,' he cried in alarm as he took in her wet and muddy clothes and her tear-streaked face. 'What on earth has happened to you?'

'Justin!' she croaked. 'Justin! He's in the river. By the weir.' And with that she gave in to her weakness and collapsed at Fortune's feet.

After that everything moved very quickly. Sir Philip was called, and immediately Fortune reported what Miss Frances had said before she fainted, a search party was despatched to the river.

They had no idea of what they were going to find. Frances had collapsed without telling them whether Justin was still alive, but they went equipped with a strong rope and a blanket, ready to haul him to safety.

They found him as Fran had left him, tethered to the small bush on the bank but still floating with his face in the water, his hair a dark halo about his head. There was nothing they could do for him but draw him in to the bank and lift him out of the water. It took four men to drag him ashore. The water streamed from his clothes, draining out of the waders that had drowned him.

It was a sad procession that trailed back towards the house, Fortune and Sir Philip's man, Scott, carrying Justin, wrapped in the blanket, while Jack the stable lad and Harris, Justin's valet, carried the things that Justin and Frances had left on the shingle beach.

When they reached the house they laid Justin upon his bed. Lady Chalfont was at Frances's bedside, but when she heard the men come in, she left her daughter, now dozy from a dose of laudanum, and hurried down to be with Justin. The moment she saw him lying inert on the bed, she knew her son was dead and gave a cry of despair. Sir Philip was already at his side, standing looking down at the pale face with the bruise at the temple, his own face a mask of anguish. After a moment he turned away, and as he walked out of the room he said, 'Send for Rupert.'

Chapter 25

Rupert spent the next month at Le Coq d'Argent. He had come to terms with the landlord and negotiated a special rate for his room and board. Joseph Fermont was pleased to be able to say that he had an 'English milor' making an extended stay at his inn. It could only be good for business, but though he was indeed staying, he seldom ate more than his breakfast at Le Coq.

Once the St Clairs had accepted him as a frequent visitor to their home, he was often made one of the party at dinner or included in family picnics taken by the river or beneath the trees in the nearby woodland. He was allowed to drive Hélène about the countryside in the chaise he had hired from the stables in town, with Annette sitting quietly in the seat beside her, a silent chaperone.

It was as they were walking in the Place in St Etienne, looking at the market stalls one afternoon, that they encountered Simon Barnier. Annette was still in close attendance, but at first Simon did not see her, perhaps did not realise that she was anything to do with the couple, who were looking at some lace being displayed to them by an old woman who brought her work to the market once a week.

'It's beautiful,' Hélène was saying, 'and just what I need to trim my new tea gown.' She carried a small purse and was reaching for this from her reticule when Rupert said, 'Allow me,' and handed the woman the few coins she asked for the lace.

Simon Barnier, who had seen them across the square, stared in amazement as the damned Englishman took the lace and handed it to Hélène with a smile and a slight bow. Hélène put a hand on his arm and was thanking him when Simon could bear it no more. He crossed the street and approached as if he had only just seen them.

'Mademoiselle Hélène,' he said, ignoring Rupert and greeting her with a bow. 'Good day to you. I trust you are well.'

'Yes, indeed, m'sieur,' Hélène replied with the slightest of curtsies. 'I thank you.'

'It is such a hot day, I'm surprised to see you out and about. I was about to take a glass of lemonade at Le Coq d'Argent; if you would care to join me, I would be delighted to escort you.'

'Thank you, m'sieur, but as you see I already have an escort' – she indicated Rupert, who was standing at her side – 'and we have just now taken a glass of lemonade.'

'I beg your pardon, Mademoiselle Hélène.' Simon still ignored Rupert. 'I assumed you were attended by your maid and had only stopped to pass the time of day with Monsieur Chalford.'

Rupert made no effort to join in the conversation. It seemed to him that Hélène was managing very well on her own.

'Monsieur Chalfont and I are about to return to Belair, monsieur.' Hélène made no effort to correct Simon's mispronunciation of Rupert's name, deciding not to dignify the deliberate mistake with any attention. 'So if you will excuse us.' She held out her hand, which he had hardly touched with his own before she withdrew it to rest on Rupert's arm. 'It was a pleasure to meet you, m'sieur.'

'Good day, m'sieur,' said Rupert, with an inclination of his head, and together they walked away. Annette stepped forward to follow a discreet few metres behind them, but as she passed Simon Barnier, who stood stony-faced looking after them, he put out an arm to stop her.

'You're Mademoiselle St Clair's maid?'

Annette curtsied. 'Yes, sir.'

'And you always attend your mistress?'

'Yes, sir.'

'I very much fear for her with that man.' He glanced after the departing Rupert. 'I think he is an adventurer after her money.'

Annette made no reply, but her mind raced as he went on, 'I would make it worth your while to keep an eye on them for me. The St Clairs are old friends of my family.' He jingled some coins in his pocket. 'It would be doing us all a service if you happened to find out anything about him. He is too free with her and we must guard her reputation, must we not?'

'Indeed we must, m'sieur,' agreed Annette. 'I will keep careful watch.'

Simon Barnier nodded his approval and, slipping a coin into her hand, turned away, allowing her to catch up with Hélène and Rupert without them having noticed that she had been waylaid.

They took the path through the fields, and when they reached Belair they joined Rosalie, who, with a book in her hand, was reclining beneath the ancient apple tree that offered welcome shade. She looked up and smiled as they approached.

'Hélène, my dear,' she said. 'Do come into the shade or

you'll burn and look like a peasant!' She turned to Rupert.
'Good afternoon, m'sieur. Pray do please take a seat and join
me. Didier will be bringing some refreshment directly. Louise
will be out in a moment, when Mademoiselle Corbine releases
her. It really is too hot to remain indoors in the schoolroom,
is it not?'

Rupert agreed that it was and sat down as requested,
listening as Hélène told her mother about the lace she had
bought. It was hot, even here in the shade, and for a moment
Rupert's thoughts drifted away from the Belair garden as
he pictured the spreading oak tree in his family's garden in
England. How often had his mother sat as Rosalie St Clair
was sitting now, about to dispense cool drinks and cakes on a
summer afternoon, the gentle drone of bees busy among the
flowers a soft accompaniment to the heavy stillness of the day?

Would Hélène be comfortable at Pilgrim's Oak? he
wondered. He was certain that she and Fran would get on
well, that Fran would ensure her welcome whenever they
visited, but it would not be their home. He had no idea where
that might be, but he was quite happy to settle anywhere
Hélène might choose – Paris, maybe, or London.

His thoughts of the future were interrupted and he was
drawn back to his immediate surroundings when Louise
appeared from the house, running out into the sunshine,
having finished her lessons for the day. He was surprised to
see that she was accompanied by her governess, and when
Louise flopped down into a chair with a sigh, Angèle Corbine,
uninvited, also joined the group.

Mademoiselle Corbine had been the girls' governess ever
since they had returned to Paris seven years earlier, and
Rosalie was beginning to think that they had no further
need of her services. Louise would be out of the schoolroom

and launched into the world next summer, and there was little that Mademoiselle Corbine could teach her now that could not be learned from visiting tutors like the dancing master and the drawing master who already came to the house. In the last few months Rosalie had been aware of Mademoiselle Corbine in a way that she had not before, aware of her growing confidence of her place in the household. A governess was always in rather an equivocal position within an establishment – neither a servant nor one of the family – but recently Rosalie had realised that Angèle Corbine expected to be treated almost as an equal, and that Emile seemed quite comfortable with this state of affairs. It was, Rosalie decided as she listened to her speaking to Hélène, time for Mademoiselle Corbine to move on. She would speak to Emile about it when she could get him alone. He would understand, she thought now, and acquiesce. He had strayed before and she had always turned a blind eye, but his wandering had been discreet, not carried on under her own roof.

Just then Didier appeared, carrying a tray, with glasses and a jug of lemonade and a plate of macaroon biscuits. He was followed by Lizette with cloth and plates to lay out on the table, and so Rosalie put these thoughts away to be considered later. Once the refreshments had been set out, Rosalie told Didier that they would help themselves.

'Hélène, chérie,' she said, 'will you pour the lemonade, and perhaps Rupert will pass the glasses.'

Rupert was happy enough to be thus called upon. It demonstrated to him that he was no longer considered a guest to be waited on, but one of the informal family group.

It was as he picked up a glass of lemonade, and was carrying it over to Rosalie, that he was struck by a sudden shaft of pain in his head, making him stagger. He cried out, dropping the glass onto the ground, the lemonade spraying over his hostess's skirt. For a moment he clutched his head in his hands and then the pain was gone, leaving him unfocused and giddy.

'Rupert!' Hélène cried, leaving the table and rushing to his side. 'Are you all right? What happened?'

For a moment Rupert thought he might collapse but then the dizziness passed and, seeming to recover, he apologised profusely to Rosalie for his carelessness.

Rosalie had looked up in alarm as he'd dropped the glass, and as she heard his apologies, she saw that all colour had drained from his face, leaving him deathly pale.

'My dear Monsieur Chalfont,' she cried. 'You are unwell. Please, sit down, sit down.'

'Really, madame,' he said a little shakily, 'it is nothing. Perhaps the heat or a little too much sun.' But he followed her instruction to sit, nonetheless, and was glad to do so. Hélène was at his side at once, fear in her eyes.

'Rupert,' she said again, more quietly this time. 'What is the matter? You look quite ill.'

'Nothing,' he answered with a weak smile. 'I'm fine, really. Just a moment's dizziness, which caused me to spoil your mother's dress.'

'Just stay sitting where you are,' Hélène said, taking charge. 'You mustn't get up again until you're feeling better. Louise, will you run indoors and ask Didier for some brandy for Monsieur Chalfont? He needs a restorative.'

'Yes, hurry up, child,' Rosalie said. 'Ask him to bring it at once.'

Moments later Rupert was sipping from a generous measure of brandy, and as he felt the warmth of the spirit trickling down his throat, he did indeed feel better. A little colour crept into his cheeks and again he apologised to Rosalie, who dismissed his words with a wave of her hands.

'Think nothing of it, m'sieur,' she said. 'Yvette will have that set to rights in no time. It is you who must concern us now. How are you feeling?'

Rupert smiled and said, 'Much better, madame, the brandy has done me a world of good.'

The accident seemed to have brought the party under the tree to a close, and it was not long before they all repaired indoors to the cool of the drawing room, saying that it really was much too hot to be sitting outside.

Rupert was grateful to be out of the heat; that must have been what had caused his giddiness, but though the piercing pain had gone, he was still feeling decidedly strange. Was it really too much sun?

'I think I should go back to Le Coq,' he said quietly to Hélène.

'I will ask Pierre to drive you,' said Rosalie, who had overheard him. 'Hélène, run and ask Pierre to put the horse to at once.'

'Really, madame,' protested Rupert as Hélène hurried from the room, 'there is no need to trouble Pierre. I can easily take the path through the fields.'

'Certainly not, m'sieur,' replied Rosalie firmly. 'Pierre will drive you.'

Ten minutes later the message was brought that the chaise was at the door.

Rupert got to his feet and walked a little unsteadily out to where Pierre was waiting. Hélène went with him and he paused before climbing up to take his place.

'Really, Hélène,' he said softly, 'there is nothing to worry about, I am sure. I will call on you again tomorrow, if I may.'

'Of course you may,' smiled Hélène, holding out her hand. 'I shall look forward to it, but in the meantime, Rupert, I shall be thinking of you.'

Rupert raised her extended hand to his lips. 'And I of you, my darling girl.'

Colour flooded Hélène's cheeks as she murmured, 'Really, M'sieur Rupert—'

'Just Rupert will do, you know,' he interrupted, still holding her hand.

'Rupert, you should not address me as such.'

'Why not, my darling girl? It's what you are.' And with that he touched her hand to his lips once more before climbing up into the coach.

Though he would never have admitted it to anyone else, he was relieved that he did not have to walk back to the village across the fields under the summer sun. The pain and giddiness had passed, but he felt strangely tired.

They made the short journey at a leisurely pace, and as he drove, Pierre considered what Annette had told him on her return from the village. Should he pass the information on to this Englishman who now seemed to have become so important to Miss Hélène? He, Pierre, had a great fondness for Hélène. He had been among those who had searched for her high and low when she had gone missing during the siege six years ago, and he had admired the courage with which she had managed to keep herself safe in the war-torn city. If Annette was right in her thoughts on Monsieur Barnier's proposition, surely Monsieur Rupert should be warned.

'Monsieur Chalfont,' he said. 'I think there is something you should know.'

'I beg your pardon,' said Rupert, whose thoughts had been drifting away again as he dozed to the rhythm of the chaise. 'What did you say?'

'This afternoon as you were leaving St Etienne, I believe Miss Hélène was approached by Monsieur Barnier.'

'Yes.' Rupert remembered the encounter with a wry smile. 'So?'

'So, afterwards he approached the maid, Annette.'

'Did he? How interesting. And what did he want?'

'He offered her money to spy on you and Miss Hélène... particularly on you, and to tell him anything she learned about you.'

'Well now... and what did she say?'

'She took his money. She was quick-thinking enough to realise that if she didn't, someone else would and we'd have no idea what he was up to. Better to *be* the spy than for there to be another who we know nothing about, don't you think?'

'We?'

'Annette and me. We both want to protect Miss Hélène from that man, so it is better to know the information he's being given.'

'I see. And do you know why he wants this information?'

'Simply to discredit you. The talk below stairs is that he wants you out of the way and Miss Hélène for himself.'

'And is the below-stairs gossip reliable?' asked Rupert, though he knew for sure it would be at Pilgrim's Oak.

'Oh, yes, sir,' said Pierre, 'and we are all fond of Miss Hélène.'

'And what about me?' asked Rupert with a grin. 'Do you think she needs protecting from me?'

'That remains to be seen, sir,' replied Pierre.

That made Rupert laugh out loud. 'You believe in plain speaking, Pierre!'

'Yes, m'sieur, as you do yourself.'

'Perhaps we should assume the worst about Monsieur Barnier,' said Rupert ruminatively. 'Is the maid, Annette, going to speak to Miss Hélène about what she's been asked to do?'

'Yes indeed, m'sieur, when she gets the chance to speak with her alone. She must be warned.'

'Will she also warn Madame St Clair?'

'No, sir. There would then be the risk of Monsieur Barnier learning that his spy was no friend of his.'

'But why?' demanded Rupert. 'Why are Miss Hélène and the maid so close? Because I know they are.'

Pierre was silent for a moment as he considered his reply. 'That's not for me to say, m'sieur,' he said at length. 'Maybe Miss Hélène will confide in you when she is ready to.'

When they reached the inn, Rupert descended from the chaise and turned back to Pierre. 'I'm glad we have had this little talk on our way home. You are completely right that Miss Hélène must be protected from this man. I shall be there to protect her, but if you or Annette hear anything that I need to know, you must come to me at once. And if for any reason you cannot then you should go to Madame St Clair.'

Chapter 26

The telegram arrived the next day. Rupert had already set out for Belair in his hired chaise with a picnic basket packed by the inn, in the hope of tempting Hélène out for a drive. He wanted to talk to her alone about what Annette had been asked to do. Of course Annette would be with them, but it was clear to Rupert that she was special for some reason and he decided it was time he got to know her better.

When the post boy arrived at Le Coq d'Argent, Joseph Fermont directed him to Parker, who was outside in the yard, cleaning his master's boots.

Parker took the telegram and saw that it came from England. How important is it? he wondered. Will it keep until Mr Rupert returns, whenever that is, or should I take it at once and hope to catch him before he sets out from Belair on his picnic?

Telegrams usually brought bad news, he thought. Why spoil the day? Surely another few hours would make no difference. He put the envelope into his pocket and got on with polishing the boots, but as the day wore on, he became more and more conscious of the telegram, rustling in his pocket, and at last he got to his feet and set off to walk to Belair.

As he arrived in the stable yard, the chaise was returning

along the drive. It drew up in front of the house, and Henri the stable lad ran to take the horse's head while Rupert handed Hélène down. He looked surprised as he saw Parker coming round the side of the house.

'Parker?' he said. 'What's up?'

'Telegram for you, sir,' Parker said, handing him the envelope.

For a moment Rupert looked at it, premonition flooding his mind, then he ripped it open and read the message...

JUSTIN KILLED IN ACCIDENT STOP COME HOME IMMEDIATELY STOP CHALFONT

... and the colour drained from his face.

'Rupert?' Hélène put her hand on his arm. 'Rupert? What is it?'

'My brother,' Rupert said. 'My brother!' And he crumpled the telegram in his hand.

'Let's go indoors,' Hélène said, and taking him by the hand as she would a child, she led him into the house.

Annette had climbed out of the chaise and turned to Parker. 'You're Mr Rupert's man?'

'Yes,' he replied, and as he spoke he knew he should have brought the telegram straight away. He didn't know what it actually said, but it was clear there was something wrong with Mr Justin.

Hélène had taken Rupert into the morning room where, when she had closed the door, they could be private. Once inside, she turned to face him and took both his hands in hers. His face was as pale as it had been the day before, but this time she saw tears in his eyes.

'Tell me,' she said softly.

'It's Justin,' Rupert murmured. 'Justin, my brother. There's been an accident.' His voice broke on a sob. 'He's dead.'

Without further thought Hélène gathered him into her arms, pressing her cheek against his, wet with tears. She said nothing. There were no words that she could say that would be of any use. She just held him close as his tears slid silently down his face. She had never seen a grown man cry, but he was her Rupert and she held him tightly to offer him comfort.

She could hear voices outside in the hall, but she did not let him go. She never wanted to let him go again. She knew he loved her and she loved him. He was hers and there would never be anyone else.

At last he put her gently away from him, saying, 'I'm sorry.'

'Don't be,' she said. 'Just remember I'll always be here.'

Rupert looked down into her eyes and despite his great sorrow found he was smiling, smiling through his tears. 'I love you, Hélène,' he said.

'And I love you, Rupert.'

He pulled her back into his arms, holding her close against him. 'It's not the time to ask,' he said into her hair, 'but will you marry me?'

She reached up a hand and touched his cheek. 'Of course I will.'

At that moment the door opened and Rosalie came into the room. 'Hélène,' she said, 'what are you doing in here?' As she saw her daughter still standing within the circle of Rupert's arms, she went on, 'Well, I can see, but it is most unseemly of you.'

Hélène stayed where she was, safe with Rupert, and said, 'Rupert has just learned that his brother has been killed in an accident, Maman.'

'That is very sad news,' replied her mother, 'but it is a good thing that it was I and not one of the servants who found you like this. You should not be shut away, alone, with an unmarried man. If there was news of this, your reputation—'

'My reputation is quite safe, Maman,' Hélène interrupted. 'Rupert and I have just become engaged, so it must be perfectly proper for me to comfort him in his distress at this dreadful news.'

'Engaged!' Rosalie latched on to that word, hearing little of the others. 'With no reference to your father... or to me?'

'Papa has already given Rupert permission to address me...'

'But not for a formal betrothal...'

'It is quite decided between us, Maman,' Hélène said, glancing up at Rupert with a shy smile. 'Is it not, Rupert?'

'Quite decided,' echoed Rupert. He stepped away from Hélène and said, 'I hope you do not completely disapprove, madame.'

Rosalie looked flustered, but at last came back to the news brought by the telegram. 'But with this news of your brother, surely this is hardly the time...'

'It is just the time, madame,' Rupert asserted. 'I shall have to return to England at once. My family needs me there, and there will be much to arrange, but I shall come back as soon as I may to claim Hélène and take her to Pilgrim's Oak.'

'Pilgrim's Oak?'

'My family home, madame.'

'This is not at all as it should be,' Rosalie tried again, but she recognised in her daughter's expression the look of determination that had carried her through the dark days of the siege. 'I don't know what your father will say.'

'I hope he will give me his blessing,' Hélène said. 'But whether he does or not, I shall consider myself engaged to

Rupert and will wait for his return, however long he's needed in England.'

The news of Justin's death was quickly spread below stairs.

'Pierre says it means that Mr Rupert is now the heir,' Annette told Agathe. 'He will be *Sir* Rupert one day, and Hélène will be Lady Chalfont.'

'If they get married,' interposed Agathe.

'I'm sure they will,' Annette said. 'Pierre says that Mr Rupert is besotted with her.'

'Does he now?' commented Agathe. She had noticed recently that Annette was giving a great deal of weight to what Pierre said. She wasn't sure whether she was pleased or not. Annette had had a dreadful experience at the hands of Father Thomas, and Agathe was afraid that it might have made her fearful of every man. She liked Pierre, he was a good steady man, but would he understand the very gentle care Annette needed if she were ever to marry? There was nothing she could say in warning – she was bound by her promise to Rosalie that no hint of Annette's real situation should become known at Belair – but she was also afraid that Annette could be damaged further if she were to marry and her husband expect his conjugal rights without knowledge of what had gone before.

'Well,' she said, 'I'm sure he isn't thinking of that just now. He will be mourning his brother. They were twins, I believe, which probably means they were very close. I'm sure titles will be the last thing on his mind.'

In the propriety of the drawing room, with Rosalie in attendance though not within earshot, Hélène and Rupert sat in the window embrasure.

'Does it say what happened?' Hélène asked.

'No, just an accident.'

'And when?'

'Yesterday,' Rupert replied. 'It must have been yesterday when I was taken ill; but I didn't recognise it for what it was.'

'When will you leave?'

'First thing tomorrow. We shall take the train to Paris and then to the coast. I've sent Parker to the telegraph office to send a reply saying that I am on my way.'

'Oh, Rupert! I wish I could come with you!'

Rupert flashed her the smile she had come to love. 'So do I, my love, but we have to agree that that is impossible.'

'We could elope?' she suggested hopefully, and was rewarded with another smile.

'So we could,' he agreed, 'but it wouldn't answer. It would just upset everyone further still. Remember, we still have to brave your father's anger!'

That turned out to be less of a trial than they had expected. Emile had grown to like the charming Englishman laying siege to his daughter, and he too had realised that now the elder brother was no longer in the way, Rupert would eventually inherit his father's title. Of course he made no mention of this now, but it was in his mind as he gave his consent.

'There can be nothing formal until you return,' he told Rupert when he applied to him later that evening. 'Hélène is very young, but if, after a period of mourning for your brother, perhaps in the spring, you are both of the same mind and wish to announce your betrothal, then we shall be happy to give you our blessing.'

It was almost dark when Rupert finally took his leave. Hélène's parents gave them a few moments' privacy to say goodbye before he climbed up into his chaise and drove back to the village. For a long moment as he held her close, she felt the warmth of his body against her own. 'Never forget how much I love you, darling girl,' he murmured into her hair, and then, with a gentle kiss upon her lips, he let her go.

'It was such a lovely day,' Hélène said with a sigh, 'until you got the telegram.'

As he drove back to the village through the gathering gloom, he thought of the brief conversation he had managed to have with Annette, the maid.

'Look after your mistress while I'm away,' he'd said.

'Of course,' she had replied. 'No harm will come to her. Pierre and I will see to that.'

'Send word to me if necessary,' Rupert had added, giving her his direction at Pilgrim's Oak.

Once back at the inn he found Parker had packed all his belongings in readiness for the journey, and so he retired to his room, where he spent the night alone with his grief. Justin was dead, the other half of himself was missing and would never return, and having held himself together while he was at Belair, at long last he was able to give vent to his misery.

When the chaise was out of sight, Hélène had turned back into the house. She missed him already, but they had agreed to write and she would send her first letter the very next day and then wait to receive his reply. As she lay in bed, staring out into the night sky, she relived the day, the day which had been such a mixture of sadness and joy, the day she had engaged herself to marry Rupert Chalfont.

Chapter 27

'He's on his way home,' Sir Philip said as he opened the telegram. 'He'll be here in a couple of days.'

Pilgrim's Oak was a house in mourning. The curtains were drawn against the daylight, voices were hushed, footsteps light upon the stairs. Everyone was dressed in black, hurriedly ordered by Fran to show respect for the unexpected death.

Fran couldn't wait for Rupert to get home. She had had to carry the weight of her parents' grief alone. Her mother had been prostrate ever since she had seen Justin's body laid out in the morning room.

'I shall never be able to go into that room again,' she had wailed. 'What can have happened to him? How did he drown? I always hated him fishing!'

Sir Philip had been as strong and withdrawn as any man of his age faced with the death of a son. There was no wailing or tears from him, just a rigidity of body and mind as he had to accustom himself to the fact that Justin would never again walk in through the house in muddy boots, or be scolded by his mother for doing so.

Fran took on the arrangements for the funeral, for the notices to *The Times* and *The Morning Post*. It was Fran who consulted with Mrs Darwin about the baked meats to be served at the house to those who returned there after the service; with Mrs Crowley, the housekeeper, about which rooms should be prepared for Lady Chalfont's sister and her husband, Lord and Lady Devenish, who were coming to stay for the funeral. And all the while she was worried Rupert would not arrive in time. How long had the telegram taken to find him? How long had his reply been in coming back?

There was also Kitty to consider; she and her family were almost as devastated as Justin's own. They had liked and respected Justin as a person, but Sir James had been particularly pleased with the alliance because, as he had no male heir, Kitty's sons would inherit from both sides of the family. It was a blow to his plans, as he didn't hesitate to say to his wife.

'Well, please don't put it in those terms to Katharine,' she retorted. 'It's her fiancé we're talking about here, the man she was going to marry. Do you not take her feelings into consideration when you speak like that?'

'Feelings are all very well,' returned her husband, 'but this was more than a question of feelings and—'

'Not for Kitty it wasn't,' snapped his wife. 'And poor Frances is having to look after everything at Pilgrim's Oak, as her mother has gone into a decline. Understandable, I know, but leaving a lot on Frances's shoulders.'

'Well, I hear that she telegraphed for Rupert to come home; he can take control of all that when he gets here. After all, he's the heir now.' He looked thoughtfully at his wife and added, 'Isn't he.' And it wasn't a question; to him it was a thought worthy of consideration. After all, there was not only land at stake here, but a title as well.

Kitty had been achingly miserable since she'd heard the news, but she had controlled her tears and they had only been shed in the privacy of her own chamber. She had of course put on mourning and paid the required visit to Pilgrim's Oak. Fran had greeted her with a quick embrace and then led her to where Justin was lying in his coffin for her to make her farewells. Left alone in the morning room, she had looked down at his pale face – only it wasn't Justin's face any more, it was stiff and waxy and cold. She reached out with one finger and touched his cheek. The chill and texture of it made her draw back in horror, wiping her finger on her sleeve as if to wipe away the feel of his skin.

She looked down at him, and having ensured she was alone in the room and that the door remained closed, she murmured, 'Goodbye, Justin. We could have been happy, you and I. I shall miss you.' There seemed no more to say. She hadn't loved him as a wife should, but she had loved him as an old friend and she was full of sadness at his sudden demise. She dashed away the single tear that had escaped and trickled down her cheek. No! No more tears. She would not cry. Now she had to get through all the condolences and sympathies which would be heaped on her by well-meaning friends and family. They would mention the wedding, they would regret her single state, they would talk about the Justin *they* knew with little thought to her own memories of him, private and sad. With one last glance at the man she might have married, she turned away, opened the door and went out to face the world.

Rupert arrived home three days later and was immediately aware of the invisible mist of sorrow that had drifted through the house, invading every corner, ever since Justin had been brought home. Servants moved silently about their business, voices were low, the sounds of the living quieted by grief for the dead.

Fran had heard the carriage bringing her brother home from

the station and was out to greet him before the coachman had had time to let down the steps and open the door. Rupert was tired after the uncomfortable journey by train, ship and coach, but as soon as he saw Fran's eyes, glistening with unshed tears, peering up at him from her strained, pale face, he jumped down from the coach and enveloped her in a bear hug.

'My poor girl!' he murmured. 'Tell me what happened. Was he thrown from his horse?'

'No,' said Fran. 'He fell by the weir, hit his head and was drowned.'

'Drowned? But he could swim like a fish.'

'He was fishing, he missed his footing on the rocks and hit his head. I found him face down in the river.'

'You found him? Oh, Fran, my poor Fran.'

'Let's go indoors so we can talk properly,' said his sister, taking his arm. 'We need to discuss the arrangements I've made so far.'

'You? Has everything landed on you! Never mind, I'm here now and we'll sort things out between us. How's my father? And dear Mama, how is she?'

'Papa is well enough,' Fran replied as together they turned towards the front door. 'He's very sad, of course, but determined to show no emotion. He seems to carry on as normal, but spends most of his time in his library and has left all the arrangements to me. Mama, on the other hand, is *all* emotion. She is prostrate and has retired to bed.' Fran bit her lip before she went on softly, 'Rupert, I'm so glad you've come home.'

Rupert gave her hand a squeeze. 'So am I,' he said. 'I'm sorry it took this long. Where is he?'

'In the morning room,' replied Fran, 'but you can't see him. I'm afraid we had to close the coffin.'

'Of course you did,' said Rupert gently. 'Anyway, I'd rather remember him as he was last time I saw him, young and vigorous and in good health.'

Together they went up the steps into the house, where Mitchell stood in the hallway waiting to welcome Rupert home.

'Good afternoon, sir,' he said. 'Sir Philip asks you to find him in the library as soon as is convenient.'

'Thank you, Mitchell,' Rupert replied. 'Perhaps you would tell him I'll be with him just as soon as I've washed off the dust of the journey.'

Rupert went up to his bedroom, where he found Parker already waiting for him.

'Your luggage will be brought up directly, Mr Rupert. Will you change your clothes, sir?'

'No, for the moment I'll just get washed and then I must go to Sir Philip.'

He found his father sitting in the library beside a log fire. Despite the fact that it was the height of summer, the room still felt cold, and the old man sat in an armchair, huddled into his clothes. He got to his feet to greet his son and Rupert was struck by how much his father had aged in the few weeks since he'd last seen him. His face was gaunt, the skin loose about his cheeks, his eyes dull, smudged with dark shadows. The hand he extended to Rupert was dry and bony, more like a claw than a hand, Rupert thought as he grasped it in his. Was this change sudden? Due entirely to Justin's unexpected death, or had it been happening gradually, unnoticed, over the last few months?

'Father,' he began and then had no idea what to say next. He added rather lamely, 'Here I am, sir. I came at once.'

His father nodded and turned back to his chair by the fire.

He sat down heavily and waved Rupert to the chair opposite. For a long moment a silence lapsed about them and then Sir Philip said, 'He was about to get married; did you know?'

'Yes, sir,' replied Rupert gently. 'I was to be his best man.'

'It's great pity you weren't here, instead of gallivanting off to France. If you'd been here it might not have happened.'

Despite the unfairness of this remark, Rupert didn't dispute it. He realised that his father needed someone to blame for Justin's accident.

'I believe Fran has been making all the necessary arrangements,' he said to change the subject.

'Frances has been very good,' agreed Sir Philip. 'Your poor mother is in no fit state to arrange anything.'

And nor are you, Rupert thought, but he did not put this thought into words. He was shaken by how his father looked and knew he must share the burden Fran had been carrying.

'And of course there is Katharine. You will have to visit her. The funeral is on Friday – we had to allow enough time for you to get home – but you should pay a call at Marwick House before we all meet at the graveside.' Sir Philip's voice was matter-of-fact, and Rupert realised that that was how his father was coping with Justin's death.

'Of course I will, sir. I will ride over tomorrow.'

When Rupert went upstairs to see his mother, he found her in her bedchamber. She was not in bed, but wrapped in several blankets, sitting in an armchair before a glowing fire. The room was stiflingly hot, but the windows were tight shut.

Rupert crossed the room and knelt down beside her, taking her hands in his. 'Mama,' he said softly, 'Mama, I'm home.'

She looked at him with blank eyes. 'Rupert,' she said. 'Do

you find it very cold in here? Will you put more coals on the fire?'

He did as she asked, adding a single coal to the fire before taking a seat opposite her.

'I came as soon as I could,' he said. 'Dearest Mama, I'm so sorry.'

'Justin's in the morning room,' said his mother. 'Have you seen him? I don't go in there any more.'

'No, Mama, I haven't been in there yet. I wanted to see you and my father first.'

It was ten minutes later that Rupert left his mother. She had uttered not another word and didn't seem to notice when he got quietly to his feet and slipped out of the room.

Then at last he went down to the morning room and softly opened the door.

Justin's coffin lay on two trestles. As Fran had told him, it had been closed the day after he'd been brought home, but she had put two vases of lilies, one at the head and one at the foot, and the room was filled with their heady scent.

Rupert went and stood by the coffin, laying his hand on its polished oak surface. He felt he ought to be saying something to his dead twin, but found that the words would not come. His throat had closed and he stood there with his eyes shut, trying to conjure up Justin's face. The scent of the lilies was cloying and he knew that whenever he smelled them again it would remind him of this minute, of his farewell to Justin, the best brother a man could possibly ask for. With his hand still on the coffin lid he managed to say, 'Goodbye, old man,' before he turned away, blew his nose, wiped his eyes and went back to his grieving family.

Later that evening, when they had had their dinner, he and Fran sat alone in the drawing room. Lady Chalfont had taken her meal upstairs, as she had ever since Justin had been found. Sir Philip had eaten with his children, but had now withdrawn once again to his library.

For a while the two of them sat in a comfortable silence. Rupert looked out of the window at the familiar view of the garden. The sun was setting and the sky was painted a glorious rose gold, streaked with orange. Justin was lying in his coffin and yet the world was still unimaginably beautiful.

'Do you think Mother will attend the funeral?' he asked Fran.

'I doubt it,' Fran replied. 'You've seen her. She's in no fit state to appear in company, is she? I thought when the first shock was over she might rally, but there has been no sign of that.'

'And my father?'

'Oh, certainly he'll be there; whatever torment he feels, he will stand at the graveside and do his duty,' she said, adding almost as an afterthought, 'as will you and I.' She glanced across at him and asked, 'Why were you away for so long in France? We had no word of you for ages. We didn't even know where you were until Parker arrived here to collect your luggage. What kept you so long?' She softened the question with a faint smile. 'I bet it was some woman you met.'

'Well, I admit it was a woman...' began Rupert.

'I knew it!' cried Fran. 'It always is with you!'

'Well, you're wrong,' Rupert said. 'It was not "some woman", it was the woman to whom I've become engaged and whom I intend to marry.'

'What?' Fran stared at him in amazement. 'What did you say? You're engaged?'

'As good as,' Rupert said with a smile. 'Hélène's very

young, but if we are still of the same mind in the spring, we have her father's blessing.'

'Have you told Papa? Or Mama?'

'No,' replied Rupert. 'This is hardly the time. I've only told you, and I'm trusting you not to mention it until the time is right.'

'Of course I won't,' Fran said. 'And I think you are quite right to say nothing for the time being. Papa is expecting you to stay here now and take over Justin's role. You're the heir and you have to learn about the estate.'

'I realise that everything has changed,' Rupert conceded. 'Everything here at Pilgrim's Oak – but my feelings for Hélène won't change, I promise you.'

Chapter 28

The next morning Rupert rode over to Marwick House to call on Kitty Blake and her parents. He was greeted in the hall by Campbell, who took his hat and gloves and, as a retainer who had known the Chalfont twins since they were babies, offered his condolences in a muted tone before saying he would ascertain whether Sir James and Lady Blake were at home and receiving visitors.

He was back almost at once and Rupert was shown up to the drawing room, where Lady Blake sat stitching at some tapestry. Immediately she set it aside and, as Rupert crossed the room to her, held out her hand in greeting.

'My dear Rupert,' she said. 'You're home again, but on such a sad occasion. When did you arrive?'

'Yesterday afternoon, Lady Blake.'

'And you've come at once to call on Katharine. It is very good of you to do so. The poor girl is distraught, losing Justin so unexpectedly and so close to their wedding day. Sir James is from home, I'm afraid, but I'm certain Kitty will want to receive you. She's not receiving callers at present, of course, but I've no doubt she'll make an exception for you.' So saying, she reached for the bell pull, and when a footman came in answer to her summons she said, 'Ah, John. Please will you inform Miss Kitty that Mr Rupert has called and ask her to join us.'

The footman went off on his errand and while they awaited Kitty's appearance, Lady Blake asked, 'And how is your dear mother? I believe she has been extremely unwell since your brother's accident.' There was something in her tone of voice that seemed to imply that she should not have been so stricken, and Rupert, who had never really liked Lady Blake, found himself rising to his mother's defence.

'Of course she is most upset,' he replied, keeping his voice even, 'which is only to be expected. However, she is a little better each day, which is a comfort to my father.'

'Will she attend the funeral, I wonder?' mused Lady Blake. 'In our family it is not the custom for the ladies to attend funerals, it is left to the gentlemen to show that respect, so I shall not be there; however, I know that Katharine, despite our wishes on the matter, intends to be present.'

At that moment the door opened and Kitty came in. She was dressed in deep mourning, which a detached part of Rupert noticed suited her well. Her face was very pale, but she greeted him with an attempt at a smile, which didn't quite reach her eyes.

'Rupert!' she said as she crossed the room to greet him. 'How very kind of you to come. I'm so glad you managed to get here in time for the funeral.'

'I was just telling Rupert, my dear, that you are intending to go to Justin's funeral on Friday, despite your father and I feeling it is not quite proper for you to appear in public so soon.'

'As I've told you, Mama,' responded Kitty, 'I shall only go to the church. I shall wear a heavy veil and no one shall see my face. I have no intention of meeting with other people after the service, but shall return here immediately.' It was clear from the resignation in her voice that she and her mother had already had this conversation more than once and that she was not going to change her mind.

Lady Blake sighed and said, 'Well, I suppose you will do as you please, but I don't know what Sir Philip and Lady Chalfont will think – nor you, Rupert, for that matter.'

'Kitty must do as she thinks best,' replied Rupert. 'But I'm sure you know, Kitty, that you will be more than welcome at the church.'

Lady Blake said no more on that subject, but getting to her feet, she said, 'Kitty, my dear, please ring the bell and ask Campbell to bring us some refreshment. I have to speak to Mrs Carson, but will be back with you directly.' Campbell came in answer to the bell, and Lady Blake gave him her orders and then left the room, leaving Rupert and Kitty alone together.

Kitty took a seat by the window and invited Rupert to do the same.

'I'm sorry I've only just got home,' Rupert said. 'It must be a very difficult time for you.'

'And for you,' returned Kitty. 'He was your brother, after all.' She gave him another smile and said, 'And everything seems to have fallen on poor Fran's shoulders. She must be extremely glad to have you home again.'

Rupert smiled back as he said, 'Yes, I think she is, with all the arrangements that have had to be made. Still, I'm here to take some of the load now and to comfort my parents in their grief.'

'I believe you were in France,' Kitty said. 'Justin told me that you'd been invited to a wedding.'

'Indeed I was, but the countryside there was so beautiful I stayed on a while to explore.'

'He did wonder why you didn't come home when he wrote and told you about our engagement. He hoped you would.'

'I know, and of course I wish now with all my heart that I had, that I hadn't left it too late, but such regrets are of no use. Now I must do all in my power to ease my parents' sadness. I shall stay at home and try to learn what Justin was brought up to know.'

It was on the tip of his tongue to confide the secret of his understanding with Hélène St Clair, but as he hesitated the moment was lost as Lady Blake came back into the room, followed by Campbell with a tea tray and a dish of cakes and biscuits.

They drank their tea and ate the sweetmeats, and as soon as he decently could, Rupert left Marwick House with a promise to return to call on Sir James in the next few days. As he rode home, Rupert thought about Kitty and her reaction to Justin's death. Her mother had described her as 'distraught', but Rupert had seen no sign of that. Kitty had been dignified in her determination to attend the funeral in two days' time, and she had spoken of Justin in a tone of affection, but without the depth of love he would have expected from a fiancée. Perhaps, he thought, it is the only way she can get through the days, the only way she can hold herself together until the ritual of the funeral is over and Justin is committed to the ground.

When he got home again, he and Fran went over all the arrangements she had made.

'How did you find Kitty?' Fran asked.

'Calm, dignified, determined.'

'Determined?' Fran looked at him sharply. 'Determined about what?'

'Determined to come to the funeral. Well, to the church, anyway. Her parents don't approve.'

'She usually gets what she wants,' remarked Fran. 'So I'm sure she'll be there.'

The following day Lord and Lady Devenish arrived and the house was in a flurry of welcome. Lady Chalfont, encouraged by Rupert and Fran, made the effort at last to get dressed and come downstairs. It was the first time she had left her chamber and she walked unsteadily down to the drawing room, leaning on her son's arm.

'Amabel!' cried Lady Devenish. 'How do you do? You look very pale, my dear sister.'

'I'm very tired, Grace. I haven't slept in days. There's been so much coming and going in the house and poor Justin lying in his coffin in the morning room.' She let go of Rupert's arm and sank into an armchair as if her legs would no longer hold her.

Dinner was a quiet affair, with little conversation from either side of the table. Sir Philip had always found his sister-in-law difficult and tonight was no exception. The men did not linger in the dining room and the ladies retired to bed soon after the tea tray was brought in.

Rupert went to his room and, having dismissed Parker, closed the door behind him and sat down at the table to write a letter to Hélène. It was the first chance he had had to put pen to paper since he'd left France. How he missed her. He summoned a picture of her face, remembered the feel of her warmth in his arms with an almost physical ache. He longed to talk to her, to hear her voice, to explain the loss he felt at Justin's death and be comforted by her presence. He couldn't speak to her, so writing to her was the next best thing, and hoping she would reply at once, he picked up his pen.

Chapter 29

The morning after Rupert's departure Hélène felt completely bereft. How could this strange yet charming Englishman have invaded her being to such an extent that she felt only half herself without him? He had promised to write as soon as he got home and had given his own direction at Pilgrim's Oak so that she could write back to him. This correspondence had received the consent of her parents, though when Rupert had made his final farewell Rosalie had insisted that Hélène should not be the instigator of this exchange of letters.

'It would be unbecoming and forward to write first,' Rosalie explained when Hélène announced next morning she would write immediately. 'You must wait to hear from him, and then, if he does write, you may answer.'

During the following week Hélène waited eagerly, checking the postbag for his letter, for she had no doubts that he would write as soon as he was able. In the meantime she began writing to him so that when the longed-for letter from England arrived, she would have the beginnings of a reply ready to send. She knew she must be patient and that Rupert would not fail her.

Indeed, he did not, and ten days after he had set out for

England the letter arrived. Didier had brought the post in to her mother, who, seeing the letter with an English stamp, had summoned Hélène into her parlour.

'I think the letter you've been waiting for has arrived, Hélène,' she said with a smile. 'I shall not insist on reading it,' she went on, 'as I trust Monsieur Chalfont to write only what is proper, but should you find anything improper, I must rely on you to tell me so that I can deal with the matter.'

She fixed Hélène with an assessing eye and Hélène held her gaze. 'Of course, Maman,' she said, and then, at a nod from her mother, she took the envelope and carried it away to her own room.

As she watched her leave, Rosalie wondered if she had been too lenient. Would she, she thought, have been allowed to receive uninspected letters from Emile before they were formally betrothed? Almost certainly not but, she decided with a sigh, the modern young lady seemed to be allowed far more licence than had been accorded to her, and she had no wish to read her daughter's love letters, for love letters they were sure to be. She turned her attention to the rest of the post, while laying aside a letter addressed to Agathe Sauze.

Agathe had, indeed, been a great success. Rosalie found herself relying on her more and more. The running of the house had become much smoother and more efficient since the departure of Madame Choux. Annette was now being trained by Yvette to be Hélène's personal maid. Lizette had blossomed under Agathe's strict but fair tutelage and, less afraid of her own shadow, worked hard in her new capacity as housemaid.

Rosalie rang the bell and Agathe Sauze was soon knocking on the parlour door.

'You wanted me, madame?'

'I just wanted to go over the arrangements for tomorrow evening, our welcome dinner for young Monsieur and Madame Barrineau.' She said the names with a smile, as describing Clarice and Lucas in these terms still pleased her. Briefly Rosalie ran through the guest list: Clarice and Lucas, of course, and Lucas's parents and sister. Louise could not be left out of her sister's homecoming celebrations, but she and Lucie, much of an age, would be surely be glad of each other's company. After some thought she'd added Simon Barnier to the list to balance her table, and now she passed the seating plan to Agathe.

'Oh, and there's a letter for you in this morning's post, Madame Sauze.' She held out the envelope, which Agathe took and pushed into her pocket, wondering who might be writing to her here. Fleur? But at first glance the script on the envelope was not familiar.

Having been thus dismissed by Madame St Clair, Agathe retired to the kitchen, where Lizette was just making the staff's mid-morning coffee. As the gardener, the stable lad and Pierre came in from the outside, she picked up her own coffee and went into her little sitting room to drink it in peace as she opened her unexpected letter. It clearly wasn't from Fleur – it was not her handwriting, and anyway, over the last few weeks her brief letters had arrived less frequently. Agathe had been planning to travel to Paris on her next free day to see how her sister was, but somehow the time to spend a day away from Belair had never been right, and while she was new to the post Agathe had no intention of jeopardising her position.

She set her cup down and withdrew the letter from her pocket. The envelope gave no clue as to who had sent it. She slit it open and pulled out the single sheet of paper it contained. There was a name and address across the top – a firm of lawyers in Paris – written in black ink and a letter in the same ink.

Dear Madame Sauze

It is with regret we have to inform you of the sudden death of your sister Fleur Bastien on 23rd August. At her written request, in case of her death, we have contacted you as next of kin and have to tell you that you are the sole legatee named in her will, which was signed and witnessed in our offices on 1st August 1877.

We request that you visit us at our offices at the above address at your earliest convenience, to arrange the funeral and sign the various documents required.

I remain, madame, yours faithfully…

The signature was undecipherable, but below it the name R. J. Colet was printed.

Tears sprang to Agathe's eyes at the unexpected suddenness of Fleur's demise. Why hadn't she made the effort to go and see her? And now it was too late. Fleur was dead. Her sister was dead and Agathe hadn't even known that she was ill. Why hadn't Fleur told her? The letter gave no clue to the cause of death. Perhaps she hadn't been ill at all; perhaps there'd been an accident. Agathe felt stunned by a mixture of grief and regret. They had never been really close, but Fleur had taken her in when she'd had nowhere else to go. Now she was gone and Agathe hadn't even had the chance to say goodbye.

She continued to sit, silent, the letter clutched in her hand, while her coffee cooled unregarded beside her. She must go to the lawyer's office as soon as possible. She would have to ask Madame St Clair for several days' leave of absence to deal with all the necessary arrangements. When would she be able to go? Tomorrow was the family dinner for the returning married couple. Everything was in place for that. Madame St Clair had agreed the menu with Cook and Didier was in overall charge; surely they could manage without her.

Well, she decided, it was no use sitting wondering. She must explain the situation to her mistress and obtain the necessary time off to go to Paris. Reluctantly she got to her feet and went back to knock on Madame St Clair's parlour door.

Rosalie listened to her request and sighed. 'Of course, you must go,' she agreed. 'And the sooner the better. Where will you stay in Paris?'

'My sister lived in an apartment in Batignolles. I think I may be able to stay there.'

'Better you stay in the Avenue Ste Anne,' said Rosalie. 'I'm planning to go to Paris myself next week and you can advise Madame Vernier of my arrival. I shall take Hélène with me; she needs a change of scene. You must be back here before I go, as I will need to leave everything here in your capable hands.'

So it was agreed. Agathe was to leave the same afternoon and present herself at the lawyer's office first thing next day.

Unaware of anything else going on in the house, Hélène opened her letter from Rupert. It wasn't as long as she'd hoped, obviously written in some haste, but began with the decidedly welcome words:

My darling girl,

Warmth flooded through her and she went on to read,

How I miss you! After a tiresome journey I'm here at home and find the house full of understandable melancholy. My mother is distraught at Justin's death and my father, though stoical in the extreme, seems suddenly very much older. My sister Frances has coped wonderfully, but obviously she too is desperately sad. I'm doing what I can to support them all, but there has to be an inquest, now set for this coming Thursday, before we can have the funeral on Friday. These things make it even harder to deal with.

I think of you all the time, my darling, and wish you were here at my side, but since that can't be just now, believe me when I tell you how much I love and miss you. A letter from you would cheer me greatly, for I too am struggling to come to terms with Justin's death. I could not have wanted a better brother.

I will write again soon. Though from the look of things I shan't be able to return to you as soon as I would wish, I remain now and always, Your Rupert.

Hélène read the letter through several times, dwelling with pleasure on his endearments and promised love. The letter contained nothing to which her parents might take exception, and Hélène decided if Maman spoke of it again to offer her the chance to read it for herself. For, thought Hélène, once her mother had satisfied herself that Rupert's letters were entirely proper, she would not concern herself with them again, when perhaps their content might have altered.

It was later that she heard from Annette about Madame Sauze's unexpected departure for Paris.

'We stayed in her sister's apartment before we came here,' Annette explained. 'Aunt Agathe lived with her when Father Thomas threw her out, and she took me there when I left.'

'Do you think she'll leave us,' asked Hélène, 'and go back to live in Paris?'

'Doubt it,' replied Annette. 'She loves working here. It's the sort of job she's always dreamed of.'

'Didn't she like working for the priests?'

'Oh, she was happy enough when Father Lenoir was alive, but when he died everything changed,' answered Annette. 'With Father Thomas... well, I told you about Father Thomas. But I'm sure she doesn't want to go back to the city.'

Annette was right. When Agathe had left for Paris the previous day, she had had every intention of returning to Belair as soon as possible. She spent the night in the Avenue Ste Anne, where she had been welcomed by Madame Vernier, the housekeeper who, with the aid of a housemaid, looked after the house when the family were in the country. Agathe passed an anxious night, but the following morning she presented herself a little nervously at Monsieur Colet's office.

The lawyer rose to greet her with an outstretched hand, invited her to sit down and offered her coffee. She took a seat on the chair opposite his desk but declined the refreshment, surprised that it had been offered. She looked across at him expectantly. He was a dapper little man who looked surprisingly small behind his large desk. He was younger than Agathe had expected, too, no more than thirty-five, with a fine head of hair coming to a widow's peak on his forehead and beetling black brows from beneath which a pair of shrewd brown eyes assessed her. Agathe raised her chin a little and he smiled.

'It's a pleasure to meet you, madame,' he said, 'despite the sad circumstances that bring you here. May I offer you my condolences on the loss of your sister.'

'Thank you,' Agathe replied gravely. 'Please can you tell me what happened to her? Was she ill? I haven't seen her for some time and though we've had occasional contact by letter she never mentioned that she was ill, and I've no idea how she died.'

'She was indeed ill,' replied Monsieur Colet, 'but I don't think even she knew quite how bad she was. She must have had some idea, as she came to me so recently to remake her will.' He looked enquiringly at Agathe. 'Were you aware that she had done so?'

Agathe shook her head. 'No,' she answered, 'as I said we'd had little contact since I took up a position outside Paris.'

'Well, in her new will she left everything she had to you. That is, her apartment...'

'Her apartment?' echoed Agathe faintly.

'Certainly,' replied Monsieur Colet. 'And also the money she had in her bank account.'

'Bank account?' murmured Agathe. 'But she didn't hold with banks.'

'That may have been her stance, but she certainly had one with a reasonable balance.' He tilted his head a little as he went on, 'I believe her late husband was a man of some substance?'

'He was a butcher with his own business,' Agathe agreed, 'but...'

'There you are, then. She had money and as far as I can see

she used it shrewdly. She owned the other two apartments in the building, which she rented out, and the butcher's shop on the ground floor.'

'She owned all that?' Agathe stared at him, stupefied.

'Her husband acquired those some years before he died. When he was killed in a road accident, he died intestate and everything automatically came to your sister.' Monsieur Colet paused for a moment and then added, 'And now it all comes to you.'

Agathe was silenced by this explanation. She'd not even known for sure that Fleur actually owned the apartment in which she had lived, let alone any others.

'She never told me any of this,' she said at last. 'When Yves was killed I thought she was left with very little.'

'Apparently not,' said the lawyer with a smile. 'So, I must congratulate you, madame, you are now a woman of some substance. You will have no need to work, and could, if you wished, employ a servant of your own.'

The silence that followed these remarks lengthened until Monsieur Colet broke it by saying, 'The first thing that must be considered is the funeral. Afraid that we might not be able to contact you in time, I, as Madame Bastien's executor, have made arrangements for her funeral, which will take place tomorrow at the Church of the Holy Virgin in the Rue du Boiselles. As you will understand, such things cannot be delayed.'

'I see,' murmured Agathe.

She did understand that the funeral must take place sooner rather than later, but everything else? How on earth was she going to cope with everything else? She had no head for business, as Fleur had apparently had. How was she going to manage? She had no wish to come back to live in Paris, she was entirely settled where she was. Her confusion showed in her expression and Monsieur Colet saw it.

'If I or my firm can be of assistance to you,' he suggested, 'in any capacity, we would be happy to continue to act for you on the same terms as for Madame Bastien. But now is not the time to come to such decisions. There will be plenty of time to make those when the will is proved. However,' he went on, 'I'm sure you'll want the keys to the building and to your own apartment, so that you can come and go as you choose. I can see no problem with the will – it is a simple one – and very soon everything will be legally yours.' He opened a drawer in his desk and took out a set of keys. 'You have tenants in the other two apartments and there is no reason for them to move. Their rent will eventually be paid to you.'

Agathe left Monsieur Colet's office in a daze. She had been with him for less than an hour and in that time her whole world had been turned upside down. She would attend the funeral Mass tomorrow and thus make her farewells to her sister, the sister she now felt she'd hardly known. With her mind still in a blur, she made her way back to the Avenue Ste Anne; the apartment could wait until the following day.

After Fleur's funeral, attended only by herself and Monsieur Colet, Agathe paid a visit to the apartment. When she opened the door and stepped inside, the place had the musty smell of emptiness and neglect. As Agathe walked slowly through the rooms she was struck by how much smaller it seemed than she remembered. Pale sunlight, dust motes dancing in its brightness, shafted through the grubby windows, illuminating the general tiredness of the decor. Old-fashioned, uncomfortable furniture still crowded the rooms, and when she opened the wardrobe in Fleur's bedroom she found it full of her sister's clothes. She paused for a moment in the kitchen where she had cooked meals for the two of them, but there was no resonance of her time there and she knew that she would never return here to live. She would come back once more to clear the place out and then ask Monsieur Colet to arrange for it to be let. With a feeling of relief, she left the apartment and closed the front door behind her.

When she arrived at Belair, Agathe simply thanked Rosalie for allowing her the few days she'd been away and returned to work in the normal manner. To no one did she mention her sister's will or the change it could bring to her life. Monsieur Colet had said the process of proving the will would take a while, and Agathe was perfectly happy to relegate future changes to the back of her mind.

Chapter 30

Hélène's reply to Rupert's letter was carefully composed. It was not the letter she'd been writing in instalments before his arrived. Having read the depths of his family's sorrow at his brother's accident, her letter prattling generally about what had been going on at Belair since his departure seemed shallow and insensitive. Despite his protestations of love in his letter, Hélène felt that it would be somehow forward to pour out her heart to him. How easy it had been to tell him she loved him face to beloved face, but somehow putting the words down on paper seemed different.

The result of this dilemma was a slightly stilted missive, offering condolences for the loss of his brother and greetings to his family, after which she went on:

Of course I understand that your duty to your family is the most important thing just now but I do miss you, Rupert, and am longing for the day you come back to me.

In a few days' time Maman and I are going to our house in the Avenue Ste Anne in Paris. I'm not sure how long we shall stay, but you have the address and could write to me there.

She had been going to tell him about the dinner party that had been given to welcome Clarice and Lucas back from their honeymoon, but when she reread what she had written it seemed so trivial compared with the difficulties Rupert was facing at home that she discarded that page, simply saying the Clarice and Lucas were home again and her parents had given a dinner to welcome them back.

Hélène hadn't particularly enjoyed that evening. It was lovely to see Clarice and to hear about Venice and Florence and Rome, but that had been in the privacy of Clarice's old room, where she had laid her cloak and tidied her already beautifully coiffed hair before descending to the drawing room. Hélène had then told Clarice about Rupert's proposal and how she had, with Papa's qualified blessing, accepted him.

Clarice was surprised and mildly condescending. 'Doesn't Papa think you're a little young to be considering marriage? I'm twenty and it was only in the last few months that Lucas and I became engaged.'

'That's because Lucas wasn't here,' retorted Hélène. 'I bet you'd have accepted him if he'd proposed to you when *you* were seventeen!'

'Perhaps,' conceded Clarice, 'but there's a lot more to marriage than dancing with a handsome man.' She patted Hélène's hand and added, 'I'm sure Maman will explain what I mean when the time comes. Come on, we'd better go down.'

They found the others waiting for them in the drawing room. Almost immediately Didier announced dinner and Rosalie, offering her hand to Lucas, their guest of honour, led the way into the dining room. Hélène found she had been seated between Monsieur Barrineau and Simon. She knew both of them well and it should have been an easy dinner placement, but, somehow, she found she had very little to say to either of them. Monsieur Barrineau was jocular, speaking to her almost as a favourite uncle might. Simon, on the other hand, seemed rather stiff and formal and gave much of his attention to Lucie, sitting opposite to him. How Hélène wished Rupert were there to lighten the table with his easy flow of conversation.

It was Clarice who, unwittingly, disturbed the general equilibrium by saying in her clear voice, 'I hear that Hélène is to be married, Papa,' before turning to her husband and adding, 'and to that strange Englishman you invited to our wedding, Lucas.'

With only eight at the table, her words were clearly audible to all. Hélène felt hot colour flood her cheeks and she glared at Clarice for mentioning what she had told her in confidence. There were immediate expressions of amazement and Rosalie stepped in at once and, addressing herself to Clarice, said, 'Monsieur Chalfont has asked your father's permission to address Hélène and I believe there is some sort of understanding between them, but there is no formal betrothal and any thoughts of marriage are a long way off.' She smiled across at Hélène, hoping to soften her words. 'We shall consider the matter seriously when he returns.'

'But where is he?' asked Clarice. 'Why isn't he here?'

'Because his brother died,' snapped Hélène. 'He's gone home to his family. Where else would he be?'

'Where indeed?' murmured Simon. 'He has to claim his inheritance, after all.'

'What did you say?' demanded Hélène in unsuppressed rage. 'That doesn't matter to him!'

'Oh, I think you'll find it does,' replied Simon equably. 'Such things matter to everyone.'

'His inheritance?' Suzanne Barrineau queried and then, realising, went on, 'Of course, this means he's now his father's heir. A good catch for the daughter of a Paris architect.'

'Mother!' exclaimed Lucas.

'Suzanne, my dear,' her husband spoke repressively from the other end of the table, 'such things are hardly any business of ours.' And before she could reply he eloquently changed the subject, asking Rosalie if his gardener might take cuttings from some of her roses to graft to his own.

After a moment the talk became general again and Rosalie rang for the dinner plates to be removed and the cheeseboard to be brought. For a long moment it was all Hélène could do to remain seated in her place. She glowered at Clarice along the length of the table. How could she? How could she have broken such a confidence? But then, Hélène suddenly realised, she had not actually said that the matter was for family ears only; her sister had assumed that everyone must know of the understanding, even if it were not a formal betrothal. Clarice gave Hélène an apologetic smile and, sighing, Hélène smiled half-heartedly in return.

No further mention was made of Clarice's revelation, and when the ladies retired to the drawing room it wasn't long before the gentlemen joined them. The evening had not been spoiled by the interchange, but it had cast a shadow.

No, Hélène decided now as she recalled her own feelings of dismay, that was not something more to lay on Rupert's shoulders. Her final paragraph should be one to give him comfort.

I so wish I were with you to share in your grief. I send my love and shall count the days until you come back to Belair... to me. Your own Hélène.

★

In Pilgrim St Leonard, the inquest was little more than a formality. The succession of events that had led to Justin's untimely death were fairly clear; there was no question of foul play or suicide. The coroner, local solicitor Martin Flugue, heard the evidence given by Frances, Fortune and Scott. It was accepted that Justin had slipped on the rocks, banged his head and while unconscious face down in the water had drowned, and a verdict of death by misadventure was brought in.

The funeral was held the following day. Amabel Chalfont did not attend and nor did Lady Blake, but both Frances and Kitty, heavily veiled and dressed in unrelieved black, insisted on being at the church and the graveside, after which Kitty returned to Marwick House. Fran, however, played the part of her father's hostess and joined him in welcoming the few guests who chose to come back to Pilgrim's Oak. No one stayed long and it was with enormous relief that both Rupert and Fran heard the sound of wheels on gravel as the last carriage drove away and Mitchell closing the front door behind it.

It seemed to both of them that the house that had sheltered them all their lives settled round them as a silent shield. Sir Philip had retired to his library, where despite the warmth of the day a fire had been lit and a tray with brandy and glasses had been laid out. They did not join him, but went into the quiet of the drawing room and sat down together.

'Thank goodness that's over,' breathed Fran. 'I'm exhausted.'

Neither of them had partaken of the refreshments prepared for the guests.

'You should eat something,' Rupert said. 'I'll ring for Mitchell.'

'I'm not hungry,' said Fran wearily, 'really, Rupert.'

'A bowl of soup and some bread and cheese,' Rupert said firmly. 'We have to keep up our strength.' He reached for the bell and when Mitchell came in answer, he asked for the food.

'I saw you talking to Sir James,' Fran said as she leaned back in her chair and waited for their supper to appear. 'What did he want?'

'To tell me my business,' retorted Rupert, his eyes darkening at the memory of his conversation with Kitty's father. Before he returned to Marwick House, Sir James Blake had crossed the room to where Rupert had been speaking with Mr Flugue, thanking him for his thoughtful handling of the inquest the previous day.

'No point in dragging things out,' said the coroner. 'Difficult enough for all concerned.'

Sir James did not exactly interrupt, but standing beside Rupert in a proprietorial way he made it clear that he wanted a private word and the coroner took himself off.

'Sad day,' Sir James said, glancing round the room. 'Very sad. Poor Kitty would come to the church, though her mother and I argued against it. Very hard for her.'

Rupert gave a nod of agreement and said, 'And very brave.'

'Your father was finding it difficult... you could see.'

'That's hardly surprising, sir,' replied Rupert. 'It's been a dreadful shock to all of us.'

'Well,' went on Sir James. 'Sir Philip's still got you. He's not getting any younger and he'll be depending on your support, I dare say.'

While making these comments, Kitty's father had not made actual eye contact with Rupert, seeming, Rupert thought when he considered the conversation later, to have been addressing himself to the air between them. 'No more going off on your travels, eh?' And now Sir James did look directly at him. 'Duty before pleasure, I suppose. Yes, I expect you'll be taking over the running of the estate, like your brother was.'

Rupert could feel the anger rising in him and he replied tersely, 'That, of course, is a matter I shall be discussing with my father, sir, at an appropriate moment.'

'Quite so,' agreed Sir James with an approving nod. 'Well, I must be going. Please pass my compliments and condolences on to your mother.' And with that he half raised his hand, turned away and went out into the hall.

Another old family friend came up to bid him farewell, and Rupert managed to suppress the anger Sir James had aroused in him to shake the man's hand and thank him for coming to pay his respects.

Rupert knew that some of his anger was due to guilt. Now that there was no Justin between him and the title, he felt trapped. He had never wanted the title, or the trappings and duties that went with it. He had been completely happy in his own selfish way with no one to consider but himself. Now, all of a sudden, the title, with all that went with it, had been thrust upon him; there was no escape. The only bright light on his immediate horizon was Hélène; now he could offer her far more than before, and though he felt sure that the title would be of little importance to Hélène herself, he was certain it would be of great consequence to her parents, paving the way to their acceptance of a formal betrothal sooner rather than later.

Hélène was so precious to him he wished he could go to her straight away. He hoped she had got his letter and that he would soon have her reply.

Chapter 31

The day after the funeral Lord and Lady Devenish took their leave, and with their going the whole household at Pilgrim's Oak seemed to relax a little. Rupert and Fran privately discussed the situation as it now stood, and Fran pulled no punches.

'You've seen how our parents have aged,' she said as she and Rupert lingered at the breakfast table a few days later. 'Papa has become very frail. Not mentally, of course, but physically. He eats less than a sparrow and is exhausted most of the time. I fear for his life, Rupert. It isn't just Justin's death; he was going downhill before that. I'm sure there is an underlying illness.' She looked over at her brother and went on, 'Do you remember how our grandfather looked just before he died? All skin and bone?'

Rupert nodded. 'You think this is the same thing?'

'I don't know, not as bad maybe, but very like. Justin was taking the weight of the estate off his shoulders and now you've got to do the same thing.'

'Trouble is,' replied Rupert, 'I don't know anything about running the estate. It was never going to be my province.'

'Well, it is now,' asserted Fran. 'Justin was working with Foxton to see how the estate was run. He'd been going round to all the tenant farmers and reassessing the rents. You must do the same. You need to know how the place works to the advantage of all concerned. It's not something you can learn in a few weeks – you need to be here, living here, to get a proper feel for the place.'

'I see.' Rupert was surprised at this sudden onslaught. 'So what you're saying is that I must come home to live permanently and take control.'

'That's exactly what I'm saying,' said Fran. 'Papa and Mama need you here. Like it or not, you're going to be the head of this family, and if Papa's health is any guide, maybe sooner rather than later.' She paused and when Rupert made no comment, she continued, 'You can see that Mama has withdrawn into a world of her own. It's up to you now. You're going to have to pull this family through, and one of the best things you can do is to produce an heir before Papa dies.'

'Produce an heir?' echoed Rupert. 'Just like that? Probably have to get married first, wouldn't you say?'

'Exactly,' Fran said firmly. 'You must get married and get on with starting a family.'

'Nothing I'd like better, but I can't see Hélène's parents agreeing to anything that quickly.'

'Hélène?'

For a moment Frances looked puzzled and Rupert said, 'Remember? I told you about her when I came home. I have an understanding with the most beautiful French girl. I told you I was going to marry her.'

'Oh, yes,' replied Fran flatly. 'I do remember you saying something like that, but I didn't think it was serious. I mean that was all before… while you were away. I mean you're not actually engaged, are you?'

'Yes, we actually are. Well,' he amended, 'I've asked her to marry me and she said yes. She's only seventeen and so her parents have insisted that we wait until the spring before our betrothal becomes official, but as far as I am concerned, we're engaged to be married.'

'Oh, Rupert,' sighed Fran. 'What have you done?'

'What have I done? I've proposed marriage to the woman I wish to marry and she has accepted me. It happened before I left France.'

'Before you heard about Justin,' Fran said flatly.

'Well, no, not exactly.' Rupert felt the need to be scrupulously honest. 'It was when I knew I had to come home that I proposed, but her father had already given me permission to address her. There is nothing hole-in-the-corner about our engagement, but we both accepted his stipulation that there should be no formal betrothal until next spring.'

'So, you are not formally engaged,' stated Fran firmly. 'You can get out of it with no loss of honour.'

'If I tried to do any such thing,' Rupert said, 'it would be with great loss of honour. I have given my word. But, Fran, why should I want to?'

'You may not want to,' conceded Frances, 'but I think Papa will want to discuss this with you.'

She was quite right, and it was the very next morning that Sir Philip summoned Rupert to the library. He was already ensconced in his armchair and he waved Rupert to the one on the other side of the fireplace.

'Now then, my boy,' he said with something of his earlier manner, 'we've got some serious thinking to do. It's time to consider the future.'

'Indeed, sir,' said Rupert, readying himself to speak of Hélène, but his father completely took the wind out of his sails by continuing, 'You can see for yourself, Rupert, that I'm not very long for this world. I have the wasting sickness.'

'Papa—' exclaimed Rupert, but Sir Philip simply waved him to silence.

'Just like my own father. It must be obvious to anyone who knows me. I have been to see Dr Evans and he has confirmed that it's just a matter of time and there is nothing to be done.'

'But we must have a second opinion!' cried Rupert. 'You must see someone in London.'

'Indeed,' replied his father, 'and I have. Not long ago I went up to town for a few days, and while I was there, I took the opportunity of consulting Mr Ernest Young in Harley Street. He was of the same opinion as Dr Evans. The condition is fairly well advanced and there is no cure. Mr Young gave me about six months to live, but said that was only a guess based on previous cases he'd treated.'

'Have you told Mama?' asked Rupert quietly. 'Or Fran?'

'No, not yet. There is no point in alarming your mother at this stage. Since Justin's death I fear for her sanity; I won't put anything further on her. As for Frances, she's been a tower of strength to me over the past days, and I'm loath to ask any more of her.'

'I think she already knows, sir,' said Rupert. 'She has seen for herself.'

'Has she? Then I'm sorry. She's had too much to bear. I just thank God you're home at last and can take the weight from her shoulders... and mine.'

'Did Justin know?'

'He guessed and I admitted it to him just before he died. He began to deal with estate matters at once.'

'I shall try to do the same, sir,' Rupert said. 'I have an appointment with Foxton later this afternoon to discuss how things are on the estate. Fran told me that Justin had already been dealing with some of the estate business, and I need to be brought up to date with the state of things.'

'Justin was setting his hand to the plough,' agreed Sir Philip, 'and now it's up to you. At least there's nothing to keep you away from home these days, and while I'm still here we can make plans for the future together.'

Rupert looked across at his father, so suddenly small, but still with fire in his eyes. How could he tell him that there was something, or rather someone, to take him away from Pilgrim's Oak, at least in the short term? How could he tell him about his engagement to Hélène? And yet he must, because she was part of the future they were going to discuss.

'I shall be very grateful for your advice, sir,' he began. 'I know that Foxton is an experienced man, but you have been living here at Pilgrim's Oak all your life. There's no one with a greater knowledge of the place than you. However, there is one piece of news that I need to share with you, and I hope you will be pleased when you hear it...' Rupert paused, seeking the right words to tell his father about Hélène. In the end it seemed that simply to tell him would be the easiest way for them both.

'I am engaged to be married, sir.'

Sir Philip stared at him for a long moment and then asked, 'To whom?'

'To a young lady in France, Hélène St Clair. Her father is an architect in Paris.'

'And when did this engagement take place? Why were your mother and I not immediately informed of this?'

'With her father's permission I have been paying my addresses to her for the last month. She was the reason that I stayed on in France. When I heard about Justin and I was going to come home, I proposed to her and she accepted my proposal.'

'I see.' Sir Philip's tone was chilly. 'And what did her father say to this sudden proposal?'

'He said there must be nothing formal until the spring as Hélène is still quite young, not yet eighteen, but if we were still of the same mind in the spring, he would give his consent.'

'Did he now? Of course by this time they will have realised that Justin's death meant that you will one day have the title.'

'I doubt if that was a factor in his consent,' Rupert said.

'Do you? Then you're a bigger fool than I took you for.' His tone softened as he went on, 'Put her out of your mind, Rupert. The daughter of a French architect has no place in your future. You will be the tenth Baronet Chalfont, and your wife must be a lady of your own class, so that the bloodline of good English stock will continue in your children as it would have in Justin's.'

'I shan't desert her,' Rupert said quietly. 'Hélène is the love of my life and I would find no other love like her.'

'What has love to do with it?' Sir Philip demanded petulantly. 'People of our class don't marry simply for love; there are other considerations that are more important.'

'Not to me, sir.'

'Well, there should be,' retorted his father. 'Love comes later, when you grow together in marriage. Look at your mother and me.'

'But you love my mother,' asserted Rupert.

'Of course I do, but that wasn't why I married her. I liked her, certainly, and she was a suitable bride, but the love came later. The marriage was proposed by your grandparents. Everyone could see that it was a good match and we've been very happy together. If I'd married the first young woman I'd fallen in love with, it would have been a disaster. No, Rupert, you must put this young French girl out of your mind and settle down and start a family with an English girl of good family.'

For a long moment Rupert said nothing. He was still shocked by his father's revelation about his illness. He should have realised, and perhaps he would have if he'd seen his father before Justin died, but as he hadn't he had put down Sir Philip's frailty to the suddenness of Justin's death. He knew he should say nothing further about Hélène and their understanding – he must let his father get used to the idea. There was nothing wrong with marrying a French girl; she came of a respectable family with an independence of her own upon her marriage, and once his family met her, he was certain they would understand his love for her and learn to love her too.

'So,' Sir Philip took up his theme again, 'no more of this French girl. You must write to her and tell her that you will not be returning to France and it is with regret that you must release her from any understanding that was between you.'

'And break her heart.'

'My dear boy, if she's as young as you say – seventeen, was it? – she will soon recover from her broken heart and go on to lose it again to someone else.' He shifted in his chair as if to get more comfortable and said, 'You need someone like Kitty Blake.'

'Kitty?' Rupert couldn't hide his astonishment. 'But she was engaged to Justin and has only just lost him. She's hardly likely to be looking for another husband yet!'

'There were good reasons for her engagement to Justin,' said Sir Philip. 'It was an excellent match, with advantages to both families. Those advantages still remain, Rupert. Worth thinking about.'

Rupert could hardly believe his ears. He stared at his father in stupefaction, but Sir Philip had picked up his newspaper again, indicating that he considered the interview to be over. As Rupert got to his feet and moved to the door, he lowered the paper again and said, 'I trust you haven't spoken to your mother about this girl?'

'No, sir, I have not.'

'Glad to hear it,' grunted his father. 'Don't want her getting any silly romantic notions in her head. What about Frances?'

'She's of the same opinion as you,' Rupert replied.

'Good. She's a sensible girl. Got her head screwed on properly.'

Rupert went back to his own room, his mind in a turmoil. Was his father really suggesting that he should take his brother's place in everything, including the marriage bed? Justin was hardly in his grave and such a suggestion sickened him. What on earth would Kitty think if she knew she was being touted about as a prize to be seized? Then he remembered Sir James's comments at the funeral. Surely his thoughts weren't running parallel with Rupert's father's, were they? Was one of the 'duties' Sir James had mentioned to marry his daughter now that his brother was dead and it was he who had the title and the land?

His thoughts were interrupted by Mitchell knocking on his door and handing him a letter. 'Your post, Mr Rupert.'

Rupert almost snatched it from his hand and the moment the butler had closed the door he tore open the envelope.

Hélène's letter was the only bright spot that day. When Rupert had read it through several times, he was almost word perfect. He placed it in a drawer by his bed and, fortified by her words, went down to have lunch with his family.

No mention was made of the conversation between him and his father that morning, and as soon as the meal was over Rupert went out to meet the steward, Jack Foxton.

'Things need looking at, Mr Rupert,' Foxton said. 'I don't want to say nothing against Sir Philip, mind, but things have slid a bit, if you get my drift. I explained it all to Mr Justin and he realised that we needed to take stock of exactly how things were. Reckon you'll be taking over from Sir Philip, now, sir. Him being not well.'

Rupert felt a stab of guilt at this comment. How had everyone noticed the decline in his father's health when he had not? Because he'd stayed away too long; because he'd assumed it was due to Justin's death. Why hadn't Justin told him? Or Fran? Then he thought back to the letters he had received from them while he was in St Etienne and he remembered Fran had mentioned something about Papa not being well. He found her letter again now and reread it. Yes, there it was;

Papa has not been well lately and Mama is relying on me more and more about household matters. They're suddenly older, Rupert. Don't leave it too long before you come home again.

Fran had mentioned that her father was not well and suggested that he come home, but there had seemed no urgency in this. He read the letter again. He should have understood that she was worried. He should have come home, if only for a visit, and seen for himself, but he hadn't wanted to. He hadn't wanted to leave Hélène, leave her to the likes of Simon Barnier. He had put his own wishes before those of his family. He'd thought there was plenty of time, that he and Hélène had their whole lives before them, and now everything had changed. Now he was needed at Pilgrim's Oak.

That evening he sat down and wrote back to Hélène. She was probably already in Paris and so as she had suggested he would send the letter there. He was pleased that she and her mother were going there – it removed Hélène from St Etienne and from Simon Barnier.

My darling girl...

Chapter 32

Hélène and Annette accompanied Rosalie to Paris the following day. They were both pleased to be going, Hélène because she was missing Rupert too much at Belair and Annette because she wanted Hélène safely away from Simon Barnier. They travelled up by train, but Emile had sent Pierre with them so that he could drive them in the light chaise that they kept in town, and the first few days were spent shopping and visiting friends.

Pierre was delighted to be able to spend time back in his loft above the stables. Over the ten years he had worked for the St Clairs it had become entirely his place, and he felt far more at home there than in a similar loft above the stables at Belair. It was there that the street urchin, Jeannot, would visit him whenever he heard that Pierre was back in the city. Pierre never knew how Jeannot learned of his arrival so quickly, but he clearly had his sources, as Pierre could be sure of seeing his grinning face looking round the stable door within a day or two of his arrival.

Jeannot had prospered after the Communard siege. Having removed fifteen francs from Emile's desk when the house had been left empty for a while, he'd used his new-found capital to start his own business. He employed street boys like his former self and had a booming trade in pickpocketed goods and, even more lucrative, information. Jeannot was now a main man, respected in the Paris underworld, a man to be reckoned with.

Together, two children alone, he and Hélène had survived the siege and the bloody civil war that ended it. With the arrival of peace, their lives had taken very different paths and though he seldom had the opportunity to see Hélène, Jeannot continued to feel protective of her. It was for this reason that one of his scouts kept an eye on the house in the Avenue Ste Anne, how Jeannot always knew when the family was in residence. The last time he had seen Hélène was at her sister's wedding. He had travelled down to St Etienne and joined those lining the street to watch the bride and groom ride home after the ceremony, and in the second carriage he had seen her, Hélène, dressed in pale yellow with flowers in her hair, her sister's bridesmaid. He had risked a visit to Pierre in the Belair stables the next day, but had caught no glimpse of her.

Pierre had always had a soft spot for the boy and was not surprised when Jeannot put his head round the door the day after they'd arrived in Paris this time.

'Well, Jeannot,' he said. 'Thought we might see you.' The two men sat together on the bales of straw, sharing a beer and chatting as comfortably as they always had.

'Who's here?' Jeannot asked casually.

'Madame St Clair, with Miss Hélène and her maid, Annette.'

'She has her own maid now, does she?' Jeannot said, raising his eyebrows.

'I thought it was you!' The voice from the doorway broke in on their conversation and the two men turned to see Hélène standing on the threshold. Both stood up as she walked into the stable to join them, saying, 'I saw you from my bedroom window, Jeannot, creeping into the yard.'

'I didn't creep, Hélène, I walked in like a Christian.'

'Miss Hélène,' murmured Pierre, 'you shouldn't be in here with us.'

'Why not?' Hélène shot back. 'I always was before.'

'And remember the trouble it got you into? Madame would not be pleased.'

'My mother is out,' replied Hélène. 'She took a fiacre to visit her dressmaker.'

'It still isn't proper for you to be out here,' Pierre maintained, 'without even your maid.'

'Oh, if that's the problem,' Hélène said cheerfully, 'I'll call Annette, shall I?'

Jeannot looked at her and realised she'd changed. Last time they had sat together in this stable had been just before Clarice's wedding. Hélène had been a young girl, full of excitement about the wedding, telling Jeannot of all the important people who would be attending, the latter information interesting him very much. Now, however, she was different. That girl was gone and in her place was a young woman, an adult, relaxed and confident.

At that moment Annette appeared at the door. 'Miss Hélène,' she said breathlessly, 'your mother has returned, she's paying off the fiacre.'

'Then I suppose I'd better go indoors,' replied Hélène, 'but I shan't need you for a while, Annette.' She gave Pierre a grin and disappeared, leaving the other three staring after her.

'She's changed,' Jeannot said.

'She's in love,' replied Annette as she sat down beside Pierre on his straw bale.

'In love?' laughed Jeannot. 'Is that all?'

'With an Englishman.'

'An Englishman!' Jeannot was horrified. 'What's wrong with someone French?'

'He's a good man,' Annette said. 'He'll look after her.'

'What about you two, then?' asked Jeannot with a grin as he saw Pierre with his arm round Annette's waist. 'You look pretty close an' all.'

'None of your business!' retorted Pierre, though he grinned back as he said it.

'The coachman and the lady's maid,' Jeannot said. 'Sounds like a bar room song to me!'

'Does it?' growled Pierre. 'Well, you can keep such thoughts to yourself, my lad!'

'All right, all right, keep your hair on. I'm going anyway.' He stood up and turned to Annette. 'Nice to meet you, miss. Hope you know what you're taking on.' He nodded in Pierre's direction. 'Bit of a reprobate this one, yer know!'

'Who on earth is he?' demanded Annette when he'd gone, and she settled herself more comfortably against Pierre.

'He's a lad who used to work for the St Clairs,' answered Pierre. 'Then he and Hélène got trapped in the city during the siege. As you see they both survived, but it made them close despite their different backgrounds. The St Clairs were grateful he'd helped her, but they didn't want to continue the association, so Hélène sometimes sneaks out here to see him.'

'And you let her?'

'I can't stop her. There was no real harm in it,' insisted Pierre. 'I don't encourage them, but I don't give them away either.' He tightened his arm round Annette and added, 'I can tell you one thing, though, she has nothing to fear from Jeannot. He wouldn't harm a hair of her head.'

Annette heard voices out in the yard and wriggled free of

his arm. 'I must go in,' she muttered. 'That Madame Vernier will be after me.' And with that she was gone, leaving Pierre wishing he'd kissed her. He hadn't yet, but found himself increasingly longing to do so. His instinct was to hold back, to take things slowly. She had lost a husband, she'd lost a baby, but the more he saw of her, the better he got to know her, the more he wanted her; he had never wanted anyone more.

When Hélène got back inside, she found her mother standing in the hallway, looking at the post that lay on the table.

Rosalie looked up and smiled. 'One for you, chérie,' she said and passed Hélène the envelope.

Hélène took the letter and hurried up to the privacy of her room to open it.

My darling girl,

Hélène smiled. She loved the way he called her his darling girl.

In the first part of the letter he told her about the funeral and the difficult days that followed, preparing her, she thought as she read the rest of the letter, for the disappointing news it also contained.

I shall be needed here for some while yet, my darling. There is much to do, as my father is not well and I have to take over the running of the estate. Justin had already begun to take my father's place and now I must do the same. As I feared, it does mean that I shan't be able to come back to St Etienne for a while yet, but I know you'll understand why. Darling Hélène, remember how much I love you, how I long to hold you in my arms. You are my beloved and one day I shall bring you here as my bride;

in the meantime I shall live for your letters. Believe me,
I'm forever yours, Rupert.

Well, she thought with a sigh, I am disappointed. I really
hoped he might be back soon, even if only for a short visit,
but I suppose I do understand that his family must come first
for the time being.

She read the letter again, several times, hearing his voice,
cherishing his endearments, before she slipped it back in its
envelope and put it into the cherrywood box she had bought
especially as a repository for his letters. Two rested now
beneath its smooth polished lid, and she turned the key to
keep them safe.

I shall live for your letters, Rupert had said, and so after
dinner that evening, Hélène sat down to write to him again.

What made Fran do it she wasn't sure. It was simply an
impulse and she followed it. The postbag from the village
lay on the hall table. Mitchell had not yet sorted its contents
and Fran, expecting there to be more letters of condolence
to be answered, flipped it open and pulled out the letters it
contained. There she saw it, a letter addressed to Rupert in
flowery foreign script. It had a French stamp and a name on
the back of the envelope. *Hélène St Clair.*

Fran glanced round, but there was no one to see her.
Hurriedly she stuffed the letter into the pocket of her skirt
and, pushing the rest of the post back into the bag, left it as
she had found it, lying on the hall table. With another guilty
glance over her shoulder, she hurried upstairs to her bedroom
and closed the door behind her. She flopped onto the bed,
almost unable to believe what she had done. She had stolen

Rupert's letter. She took it out of her pocket and looked at it. The envelope beckoned, as if urging her to tear it open, but with sudden resolution she resisted the temptation. She had the letter in her possession, but she wasn't quite sure what she was going to do with it. Perhaps, after some thought, she could replace it in the postbag another day. No one would know when it had actually arrived, so if she decided to do that there was nothing to stop her and no one would suspect. In the meantime, she certainly wasn't going to open it. It was clearly from the girl in France and Fran had no desire to know what she'd written to Rupert. It was one thing to divert the mail for a couple of days and quite another to read her brother's private correspondence.

At that moment there was a tap on the door. Fran looked round for somewhere to hide the incriminating letter and hastily stuffed it down the side of the armchair that stood in the corner of the room before calling, 'Come in.'

'Excuse me, Miss Frances.' The parlourmaid put her head round the door.

'Yes, Hilton? What is it?'

'Beg pardon, miss,' Hilton said, 'but Lady Chalfont says will you come to her in her parlour.'

'Yes, of course,' Fran replied. 'Please tell Lady Chalfont I'll be there in just one moment.'

'Yes, miss.' Hilton disappeared, closing the door quietly behind her.

Fran hastily retrieved the letter from the chair and looked round for somewhere better to hide it. She decided on the back of her dressing table drawer, and pulling it right out, she carefully secreted the letter behind it. It wasn't the perfect hiding place, but unless someone was actually looking for something, it was unlikely to be discovered by accident.

And it isn't as if it'll be there for long, Fran thought as she went along the landing to the parlour, where her mother was waiting for her. She would probably put it back in the postbag tomorrow.

She did not. When the post came the next day, Mitchell received it from the postman and, immediately sorting the letters, took them round to their various recipients. There were two more letters of condolence from people who had only just heard about Justin's accident, and it was Fran who replied to those. Rupert had been spending most days with Foxton, visiting the tenant farmers, and said that he could not be responsible for answering the letters as well.

The days went quickly and September passed in a blaze of colour. The trees were dressed in flaming orange, reds and gold, made brilliant by the September sun. In the evenings there was an autumnal smell in the air as wood fires were lit and stoked to fight the night-time chill. Rupert was tired at the end of each day and found himself happy enough to settle by the fire after an early supper and chat with his sister. His only disappointment was the lack of letters from Hélène. At first he explained this to himself quite rationally. Hélène and her mother were in Paris and perhaps his letter had gone astray. Perhaps he had not put the correct address on the envelope. Perhaps there had been a change of plan and they had not gone to Paris at all; they were still at Belair and his letter was waiting for her in the Avenue Ste Anne. He made no mention of the expected letters to his family. They had, for the time being, stopped talking about his future, leaving the thoughts they had implanted in his mind time to take root and put up shoots. He asked Mitchell if there had been any post for him, and the butler shook his head.

'I'm sorry, Mr Rupert,' he said a little stiffly, 'but if there had been I'd have given it to you, sir.'

Rupert sighed. 'Yes, I'm sorry, of course you would.'

The day that Kitty and Justin were to have married came and went. Everyone remembered it, but no one mentioned it except for Amabel. She still took most of her meals in her room, but on this occasion she had come down for luncheon.

There had been little talk during the meal when she sudden announced, 'Today is Justin's wedding day. Poor Kitty.'

Poor Kitty indeed. Rupert had been over to Marwick House to see her a couple of times. Neither time had she seen him alone, but knowing what his own father was suggesting and what Sir James had hinted at the funeral, he was disappointed that they had no opportunity for private conversation. He wanted to know if the outrageous suggestion that he should now marry Kitty in his brother's place had actually been made to her.

'It would have been a lovely wedding,' Amabel went on, entirely unaware of the effect her words were having on the rest of the family. 'Poor dear Justin. Everything was arranged. And they'd have had babies, wouldn't they?' Her voice broke on a sob.

'Now then, Mama,' Fran said quietly, taking her hand. 'You mustn't distress yourself so. We all miss Justin, but we have to look forward now. Rupert's here to look after Pilgrim's Oak.'

'Then he must have babies,' whimpered her mother.

Nothing more was said at the table. Frances took her mother back up to her parlour and settled her down for an afternoon nap, but her words could not be unsaid and now stood between Rupert and his family. Rupert knew that it was his duty to step into Justin's place as his father's heir, and he knew he would stay, but if they wanted a new generation, they must accept his marriage to Hélène.

That night, despite having heard nothing from Hélène since her first letter, Rupert retired upstairs and wrote to her again. He poured out his heart to her, telling her how much he missed her and asking her to write to him very soon.

I miss you every minute of every day, he wrote. *Write to me soon, my darling girl, and tell me news of your family and Belair.*

This time he addressed the letter to her at Belair, for surely they must have returned from Paris by now. He thought of her, back in the social circle in St Etienne, and the fear began to grow that she had become so involved in the social life there that she had started to forget him. Perhaps Simon Barnier had begun to court her. The thought made him go cold but he dismissed it at once. Hélène didn't even like Simon Barnier.

Remember how much I love you, darling girl, and send me a letter bringing me your love.

Your Rupert

This he added as a postscript to his letter before sealing it into its envelope.

In the morning he put it in the postbag to go to the post office. Today it would be on its way to St Etienne, and surely Hélène would reply. With a lighter heart he went out to the stable.

From the shelter of the half-open dining room door, Fran watched him leave the house. She stole across the hall and silently slipped her hand into the postbag. There were three letters waiting to go, and glancing at them, she removed the one addressed to the girl in France.

Even as she went quickly upstairs with the letter in her pocket, she felt sick at what she was doing, but it was too late to go back on everything now. She already had two letters from France hidden in her dressing table. How long before Rupert came to accept that the girl wasn't going to write to him, that the romance had meant nothing more to her than a mild flirtation? In many ways Fran wished she had never started the deception, but it was too late to repine. After all, she was doing all this with the best of intentions; she was doing it for her family. Rupert might never forgive her if he ever found out, so she must ensure that he never did, but it was Rupert's duty to marry Kitty and all she was doing was helping him to make the right decision. She had never opened the letters; they were still private. He could never accuse her of prying, she wouldn't dream of reading anyone else's letters... and thus she tried to salve her conscience. She was doing the right thing.

Chapter 33

Rosalie stayed in Paris for a week before returning to Belair. To begin with Hélène was buoyed up with the thought of Rupert's letters, but as the days passed and nothing was heard from him, she began to worry. Without letting her mother know, she had written to him again, getting Annette to post the letter in the village rather than putting it in the household postbag. She had no reason to think that it would not have been posted that way; it was simply that she had disobeyed her mother in not waiting for another letter from Rupert before writing again. She realised that he must be extremely busy with everything he needed to do at Pilgrim's Oak, with perhaps no time to write, and she hoped that another letter from her would cheer him, but as the days turned into weeks and she heard nothing further, she began to believe that he had changed his mind and forgotten her; her heart ached and her spirits sank lower.

Rosalie saw the change in her. She had, of course, noticed that there had been no letters from England after the one which had arrived in Paris. She wondered if another had been directed to the Avenue Ste Anne and was simply waiting to be picked up. She wrote a brief note to Georges and asked him to go to the house next time he was in Paris and see what post, if any, was there. Within three days she had a reply from him, saying there was nothing.

Were you expecting something important, Maman? he wrote. *I shall be in Paris again very soon and can go to the house again to see.*

Rosalie replied that there was nothing and not to bother. If Rupert hadn't written to either place by now, it was clear to Rosalie that he wasn't going to. He had left Belair and Hélène behind, gone home to claim his inheritance, and he wasn't coming back. She saw her daughter's misery, but there was little she could do to alleviate it.

Since the dinner party revelation, word of her understanding with Rupert had become generally known and those in their social circle had accepted the fact that Hélène was spoken for. Rosalie wished with all her heart that Clarice had not spoken out as she had that night. If the understanding had been kept within the family, Rupert's desertion would have passed almost unremarked. She had noticed that Simon Barnier, a frequent caller at Belair for some time, visited less often. Rosalie thought that this was most unfortunate; Simon would have been an eminently suitable match for Hélène had there been no Rupert Chalfont. He had returned from a sojourn abroad a year ago and had quickly made his way to the top of the list of eligible bachelors. Several young ladies had had hopes of him, but so far none had captured his heart. Rosalie had seen how he had looked at Hélène recently and wished she could see a reciprocal spark of interest in her daughter's eyes, but she knew that at present Hélène only had thoughts of Rupert.

Well, Rosalie thought bitterly, he doesn't seem to have any thoughts of her.

'I don't understand it,' she confided to Emile. 'I thought he was a man of honour... and that he really loved her.'

Emile shrugged. 'He's probably found a better prospect at home,' he said. 'He'll be able to take his pick now that he'll inherit a title.'

'I thought Hélène *was* his pick,' muttered Rosalie.

'Well, Hélène's young. If he has changed his mind, she'll soon get over him.'

Rosalie wasn't so sure, but she made a point of taking Hélène with her wherever she was invited. The girl was not wearing an engagement ring, there had been only an informal understanding; it was important that people realised Hélène was under no obligation to the Englishman who had disappeared home.

'Why doesn't he write?' Hélène cried to Annette in the privacy of her bedchamber. 'What's happened to him?'

'I don't know, Hélène,' Annette replied. 'You could write again, I suppose.' They had grown closer since Annette had become Hélène's personal maid, and when alone together, they spoke as equals.

'No.' Hélène was adamant. 'If he doesn't want me after all, I'll not chase him.' She stuck by this resolve and whenever she went into company her pride kept her smiling. She was not the life and soul of the party, but neither was she seen to droop.

On one occasion when Annette was in the village running an errand for Rosalie, she was cornered by Simon Barnier.

'You were going to keep me informed about the Englishman,' he said, 'but I've heard nothing from you.'

Annette bobbed a curtsy. 'There's nothing to tell, sir,' she replied. 'He's gone back to England.'

'I know that, stupid girl,' he snapped, 'but what news from there?'

'I don't know, sir. Miss Hélène doesn't talk to me about him, so I can't tell you nothing.'

'Hmm. Well, if you hear anything, make sure you do!' And with that he strode off across the square, unaware that she stared after him with visible dislike.

Back at Belair, Annette didn't tell Hélène that Simon Barnier had been asking questions – there was no need to worry her any more than she was already. However, as soon as she got the chance, she spoke to Pierre.

'What should we do?' she asked. 'Monsieur Chalfont asked us to look after Hélène and keep her away from Monsieur Barnier. Should we write to him – Monsieur Chalfont, I mean?'

Pierre gave the idea serious consideration before he said, 'One letter, perhaps. But if there's no reply to that, well, we've done what we promised.'

'You'll have to write,' Annette told him. 'It would be better coming from you. What will you say?'

Pierre sighed. 'I don't really know. Just that Hélène's pining for him and he must come back?'

They decided that was enough and that evening Pierre wrote a brief note and sent it to the address Rupert had given him.

'Now all we can do is wait,' he said. And wait they did until the letter came.

At Pilgrim's Oak, Rupert was also waiting. There had been no word from France for the past month. He had given up looking expectantly at Mitchell when he came in with the post. He had written once again, but when that letter produced no response, he finally accepted that Hélène had changed her mind and had written no more. He briefly considered going over to France to see her. He even mentioned the idea to Fran.

'If I could just see her,' he said, 'perhaps I'd understand.'

Fran had a vision of the letters in her drawer and knew an appalling guilt, but she said, 'I don't think that would answer, Rupert. It would reopen wounds for both of you. If she's changed her mind and stopped writing, she must feel that a clean break, without long explanations about why, would be the easiest thing for both of you.'

'But if I could just see her...'

'What good would it do?' Fran asked. 'You'd just be hurt all over again.' She thought of the last letter that had arrived. It was not addressed in the same hand as the others, but Fran was not prepared to risk Rupert receiving it, even if it wasn't from his Hélène girl, and she had squirrelled it away with the rest.

No further mention was made of 'the French girl', but one windy afternoon in late October, Rupert was summoned to the library.

'It's time you sorted yourself out,' said his father. 'I want to see you settled before I die. I want to see you married.'

'I told you I was engaged, sir,' began Rupert.

'To the daughter of some French architect—'

'He's a professional man,' interrupted Rupert, 'and perfectly respectable.'

'To a foreigner and a Catholic,' continued Sir Philip, as if Rupert had not spoken. 'Neither of which is suitable or acceptable for a Chalfont of Pilgrim's Oak.'

'I really think, sir—' Rupert tried again.

'That's the trouble, Rupert! You don't think at all. Our land marches with Sir James Blake's. Neither estate is large enough to survive much longer alone, but combined... now that's a different thing altogether.' He looked at Rupert with steel in his eyes. 'Only you can save the place now, you know.'

Rupert did know. He'd been working with Foxton for

nearly two months now and had seen that much of the estate was no longer viable as it stood.

'We have to modernise, Mr Rupert,' Foxton had urged. 'If we don't do that, we'll end up selling off land simply to survive. You can't just raise the rents, because your tenants won't be able to afford them, not without help to bring the farms up to date, and to do that you need an injection of capital.'

Rupert knew Foxton was right, and it had been made clear to him that such capital might come from Sir James if he thought it advantageous to his family, to Kitty and her children.

'You can't marry this French girl, Rupert,' insisted Sir Philip. 'It won't do. You have to break any agreement you had with her... and do it straight away.'

'It's not as simple as that, sir,' Rupert said.

'Yes, my boy, it is. Once done, you propose marriage to Katharine and all will be well.'

'She might turn me down,' said Rupert.

'I very much doubt that,' replied his father.

'She loved Justin,' Rupert pointed out.

'And she'll come to love you,' came the sharp reply. 'For goodness' sake, man, look at the bigger picture. The continuance of our family, our name, our land...'

'That wouldn't change either way...'

'You have a duty to your heritage. Against which you're setting an unsuitable marriage to a chit of a girl from France, and a Catholic at that.'

Rupert got to his feet. 'Thank you, sir,' he said, his voice tight with emotion. 'You've made yourself perfectly clear. I will consider what you've said. And now if you'll excuse me...' He let his words hang in the air, unable to finish, and left the room, closing the door softly behind him... a closing that demonstrated his feelings far better than a slam.

Rupert knew that the time had come for him to make a choice. Hélène, who appeared to have cut him off, or his family, who made it very clear where they believed his duty lay. He thought of Kitty and wondered what her reaction would be if he went to her and suggested that they should get married, and married with Justin only two months in his grave. He could explain that the questionable haste was due to his father's illness, but wouldn't Kitty think it unseemly to accept him so soon after Justin's death?

There was, he decided, only one way to find out and unknowingly following Justin, he made his way out to the stables, where Jack saddled Rufus, and without a word of where he was going, he rode to Marwick House.

This time Kitty was alone when she received him. She offered him refreshment, but he turned it down. Having got here and able to speak to her privately, he wanted to get their conversation over before they were interrupted by her parents or one of the servants.

'Kitty,' he began, 'we need to talk.'

She watched him pacing the floor and said, 'Do we, Rupert? If that's the case, do stop pacing about and sit down, you're making me giddy.'

Rupert did as she asked, perching for a moment on a chair by the fire, before getting to his feet again and walking the floor once more.

'It's difficult,' he began.

'Is it? Well, I shan't know what you're talking about unless you tell me, so do come straight to the point. I always think that's best when you have something unpleasant to say.'

'It's not unpleasant, it's just difficult.'

'For goodness' sake, Rupert, tell me.'

'Right.' And Rupert took the plunge. 'My family think it would be beneficial all round if you and I got married.'

'I see,' Kitty responded coolly. 'But you don't want to.'

'It's not that exactly…'

'Then what is it… exactly?'

'I wanted to know what you thought of the idea,' Rupert said, then continued without giving her time to answer. 'I mean, it's far too soon for you to be thinking again of marriage. You loved Justin and you can't simply take me instead, like replacing a pair of lost shoes.'

'So why are we talking about it?' asked Kitty quietly.

'My father is dying,' Rupert told her. 'He has the wasting sickness, like my grandfather. He knows he hasn't long to live.'

'I'm so sorry,' murmured Kitty.

'He is anxious to see me settled at Pilgrim's Oak.'

'Well, you are, are you not?'

'Of course. It's my duty to stay.'

'And you feel it's your duty to marry me?' Kitty gave him a quizzical look.

'It's something we both wanted once,' he replied quietly.

'And now you don't, because of Justin's death.'

'Something like that, I suppose.'

'I do understand, Rupert,' Kitty said. 'If Justin hadn't died there would be no question of our being married. But we can't bring him back, much as we'd like to, so we have to look to the future. If we agree that we should marry at some time in the future and it is only the speed with which we are contemplating it that concerns you, well, that is nobody's business but our own. Wishing to be married before your father dies puts a completely different complexion on the whole thing; it can give offence to no one.'

'But what about you, Kitty? It may not be something you want, ever.'

'I want to be married,' she answered. 'I want to have children. With you I could do both. Of course it would be more seemly to wait, but in the circumstances, it would be unkind to your father to do so.'

'Your parents may not agree,' Rupert warned. 'Your mother will surely worry about the proprieties.'

'She may,' agreed Kitty, 'but my father will not. He has always been keen for an alliance between our families.'

'He's a practical man and thinks of the estate,' remarked Rupert, remembering his conversation with Sir James at the funeral.

'He does, but he also wants to see me comfortably established. If we did decide to marry, he would be happy for both reasons.' She smiled at him and added, 'But it must be your decision, Rupert. You will have to propose our marriage. It won't come from me.'

Rupert rode home with his mind in turmoil. There was no doubt that news of his visit to Kitty would soon come to Sir James's ears – the servants would see to that – and Sir James would put two and two together and be expecting a visit from him. Speaking with Kitty he had almost proposed to her there and then, firmly dismissing any further thoughts of Hélène, but he held back, as one tiny corner of his mind warned, 'Suppose you get home and find a letter waiting – it will be too late.'

There was no letter. The following day he rode back to Marwick House to ask Sir James's permission to marry his daughter.

They were wed three weeks later in a quiet ceremony at the village church and together moved into the Dower House, as Kitty and Justin had planned.

No one mentioned Hélène St Clair, and if Kitty suspected there might have been someone else, she asked no questions. She had accepted Justin as second best and hoped he wouldn't realise it, and she didn't want to know if Rupert had accepted her in the same way. With a heavy heart, Rupert wrote one last time to Hélène, telling her of his marriage; and to save any awkward questions from Kitty, he walked to the village and posted the letter himself.

Chapter 34

The letter arrived at Belair on a cold morning in early December. The world beyond the windows was white with overnight frost, unmelted by the pale winter sun. Hélène was sitting in the morning room by the fire reading when Didier brought in the post. He had seen that there was a letter from England, and knowing how long Hélène had been waiting for one, he brought it straight to her. When she saw the handwriting, the blood drained from her face. Rupert!

Didier saw her change of countenance and ventured to ask, 'Are you quite well, Miss Hélène?'

'Yes, of course, Didier,' snapped Hélène. Then, realising how rude she had sounded, she said, 'I'm sorry, Didier, but I'm quite all right.' She thanked him for bringing her post, and as soon as he had withdrawn, she hurried up to her room where she could lock her door and be undisturbed.

Didier was unconvinced, and knowing that Madame St Clair was out, he went in search of Annette, who was in the kitchen with Agathe Sauze.

'A letter has come for Miss Hélène,' he told them. 'From England. She went quite pale and I think she almost fainted. Madame is out, but I think someone should go to her in case it's bad news.'

Annette was on her feet at once. 'I'll go. Where is she?'

'In the morning room,' replied Didier.

Annette hurried to the morning room but when she found it empty, she ran upstairs to Hélène's bedroom and tapped on the door. No reply came from within and she knocked again before trying the handle, only to find the door was locked. She called Hélène's name but received no reply.

Hélène heard her knock, but she was beyond answering. She had just opened and read her letter and her world had crashed about her ears. She couldn't speak. Tears streamed down her cheeks as she understood what he had written. No *my darling girl*, the opening words she loved so much – it simply began,

Dear Hélène,

The letter was short, but its content felt like a hammer blow, and she sank down onto her bed, overcome with a physical pain in her chest.

When you stopped answering my letters, I realised that you must have changed your mind about our engagement. Obviously you thought a clean break was for the best and so, though I don't understand what made your wishes change, I respected your decision and ceased writing to you.

This is the last letter you will have from me but I felt the necessity of letting you know that, at the behest of my family, I am now married to a young lady whose family land is neighbour to our own. As I have known her since childhood, it seemed a sensible way forward and both families are pleased with this union.

The time I spent with you at Belair will always be precious to me, but I can see now that it would have been difficult for you to uproot yourself and move to another country where you knew no one and didn't speak the language, and I understand your change of heart.

I wish you every happiness, Hélène. Think kindly of me, as I do of you.

Yours, Rupert Chalfont

Hélène cried until she had no more tears and lay, exhausted, on her bed. The door was still locked, and hearing nothing from inside, Annette was terrified that Hélène might have harmed herself. What on earth could have been in that letter to provoke such a reaction? She hurried down to the kitchen to consult with Madame Sauze as to what they should do. They both went back upstairs, but no amount of knocking elicited a response.

'Should we break open the door?' Annette cried. 'What can she be doing in there?'

The decision was taken for them by the arrival home of Madame St Clair. Immediately she heard what had happened she rushed up the stairs and banged on Hélène's door. When there was no response, she sent Annette to fetch Pierre from the stables. 'And tell him to bring a crowbar,' she called after her.

Within minutes Pierre appeared, crowbar in hand. 'Get the door open somehow, Pierre,' Rosalie instructed.

'It'll damage the door, madame,' he said.

'Just do it!' snapped Rosalie and she watched as Pierre set to work, attacking the door about its lock.

Moments later, with a loud cracking of wood, the door flew open and Rosalie rushed into the room, closely followed by Annette. Hélène lay, a still form on the bed, the crumpled letter beside her. Annette went immediately to the bedside and gave a cry of relief when she saw that with the sudden invasion of her room, Hélène had opened her eyes and was staring unfocused at the crowd. She was pale and tear-stained, but she was struggling to sit up.

'Hélène!' Annette cried. 'Thank God you're all right.'

Rosalie picked up the letter and read it quickly. It explained everything. No wonder Hélène had been in despair. Not only had Rupert married someone else, he had done so without warning Hélène that he considered their engagement over. It was done and there'd be no going back. The mention of no letters was clearly an excuse to get him off the hook of an unwanted betrothal. Rosalie seethed with anger. And she had thought him an honourable man!

Seeing her daughter's confusion, Rosalie shooed them all from the room before returning to the bedside to take Hélène's hands in hers. She looked down at the tear-streaked face, the eyes swollen with crying, and, gathering her into her arms, rocked her like a baby.

At last Hélène broke free and scrubbed her eyes with the handkerchief her mother handed her.

'He's married,' she said flatly. 'Rupert's married.'

'I know,' Rosalie said gently.

'He says I didn't write, but I did, several letters' – her voice broke on a sob – 'but he never wrote back.'

'Perhaps he didn't receive them for some reason,' murmured Rosalie, though she didn't believe that for a minute; he had just used that as an excuse.

Hélène latched on to this and said, 'That must be the answer. I can write and tell him I did write.'

'But if he didn't receive your other letters, chérie, he probably won't get that one either. And you have to accept,' she continued firmly, 'that it doesn't matter now, one way or the other. He's married to someone else and that's an end to it.' She knew it sounded unfeeling, but there was no way she was going to allow Hélène to write another word to the monster who had led her on in such a dishonourable way and then pushed her aside when someone else came along. 'A better prospect,' Emile had suggested and it seemed he was right. Hélène had been brushed aside for 'a better prospect', and Rosalie felt the rage build up inside her.

Well, she thought, she'll not give him the satisfaction of any more tears. 'Think kindly of me'! Huh, they would never think of him again.

'Come along now, chérie,' she said briskly. 'You must get up and wash your face and then come down for lunch. This afternoon you must have a rest in the drawing room, ready for this evening.'

'This evening?' Hélène looked at her blankly.

'This evening... at Gavrineau. Madame Barnier's card party.'

'Oh, Maman, I couldn't possibly...'

'Yes, my dearest, you could and you must. You cannot allow the world to see you so distressed. Face the world proudly, with your head held high and a smile on your face, and people will soon forget that you ever met Rupert Chalfont, let alone became engaged to him. Come along, now. Up you get. I'll send Annette to you, and when you're ready just come downstairs. Don't worry, no one will say anything.

I shall speak to your papa, and Rupert Chalfont will never be mentioned in this house again.'

Rosalie was glad that they had an evening engagement. It would stop Hélène sitting at home brooding on Rupert's perfidy. Rosalie had been delighted when they received the invitation to Madame Barnier's card party at Gavrineau. It was clearly a select gathering, just four card tables and a light supper, and it would be a chance for Hélène and Simon to spend some time together. Now she was even more pleased; Hélène had received a blow to her confidence and the sooner she had another man paying court to her, the better. The quickest way to forget all about Rupert was to fall in love with someone else. Simon was tall and good-looking and could be extremely charming when he chose. She had no doubt the news that Rupert Chalfont had married someone else would percolate through to become general knowledge, but if Hélène could be seen to be unmoved by it, it would be clear she was, perhaps, ready to consider another proposal.

She would share none of these thoughts with Hélène, but she was determined that all memory of Rupert should fade as quickly as possible from local recollection. They had all been taken in by him and the sooner he was forgotten the better.

When her mother left the room, Hélène crawled off the bed and, crossing to the window seat, looked out at the garden. In her mind's eye she saw not the bare flowerbeds of the winter garden, still gleaming frostily in the pale sunshine, but the pavilion that had been erected for Clarice's wedding, the rose garden in fragrant and colourful bloom and the seat where she had sat with Rupert, Georges and Sylvie. She would always remember that night, the night when she had first seen him, standing at the bottom of the stairs, and her heart had begun to thud.

On the day he'd left to return to England they had declared their love to each other, and when she had said, 'I shall remember today as long as I live, sitting with you beside the river and having our picnic,' he'd replied, 'It's the day you said you'd marry me; for that reason it will be with me all my life.' With his promise and a kiss, he had left her, and now he was married to someone else.

When Annette came back upstairs, bringing hot water to wash with and a soft, warm towel to dry her face, she found Hélène sitting, staring dry-eyed down at the garden.

'He's married,' she said. 'He's married someone else, Annette.'

'Then you must forget him,' stated Annette firmly. 'He belongs to her now.' She poured the warm water into the china bowl on the dresser and, as if speaking to a child, encouraged Hélène to sponge her face and wash her hands. Then she made her sit down in front of the dressing table and released her hair, which she brushed soothingly until it was shining. Yvette had taught her well and it wasn't long before Hélène, though still looking pale, was ready to go down to the dining room for the midday meal.

'Are you all right?' Annette asked as she paused on the landing. 'Is there anything more I can do for you?'

'No,' Hélène replied quietly. 'There's nothing anyone can do.'

By the time she reached the dining room, Rosalie had spoken with Emile and impressed on him the importance of saying nothing about a letter coming, or anything that might upset Hélène's fragile equilibrium, and the meal passed off easily enough.

'Don't worry about her,' Emile said to Rosalie. 'She'll soon get over him. She's a strong character – remember how she survived during the siege?'

Rosalie did remember; it was a memory she would have preferred to forget, for it still frightened her.

After luncheon, as she rested in front of the drawing room fire, Hélène considered whether she would write one last letter to Rupert, to tell him that she hadn't cut him off. But the more she thought about it, the more she came to the conclusion her mother had been right. Whatever the rights and wrongs of the correspondence, Rupert was married; it was too late to alter that and he was lost to her.

Following her mother's instructions, Hélène dressed to go out for the evening, in gown the colour of clotted cream that set off her gleaming dark hair to perfection. Annette had dressed it in a simple but becoming style and threaded cream ribbons through her curls to hold them in place. She looked at herself in the mirror, and seeing how pale she was, she pinched her cheeks to bring some colour to her skin.

Pierre drove them to Gavrineau, and when they walked into the drawing room to be received by Madame Barnier, remembering her mother's advice, she held her head high and smiled as she greeted her hostess. From across the room Simon watched her, and the sight of her, elegant and upright in the simplicity of her cream dress, took his breath away. She had never looked more beautiful. As yet he knew nothing of Rupert's marriage, but he was already determined to supplant the effete Englishman in her affections.

Chapter 35

The following days were difficult for Hélène. She managed to maintain a hard-won steadiness when she was in company, and even with her family, but once she had retired to her own bedchamber, she allowed her rigid self-control to drop and cried herself to sleep, her head buried under the pillow to prevent her sobs being heard. When she awoke, early in the morning, often before the daybreak, there would be one blissful moment before she remembered, and then the cloud of misery would descend upon her once again. Only Annette really knew of the despair that threatened to break her resolve.

Rosalie had been right. When the news of Rupert's marriage filtered through to their friends, few were surprised. He had been a bird of passage and had gone home to his family three months ago. Now he was his father's heir, no one had expected him to return. The rumour of his engagement to Hélène was soon forgotten when it was seen that she was apparently unmoved by the news. The social life of St Etienne settled back into its familiar pattern of dinner parties, musical evenings, cards and the occasional informal dance, organised in someone's home.

Gradually, Hélène was drawn into the social round and

though Rosalie often had to persuade her to accept the invitations she received, when she did go, she found that a convivial evening with old friends could pass without her thoughts being drawn back to Rupert.

Rosalie watched with relief as Hélène seemed to be recovering something of the bloom which had seemed to capture Rupert's heart.

When Simon Barnier made his surprise visit to Emile, to ask his permission to address Hélène, Rosalie encouraged Emile to agree.

'Hélène's taken a blow to her self-esteem,' she told him. 'She needs to feel loved and admired, and the sooner she has another beau, the sooner she'll forget Rupert Chalfont and look forward rather than back.'

Emile did not need much encouragement. He knew that an alliance with the Barnier family would be another rung up the social ladder. He still had to work for his living, but that living was good. He was a professional man, much respected in his world, and before very long he would be able to retire from practice and live as a country gentleman should.

'Have you spoken to Hélène yet?' her father asked.

'Certainly not, sir,' replied Simon, shocked. 'It would be most improper to approach her before receiving your permission to do so.'

'What? Oh, yes, of course.' Emile held out his hand. 'Well, you have it, so you may approach her whenever you feel the time is right.'

Simon left Belair that afternoon feeling very satisfied with the move he had made. He had not loved Clarice when she was snatched from under his nose by Lucas Barrineau and he did not love Hélène, either, but he desired her with every fibre of his being. He longed to possess her and make her entirely his own, thus banishing any lingering feeling for Rupert Chalfont.

For the next few weeks he set about courting Hélène, paying her marked attention at any gathering and generally making himself agreeable. Hélène was aware of him as she had not been before, but she didn't attach any significance to his behaviour. She had no idea that he had already approached her parents and that at any time now, Simon might propose marriage to her. Thus it was that when, three weeks later, he arrived unannounced at Belair and he found her sitting alone in the morning room, reading, she was surprised to see him. She was even more surprised when, having discovered her alone, he did not leave the room with an apology, but closed the door behind him and advanced towards her. She got to her feet, feeling somehow at a disadvantage as he approached.

'Hélène,' he said, smiling. 'I trust I see you well on such a beautiful morning.'

'Very well, thank you, monsieur,' she replied. 'Allow me to let my mother know that you have called.'

'Perhaps, in a while, but it is you that I have come to see.'

Surprised, and uncomfortable, she fell back on the requirements of hospitality, and with an anxious glance at the door, she said, 'May I offer you some refreshment? Some coffee? A glass of wine?' She moved towards the bell, about to summon Didier, but Simon put a hand on her arm to stay her.

'I require nothing, thank you,' he said. 'Just a moment of your time. Indeed, I'm delighted to find you alone for a moment or two this morning, as I have something particular that I wanted to say to you.'

'Really, monsieur,' she began, taking a step backwards, 'I can't think what it can be.'

'Can't you? Well, I shan't detain you long; I trust you can spare me just a little while.'

'Of course, monsieur,' Hélène replied uneasily. 'We are old enough friends, I'm sure.'

'Indeed we are,' he agreed with a smile. She had given him the way to introduce his proposal. 'Hélène, my dearest girl...'

Hélène seemed to freeze. 'I'm not your dearest girl,' she murmured.

'Perhaps not. Not yet. But I want you to be. I want to be more to you than an old friend. All marriages should be founded on friendship, don't you think?'

'Marriage!' Hélène's voice was almost a squeak. 'Why are you talking of marriage, monsieur?'

'Because that is what I have come to ask you,' replied Simon. 'You must know that I have admired you from afar for some time, and now I want to be closer. These last few weeks I have come to know you as I never knew you before. You are beautiful and gentle and kind, and I have fallen in love with you, my dearest girl. I want to marry you if you will have me.'

As she stared at him in astonishment Simon dropped on one knee before her and, reaching for her hand, said, 'My dearest Hélène, will you do me the honour of becoming my wife? I love you dearly and hope you will come to love me in return. Will you marry me, Hélène? Will you be my wife?'

Hélène was stunned. With Rupert's desertion she had already decided that she would never marry, and now here was Simon Barnier, whom she'd known most of her life, on his knee before her asking for her hand. She was at a loss for words.

'Monsieur...' she tried.

'Simon,' he corrected.

'Simon, I don't know what to say.'

'You could say yes,' he suggested hopefully, her hand still held in his.

'It isn't for me to say,' she said, her brain racing as she tried to escape his proposal. 'You must first apply to my father.' She pulled her hand free and turned away.

'Of course,' replied Simon, getting to his feet. 'But I already have. Your father gave me permission to address you some weeks ago.'

Hélène stared at him. 'You went to him without ascertaining my wishes on the matter?'

Simon smiled at that. 'Well,' he said, 'you can't have it both ways, you know. You say I must apply to him first and when I say I have, you tell me that I should have asked you first.'

'It's all too sudden,' Hélène told him firmly. 'I have no thought of marriage at present, to you or anyone else.'

'My dearest girl,' he said, 'the idea of our marriage is new to you and I understand that, but you must understand that it has been near to my heart for some time. I'm offering you my hand, my heart, my home, and dearest girl, when you have thought about how happy we could be together, I hope you will accept my proposal and become my bride.'

Hélène moved across the room and pulled the bell. 'I'm honoured by your proposal, Simon,' she said, 'but it is so unexpected that I cannot give you an answer.'

'At least you haven't refused,' Simon said. 'So I can live in hope. Perhaps I may call on you again very soon.'

'Perhaps,' she agreed, wishing he would go. She felt trapped with him there in the room and was relieved when Didier came in answer to the bell. The relief showed in her voice as she said, 'Didier, Monsieur Barnier is just leaving; please will you show him out?'

'Thank you for your time, mademoiselle,' Simon said formally. 'I look forward to seeing you again soon.'

When he had gone and she had watched him ride away down the drive, Hélène sank back into her chair, exhausted. Why had Simon Barnier come to propose to her? Did he really want to marry her? He knew perfectly well that she was... had been... in love with Rupert and had thought she was going to marry him. She had seen the two men together on several occasions and knew that neither liked nor trusted the other. Simon had clearly decided that he had been right not to trust Rupert and was trying to take advantage of his disappearance. Rupert would have hated to know that his place might be taken by Simon Barnier. But that didn't matter now. Rupert hadn't any rights in her life any more. They all knew that Rupert wasn't coming back.

When she considered the past weeks, she realised that Simon had been demonstrating a decided partiality for her company. Until now she had accepted it without thought as she had struggled to appear in public, apparently unconcerned about her broken engagement. Now his attentions took on an entirely different meaning. He was serious, serious enough to have asked her father's permission, and for Papa to have given it. She needed to talk to Papa.

With a deep sigh, she heaved herself out of the chair and went in search of her father. When she discovered he was out of the house, she went and tapped on the door of her mother's parlour.

'Hélène,' Rosalie exclaimed. 'Come in, chérie.' She patted the place on the sofa next to her. 'Come and talk to me.' She had seen Simon arrive and depart and had guessed the purpose of his visit. If she was surprised he had decided to propose so soon, she would not say so to Hélène.

However, she did want to introduce the subject of his visit, so she said, 'Was that Simon Barnier I saw riding down the drive?'

'Yes, Maman,' Hélène answered.

'What did he want?'

Hélène looked across at her mother and said, 'I think you know, Maman. He has already spoken to Papa and I'm sure you know that he has.'

'I see.' Rosalie smiled at her. 'So, don't keep me in suspense. What did he say to you?'

'He asked me to marry him.'

'And what did you say?'

'I said it was very sudden and I wasn't thinking of marriage.'

'A very good answer,' said Rosalie. 'It would not have been proper to accept him at once, and without reference to your papa.'

'He says he already has Papa's permission to speak to me,' Hélène said. 'But no one thought to ask me what I think about the idea. I have no intention of marrying anyone and now I have to tell him so. If Papa had asked me, he could have headed him off before he knelt down and asked me to be his wife.'

'I'm sure his offer was unexpected,' said her mother gently, 'but I think you should not dismiss it out of hand, my dear. Take time to consider the advantages of such a match. You would have a loving husband and be mistress of your own establishment. Your position in society would be assured.'

'But I don't love him, Maman.'

'My darling, that will surely come in time, and over the years you'll grow together. You'll start a family and your children will bring you joy.'

'You loved Papa when you married him,' Hélène said, then

added with a perception her mother had not expected, 'but you have grown apart.'

For a moment Rosalie knew a pang as she remembered the bitterness in Mademoiselle Corbine's eyes when Emile had terminated her employment. 'I loved him dearly when we married,' Rosalie replied, 'and I still do, but as you grow older it becomes a different kind of love. You don't have to be passionately in love to have a good and happy marriage. Indeed, it is sometimes better to have a union based on friendship.'

'That's what Simon said,' Hélène admitted reluctantly.

'It isn't a bad basis for marriage,' said Rosalie. She reached out and took Hélène's hand and continued, 'All I'm asking you to do is to take the time to consider Simon's proposal. He's an eligible young man with whom I think you could be happy. Give the idea some time and thought before you give him your answer.'

Chapter 36

The date of Hélène's marriage with Simon Barnier was set for the beginning of February. Gradually, over the weeks that followed Simon's initial proposal, she had been worn down in her refusal by both her parents and Simon himself.

Her mother had been gentle in her persuasion. 'I know you say you don't love him, but you don't dislike him either. I know he's not Rupert, but no one is going to be, are they? You have to set aside any feelings you still have for him and look forward to the rest of your life. You'll have your own establishment in the Gavrineau Garden House, your own staff. And, sometime in the future, you'll move into Gavrineau itself as one of the most important hostesses in the area. Simon loves you and wants you as his wife, but if you turn him down you may lose him completely; a man won't wait for ever for a capricious bride. Think before you throw all this away, chérie.'

Her father was altogether more forthright. 'If you're still languishing for that Rupert Chalfont, it is time you faced facts. He is no gentleman but a dishonourable man who doesn't stand by his given word. The sooner you get him out of your head the better it will be. Simon Barnier is first and foremost a man of honour and he expects everyone else to have the same standards.'

'You thought that of Rupert once, Papa,' Hélène said hesitantly.

'Maybe I did, but I was entirely wrong, wasn't I?' Emile retorted. 'He had us fooled. I should have suspected he was after your money all along. He admitted he knew that you came into your grandmother's money on your marriage, but he assured us he would not touch a penny of what would be yours. And we believed him! We hardly knew the man and yet we believed him and allowed him to court you. We were wrong. We should never have allowed such a thing. As soon as he discovered he'd become his father's heir, he no longer needed any money of yours and he was off back to England without a backward glance. I blame myself, Hélène, and I'm not going to make the same mistake twice.'

'Simon might be after my money as well,' Hélène pointed out.

'Don't be ridiculous, child,' snapped her father. 'We've known the family ever since they came to St Etienne. We all move in the same circles and have the same standards of behaviour. You will be marrying into your own kind, which is the best kind of marriage.'

'But I don't love him,' Hélène said flatly.

'My dear child' – there was a pitying note in Emile's voice – 'what has that to say to anything? Simon Barnier is an excellent match and should you turn him down, I wash my hands of you.'

Simon himself was far more subtle. 'I'll give you all the time you need,' he promised. 'After all, that gives me time to teach you to love me.'

When Hélène told Annette that she had finally given in and

agreed to marry Simon, she said, 'But you will come with me to Gavrineau, won't you? I couldn't go without you.'

There was only a fractional hesitation before Annette smiled at her and said, 'Of course I will.'

'You'll still be able to see Pierre,' Hélène said. 'I promise you that.'

'Pierre?' Annette gave a wry smile. 'I doubt if he'll mind one way or the other.'

'I think he will,' asserted Hélène. 'I've seen the way he looks at you.'

Annette smiled again. 'We'll have to wait and see,' she said. She was very worried about Hélène's forthcoming marriage. She had never liked Simon Barnier, especially since he had tried to use her as a spy. She had seen the way Simon looked at Hélène and it was not the way Rupert had looked at her, nor, if she were honest, the way Pierre looked at *her*. She was loath to move from Belair to Gavrineau, but she was not about to let Hélène go there without her.

'I have to go with her,' she confided to Pierre when she had slipped out to the stables one evening to sit and talk, cosy in the lamplight. 'I can't leave her alone with that man. I simply don't trust him, not after he paid me to spy.'

'Of course you must go,' Pierre agreed reluctantly. He didn't want her to leave; he would miss her more than he'd thought possible. 'You could stay with her to begin with, but if everything is all right when she's settled in, you could come back and marry me!'

Annette stared at him, stunned. 'What did you say?' she whispered, unbelieving.

He grinned at her and said, 'You heard.'

'You want to marry me?' She shook her head. 'But you don't know anything about me.'

'I know all I need to know,' Pierre assured her.

'No, you don't,' Annette said softly, 'and you can't even think about marrying me until you do.'

'Go on, then,' said Pierre. 'Tell me.'

Annette drew a deep breath and got to her feet. Pacing the stable floor, she told him the truth about Father Thomas, the baby and her disgrace. When she had finished Pierre reached for her hand, making her pause in her pacing.

'Do you think that makes any difference to how I feel about you?' His eyes were fixed on hers and she looked away.

'I don't know,' she murmured, 'do I?'

'Well, it doesn't,' stated Pierre. 'Annette, I don't care about your life before you came here. I love you and I want you to marry me. Will you?'

'I can't,' whispered Annette. 'I have to go with Hélène.'

'I quite see that,' responded Pierre, 'but when the time comes that you're happy to leave her, I shall be waiting for you.' He got to his feet and gently drew her into his arms, and for a moment the feel of his body against the length of her own made her stiffen. Very gently he kissed the top of her head and said, 'It's all right, Annette, I'm not Father Thomas.' After a moment he felt her relax again, and looking down into her face, he said, 'I love you, Annette Dubois.'

'My name's not Annette Dubois,' she said. 'Just Annette. I have never had a surname.'

'Well, it won't be long before you have mine,' said Pierre, and he shared with her her first truly loving kiss.

Once Hélène had finally given in and accepted Simon as her future husband, all seemed to be well. The only stand she had to make, with the firm backing of her mother, was that Annette would move with her as her personal maid. Simon had vetoed this to start with, but Rosalie had said, 'She needs a maid of her own.' At which Simon had said, 'And of course she may have one, but it will be a new household and I think it better that we start with entirely new staff.'

Rosalie appeared to relent. 'I understand that,' she said, 'but marriage is a completely new way of life for a young girl and it would be comforting to have someone with whom she is at ease to look after her.'

Simon had given in, but with bad grace, saying, 'Well, if you really think it's that important, then of course she may bring her maid with her. I only want what will make Hélène happy.'

So, Rosalie was able to tell Annette that she would be moving to Gavrineau with Hélène. 'I am sure you'll want to move with her as her personal maid, Annette; she'll feel less strange if she still has someone familiar living with her.'

'I'm very happy to go with her, madame,' Annette replied, and she truly meant it. She considered writing to Rupert and telling him what was happening, but when she consulted Pierre about the idea, he discouraged her.

'There's no point, my love,' he said. 'There's nothing he can do. It's too late. He's married.'

Even so, Annette continued to think about Rupert. She was angry with him and he deserved to know that it was he who had caused Hélène to accept Simon Barnier's proposal.

A few nights before the actual wedding, Simon cornered Annette in the corridor when he was visiting Hélène at Belair.

'I hear you're coming with Miss Hélène when she moves to Gavrineau,' he said.

Annette lowered her eyes and murmured, 'Yes, monsieur.'

'Well, let me warn you, you're there for the time being on sufferance. Just make sure you do nothing to jeopardise your position.' He put his hand under her chin and tilted her head towards him. 'Understand?'

'Yes, monsieur,' she whispered.

'Well, I hope you do.' He let her go and strode across the hall into the drawing room, where Hélène and her mother were waiting for him.

It was this encounter that convinced Annette as to what she should do, and that evening she set pen to paper and wrote to Mr Rupert Chalfont at Pilgrim's Oak.

The wedding day drew nearer and Rosalie knew that she must have a very serious talk with Hélène before the big day. It was only six months since Hélène had begun her monthly courses and Rosalie had had to explain to her when Hélène, terrified, had come to her, fearing that she had some dreadful internal disease. 'It happens to all women,' Rosalie had said. 'It means that you are ready for marriage, that you are old enough to bear children. This is one of the most important days of your life.'

She knew that she should have explained before, so that Hélène would not have been frightened, but she had continued to put off the explanation for fear of reviving memories of what had happened to her during the siege. Now she must risk that, so that Hélène would be ready for the bedchamber on her wedding night. She could only hope that Simon would be a careful and gentle lover. She could procrastinate no longer and summoned Hélène into her parlour.

'Shut the door, chérie,' she said, 'and come and sit by me.' Hélène did as she was told and waited.

'Hélène, you remember I told you when your monthly courses started that you were now ready for marriage.'

'Yes, I remember.'

'Well, when a man and a woman are married, they have a very intimate life with each other. Very often they share the same bed and when they are sleeping close to each other they become...' She paused, looking for the right word. '...entwined.' She paused again before she went on, 'It may take you a while to get used to sleeping next to someone like that, but it can be very comforting to fall asleep in a man's arms.'

For a moment Hélène remembered the feel of Rupert's arms about her, but she forced it away. That way led to misery. It was Simon's arms in which she would fall asleep.

'And after such a night together, you may find you are carrying his child.' Rosalie had still not explained how this last was achieved, but, she reasoned, very few brides actually knew before their wedding night exactly what was expected of them. It wasn't customary to go into detail; a new wife learned as she went along, and once she had found herself expecting a baby, as Clarice was now, she accepted that whether she enjoyed the experience or not, that was the way babies were created.

That evening Hélène sat at her dressing table while Annette brushed out her hair, and looking at her maid in the mirror, she wondered about Father Thomas. Annette had said he used to come to her bed at night. That was what her mother had just explained would happen when she and Simon were married. She was very tempted to ask Annette about it, but she knew Annette had hated what had happened, and surely that couldn't be the same for all women, or there would be no children. So, she asked nothing and relaxed as the strokes of the brush soothed her. She wouldn't know what to do, but she guessed Simon would, and they would have babies.

Chapter 37

It was extremely cold. Rupert walked over from the Dower House to Pilgrim's Oak to visit his father. Sir Philip was dying. They knew it and he knew it and he was facing death with his usual fortitude. In the chilly weeks after Christmas he had contracted a loud and hacking cough, but he had only taken to his bed when his temperature had risen to thirty-nine degrees. Fran was at his bedside. She held a cup of wine mixed with a little warm water to his lips and said, 'You must try, Papa.'

'Don't fuss, Frances,' he muttered as she tried to sit him up so that he could drink, but the effort simply brought on another bout of coughing. Amabel, now living in a world of her own, took no part in nursing her husband; it was probable that she had no realisation of his illness. Kitty was expecting a baby and had been so sick herself that she was unable to help with the nursing, so the responsibility fell on Fran, ably helped by Mrs Crowley. Fran had wanted to employ a proper nurse, but her father had been adamant.

'I'm dying, Frances,' he'd said, 'I don't want anyone fussing round me. Let me go with dignity.'

Fran had understood and accepted his wishes. Rupert visited every day, only to see his father growing progressively weaker. Dr Evans had paid several visits, but admitted that there was no more he could do and that it was just a matter of time.

'His cough is in his chest and there is almost certainly fluid in his lungs,' he said. 'That means pneumonia, and in his weakened state it could carry him off any day. I'm afraid you must prepare yourselves.'

Rupert, Fran and Kitty all knew of this diagnosis, but they had kept the news from Amabel. She was in no fit state to hear it. Time enough when the worst happened and she had to be told.

Rupert opened the bedroom door quietly and went into the room. Fran was still sitting holding the cup, but Sir Philip was lying back on his pillows with his eyes shut.

'How is he?' whispered Rupert.

Fran gave a faint shrug and, keeping her voice low, said, 'Much the same.'

'I can hear you talking,' said the voice from the bed. Sir Philip opened his eyes again. 'I'm not dead yet.'

'How are you, sir?' asked Rupert, knowing as he posed the question what a stupid one it was. The old man was a shadow of his former self, wasted to the size of a child, his skin the colour and texture of parchment. He lay under the covers with only his hands above the sheet, but his eyes were open again and he fixed them on Rupert.

'Never better,' came his reply. It was followed by another bout of coughing, great rasping coughs that shook his whole body. When at last it stopped, he said, 'How's that wife of yours?'

'Still feeling sick, I'm afraid,' Rupert replied. 'At the moment she's staying in bed on Dr Evans's orders, but she's very anxious to get up and come over to see you.'

'Tell her not to,' said Sir Philip. 'No point in putting that baby at risk; he's the future.' Ever since he had heard there was a baby on the way, Sir Philip had referred to it as 'he'. 'I didn't think I'd live to see my grandson,' he'd said when he heard the news, but now he knew he'd been right – he would be in his grave before the baby was born.

It was later, when he had fallen into an uneasy doze, that Rupert left Fran watching over him and went to see his mother. She was in her parlour, sitting by the fire, which, recently made up, was throwing out a comfortable heat. She looked up as he came in and gave him a dreamy smile.

'Hello, dear,' she said. 'I thought you were Justin. Where's he?'

'He's out, Mother,' Rupert answered. They had all long since stopped trying to tell her that Justin was dead. That had upset her every time she asked. It was as if she had to come to terms with his death anew each time she heard of it. Now, at Dr Evans's suggestion, they simply told her he was out and she accepted that quite happily, sometimes saying, 'Ask him to come in to see me when he gets back.'

'I just looked in to see how Papa is,' Rupert said.

'Is he well?'

'He's coughing a bit.'

'Poor Philip. His usual winter cough. We must find some camphor and red flannel for his chest. That always makes him more comfortable.'

'Good idea, Mama,' said Rupert. 'I'll suggest it to Fran.'

He stayed with her for ten minutes longer and then kissed her on the cheek and went back downstairs. As he crossed the hall, Mitchell came in with the postbag. Since his marriage, Rupert's mail was addressed to him at the Dower House, but this time Mitchell said, 'There's a letter for you here, Mr Rupert. Must have got put in the wrong bag,' and he handed him an envelope. Rupert glanced down at it and it seemed for a moment that his heart had stopped. The writing was not known to him, but the letter came from France. He stared at it for a second and then shoved it into his pocket, saying as he did so, 'Thank you, Mitchell. Please will you tell Miss Frances that I've gone back to the Dower House. I'll come over again later. Perhaps you'd ask Mrs Crowley if she could sit with Sir Philip for a while to give Miss Fran a break. I think she sat up with him most of the night and she ought to get some sleep.'

'Of course, sir.' Mitchell disappeared towards the kitchen to find the housekeeper and Rupert left the house to walk slowly home. When he got there, Kitty was still obediently in bed, so he went into his study and shut and locked the door. He could feel the letter in his pocket, as if it were burning a hole, but for a long moment he waited, afraid to pull it out.

At last he did so and looked at the envelope. The writing was ill-formed, definitely not Hélène's, but his name and the address at Pilgrim's Oak were spelled correctly, and the stamps were French. He sat down behind his desk and picked up his paper knife. For one moment he shut his eyes, then with a quick movement he slit the envelope open and drew out the single sheet it contained.

Dear Mr Chalfont

This is to let you know that Miss Hélène is going to be married to Monsieur Barnier next week. She was very upset when she heard you were married having heard nothing from you after your first two letters even after Pierre wrote and told you how sad she was. It was cruel

*of you to cut her off like that, and not write any more
letters until you was actually married. You may have
changed your mind, but she didn't deserve that. Shame
on you! Miss Hélène is nothing to do with you now, but
I thought you should know the misery you have caused
her by your desertion and now she's being pushed into
marrying Monsieur Barnier.*

*You may think I have no right to take you to task, but
Hélène is my friend and we look out for each other so I
have every right. I am going with her to Gavrineau, so
she won't be on her own but I hope you feel as sick as
I do at the thought of her being married to M. Barnier.*

Annette Dubois

Rupert read the letter through again and did, indeed, feel
sick. Hélène was going to marry that cold, autocratic man.
How could she? How could she even consider the idea? And
what did Annette mean by saying he hadn't written more than
once? He'd written several times and received no replies. It
was only because Hélène had cut him off that he had allowed
himself to be pushed into marriage with Kitty. Pushed into
marriage. The words that Annette had used struck him
forcibly. His Hélène was being forced into marriage with
Simon Barnier – only, of course, she wasn't his Hélène any
more. But who was forcing her? Her parents? Simon Barnier
himself? Did he have some hold over her? Rupert wished he
could talk to Annette and get her to answer all his questions.
She said Pierre had written to him as well. Where was that
letter? If he had addressed it as this one from Annette was
addressed, it must surely have arrived. The same with Hélène's

letters. He had given them all the same address to write to, but this was the sole letter that had arrived since Hélène's first and only one. Annette said Hélène had heard nothing from him after the letter he'd sent on his arrival. Surely all his other messages couldn't have gone astray. She obviously received the one he'd sent after he and Kitty were married. Why not the others?

And then a thought struck him; he'd taken that one to the post office himself. He had not put it in the postbag in the normal way, to be posted by one of the servants, and that letter had arrived at Belair.

Surely that wasn't the answer, that thought that had slipped into his mind, something so unthinkable that he dismissed it at once. But as he sat reading and rereading the letter from Annette, it returned to weigh in upon him. If his letters, the ones he'd put into the postbag in the hall, had never been sent, that would account for what Annette was saying. But surely, no one at Pilgrim's Oak would have had any reason to tamper with the postbag. But if they had, who had it been? Once the unwelcome thought had been planted in his mind, it began to take root, and he then took the next logical step. What had happened to the letters that Annette said Hélène had written to him? The servants would have had no knowledge of letters that might come from France. His mother knew nothing about Hélène – Rupert had never mentioned her existence to Amabel – which left his father and Fran. It seemed to him incredible that either of them should have taken such a reprehensible step, but who else was there? They had both been determined that he should marry Kitty, but determined enough to steal his letters? Because that was what it came down to: theft of both incoming and outgoing post. How could they have done such a thing? And how could he accuse them of it? He had no proof and if he were wrong, it was the sort of accusation that could never be repealed or forgiven.

At that moment there was a knock on the study door and he heard Parker's voice calling through to him, 'Are you in there, sir? Message from Miss Frances.'

'I'm coming, Parker,' he said, and putting Annette's letter in his desk drawer, he unlocked the door and went out.

'Message from Miss Frances, sir,' Parker repeated. 'Please can you come over to the house at once.'

Rupert didn't ask him why, simply nodded and hurried over to the main house.

Mitchell was in the hall waiting for him. 'Miss Frances is in with Sir Philip, Sir Rupert,' he said; and those words told him all he needed to know. His father had closed his eyes for the last time. He was now Sir Rupert. He went upstairs to his father's room and found Fran sitting quietly beside the bed. There was a stillness in the room; the hacking cough was silent and the face of the man lying in the bed, eyes closed, was peacefully smooth. Fran turned round as Rupert came in.

'He's gone,' she said. 'One minute he was here, you could hear his breathing across the room, and the next minute, nothing.' She looked up at Rupert, dry-eyed, and said, 'It was a merciful end, you know. He never complained, but he was in great pain.'

Rupert nodded. 'Yes,' he murmured, 'I know.' He crossed to the bedside, and for a moment he rested his hand against his father's cheek and wished he could have said goodbye properly. Fran was right, of course, Papa had been in pain and now he was free and at peace, but even so, who he had been to each of them would leave an empty space in their lives.

'We must tell Mama,' he said. 'Perhaps we should do that together.'

'And we must send for Mrs Fender from the village to come and lay him out properly,' said Fran. 'Oh, Rupert, how we'll all miss him.'

Rupert saw now that tears were beginning to slip down her cheeks and he went and put his arms round her, to comfort them both.

After a while she pulled free and, taking her hankie out of her pocket, blew her nose. 'Well,' she said, 'at least he knew that Kitty is expecting. He knew that the future he wanted was taken care of. He was pleased about that.'

Rupert nodded and, with the flick of a thought to the letter lying in his desk, said, 'Yes, I know.'

Together they went to see their mother in her parlour. Amabel was sitting in her usual chair by the fire and looked pleased to see them as they came in.

'Have you come to take me down to lunch?' she asked. 'I told Mrs Crowley I'd come down today. I want to see Justin.'

'No, Mama,' Fran said softly. 'I think you're having your lunch up here today. Justin's out.'

'Is he? Well, perhaps, then, you'll tell Mrs Crowley that I've changed my mind. I will have my lunch up here.'

'Mama,' Rupert said, 'I'm afraid we've got some sad news.'

'Have you, dear?'

'You know Papa has been very ill—' he began.

'I told you to put red flannel on his chest,' interrupted his mother.

'We did that, Mama,' interposed Frances, 'but it didn't do any good. Dear Papa passed away this morning.'

'Passed away?' echoed Amabel.

'Yes, Mama,' said Fran.

'Passed away,' repeated her mother. 'Poor Philip.'

For a moment none of them spoke and then Amabel turned to Rupert. 'You will tell Mrs Crowley about lunch, Rupert, won't you?'

'Of course, Mama,' he replied, and then he and Frances left her sitting contentedly in her chair, gazing into the fire.

'We've lost them both now,' Fran said sadly as they closed the door behind them. 'Mama isn't Mama any more. Now there's only you and me.'

'And Kitty,' Rupert reminded her. 'I must go and break the news to Kitty. Will you send for Mrs Fender?' Fran said she would, and they parted in the hall.

With his father's death and all the arrangements that had to be made about the funeral, Kitty's continued sickness and his mother's disconnection from the world, Rupert had little time to give further thought to Annette's letter and what it might indicate. It was not at the forefront of his mind, but neither did it rest quietly at the back. In moments alone, her words slid forward into his consciousness: *I hope you feel as sick as I do at the thought of her being married to M. Barnier.* And he did. His instinct had been to rush over to France, to see Hélène... And what? His saner, more sensible self enquired. Ask her not to marry Simon Barnier? Hardly. No, such a journey would achieve nothing, nothing but to open old wounds for both of them; and it was too late. In her letter Annette had said Hélène was getting married *next week*. Taking into consideration the time Annette's letter had taken to reach him and the time he must give to respect his father's passing, it was almost certain that Hélène was now married and they were each beyond the reach of the other.

He would write back to Annette, Rupert decided, and ask her all the questions to which he wanted answers. Perhaps then he might tackle Fran about the missing letters, but maybe that too would do more harm than good. There was Kitty, and her feelings must be considered. She had known nothing about Hélène and their engagement, and since there was nothing to be done, perhaps it would be better to let sleeping dogs lie.

Chapter 38

It had been decided that Hélène and Simon's wedding should
be a quiet one, just the families on both sides and a few close
friends. Hélène was glad; she didn't want the huge celebrations
that had attended Clarice's nuptials, bringing unwelcome
memories of the day when she'd first seen Rupert. The actual
marriage would take place in the Mairic followed by a service
conducted by Father Bernard in the church, but it would be a
low-key affair without bridesmaids or other attendants. There
would be a select group invited to the wedding breakfast at
Belair, after which the newly married couple would quietly
retire to their new home to begin their married life.

Annette had been told she would be moving with Hélène,
and safe in the knowledge that Pierre was waiting for her, she
was happy enough to go.

When Hélène is thrust into that house of strangers, Annette
thought, she'll need me as a friend to confide in, as well as a
maid to look after her.

She was folding Hélène's clothes into a trunk for
transportation to the Garden House when Lizette appeared,
breathless, at the bedroom door.

'Annette, Madame wants you in the drawing room,' she
said. 'Right away.'

Annette smoothed the blue silk evening dress she had been folding into the case and, getting up from her knees, hurried downstairs. In the drawing room she found Madame St Clair and Hélène seated by the fire, and Simon Barnier pacing the floor like a caged lion.

'Ah, Annette,' said her mistress. 'Monsieur Barnier is taking Miss Hélène over to Gavrineau directly. The carriage is waiting outside. Please be ready to attend them.'

Annette bobbed a curtsy and said, 'Yes, madame, at once.'

She quickly collected her own hat and coat and then helped Hélène into hers, a new fur, a present from her father. Ten minutes later they were bowling down the drive in the Gavrineau chaise, driven by Simon himself. Hélène and Annette were seated side by side behind him. Neither of them spoke, anxious, in front of Simon, to maintain the relationship of mistress and maid. Though shafts of pale winter sunshine occasionally burst through the clouds, there was also a chill in the air and despite her new coat, Hélène shivered.

The carriage turned in through the gates of Gavrineau and made its way along the tree-lined drive, the bare branches of the winter avenue stark against the grey January sky. Ahead of her Hélène could see Gavrineau itself, standing sombre and tall. It was an imposing house with echoes of the chateau it might have been in earlier days, but its turrets were now to add grandeur rather than for fortification, and its windows were wide and high to let in light and to offer a view. Hélène knew the house from childhood, but it was not yet to be her home and she was glad. Used as she was to the easy comfort of Belair, she found Gavrineau too grandiose for her taste, with its sweeping staircases and marble floors. She and Simon were to live in the much smaller Garden House, which had been built for Simon's great-grandmother when she was widowed.

'I've never been into the Garden House before,' Hélène had confided to Annette earlier that day when she'd had a message to say that Simon intended to take her there that afternoon. 'I've been to Gavrineau many times, but until she died last winter, old Madame Barnier, Monsieur's mother, was living in there. I wonder what it will be like inside.'

Annette wondered too. If nothing had changed since the old lady had died, it might be rather old-fashioned. Perhaps Monsieur Barnier would let Hélène redecorate it, at least that would give her something interesting to think about; but for the moment Annette kept those thoughts to herself – they were suggestions for another day.

When the carriage reached the wide gravel sweep in front of the portico, it did not stop but proceeded slowly round the side of the house, following the extended drive until it drew up in front of the Garden House, and Hélène saw her future home. Simon handed her down from the chaise and, turning to Annette, said brusquely, 'You can wait outside. I prefer to show Miss Hélène round her new home in private.'

Annette saw a look of anxiety flit across Hélène's face, but it was gone as soon as it had come, and raising her chin, Hélène preceded her fiancé up the steps to the front door.

Annette knew she would have to do as he ordered, but as soon as Simon had unlocked the door and they'd stepped inside, she moved quickly to stand in the porch, which would give her some protection from the east wind... and keep her closer to Hélène.

As she reached its shelter, she heard Simon say, 'I have employed an entirely new staff for the house. My grandmother's servants were well past the age of service and I turned them off. I have chosen the new servants very carefully, experienced staff who know how a household should be maintained; they will answer to me until you have established yourself as mistress. I will see them installed tomorrow, ready for when we come home from Belair the following day.'

'You seem to have thought of everything,' Hélène said softly, and then, although she continued speaking, they passed out of her hearing and Annette could only hear her voice, not what she was actually saying.

She waited in the porch for some time as Simon took Hélène into the reception rooms on the ground floor. Their footsteps returned across the hall and Annette heard Simon saying, '... and of course you may furnish your parlour as you choose. Now, let's go upstairs.'

Hélène had liked the principal rooms downstairs, elegant and tasteful, nothing too grand or stately. She followed Simon up to the first-floor landing, where the corridor divided, leading to the two wings that projected from the back of the house. He turned left and led her past two closed doors before flinging a third one wide and standing aside to let her enter.

'This will be your bedchamber, Hélène,' he said. 'It was my grandmother's, but I have had it redecorated, ready for you.'

Hélène walked to the middle of the room and looked about her. The walls had been covered in pale grey silk, and the hangings were of a deep rose pink; not what she would have chosen but inoffensive enough. The room was comfortably furnished with a large bed, dressing table, wardrobe and chest of drawers. Two easy chairs stood on either side of the wide fireplace, in which a fire was already laid, simply awaiting a match. At one end of the room was another door, leading to a cabinet furnished for her ablutions, and beside it was yet another door, but when she tried the handle, thinking it a further closet, Hélène found it was locked. She looked questioningly at Simon and asked, 'Why is this cupboard locked?'

'It's not a cupboard, my dear, it's the door that leads to my bedchamber, the next room. When I come to your bed, I will simply unlock it and walk through.' He reached for her hand and said, 'Nothing could be more convenient.'

'And where is my key?'

'Your key?' His voice hardened. 'Why would you need a key? You won't be coming to my chamber... unless I tell you to, in which case I will unlock the door for you.'

'But...' faltered Hélène.

'But what?' His grip tightened on her hand. 'Are you suggesting that there might be occasions when you'll be unwilling to receive your husband as you should?' He looked at her sardonically. 'Surely not! I'm certain your mother has explained that a husband has his needs... and it is up to you to satisfy them.' He grasped her other wrist and pulled her to him, making her cry out.

'Simon! Stop! Let go! You're hurting me.' Hélène tried to jerk her hands free, but he held them fast.

'Stop?' he teased. 'My dear girl, I haven't started yet.' There was something in his voice, a tone, a roughness that triggered a memory and made her shudder.

'I just thought,' he went on, 'that you might like a little foretaste of what will happen when I come to visit you on our wedding night.' He spoke mildly, as if explaining to a child. 'Just so that you understand what I expect of you.'

He was too strong for her, and despite her efforts to break away, he pulled her closely against him. She could feel the length of his body leaning against hers, something hard pressing against her stomach. His breath was hot on her face, but she felt an icy chill as further memories slid into her mind. 'Don't!' she cried. 'Don't! Leave me alone.'

It was a strangled cry, but Simon took no notice of her distress, simply lowering his head and kissing her long and hard, his tongue probing her mouth. She almost gagged as she tried to curl her own tongue away so that it didn't touch his. Still she had the taste of him in her mouth and it almost made her sick. Even when at last he raised his head, she could not break free, his body pressing on hers as he edged her into a corner of the room, trapping her against the wall. She struggled, still trying to pull away, and seeing the fear in her eyes, he gave a soft laugh. Fear in a woman's eyes had always been an aphrodisiac to him and it was no less so now that this woman he wanted would soon be his wife... to do with as he chose; such anticipation was exciting.

He looked down at her and smiled. 'What's the matter,' he mocked, 'didn't the Englishman kiss you properly like this?'

'Certainly not!' she cried. 'He was a gentleman!'

'Ah, but you see, husbands don't have to be gentlemen,' he told her. Holding her face firmly between his hands, he bent his head once more to claim her mouth – one last taste before, in two days' time, he could claim the rest of her. But as he lowered his lips to hers, she twisted away, letting out a piercing scream. With an oath he slapped her cheek, cutting off her scream, and let her go.

Annette, still standing shivering in the porch, heard Hélène's terrified scream and flung herself in through the front door, and took the stairs two at a time. As she reached the landing, they were coming towards her with Simon saying in a loud and hectoring voice, 'For goodness' sake, Hélène, it was only a spider! A large one, I'll grant you, but only a spider nonetheless. I'm afraid that you'll have to get used to those here. The Garden House is an old building and there are bound to be spiders.'

As he spoke his fingers gripped more tightly round her wrist, the stone of his signet ring biting painfully into her flesh. She dared not speak out, and he knew it. He turned his wrath on Annette. 'I thought I told you to wait outside,' he growled.

'I beg your pardon, monsieur.' Annette was all contrition. 'I thought perhaps Miss Hélène had had a fall. I came to help.'

'There is no need of your help when Miss Hélène is with me, and I'll thank you to remember it!'

Annette ducked her head submissively and murmured, 'Yes, monsieur.' She had seen the mark of his hand on Hélène's face, but wisely dropped her eyes again, giving no indication.

'Well,' he said briskly, 'enough of that now. It's time to get your mistress back to Belair. I'm sure she's longing to tell her parents of the arrangements I've made here for her comfort.'

They went back downstairs, and having handed Hélène into the chaise, Simon turned back to lock the house while Annette waited for permission to get in beside her mistress.

Simon, turning back towards her, gripped Annette by the wrist. 'Miss Hélène was disturbed by a large spider,' he said softly, 'and I wish to hear nothing else about it.' His voice was menacing as he added, 'You understand me, Annette? One word and I'll throw you out on the street.'

'Yes, monsieur, I understand you very well.' And she did. She didn't know exactly what had happened upstairs in the bedroom, but seeing the red mark on Hélène's face she could guess. Hélène sat beside her, pale-faced and mute, as Simon drove them back to Belair.

Simon did not stay once he had seen Hélène into the house. Before he turned back towards the front door, he said, 'My compliments to your mother, my dear, but I must beg her to excuse me. I have to return to Gavrineau directly. My mother's sister is arriving today and I must be there to greet her.' He reached for Hélène's hand and lifted it to his lips. She kept her eyes lowered but he squeezed her hand hard, his signet ring again digging into her skin, leaving a deep indentation as if in wax, as if he had sealed her as his own.

The moment Didier closed the door behind him, Hélène went straight upstairs, retreating to the sanctuary of her room, and locked herself in. She flung herself down on her bed in a depth of despair too deep for tears. She had seen the look in Simon's eyes as he'd held her face in his hands. He had been enjoying her fear, and that was the most frightening thing of all.

Chapter 39

Annette went into the kitchen, where Agathe was discussing the preparations for the wedding breakfast with Madame Paquet. Agathe took one look at Annette's face and brought her conversation to a close, saying, 'I'm sure it will be perfect, Adèle. I rely on you entirely.'

'Aunt Agathe, I need to talk to you for a moment.' Seeing how serious Annette looked, Agathe led her into her sitting room and closed the door.

'You look worried,' she said. 'What on earth's happened?'

'I am worried, Aunt. We've just been to the Garden House with Monsieur Barnier...' She hesitated, trying to find the words to explain.

'And...?' prompted Agathe.

'And something happened while we were there.'

'Something? What something?'

Annette explained how she had been told to wait outside while Monsieur Barnier showed Hélène round the house that was going to be her home.

'He's dismissed all the servants who waited on old Madame Barnier and he's hired a whole new staff. Hélène won't know any of them, except me.'

'That usually happens when a bride moves into her new

home,' Agathe pointed out. 'Even if the old servants were still there, she wouldn't know them, would she?'

'No,' agreed Annette cautiously, 'but surely a new bride should have some say in the hiring of those who will wait on her.'

'Perhaps Monsieur Barnier simply wanted to save her the trouble of engaging new servants.'

Annette shook her head. 'No, Aunt, I think he has chosen them to spy on her.'

'That's a serious accusation,' Agathe warned her. 'You must be careful what you say.'

'I'm only saying it to you,' Annette said. 'But that's not all. Something happened while we were there. I was waiting downstairs in the porch as instructed while he took her upstairs to show her her bedchamber. They had been up there for some time when Hélène suddenly screamed. Such a scream! I rushed upstairs to see what had happened, but by the time I got to them they were coming back along the landing and Monsieur Barnier was scolding her for screaming at the sight of a spider.'

'Perhaps she had...?' suggested Agathe mildly.

'That scream was not about a spider, Aunt, it was a scream of pure terror. You should have seen her face.'

'But what could he have done with you standing in the hall downstairs?'

'Almost anything,' replied Annette. 'He had certainly hit her, the mark of his hand was red on her cheek. He's a monster and she shouldn't be marrying him.'

'Well,' said Agathe with a sigh, 'there's nothing we can do about that.'

'Isn't there?' Annette looked at her. 'I know what it's like to be dominated by a man and have no escape. I was lucky. I could simply walk away, flee when he was out of the house, but if she marries Simon Barnier she'll never have that choice. Even when he's not there, she'll be surrounded by his people, watching her every move. She'll be tied to him for life.'

At that moment they heard a bell ring in the kitchen. 'That's her bell,' Annette said, getting to her feet. 'I'd better go and help her dress for dinner.'

'Annette, please tread carefully,' Agathe warned. 'You must say nothing of your own troubles.'

'Troubles?'

'Father Thomas!' Agathe whispered as if she might be overheard.

'Don't worry, Aunt, she knows about him already.'

'Hélène does? Who told her?' One look at Annette's face gave her the answer. 'Oh, Annette, how could you? If Madame St Clair ever hears that, we shall both be turned out into the street.'

'Hélène and I agreed that neither of us would tell, so if you don't, then Madame won't know, will she? Look,' she went on, 'I've been through it all, I know what it's like. Father Thomas and Simon Barnier are exactly the same. They're bullies. They simply take what they want from a woman… because they're stronger… because they can.'

The bell rang again, louder and longer than before, and Annette hurried out of the little sitting room and upstairs to Hélène.

Left alone in her sitting room, Agathe thought about what Annette had told her. She did not like Simon Barnier, but unless she changed her mind, Hélène was going to be married to him in two days' time and there was certainly nothing *they* could do about it.

She remembered the day, seven years ago, when Father Thomas had found Hélène in the church. She, as the clergy housekeeper, had been called and had taken the child back to the Clergy House to wash and feed her. Agathe had immediately realised that something had happened to her. There had been bruises on her body and it had been clear that she was afraid of men – she was certainly afraid of Father Thomas. Agathe had guessed that someone, somewhere, had been abusing her. She remembered the child's nightmares, and knew that it was for this reason that Madame St Clair had been determined Hélène should not hear of Annette's misfortunes. Annette said Hélène had screamed in terror and it was nothing to do with a spider. Agathe feared that she might be right and wondered what had occurred. Had Simon Barnier really hit her? He seemed so cultivated, with such civilised manners. But even if he had done whatever it was, there was surely nothing that she and Annette could do about it.

Upstairs, Hélène let Annette into her room, but as soon as she closed the door, she locked it again so that they would not be disturbed. Annette looked at her. The slap mark had faded, there would be nothing for her parents to see when she went down to dinner, but there was a dullness in her eyes and her face was unnaturally pale.

'Do you want to tell me?' Annette asked.

Hélène did. Speaking in a flat, monotonous voice, she told Annette everything.

'I can't bear him near me,' she said. 'The thought of him touching me, touching me in any way, makes me feel physically sick. Can you understand that, Annette?'

'Oh yes, Hélène, I understand only too well.'

'But I don't know what to do.'

'There's only one thing you can do,' Annette told her. 'You

go to your parents and tell them that you've changed your mind.'

'Changed my mind?' echoed Hélène faintly.

'Changed your mind. That you don't want to marry Simon Barnier after all.'

Hélène stared at Annette in horror. 'I couldn't.' She shook her head violently. 'I just couldn't do that. Not now. It's too late.'

'It's not too late,' insisted Annette. 'Too late is when you're married to him. Then there really is no chance of escape.'

'But it wouldn't work, just saying that. They'd all go on at me about the shame of jilting him, of how I would shame not only myself and our family by refusing to marry him but him and his family as well. I would end up having to marry him anyway, and he'd never forgive me for saying I didn't want to.'

'You could do what I did,' suggested Annette. 'Just walk out.'

'I couldn't, Annette. I really couldn't. Where would I go?'

'I didn't have anywhere to go,' Annette reminded her. 'But I knew I couldn't stay and nor can you. We'll find somewhere to go, just you and me.'

'But he'd come looking for me. He'd come looking for me and if and when he found me, my life wouldn't be worth living.'

'If you simply disappeared, before you were married, he'd have no claim on you. Do you really think he'll bother to come searching for you?'

'Yes,' replied Hélène. 'I know he will. However long it takes.'

'And you really think it's better to be married to a man like that than take the risk of leaving while you still can?'

'Yes,' replied Hélène. 'He would find me.'

When Annette returned to the kitchen for her supper, she whispered to Pierre that she and Madame Sauze wanted him to come to the sitting room once the meal had been cleared away and coffee served in the drawing room.

'What's up?' he said when they were sitting beside Agathe's fire.

'I'll tell you,' Annette said, 'but you must promise me to listen without interrupting until I've finished. All right?'

Pierre shrugged. 'All right,' he said. 'Fire away.'

Annette told him what had happened at Gavrineau, finishing by saying, 'She's terrified of him. We have to get her away from him.'

It was then that Agathe said, 'She was abducted when she was a child. She used to have nightmares.'

'We need to make a plan,' Annette said, 'and then we have to convince her that it's her only chance unless she wants to be tied to him for ever.'

They continued to discuss the matter, suggesting and discarding ideas until they had thrashed out a plan that might work. They all agreed Annette and Hélène would be safest in Paris, where they could get lost in the bustle of the city, but there was no question of using the house in the Avenue Ste Anne.

'That's the first place he would look,' said Pierre.

'To her brother? He lives in Versailles. Would he take her in?'

'Same thing,' Pierre said. 'Too obvious. We need somewhere quite different.'

'I have an apartment,' Agathe said quietly. 'You could go there.'

'*You* have?' Annette cried in amazement. 'Where? When did you get it?'

'You remember my sister Fleur, Annette? She died several months ago and Madame gave me two days off to go to Paris to settle her affairs. Well, she had many more affairs than I knew about. She had been left very comfortably off by her husband, with property and some money in the bank, and when she died she left it all to me, including the apartment where you and I stayed. No one here knows anything about it, so that's where you can go. You'd be quite safe. No one would be looking for you in that part of the town.'

'But who lives there now?' asked Annette. 'I mean, haven't you let the apartment?'

'Not yet,' replied Agathe. 'Because of the property, the proving of the will took the lawyer, Monsieur Colet, longer than he had thought, but it's all done now and everything is transferred into my name. I can write a note to him and he'll give you the key; you can stay as long as is necessary. And don't worry about money, there's plenty for now.'

'If you leave very early in the morning,' Pierre suggested, 'you can take the footpath to the village and catch the first train to Paris before anyone here realises that you've gone. I'll come with you and once I've seen you safely onto the train, I'll come straight back. No one will know I've even been out.'

'Suppose someone sees us leaving?' worried Annette.

'That's a risk we'll have to take,' replied Pierre, 'but it isn't a big one. It's very cold these winter mornings and still dark for a while. No one gets up early, as they might in the summer. They stay in bed and keep their curtains drawn against the cold outside. To catch that first train we shall have to leave in the dark. No one will see us go.'

It was agreed that this was the best plan they could come up with. All of them were fond of Hélène, had known her from childhood, and they were all prepared to risk helping her escape marriage with an abusive husband. Now all they had to do was convince Hélène.

Annette carried the plan up to Hélène when she attended her at bedtime.

'It will be easy enough,' she explained. 'While it's still dark we'll take the back stairs down to the kitchen and leave the house that way. It is only Miss Louise's window that looks out over the stable yard, and she is never one to leave her bed before she has to.'

'But where are we going? You just say Paris.'

'We have a safe place to go,' insisted Annette. 'No one will find you there. Now,' she went on, 'you can bring just a small bag with you. Pierre will go with us across the fields to the village and see us onto the train. I have money for our tickets and Pierre will buy them so that we are not seen at the ticket office. Then he will come back here, ready to hear that you've disappeared.'

'It's too risky,' ventured Hélène. 'Especially for you and Pierre.'

'There is an element of risk,' agreed Annette, 'but it shouldn't be too great and we have to get you away from here. This is your only chance if you really want to go. Think about it and make your decision.'

When Annette had left her, Hélène lay in bed, unable to sleep, and considered the plan Annette had explained. It was so risky that her heart failed her and so far she was refusing to contemplate the idea. For a long while she simply stared into the darkness, with only the glow of the fire for light and warmth, but at last she drifted off to an uneasy sleep. As the fire died to embers the chill of the night crept back into the room, and with it the night terror that had haunted her as a child.

She was alone in a cold, damp cell. It was almost dark and she was freezing. The floor and the walls of the cell were stone, wet and slippery. She sat on the small heap of straw piled into a corner, the only light illuminating her prison filtering through a barred window high above her. She curled into a ball, her arms wrapped round her body, trying to retain some warmth, but her clothes were torn and her body was bruised and she shook with cold and fear. Then she heard it, the key scraping in the lock, and when the door opened she saw his face, lit by the candle he carried. Flickering flame showed her the black beard, the scarred cheeks, the cruel eyes, now alight with lustful anticipation.

'On your feet!' he ordered. 'It's playtime!'

She screamed then, a shrill, penetrating scream of terror, a scream that woke her and left her shivering in the dark.

The bedroom door burst open and her mother was across the room and at her bedside. She gathered her weeping daughter into her arms and rocked her gently as she had done so often in the days after the siege, letting her sob great heaving sobs until, exhausted, she collapsed back on her pillows.

Annette had heard her cries and tiptoed down from the servants' landing, but when she saw that Rosalie St Clair was already there, she turned and went back upstairs to tell Agathe that they simply must persuade Hélène to follow their plan and make a break for it.

'Imagine what he'll do to her if she wakes up screaming like that when they're married,' Annette said before returning to her own bed.

Chapter 40

Hélène had her breakfast in bed the next morning and asked Annette to stay with her while she ate. In fact she hardly ate anything, simply drank some coffee and picked at a warm pastry Madame Paquet had sent up in the hope of tempting her appetite, but after one mouthful she pushed it away.

'I can't,' she said listlessly. 'I can't eat.'

'You can't not,' Annette said in a rallying voice. 'You have to keep up your strength for tonight if we're to put our plan into action. And after your nightmare last night, we really have to get you away.'

'It was only a dream,' Hélène answered. 'I used to get them when I was younger.'

'I know, you used to wake us up with your screams at St Luke's!'

'Did I? I'd forgotten.' She sighed. 'I can't remember when I last had one, but it was exactly the same dream.' And she described it to Annette.

Annette shuddered. 'Well, we know what caused it last night, don't we? Listen, Hélène, you've always had the courage of a lion. Don't give in now. You've still got one chance.'

'Running away is the coward's way out,' murmured Hélène.

'And staying is the fool's,' Annette assured her. 'We've got it all planned. All we have to do is creep out during the night and get to the station in time to catch the first train to Paris. Once we're there, even if he does come looking he'll never find us. We shall be swallowed up by the city.'

'But we've nowhere to go,' sighed Hélène. 'It's no good.'

'Well, that's where you're wrong,' Annette said. 'We have got somewhere to go.'

'Where?'

'It's not my secret,' Annette told her, 'but I can promise you, Simon Barnier will not find us.' She noticed a gleam of interest, or possibly hope, in Hélène's eye and went on, 'While you're all at dinner, I'll pack a bag for you. We can't take much, as we have to carry our own luggage, but enough to keep us going for a few weeks.'

'And what happens after that?'

'We stay safely away until we hear that he's given up looking and gone back to Gavrineau. Then we can return to Belair, or perhaps go back and live in the Avenue Ste Anne for a while until all the furore dies down.' She reached and grasped Hélène's hands in hers. They were like ice and she began rubbing them gently between her own, encouraging the blood to return to them. 'Tonight, when everyone has gone to bed, I'll come and fetch you and we'll leave the house through the kitchen and the stable yard. Pierre will be waiting for us outside by the field gate and he'll carry the bags to the station for us. We can do it, Hélène, and then you'll be safe.'

'I don't know...' Hélène still hesitated.

'Well, you've got until tonight to decide,' Annette said. 'I will have everything ready, and you can decide, but tomorrow will be too late!'

The day passed very slowly, the hours dragging through a grey morning and a wet and chilly winter afternoon. At times Hélène made up her mind that she would go to Paris, and at others that she dare not.

'We must pray for fine weather tomorrow,' her mother said as they sat together by the fire in her parlour. 'It'll be cold, but with luck the sun may break through.' Her mother took her hand and gave it a squeeze. 'Happy the bride that the sun shines on!' Hélène managed a faint smile and wondered how she could possibly creep out into the night and leave her mother to face the wrath of Simon Barnier... because she knew without doubt that there would be wrath and her mother would bear the brunt of it. She came closer then to confiding in her mother than at any other time; not the escape plan but that she might, at the last minute, refuse to marry Simon.

'Maman...' she began, but at that moment Lizette came into the parlour to make up the fire, and when she had gone, the moment had gone also. Hélène realised that she either slipped away in the night, or she married Simon Barnier in the morning.

Simon had been invited to dinner that evening and he arrived in high good humour, his manners well-bred and charming, his conversation light and entertaining. They did not stand on ceremony but ate as a family round the dinner table. Louise sat opposite Simon and thought as she watched the candlelight dance in his eyes what a lucky girl Hélène was to be marrying such a handsome, beguiling man. By this time tomorrow both her sisters would be married women, with a status in society that she had yet to attain. Louise sighed and wished that Simon had a brother.

At the end of the evening Simon took his leave and the family wished him goodnight. He and Hélène were allowed to walk out into the hall for a chaste farewell kiss. As Simon raised her hand to his lips, he murmured, 'Ah, my Hélène! Tomorrow you'll be mine and you'll learn what it means to be married!' He looked down into her frightened eyes as he squeezed her hand a little more tightly and added, 'And tomorrow there'll be no more screams!'

As the door closed behind him she realised that his final words had made her decision for her. He was right. Tomorrow there would be no more screams. Tomorrow she would not be here. Tomorrow she would be on her way to Paris before they'd even realised she'd gone.

Annette was waiting for her in the bedroom, and as soon as she'd shut the door, Hélène turned to her and said, 'I'll go.'

Chapter 41

When Annette left, Hélène locked the door behind her. She wanted no unexpected intrusions as she prepared to make her escape. Annette had been good as her word and had packed a small valise with some essentials, but Hélène moved quietly round the room adding a few trinkets and the only money she could find, just a few francs at the back of a drawer. Before she closed the bag she went to the cupboard and lifted down her cherrywood box. She had not destroyed the few letters she had received from Rupert, not even the one telling her of his marriage, but she was certainly not going to leave them here for anyone else to find and read. She couldn't take the box, it was too cumbersome, but she took out the letters and pushed them into her bag. Lastly she removed the engagement ring Simon had given her and laid it on the dressing table.

Preparations made, she did not undress, but lay fully clothed on her bed. Her fur coat remained in the wardrobe – it was far too conspicuous – but she had set her plain black winter coat, her hat and bag ready on the chair. Once she drifted off to sleep, but the nightmare pounced and she struggled to force herself awake again, shivering, the cold sweat of fear lying on her skin. She dared not close her eyes again, simply waited for Annette's tap on the door. As she lay there she wondered what they were going to do for money. Annette said she had money for their tickets and she had her few francs, but that wouldn't last them long. She thought of the inheritance that she would have had on her marriage, received from her grandmother's will. She would never marry now, so she would never inherit. She was going to have to make her own way in life, cut off from her family, at least for the foreseeable future. Her heart ached at leaving with no goodbye, no explanation except the obvious one, but now all she wanted was to get away, to vanish into thin air and never see Simon again.

At last she heard the faintest of knocks and went to open the door. Annette slipped inside, closing the door behind her.

'Ready?' she murmured.

'Ready,' replied Hélène, and putting on her coat and hat, she picked up her bag.

They doused the lamp and waited a moment for their eyes to adjust to the darkness before they stepped out onto the landing, locking the door behind them and keeping the key. Annette took Hélène's hand and led her along the landing towards the back stairs. As they passed Emile's door there was a long burst of coughing from within, and for a moment they froze. Hélène realised there was a line of light under the door; was her father awake? Annette gave Hélène's hand a sharp jerk and they set off again along the landing. Once down the stairs they felt safer. It was unlikely any of the family would see them now and even the servants wouldn't be down this early. They had decided that Madame Sauze must not be involved in their actual escape, so that when it was discovered she could say with perfect truth that she had heard nothing during the night.

Once through the kitchen, Annette unlocked the back door and they hurried across the stable yard to the field gate, where Pierre was waiting. Neither of them looked back at the dark windows of the house, neither of them saw the face at a bedroom window, where Louise, awakened by the need to use the chamber pot, thought she saw two shadows in the yard. No more than moving shapes in the darkness, they disappeared and were gone. She rubbed her eyes, but could now see nothing and, unsure she had really seen anything, she decided it must have been a trick of the light. A pale moon sailed out from behind a cloud and lit the empty stable yard. Shivering, Louise went back to bed and back to sleep, thinking no more of what she might have seen until the morning.

Pierre waited as promised in the field. He took Hélène's bag, and the one that Annette had picked up from the scullery, and led them out onto the footpath. There was no sign of the dawn, but it was not totally dark; a quarter moon drifted in and out of scudding clouds, allowing them fitful light as they made their way along the familiar path through the meadow. Once they reached the village it was easier going. The square was empty, but early lamps from some of the houses threw patches of light onto the cobbles. There was no one to see them hurrying towards the station. The platform was lit by a gas lamp, giving it an eerie green glow, and there were already several passengers standing waiting for the arrival of the early train. The girls waited in the shadows while Pierre, hat pulled down to shade his face, bought two tickets from a sleepy clerk in the ticket office. It was only a few moments later that the train steamed into the station, and Pierre opened a carriage door for them to get in, Hélène first, taking her bag. She turned back to take

Annette's bag and saw she was in Pierre's arms, sharing a last kiss before the guard blew his whistle and she scrambled up into the carriage. Even as the train began to draw away from the platform, she saw that Pierre had disappeared into the shadows.

'You're leaving him behind,' Hélène said as Annette took her seat beside her.

'For now,' agreed Annette, 'but not for ever. He'll wait for me.'

Hélène hoped that she was right, but thoughts of Rupert's promise and subsequent desertion were never far away and she didn't reply.

They spoke little on the journey. The train was a slow one, stopping at stations all the way to Paris, picking up passengers along the route, working men, mostly, with a few women bringing baskets of produce to market. They had agreed that Pierre should buy them third-class tickets, so that they would not be remembered as first-class passengers. If anyone enquired for them, it would be expected that they were travelling first class. The carriage filled up quickly and the two of them sat side by side in silence, not wishing to be drawn into any conversation. There was a buzz of it around them, but Hélène closed her eyes as if dozing and they were undisturbed.

When they reached Paris, Annette led them quickly away from the station into the jumble of streets; two unremarkable women in dark coats and respectable hats, nothing cautious or furtive about them. Once clear of the station, they took a public omnibus to Monsieur Colet's office, where Annette presented Agathe's letter explaining that she was her niece and was going to live in the Batignolles apartment for a while.

'Very pleased to meet you, Madame Dubois,' Monsieur Colet said as he handed her the key. 'I hope you will be very comfortable living there.'

'I'm sure I will,' replied Annette, and with the key safely in her pocket she shook his hand and left his office.

They boarded a second omnibus, which took them to Les Halles, from where Annette was able to lead Hélène to the apartment house with its butcher's shop at the street level and three storeys above. They were there. Simon Barnier was left behind and Hélène was free.

It was Annette who continued to take charge. She led the way upstairs, unlocked the apartment and threw open the front door. It smelled musty, and the heavy furniture was still in place, filling the rooms, but they could lock the door on the outside world.

Rosalie woke that morning with an unaccustomed heaviness in her heart. Hélène had been abnormally quiet at the family dinner last night. Was it prewedding nerves? she wondered. She thought of Hélène's nightmare two nights ago. Had that been triggered by something Simon had said or done when they were at Gavrineau? Surely nothing could have happened there with Annette in attendance. Simon was surely too cultured, too civilised, to have even mentioned the wedding night, let alone anything that might have sparked the return of the nightmare.

Thank goodness, Rosalie thought as she sat up in bed drinking the cup of chocolate Lizette had brought her, there had been no repetition of the nightmare last night. It would seem that Hélène had slept through, untroubled by dreams. Should she speak to Hélène again, explain a little more fully and try to get her to understand what her duties as a wife entailed, or was it better to leave it to Simon to teach her the ways of love? Rosalie took her breakfast in her room and considered the matter, but remained undecided.

She was not really surprised there was no sign of Hélène downstairs when she finally came down herself, but she wanted to be with her on her wedding morning and so she went back upstairs and knocked on the door. There was no reply to her first knock, nor a second one, so she tried the handle. The door, so recently mended, was locked.

'Hélène,' she called gently. 'It's Maman. Let me in, chérie.'

She knocked again and called more loudly, 'Hélène, I need to talk to you.' Still nothing. After one last knock, one further call, Rosalie gave up and went downstairs to find Emile.

'Hélène's locked herself into her bedroom again,' she told him. 'She doesn't answer and she won't come out. What are we going to do?'

'I'll deal with her,' Emile said. 'She'll open the door to me.' His knock was loud and long and echoed through the house, his voice strident with anger, but there was still no response from inside the bedroom. Frustrated at being defied and being seen to be defied, he turned on Rosalie.

'Get Pierre up here and tell him to bring that crowbar.'

Moments later Pierre appeared carrying the crowbar and before long, for a second time, he broke the lock so that the door swung open. Emile pushed him aside and strode into the room, only to find it empty, the bed unslept in, the ashes in the fireplace cold. He flung open the wardrobe door as if Hélène might be hiding inside, but all he found was the fur coat and the other clothes she had left behind.

Rosalie had followed him into the room and guessed with a plummeting heart that she had gone. Hélène had run away.

'Where's that girl of hers?' Emile demanded. 'Let's get her up here and see what she knows of this.'

Rosalie could have told him that Annette had gone too, but she said nothing other than telling Pierre to send Annette to her in her parlour.

'It's better to talk to her in private, Emile,' she said as she led the way to her room. 'We don't want the whole world to know what's happening.'

'Hmm,' grunted Emile. 'They'll already know we've had to break her door down.'

Pierre was soon back with the news that no one had seen Annette that morning.

'Well, why not?' demanded Emile. 'Where is the girl?'

'We don't know, sir.'

'I imagine she's gone too,' Rosalie said.

Emile ordered the house to be searched, but no one really expected either of the missing women to be discovered. Rosalie returned to Hélène's bedroom and looked through what she had left behind. The cherrywood box was standing on the table. She knew what it usually contained, but when she opened it, it was empty. A sudden dreadful thought struck her. Surely Hélène hadn't gone to find Rupert Chalfont! He was married to someone else and she was about to be. There was no point in her going to find him. Rosalie was well aware that, despite his desertion, Hélène had never stopped loving Rupert. She had been persuaded to marry Simon, but she would never love him. Her heart, once given, belonged to Rupert. Rosalie sighed and cursed the day that Lucas Barrineau had, on a whim, invited the Englishman to his wedding.

Rosalie went down to find Emile in his study, where he had retreated once the search of the house had proved fruitless.

'I think we have to accept that she's run away,' Rosalie told him. 'Rather than marry Simon, she's run away.' She handed him the engagement ring that she'd found lying on Hélène's dressing table. 'She left this. I think the message is clear.'

'That is ridiculous,' stated Emile. 'What's wrong with her? He's an excellent match.'

'He may be an excellent match, but she doesn't love him!'

'Love him? What romantic twaddle is that?'

'Emile, whatever the reason, she's run away.'

Emile gave an exasperated sigh. 'But where would she go?'

'I don't know,' replied Rosalie, 'but she's gone... and Annette has gone with her.'

'Well, that girl has been nothing but trouble since you decided to take her in. I told you at the time that was a mistake and so it has proved. Dead babies, and now this!' He glowered at his wife. 'And what are we going to tell Barnier, eh? Tell him Hélène has changed her mind and run off somewhere? Do we know that's what's happened?'

'Well, unpleasant as that will be,' said Rosalie, 'it seems to be the truth... though perhaps it may not be as bad as we think. Perhaps she just needs a little more time.'

'More time!' expostulated Emile. 'She's had plenty of time if she wasn't sure – several weeks. How can she simply disappear, leaving no message?'

A new thought struck Rosalie and she said, 'Perhaps she's gone to the Avenue Ste Anne. She might have, Emile, just to get away for a while.'

'And expect us to come running after her?'

'Well, we can find out, you know. We can telegraph Georges and ask him to go and see. At least we can tell Simon that's what we've done. We can make it clear that we're doing all we can to find her.'

'Better get Pierre to send the telegram, then,' grumbled Emile. 'But before he does that he must take a letter to Gavrineau to tell Barnier what's happened. I'll write it now. Please tell him to come to me at once to collect it. We can hardly leave the poor man and his family standing outside the Mairie, can we?'

Rosalie reluctantly agreed they could not, and though the engagement ring suggested otherwise, she was still hoping against hope that Hélène had simply gone out somewhere and would soon be back. 'And in the meantime,' she said, 'I'll have a word with Madame Sauze. I'll see her in my parlour.'

She was anxious to speak to Agathe Sauze without Emile's presence. It was quite possible that she might know where Annette and Hélène had gone. After all, she was the one who had come to her about Annette's plight in the first place. Everyone at Belair, Emile included, believed that Agathe and Annette were aunt and niece. Though Rosalie knew they were not, she had seen there was definite affection between them.

Her interview with Agathe was, however, postponed when Louise came downstairs to find out what all the fuss was about.

'Lizette says Hélène's run away,' she announced. 'Has she, Maman? Has she run away? Where's she gone?'

'You shouldn't listen to the servants' gossip,' said her mother repressively. 'We don't know quite where she is.'

'So she has run away,' said Louise. 'But why?'

'Louise, all these questions are not helpful. I suggest if you have nothing better to do that you go back to your own room for the time being.'

'All right,' Louise said, 'if you want me to, but I thought you might like to hear what I saw in the middle of the night.'

'For goodness' sake, child,' exclaimed her mother. 'What did you see?'

'Well, I don't suppose it was the middle of the night,' answered Louise, 'not really, but it was still almost dark. I got up and was looking out of the window and I saw them. Well, I saw somebody, in the stable yard, but when I looked again there was no one there.'

'So you didn't really see anything.'

'I did,' asserted Louise, 'and it must have been Hélène and Annette leaving. But when the moon came out they'd gone. They must have gone out into the field.'

'Into the field,' echoed Rosalie, and then she realised what that must mean. 'Louise, please wait upstairs, chérie. I have to go and speak to your father.'

With a disgruntled sigh at being sent to her room just like a child, Louise went back upstairs and Rosalie returned to Emile's study to tell him what Louise had said.

'They took the path across the fields to the village.'

'But where would they go when they got there?' snapped Emile. 'Who in the village would take them in?'

'I doubt if they went to anyone there, but they could have gone to the station and caught a train. I believe there's an early one to Paris. So perhaps they really have gone to the Avenue Ste Anne.'

'Hmm,' Emile grunted. 'Well, I suppose when Pierre gets back he'd better go and make enquiries at the station.'

'I think he's back already,' Rosalie said. 'I'll go and find him and send him to ask.' She left Emile sitting at his desk in his study and went down the passageway to the servants' quarters in search of Pierre.

Moments later, there was a crash of the knocker on the front door, and before Didier could go in answer to its summons, Simon Barnier pushed it open and strode into the hallway. Handing his coat, hat and cane to Didier, he demanded, 'Where will I find Monsieur St Clair?'

'Good morning, sir,' replied Didier diplomatically. 'Monsieur St Clair is in his study, if you wish me to announce you.'

Simon gave a curt nod and Didier led the way to Emile's study and, tapping on the door, gave Simon's name. Emile looked up and knew he needed Rosalie at his side.

'Please ask Madame to join us in here, Didier,' he said, and with an inclination of his head, the butler went in search of her.

The next half hour was not one that Rosalie would willingly repeat. Simon's anger at Hélène's disappearance was explosive. He blamed them for not keeping her under lock and key overnight.

'You seem to have no control over your daughter,' he raged. 'I will not have a disobedient wife. She needs discipline to make her understand her place. And that she'll get from me!'

If that is how you have been speaking to her, Rosalie thought, I'm not surprised she's run away. But she kept this thought to herself; there was no point in enraging Simon Barnier any further. Even Emile had no idea how to handle his furious future son-in-law. He had more sympathy with him than Rosalie did, but he had no more idea of where Hélène had gone than she had.

'We have telegraphed our son to ask him to visit our Paris house,' he explained, 'to see if she has taken refuge there.'

'Refuge?' Simon's voice was icy.

'Or whether she has gone to visit her brother,' Rosalie put in smoothly.

Simon rounded on her. 'Wherever she has gone, madame,' he said fiercely, 'she has put me in an intolerable position.'

'Yes,' agreed Rosalie reluctantly. 'I'm afraid she has... and us too.'

'I hardly think the two are comparable,' said Simon, getting to his feet. 'You will please contact me the moment you hear from her. Her desertion, for I can only call it that, will be general knowledge within twenty-four hours and I shall be a laughing stock! I will, of course, forbid my servants to speak of it on pain of dismissal, and I trust you will do the same, but you know what servants are for gossiping about their betters, a hint here, a wink there. It will not be contained for long and I want her to be back and married before this scandal breaks wide open.'

'Perhaps, Monsieur Barnier,' Rosalie said, 'you would favour me with a few minutes of your time – there is something I should explain to you.'

'Well, what is it?'

'I think we might go into my parlour, where we could talk in private?'

With an exaggerated sigh, Simon followed her into her sitting room. Rosalie sat down and invited him to do the same, but he did not. He remained standing, impatiently drumming his fingers on the table.

For a long moment neither of them spoke and then Rosalie, having taken a decision, said, 'I think this is a case of prewedding nerves. Hélène is afraid of the physical side of marriage.'

Simon made no reply, simply staring at her stony-faced as if daring her to continue.

'When Hélène was a child...' Rosalie began and then hesitated. Should she be telling Simon this? He was her fiancé and perhaps he should know, but on the other hand she had kept the secret of Hélène's abduction from becoming general knowledge when she had been rescued at the end of the siege. She had done so to protect Hélène and to allow the enormity of her experience to fade into the recesses of her mind. The nightmares had continued for several months. The doctor had warned Rosalie that this might be the case. 'But,' he had said, 'given time, her mind will heal and she will forget. Past hurts will be buried if they are allowed to remain unexplored. A wound doesn't heal if you keep picking at the scab. In my opinion it is the same with the mind. The unpleasant memories will scab over and gradually heal from underneath until the scab falls off of its own accord and they are buried for ever.'

'When Hélène was a child,' she began again, 'she was abducted, and for many days we didn't know where she was or what had happened to her. The army was besieging the Communards in Paris and Hélène was trapped in the city. She was kidnapped from our house in the Avenue Ste Anne – indeed, one of our servants was killed trying to protect her, but she was carried off by some deserter from the army. He kept her prisoner thinking to sell her on, or to use her for his own pleasure, but she managed to escape.'

'You mean your daughter is damaged goods,' Simon said icily, 'and you tried to foist her on me.'

'She is no such thing and we did no such thing,' retorted Rosalie. 'She was kidnapped by a man and kept prisoner for a few days, but she escaped. Obviously this experience was terrifying and for some time she had nightmares. Gradually these became fewer and fewer until she was only haunted by them very occasionally. Indeed I can't remember when she last had one, until the night before last, that is, the night after she had been to the Garden House with you, but for years she was afraid of any man she didn't know. Eventually things faded from her mind and she was able to move quite naturally in society.' Rosalie got to her feet, so that she could look Simon Barnier in the eye. 'I don't know what happened at the Garden House the other day, but I think you must have frightened her in some way, monsieur, and in her fear she has run away.'

'You should be grateful, madame, that despite your revelations I am still prepared to marry Hélène if she returns before the scandal becomes well known.' Simon got to his feet and walked to the door. 'I bid you good day, madame, and expect to have news of Hélène just as soon as you have any yourselves.'

When he had finally swept out of the house, Rosalie went back into her parlour and dropped into her chair by the fire. Where, she wondered, had the charming, suave gentleman whom she'd known as Simon Barnier gone? And who was this raging tyrant who'd appeared in his place? How could one man have two such different faces? How could she send her daughter back to such a man? She remembered that she had been going to speak to Agathe Sauze about Hélène and Annette's disappearance, but now she decided not to. She knew how fond of Hélène Madame Sauze was, and if she did know anything of where they'd gone, Rosalie suddenly did not want to know. If she knew, she would be honour-bound to inform Simon.

Chapter 42

Hélène and Annette gradually settled into a comfortable routine in Agathe's apartment. Hélène slowly overcame her dread of leaving the place and venturing into the street.

'I don't think you need to worry,' Annette said when Hélène admitted her fear. 'I've had a letter from Pierre and he says that Simon has told some story about you being called away to a sick aunt. No one believes it, of course, but he has to try to save face. Pierre says he made various efforts to trace us. He went to the station himself to see if anyone had seen us getting on the train but luckily no one had noticed us. The man in the ticket office told him that he hadn't even seen two young women that morning, let alone sold them tickets to Paris or anywhere else. Of course,' Annette went on, 'he must be pretty sure that's where we are, but he might as well look for a needle in a haystack. Pierre says Simon's certainly been to the Avenue Ste Anne and he thinks to Versailles to see your brother Georges too, in case you were hiding there.'

'Do you think he'll think that Pierre might have bought the tickets?' wondered Hélène.

'I suppose he might, but even if he does, Pierre will deny it and Simon can still only guess that we came to Paris.'

'But we can't stay here for ever,' Hélène pointed out. 'It's very good of Madame Sauze to lend us her apartment, but we can't stay here for ever.'

'No, I agree,' said Annette, 'but once Simon and your parents are all convinced that you will never go back to him, perhaps some arrangement can be made, so that you can come out of hiding. Perhaps I'll know more tomorrow.'

'Tomorrow? Why, what's happening tomorrow?'

Annette smiled, her eyes alight with pleasure, and said, 'Pierre's coming up to the Avenue Ste Anne with Madame St Clair today. We're going to see each other tomorrow.'

'Is that safe?' Hélène was instantly afraid. 'He's not coming here, is he?'

'No, he's not. We're meeting at Les Halles. It is so busy no one will notice us in the crowd.'

'Supposing he's followed?' said Hélène.

'Who by?' Annette smiled. 'Don't worry, he'll be careful.'

Hélène saw Annette's joy at the idea of the meeting and said, 'You love him, don't you? Does he love you? Will you get married?'

'One day, I hope, but not until you don't need me any more.'

'But doesn't it frighten you... you know, knowing what you have to do with a man when you're married? Like Father Thomas?'

'It won't be anything like Father Thomas,' Annette assured her. 'What Father Thomas did was done with hate and violence. With Pierre I know it will be with love and tenderness.'

Hélène was not convinced and shuddered at the thought of Simon's hands on her throat, the urgency of his body pressing against hers. 'I could never let a man touch me again, like that... like Simon.'

'But if you fell in love with someone else it wouldn't be like Simon. Not if you loved him; it would be quite different.'

'Well, I can tell you now, I have absolutely no intention of getting married,' Hélène asserted, 'ever! So I shall never find out. I shall never love anyone enough for that.'

Annette often wondered how things would have been if Hélène had married Rupert as planned. Would she have been seized with panic when he tried to kiss her, or would he have understood, and taken his lovemaking slowly? She had little doubt that Simon would dominate any woman he took to bed, and having suffered at the hands of Father Thomas she could quite understand Hélène's revulsion. If she *had* married Simon Barnier, Annette thought, he would have forced himself on Hélène and it would have been tantamount to rape. If Hélène was right and she never married, she was still far better off than being married to a man like that.

The next day Annette put on her hat and coat and, leaving Hélène sewing in the apartment, set out for Les Halles. At first she couldn't see him and thought he hadn't been able to come, but suddenly he was there, beside her, slipping an arm about her waist, his lips brushing her cheek, making her face flush with becoming colour.

The market was bustling with life as ever, and Pierre took her hand and led her into a side street away from the crowds.

'Hélène's afraid you might have been followed,' she told him once they were clear.

'I did wonder, myself,' Pierre said, 'but I can't really believe that Barnier would be able to have every member of the St Clair household followed. Anyway, tell her not to worry, I wasn't, I made sure of that.'

'I'll reassure her,' promised Annette, but even so she found herself glancing over her shoulder, just in case.

Pierre took her hand again. 'Come on,' he said, pointing to a small glass door steamed up from within. 'There's a café over there and we've got lots to talk about.' The café was busy, but it was warm after the chill of the day outside, and they managed to find a small table at the back. Pierre ordered two cups of coffee and some pastries. While they waited for them to arrive he smiled at her and asked, 'How have you been? Have you missed me?'

'We're well enough,' she replied, ignoring his second question with a twitch of her lips. 'The apartment isn't large, but we are comfortable. We have plenty to fill our days, and you know, I don't think I'd like to be a lady of leisure.'

'What about Hélène?'

'She's no longer a lady of leisure, either. She certainly does her share. We've had to be realistic, Pierre. Aunt Agathe gave us money to tide us over, but it won't last for ever, so we've had to find some means of support.'

'Madame Sauze said to tell you that she has made arrangements for you to draw money from Monsieur Colet if you need to.'

Annette smiled. 'How like her,' she said. 'Please thank her for us, but say we've enough to be going on with. I've actually managed to get us some sewing work from a dressmaker with a workshop nearby. I collect the work and bring it home, so they have no idea that it's a lady who's doing it. It's just plain sewing, but it's something Hélène does well and I'm getting better at. It doesn't pay much, but we don't need a lot.'

'So she's earning your livings!'

'Yes, she's teaching me to sew and I'm teaching her to cook,' said Annette, which made Pierre laugh.

'Are you indeed? And is she any good at it?'

'She will be,' Annette replied. 'Anyone can learn to cook if you show them how.'

Their coffee and pastries arrived, and once Pierre knew they would not be interrupted any further he said, 'I've lots to tell, there have been developments.'

'What sort of developments?' demanded Annette.

'Simon has dismissed his staff and moved back into Gavrineau with his parents. He's back in the separate wing where he was before.'

'Does that mean he's given up looking for us?'

'I don't know. Maybe. I doubt it some. Her disappearance on the eve of her wedding was a great blow to his pride. He wasn't left waiting at the Mairie with his family, but everyone is talking about what happened, so he might as well have been. I've a shrewd suspicion that he's employing someone to find her.'

'But why? Surely he doesn't want to marry her any more.'

'Who can tell with a man like that? He considered that she belonged to him and he's not the man to give up anything he owns.'

'You can't own a person,' stated Annette.

'I think you can try,' replied Pierre, 'if you're a man like Simon Barnier. Perhaps he thinks she'll eventually come back to Belair in disgrace. If she did, she would be completely ostracised. Maybe that's what he's hoping for: her public disgrace.'

'I doubt if she'll do that. What do her parents think?'

'Her father is so angry and ashamed that he has disowned her. He has forbidden her name to be mentioned at Belair.'

'And Madame?'

'Madame, I think, has sympathy for her. She has seen the other side of Monsieur Barnier and I think she's quite happy for her daughter to remain in hiding. I think she guesses that Madame Sauze probably knows where you are, but she hasn't asked her. I think it's the reason we've come back to Paris for a while. Madame was tired of apologising for Hélène's disappearance. She's brought Miss Louise with her and will be staying in the Avenue Ste Anne for a time. Monsieur will come occasionally, he has work to do in the city, but I think neither of them wants to be at Belair just now.'

'But they don't suspect you?'

'No, I don't think so. And,' he said, his face brightening, 'it means, if we're careful, that we can meet from time to time. I do miss you, you know!' He was rewarded with a pleasing blush on Annette's cheeks and he added a little anxiously, 'You will still marry me when this is all over?'

'Oh, Pierre, you know I will.'

He reached for her hand and, smiling into her eyes, said with great satisfaction, 'Good.'

Both of them wished that they were not in such a public place, but it would not be seemly to embrace in a café, and so they had to make do with the squeeze of a hand and a smile.

'Come on,' said Pierre, tossing some coins onto the table and getting to his feet, 'let's make the most of our afternoon. Madame's given me the day off.'

They walked arm in arm towards the river, strolling like any other couple in the early spring sunshine.

'How long will you stay with her?' Pierre asked suddenly.

'As long as she needs me,' replied Annette. She stopped and turned to face him. 'We can't let her marry that monster.' Her face darkened. 'I know what it's like, Pierre, the fear, the violence, the shame. It comes back to haunt you just when you think you're safe.'

'You'd be safe with me, Annette,' Pierre said gently.

She smiled up at him and it was like the sun breaking through. 'I know,' she said, 'and one day I will be, I promise you.'

'You look happy,' Hélène remarked when Annette came back into the apartment. 'What news from Pierre?'

'First of all he says don't worry, he wasn't followed. He doesn't think that anyone suspects him of being involved in your escape, but he says he was very careful and will continue to be so.'

'What else did he say? How are my parents?'

'Your father is still angry with you, but your mother seems much more sympathetic. She has brought Louise up to Paris and will be staying in the Avenue Ste Anne for a while now.'

'Is Madame Sauze with her?'

'No, she's been left at Belair. Pierre thinks your mother guesses that Aunt Agathe had something to do with your disappearance, but she hasn't actually asked her.'

'What news of Simon?'

'Pierre says Simon has moved out of the Garden House and back into Gavrineau with his parents. Saves him the cost of his own establishment, I suppose.' She went into the kitchen. 'Let's forget about him and think what we'll have for supper.'

'I've made it,' Hélène said proudly. 'Fish, with a sauce.'

'Good for you. What did you put in the sauce?' Annette asked, with a smile.

'Anything I liked the look of in the market,' Hélène replied cheerfully.

'Ah,' said Annette. 'The very best sort of sauce.'

As Annette and Hélène sat at the kitchen table eating their fish supper, Pierre found himself entertaining Jeannot in the stables.

'Thought you might turn up sometime,' Pierre said. 'How did you know we were back?'

Jeannot gave him a knowing look and said, 'I keep an eye on the place. Don't want no one taking advantage of an empty house, do we?'

Pierre agreed they didn't. Then an idea struck him.

'Any sign that someone's been watching the house recently?' he asked, trying to sound casual.

Jeannot shrugged. 'Don't keep a round-the-clock watch, do I?'

'No, but one of your lads might have seen something, you know, just someone hanging about in the street.'

'What's this all about, Pierre?' Jeannot asked. 'Them's not casual questions, are they?'

Pierre, who had been wondering how much if anything to say about Hélène's predicament, said, 'No.'

'So, what's behind them, then? You expecting a break-in or something? Won't happen while the family's here, will it?'

'No, nothing like that,' replied Pierre, even as he remembered how a gang of deserters had broken in all those years ago and abducted Hélène. The house had been occupied then. 'No,' he said again. 'It's just that Miss Hélène has...' He hesitated.

'Has what?' prompted Jeannot.

When Pierre didn't immediately answer, Jeannot said, 'Come on, Pierre! What's up?'

Pierre took his decision. He knew that Jeannot had always

been protective of Hélène. There could be no harm in letting him know what had been happening.

'Miss Hélène was engaged to be married to that Englishman I told you about. The English milord.'

'She didn't marry him,' Jeannot said, clearly with first-hand knowledge of this.

'No, he didn't come back from England.' Pierre explained about Rupert's marriage, Hélène's misery and her surprising decision to marry Simon Barnier.

'Very quick,' remarked Jeannot.

'He had been courting her for some time and she was encouraged by her mother to accept him.'

'Why?' demanded Jeannot. 'Was he rich?'

'His family owns a large estate near to Belair, the St Clairs' home, but whether he has any money I can't say. Maybe money problems. Miss Hélène will come in to quite an inheritance on her marriage.'

'And her ma encouraged her to marry him?' Jeannot sounded sceptical.

'I think she thought that it would help put the Englishman out of Hélène's mind, having her own establishment to run and that.'

'So, what are you telling me?'

'A couple of days before the wedding, Barnier took her to look at the house where they were going to live, the Garden House on his family estate. My girl, Annette, is her maid. They knew each other from when they were in the orphanage together. She was with them for decency's sake, but she wasn't allowed into the house with them. Barnier told her to wait outside, but it was cold and she actually waited inside the porch.'

Jeannot listened attentively as Pierre described what had

happened, both in the bedroom at the Garden House and the threats made by Simon Barnier to Annette if she spoke of what had frightened Hélène.

'Annette and I suggested that she should tell her parents she'd changed her mind, but she was too afraid of what Barnier would do to her if she did.'

'So what has happened to her?' demanded Jeannot. 'If he's harmed a hair of her head...' Jeannot glared at Pierre as if it were his fault. 'You tell me where I can find this Barnier bloke and he'll never frighten anyone ever again.'

'She's safe,' Pierre assured him. 'We finally persuaded her to run away. We got her to Paris and she's at a safe address where he won't find her.'

'How d'you know he won't? Sounds pretty ruthless to me. You asked if someone had been watching this place? Well, perhaps they have, but she hasn't been here, has she?'

'No, she hasn't, but he may still be having the house watched in case she turns up, thinking that he's no longer looking for her.'

Jeannot thought for a moment. 'What does she think he's going to do to her if he does find her? I mean, she ain't married to him, so he's got no claim on her. Law can't make her marry him, can it?'

'As I said, there's money involved.' Pierre explained about the inheritance. 'Everyone knows that the St Clair girls all come into money from their grandmother on their marriage. He may still decide he wants to marry her to get his hands on that. And because of the scandal she has already caused, she's afraid her father may say it's her duty to keep her promise and try to force her. Monsieur St Clair wants to ensure that the whole episode is quickly forgotten and his family can be restored to its place in society.'

'Well, as long as she's safe now,' Jeannot said thoughtfully, 'we must do what we can to protect her.'

Pierre told him the address of Agathe's apartment. 'No one knows of this place except Agathe herself, Annette and me. Hélène is quite safe there for the present. They're making a little money doing piecework sewing for a dressmaker nearby. Not a lot, but it all helps and it's something Hélène can do at home, out of sight.'

'I see.' Jeannot nodded. 'Well, if your girl wants to make herself a franc or two she can work on one of my stalls in the market. Tell her to go to the outside market at St Eustache and look for Benny Bonnet, sells eggs and chickens. I'll tell him to expect her, she can help with the plucking an' that.'

As Jeannot let himself out of the stable yard, he thought back to how he'd managed to rescue Hélène from the clutches of the army deserter named Gaston who had abducted her all those years ago. She was his to protect and he wasn't going to let some toff called Barnier terrify her as Gaston had done. He went to find his two henchmen, Paul and the Monkey. Together they would make some arrangements. Jeannot had a wide network of people working for him these days, many of them young lads as he had been during the siege, bright and eager to do without question whatever he required of them, for which they were always well rewarded. He would call on some of these now, while he used his information network to discover all he could about a toff called Simon Barnier.

It was several days before Pierre was able to meet with Annette again. As before, they met in the market, where they could mingle with the crowds of housewives carrying baskets to do their marketing. Annette carried hers as she carefully chose bread, eggs, onions and garlic for their evening meal.

Pierre told her about Jeannot's visit to the stable. 'He says if you want to earn some money you should find someone called Benny Bonnet who has a stall selling chickens and eggs in the St Eustache market. He says he'll tell Benny to expect you. It won't be much, but I thought you might be glad to get out of the apartment for a few hours each day. Hélène can still do the sewing you bring her and between you, you should bring in enough without having to borrow from Agathe.'

Annette was delighted with the idea. She longed to escape the apartment into the fresh air, such as it was, of the city streets. Together they went to the market in St Eustache Square, where it was easy enough to find Benny, standing beside his stall, a crate of live chickens at his side, several others, their necks wrung, hanging from hooks along the roof of the stall.

Benny was a small rat of a man, with a fringe of sandy-coloured hair around a bald pate, who greeted them with a grin displaying wide pink gums in an almost toothless mouth.

'Jeannot said you might come see me,' he said. 'Says you need a job. Well, my missus is laid low at present, so you could help me on the stall each day if you like. Dealing with the chickens an' that. Can't pay you much, just a couple of francs a day.' He squinted at Annette and added, 'You look a useful sort of girl and Jeannot says you're honest enough.' He nodded several times and then said, 'Important that, as I might have to leave you on your own at the stall sometimes when I got some other business to do.'

It was agreed, and Annette was able to tell Hélène when she got home that, thanks to Jeannot, they had another source of income.

Chapter 43

Kitty Chalfont lost her child and her life in mid-February. She had struggled with her pregnancy from the start, but was reassured by Dr Evans, the family physician, when he said that the morning sickness that laid her low would probably abate by the end of the third month.

'Still feeling a bit sick?' he had asked on one of his regular visits.

'Just a bit,' admitted Kitty. 'And some pain, in my side. I just can't seem to get comfortable.'

'Ah,' said the doctor with a smile. 'The joys of pregnancy. No bleeding, though?'

'Just a few spots,' Kitty said. She looked at him anxiously. 'I'm not going to have a miscarriage, am I?'

'No, my dear lady,' replied the doctor heartily. 'Whatever makes you think that?'

'Nothing really,' said Kitty. 'It's just that when it's your first baby, you don't know what to expect, do you? What's normal, you know?'

'Well, if you're worried, I can examine you, if you'd like me to,' suggested the doctor.

'No,' Kitty replied hastily, 'no need for that, I'm sure.' The thought of the old man seeing her naked stomach, feeling for the baby, running his hands across her belly and who knew where else, made her shudder. No one but Rupert, and possibly the midwife when the time came, should see the bare flesh of her abdomen.

It was Lady Blake, worried by her daughter's listlessness and continued sickness, who suggested sending for Mrs Harper.

'She's an experienced midwife,' she told Rupert. 'Knows far more about having babies than any doctor.'

'By all means,' he said. 'If you think it's necessary.'

Lady Blake did think so, and the message was sent.

When Mrs Harper arrived from the village an hour later, Rupert left her to his mother-in-law; it was women's business. He didn't know what the problem was or what he should be asking her.

Lady Blake took her into Kitty's room and closed the door behind her, leaving Rupert firmly outside. Once with Kitty, Mrs Harper was all efficiency.

'Now then, my lady, I'm going to have to examine you. I need to look at your stomach. Don't worry, it won't hurt, but we just have to see if baby is all right. Don't want him getting into trouble, now, do we?'

Kitty agreed that they didn't and, closing her eyes, submitted to the gentle pressure of Mrs Harper's hands.

Mrs Harper knew almost at once that there was indeed something wrong. The child was lying in quite the wrong place. She looked up and exchanged a glance with Lady Blake.

Gently she replaced Kitty's bedclothes and smiled down into her fearful eyes. 'There now,' she said. 'That's over, not so bad, you see. Now, you get some rest while I have a word with your mother.'

In Rupert's study Mrs Harper explained her fears – that

the baby was growing outside Kitty's womb and at this late stage there was almost nothing that could be done. Rupert immediately telegraphed for a doctor from Harley Street. He came at once by train but when he'd examined Kitty, he only confirmed that the midwife was right, the baby was trying to grow in the wrong place.

Kitty suffered more and more pain, and when the tube finally ruptured, as the London doctor had known it must, and she began to bleed, there was nothing anyone could do. There was no baby to save and the mother was beyond saving. As she lost too much blood, she lost her grip on life and Pilgrim's Oak suffered its third death in six months.

She was buried in the graveyard of the church where she and Rupert had been married. Apart from the priest there was no one but Kitty's parents and Rupert and Fran at the church or the graveside. Sir James and Lady Blake stood rigidly dry-eyed as their daughter's coffin was lowered into the ground, Rupert and Fran beside them. Rupert watched as Kitty's mother scattered a handful of soil into the grave, heard it clatter on the coffin lid and felt ineffably sad. He hadn't loved Kitty as a wife should be loved, but he had loved her as a childhood friend and bitterly mourned her passing. Frances stood erect and silent at his side and he wondered at her strength. Three funerals of people she loved. All that were left to her now were him and their mother.

Amabel still spent her days in her parlour, and though Rupert had told her that poor Kitty had died in childbirth, she had simply given him a sweet smile and said, 'How very sad. Poor Justin!'

Rupert moved himself and his office back into Pilgrim's Oak itself. The Dower House, with its memories of Kitty's short tenure, was too sad a place to live and he knew that

Fran would welcome his company back in the main house. Their mother was far beyond running a household, and Fran continued with the task as she had since Justin's accident. It was to her that Mrs Crowley came for orders every day.

Rupert threw himself into the running of the estate. The two estates would never be joined as Sir James and Sir Philip had planned, and it was unlikely Sir James would now fund any of the improvements Rupert had been planning. He would have to do what he could on his own, and he was beginning to consider offering some of the tenant farmers the freehold of their land.

If Papa knew I were disposing of land, he thought ruefully, he'd be spinning in his grave.

It was one evening in late March when he was searching his desk drawers for a tenancy agreement that he found Annette's letter. It was several weeks old now. With everything that had happened, he had almost forgotten about it. He had certainly never replied. He read it again, and again wondered what had happened to the lost letters. Had someone intercepted them? It was just possible, he supposed, but again he came up against the problem of who would do such a thing. Surely no one at Pilgrim's Oak. He didn't want to believe that; he couldn't believe it. Someone at Belair? But why? Monsieur and Madame St Clair had already accepted him as a suitor for their daughter. He read Annette's letter through again. Was it too late to reply to it now? She had kept her promise to write to him about Hélène, and though such a long time had passed, she deserved an answer. Before he could change his mind, he sat down at the desk and picked up his pen.

He was about to send the letter to her at Gavrineau. After all, that was where Hélène would be living now, and where she was, Annette would be too. But something made him hesitate.

If his letters had gone missing before, the same might happen again. When he had finished writing the letter, he decided to address the envelope to Pierre at Belair.

Pierre could be trusted to pass it on to Annette somehow, Rupert thought as he walked to the village to post the letter. He would rely on Pierre as he had relied on Annette, for he knew that both of them had Hélène's interests at heart.

Chapter 44

Hélène was sewing a pocket into the seam of a skirt. As she completed the task she snipped off the thread and smoothed the fabric to be sure that the pocket itself lay flat along the seam, ready for pressing. Hélène had been taught to sew as a child, but Annette had had to teach her how to iron the pocket and the seams when it had been stitched in place. Now she was proficient; she could have the sewing ready and pressed for return by the next day. Today she had been given five skirts and was supposed to be fitting two pockets into each. The sewing was simple and she found her mind wandered as she plied her needle. She was alone in the apartment and would be most of the day. Annette had already left for the St Eustache market, where she had been given work on one of Jeannot's stalls. Despite the job being menial, sometimes including the plucking of a freshly killed chicken for a customer, she had been pleased to accept Jeannot's offer of work – it gave her the freedom to come and go as she chose.

'Chickens!' cried Hélène when she told her. 'You've got to pluck chickens!'

'Isn't as if I haven't done it a hundred times before,' Annette said, giving her a sideways look. 'Working in the kitchens at

Belair, perhaps? How d'you think them birds came to the table without their feathers on!'

'I never thought about it,' admitted Hélène, thinking even as she said it that she had seldom thought about any of the jobs the servants at Belair carried out on a daily basis. 'But I should hate to do it!'

Annette laughed. 'It's not that bad,' she said. 'You could do it if you had to. You can do anything if you have to. You'd never used an iron till you came here, or cooked a meal, now you're a dab hand at both.'

'I'm getting there,' replied Hélène with a rueful smile.

Today as she sewed she thought of her mother, living with Louise at the house in the Avenue Ste Anne. Poor Maman, she thought, she has no idea where I am.

She remembered her conversation with Annette after Pierre had brought news from home. Her father had disowned her, remaining entirely unforgiving of the shame she had brought on the family, but her mother, Pierre had said, showed some sympathy. As she thought of this now, Hélène realised just how much she longed to see her mother. She wanted to feel her mother's arms around her as she explained how Simon had behaved towards her, how he had threatened more. Even though she had been away from Belair and Simon's threats for some weeks now, she still had the occasional nightmare – a throwback to when she had been in the clutches of the Gaston man.

Most of the time she could be strong, but on occasion, like now when she was alone in the apartment, she felt like a young, confused child, and wanted her mother.

She finished the sewing and thought about heating the iron on the kitchen stove but, staring listlessly at the pile of skirts, made no move to do so.

Suppose she went back to the Avenue Ste Anne, just for a short visit, just to see her mother. She need not say where she was living, but simply tell her that she was safe, and that whatever happened to her, she would never, never marry Simon. She would make no mention of Pierre or of his part in her escape. He was their link with Belair. She wouldn't mention Madame Sauze, either. They needed to remain in her mother's employ, and though perhaps Maman would not dismiss them for what they had done, if her father found out, he certainly would and she couldn't be responsible for them losing their livelihoods.

When Annette returned from the market that evening, Hélène had cooked their evening meal. Unsurprisingly, it was chicken that she had stewed in a pot with some of the vegetables Annette had brought from the market. As they sat over their meal, Hélène suggested casually that she might visit her mother.

Annette stared at her, aghast. 'Hélène! Really! You can't possibly. It would be far too dangerous. Supposing Simon is having the house watched.'

'I doubt if he is still,' answered Hélène, 'even if he was once.'

'But why take the risk? You're safe here; we are comfortable in the apartment, and we are both earning money to keep us. We aren't a burden to Aunt Agathe. Until we hear that Simon is going to marry someone else, we can stay here and he'll never find us.'

'I know,' replied Hélène with a sigh, 'it's just that my mother must be worried about me. All I'd do would be to see her and tell her I'm safe. I wouldn't tell her where we are.'

'And she'd tell your father and possibly Simon, too.'

'She might tell them that she'd seen me, but she'd still have no idea where we're living.'

405

'It would be madness,' said Annette flatly. 'Really, Hélène, you must put the idea out of your mind. Maybe in a couple of months, but why take the risk now, when you're safe?'

Hélène didn't answer and Annette went on, 'I remember you telling me that Simon would never give up looking for you. What's changed your mind? He's still the same Simon.'

'But whatever happens, I'll never marry him.'

No, thought Annette bitterly, but what about us? Pierre, Aunt Agathe and me, who helped you escape? She kept these thoughts to herself, but in all their time together, it was the first time Annette resented Hélène's reliance on them.

That night Hélène lay in bed going over their conversation. Though Annette hadn't said any more, Hélène had recognised the tension between them. Annette was right, of course; it would be stupid to give Simon any chance of finding her. She would have to wait a while longer before making contact with her mother.

Annette left the next morning, taking the skirts with her to return to the dressmaker. 'I expect there'll be some more of these,' she said as she folded them into a bag. 'With the summer coming people are going to want some lighter skirts. If there are, I'll collect them on my way home.'

Hélène had nothing to fill her day. She cleared the breakfast bowls away, thinking with a wry smile that washing up was another thing she'd learned to do since she'd left home. Once that was done, however, she had little enthusiasm for any other housekeeping duties. She looked out of the window. The day was overcast but dry. Should she go out? Take the air? Simply to get out of the apartment? She had nowhere particular to go, but she knew she could not stay alone in the apartment all day.

With sudden decision she put on her coat and hat and,

locking the front door behind her, she went quickly down the stairs and out into the street. Pausing on the pavement, she wondered which way to go, but eventually turned right and walked up the narrow road, coming out onto a main thoroughfare. She did not look behind her, entirely unaware of the man who loped along in her wake. She had forgotten how busy the city streets could be, and as she walked she was often pushed and shoved by other pedestrians as they hurried about their business. Dressed as she was in the simple clothes of a working woman, she did not receive the consideration which might have been accorded to her had she been dressed more fashionably. At first she made no conscious decision as to her direction, wandering without purpose, but as she headed further west she realised she was going in the direction of Passy, the direction leading to the Avenue Ste Anne. When at last she saw the church of Our Lady of Sorrows, the church she and her family always attended when they were in Paris, she knew that she was within a stone's throw of their house. She was nearly home.

She paused on the steps of the church and considered what she should do. Annette said it would be mad to risk going to the house, but she was so close. She hadn't set out to come here, but somehow her feet had brought her nonetheless. She knew Annette was right, she could not simply walk up to the front door; anyone might see her, and when the door was opened, all the servants would know that she had come home. Even if her mother did not speak of it, there would be no keeping her reappearance from her father or Simon. Perhaps she should simply turn round and go back to her refuge in the apartment in Batignolles.

But what if...? As she stood hesitantly on the church steps, she had an idea. When she had been hiding in the stables during the siege, her brothers, Georges and Marcel, had always come and gone by way of a small wooden gate set in the high stone wall that surrounded the garden. The gate opened onto a narrow lane outside; it was the way that Jeannot always used when he came visiting Pierre.

I could go in that way, she thought now. No one would notice me going into the stable yard. I could wait in the stables for Pierre and perhaps he could fetch Maman. I could see her in the stables and no one else in the house would even know I'd been there.

She looked down at the shabby clothes she was wearing, bought by Annette from a market stall. She hardly looked like the daughter of the house. Anyone seeing her in the street would assume she was a maid bringing a message. All she had to do was to walk along the road and turn into the lane that ran down the side of the house and it would be most unlikely that anyone would give her a second glance. She could simply slip in through the garden gate, and if that were locked, she might use the port cochère where the carriage turned into the stable yard.

She descended the church steps, and having looked carefully about her and seen only an empty street, she set off towards the house and turned into the lane. From the opposite side of the road, a pair of eyes watched her. Despite her confident walk or maybe because of it, there was something about her that drew their owner's attention and he watched her first try the garden gate, which was locked, and then slip into the yard through the port cochère.

Interesting, he thought. Would she come out again the same way, or would she remain in the house? Either way, he would be able to report her arrival to the man who employed him. He settled down again to wait, as he had waited for several long weeks. Waiting was something he was good at, especially if he received solid coinage for doing so.

Having found the garden gate locked, Hélène had to risk using the wider gates of the port cochère. The yard was empty, and with an anxious glance at the house, she slipped out of sight into the stable block. Pierre was grooming one of the carriage horses and he looked up in surprise.

'Miss Hélène!' he hissed. 'What are you doing here? Why have you come? Is there something wrong? Annette…?'

'It's all right, Pierre,' Hélène said softly, looking round to see if the stable lad was anywhere about. She had forgotten him.

'What's all right?' demanded Pierre. 'What are you doing here?'

'I came to see my mother,' Hélène said.

'To see your mother?' Pierre was incredulous. 'Is she expecting you? Have you contacted her?'

'No, not yet, but I thought if I came here, into the stables, you could fetch her out to see me.' Seeing his shocked expression turning to one of anger, she hurried on, 'I won't go into the house. No one else will see me, and I shan't stay long.'

'Have you considered the risk you're taking?' Pierre snapped. 'Not only for yourself, but for us who have been helping you? I can't believe you've simply walked in here in broad daylight. Anyone could have seen you—'

'I won't tell her where we're living,' interrupted Hélène. 'I just—'

'You just didn't think!' retorted Pierre, his anger unabated. 'You must go, now, before anyone sees you.'

'But Maman—'

'Your mother is out,' Pierre told her, not knowing if that was the case or not, but determined that Hélène should make herself scarce and do it as soon as possible. 'Go! Go now before you waste everything we've all done for you.' He shook his head in despair. 'Christ, Hélène. You had more sense when you were a kid!'

Hélène could feel the tears pricking at the back of her eyes and turned away. Pierre had never spoken to her like that before, would not have dreamed of doing so, and it was clear that he was far too angry to help her. She lifted her chin and stepped back out into the yard. As she did so, the back door of the house opened and Alice, one of the housemaids, came out carrying a pail of slops, which she tipped down into the drain in the middle of the yard. Glancing up, she saw a young girl in a dark, drab coat and hat slipping out of the gate and disappearing into the lane. She saw Pierre watching her from the stable door and she grinned at him.

'You're a dark horse, Pierre,' she chided. 'A bit of skirt on the side, eh?'

Pierre gave her a conspiratorial grin, raising a finger to his lips before turning back into the stables. He knew he should have gone out into the street to be sure the coast was clear before he let Hélène leave, but she had been too quick for him and now it would be too late. He could only hope that Alice was the only one who had seen her, and that only from behind. Thank goodness, Pierre thought, she hadn't recognised her as Hélène St Clair, daughter of the house.

Hélène strode out of the gate, along the lane. She was angry at Pierre's reaction. How dare he speak to her like that! But she was also angry with herself. She knew in her heart that she should not have come here, that Pierre was right and she had risked everything they had all done for her. With tears in her eyes, she turned out of the lane into the street and headed back the way she had come, passing the church and crossing the park behind it.

The man in the garden of the house opposite eased his way out from the bush that had concealed him. His mark was heading back into the city. All he had to do was follow her, discover where she was living and report back. It would be easy to stay far enough behind her that should she happen to look over her shoulder, he would be just another person among the press of people on the street.

Hélène walked quickly, anxious to get as far away as possible from the Avenue Ste Anne, until she suddenly realised that she had strayed into unfamiliar streets and she didn't know where she was. The street she was in didn't look familiar at all. Had she taken a wrong turning? Going towards the Avenue Ste Anne she had recognised landmarks and had found her way easily enough, but now, coming back, she was lost. Where should she turn off? Which of the smaller, meaner streets led back to Batignolles? Had she passed that church? Was that where she must turn left? She paused on a corner and looked about her. Suddenly there was a voice beside her, making her start in fright.

'All right, darlin'? Lost, are you?'

'No,' Hélène snapped. 'Of course not. Go away!'

'Just thought I might be goin' the same way as you, darlin'. We could walk together!' He reached for her arm and she shook him off, shouting, 'Let me go!'

'No need for that,' grinned the man, gripping her arm more firmly. 'Why don't you let me look after you? Pretty girl like you needs looking after!' He pulled her towards the entrance of a narrow alleyway that ran between two shops, but before they reached it and as if in an echo from her childhood, she heard Jeannot's voice. 'Bite, Hélène!' She lowered her head and sank her teeth into the man's hand. He gave a bellow of pain and let go, cradling his injured hand against himself. The moment she was free, Hélène took to her heels and ran. With no idea of where she was going she ran, pushing people out of the way, pulling loose from the hands that tried to stop her until she turned the corner into a narrow street with a bakery on the corner. Here she allowed herself to stop and catch her breath. She looked back over her shoulder, but could see no one trying to follow her. She was certainly lost now and needed directions. She knew if she got to St Eustache market she could find her way back to the apartment. But which way was it? She went into the bakery, and keeping an eye on the street outside for any sign of pursuit, she bought a loaf. It was still warm from the second batch of baking and the smell made her mouth water. As she paid for the bread she spoke to the woman behind the counter.

'Please can you tell me the way to St Eustache?'

The woman looked at her curiously and then said, 'Out of here and turn left. Follow the street to the end and then turn right, then ask again.'

Hélène thanked her and went back outside. As she turned the corner she heard someone speak her name and, spinning round, found herself face to face with Jeannot.

'Bread smells good,' he said. 'Come on, let's go back to your apartment and have something to eat.'

'Jeannot!' Hélène could hardly believe her eyes. 'What are you doing here?'

'What's it look like? Looking after you, of course. But what you thought you was doing, going back to your house when you know everyone's on the lookout for you, I don't know!'

'How do you know that's where I've been?' demanded Hélène, a little of her usual spirit returning now that she had him with her.

'Because,' he said, 'I followed you there. Saw you come out of the apartment and wondered where you was off.'

'You've been following me?' Hélène stared at him. 'All the way?'

'Yeah. Didn't want you running into no trouble, did I?'

'Well, I didn't, did I?' Hélène rounded on him. 'I got away from that man without your help, didn't I?'

'Yeah, when you heard me shout,' Jeannot concurred with a grin. 'But he weren't important, he was only after a bit of fun. No, Hélène, it was the one what was following you back from your house. Wanted to find out where you was hiding, I guess. Work for your fiancé, does he?'

'No one saw me,' Hélène asserted hotly. 'And no one's following me.'

'Well, they aren't now,' Jeannot agreed as they began to walk down the street. 'When you ran, he was after you. He ran, but I was faster. A kick in the right place sorted him. 'Spect he'll be waddling for a few days to come yet.'

'Someone really was following me?' Hélène glanced over her shoulder.

'He ain't there now,' Jeannot assured her. 'And he still don't know where you live. Doubt if he has any idea, cos you was walking round in circles. Now, are we going to get back to your place before that bread's gone cold?'

He set off through a myriad of back lanes and very soon Hélène found herself walking down the narrow street that led to Agathe's apartment building.

She led the way upstairs and opened the front door. Jeannot followed her in and looked round.

'Not bad,' he said. 'Not bad at all. Not quite like your house, though, is it? That why you went back?'

'No, of course not.' Hélène went into the small kitchen

and put some broth on to heat. Within ten minutes they were sitting at the table with the broth, the fresh bread and a hunk of cheese.

'Now then,' Jeannot said as he broke a piece from the baguette and dipped it in the broth. 'Tell me what on earth's going on.'

'It's a long story...' Hélène began.

'Well, give me the short version.'

She did not mention Rupert – well, only in passing as someone she had wondered if she might marry. She told him about Simon, how she'd been encouraged to accept him by her parents, and then how he had threatened her. She explained that she was afraid of him and didn't dare go home.

'But you went today,' Jeannot said. 'I followed you all the way there.'

'I wanted to see my mother,' Hélène said. 'She must be frantic with worry.' She paused and added, 'It's the second time she's lost me.'

'Why don't you go back, then?' asked Jeannot. 'Because of this Barnier bloke? Does he still want to marry you? After you've run off an' that?'

'I don't know, but my father is so ashamed of me, Pierre says he won't let them mention my name at Belair. I might not be allowed back.'

'Did you see Pierre while you was at the house today?' asked Jeannot.

'Yes, I did, and he wasn't at all pleased to see me. He told me I was risking everything.'

'He was right,' Jeannot said firmly. 'If I hadn't been watching your back, you'd have led your fiancé's snout straight here.'

'He's not my fiancé,' snapped Hélène.

'Well, whoever set that watch on the house wants to know where you are. And whoever it is has been very patient, and today his patience almost paid off.'

'I know it was stupid,' admitted Hélène with a sigh, 'but I can't stay in this apartment all day on my own while Annette is working in the market. I'm going mad.'

'Tell you what,' Jeannot said, 'one of my lads has been keeping tabs on you. It was only luck that I sent him somewhere else this morning and came to watch for myself. He'll be back tomorrow. From now on, when you need to go out, he'll go with you. Make sure you don't run into any more trouble.' He grinned. 'You always was one for gettin' into trouble, wasn't you?'

'Yes,' returned Hélène ruefully. 'When I had anything to do with you.'

Chapter 45

Two days after Hélène's visit to the Avenue Ste Anne, Emile St Clair arrived at the Paris house.

'I shall be staying a week or so,' he told Rosalie. 'I've been sadly neglecting my work with everything that has happened. But when I return to Belair after next weekend, I shall expect you and Louise to return with me. It is time that we get on with our lives and stop skulking in Paris.'

'I have not been *skulking*,' retorted Rosalie. 'Louise and I have been living perfectly normal lives here. It won't be long before Louise will have to be introduced to society and we have been refurbishing her wardrobe.'

'Nevertheless,' Emile insisted. 'We shall all be going back to Belair as soon as I have seen to my business affairs here in Paris.' He paused at his study door and, looking back, said, 'Tell Pierre I want him.'

Pierre knocked on the door and, when summoned inside, waited for instructions.

'I shall be going to my office tomorrow morning,' Emile said. 'Please bring the chaise round at half past nine.'

'Yes, monsieur.' Pierre spoke with great respect, wondering as he did so whether his employer had any idea of his part in Hélène's escape. But when Emile spoke again, it was evident that he had no suspicions as he said, 'We shall all be returning to Belair after the weekend. We shall take the train, but I want you to bring the chaise down to the country. I may have to come up to town now and then, but Madame will not be returning to Paris in the foreseeable future.' He looked up at his coachman and added, 'When we are back at Belair, life will revert to how it was. I want no speculation about my daughter or her whereabouts among the servants. I shall rely on you, Didier and Madame Sauze to ensure this is so. You understand?'

'Yes, sir.' There was no other answer Pierre could give. He turned to leave the room but was called back by Emile.

'I nearly forgot,' he said, opening the attaché case that lay on his desk. 'A letter came for you at Belair.' He handed Pierre an envelope, remarking, 'From England, I see.' He raised an eyebrow as if in query. Thinking fast, Pierre said, 'Thank you, monsieur. It'll be from my cousin who has a position in London.'

Emile gave a vague nod, and taking this as his dismissal, Pierre quickly left the room before any further questions could be asked. He did not know who the letter was from – he had no cousin in London – but he had once written to Rupert Chalfont and it was just possible that this could be a long-delayed reply to that letter. He went to his quarters above the stables and tore it open, only to find that the letter was not written to him at all. It began *Dear Annette* and was signed *Rupert Chalfont*.

Unable to contain his curiosity he read it through quickly, only immediately to reread it more slowly, almost not believing what it said. He stuffed the letter back into its envelope and tucked it under his pillow. He must show it to Annette as soon as he could.

Since she had begun working in the market they had been able to see each other as often as Pierre's work allowed. He would go and give her the letter tomorrow. He was certain that she needed to read it without Hélène's knowledge, and if he gave it to her in the market they could discuss its implications without Hélène even hearing about it while they decided what to do. Then he remembered he had to drive Monsieur St Clair to his office in the morning. Emile had said that they were returning to the country after the weekend; he just had to hope that his master didn't keep him fully employed until they left.

Next morning he put the letter in his pocket just in case there was an opportunity to give it to Annette. He had the chaise at the door punctually at nine thirty and it wasn't long before Emile came out, attaché case in hand. They drove across the city through the morning traffic, and when they reached the architect's office Emile went in, leaving Pierre to wait in the street. In the office, his secretary, Forquet, had a pile of mail and plenty of questions that needed answers.

'I'll just go up to the drawing office first,' Emile told him, 'and then I'll come back and deal with whatever you've got.'

The drawing office was busy with the draughtsmen carefully copying plans ready for the builders to take on site. It was several weeks since Emile had taken his design for a house off the Rue St Honoré to show Monsieur Balfour, the man who had commissioned it. Having eventually approved of what he had seen, Monsieur Balfour had decided to proceed and wanted the plans drawn up immediately so the work could begin as soon as the site was cleared. It was a good commission and Emile knew that if it went well it could attract similar design jobs. It would mean that he had to spend some time in Paris, but that did not worry him. Though he insisted that Rosalie and Louise should return to life at Belair, he knew that he himself would be happier away from the village for the foreseeable future.

When he had inspected the work, encouraging the draughtsmen to take exceptional care, he went back down to his office, where Forquet was waiting for him.

'I see your chaise is waiting in the street,' he said as Emile came back into the room. 'Your groom is walking the horse.'

'Send down to him,' Emile said. 'Tell him to come back for me this afternoon. It's not good for the horse to stand all day. Tell him I shan't be ready for him until at least three o'clock. I will eat at Le Coutelas. He may find me there.'

Forquet sent an office boy down to Pierre with the message, and Emile saw him drive away before he gave his attention to Forquet and his questions.

Pierre couldn't believe his good fortune. He had been told earlier that they would be driving round the various sites where Emile had work in progress, and he had relinquished any hope of delivering Rupert's letter to Annette that day; nor, he'd thought, would there be a chance to discuss its contents. But now Monsieur St Clair was held up in the office and did not want him to return until the afternoon, he had plenty of time. He drove the chaise to Le Coutelas in the next street, where he normally waited for Emile to send for him. He turned in under the sign of the cutlass that hung over the gate and left the horse with its nosebag and the chaise in the care of one of the ostlers. He would be back well before three to drive Emile home after he had eaten.

Telling the ostler there would be a franc for him if he had the horse ready to be put to just before three, he set off on foot for the market. Annette was working with Benny at the stall and was delighted to see him.

'What's this then?' demanded Benny. 'Love's young dream? Go on, off with the pair of you, but be back within the hour. Got some business to see to, right?'

Annette and Pierre scurried away before he could change his mind and went into the café on the edge of the market that they had been frequenting.

The patron grinned at them. 'You're early,' he remarked. 'Skiving, are you?'

He let them take their usual table in a quiet corner, and at last they could speak.

'What are you doing here?' she murmured. 'You didn't say you were coming.'

'Unexpected chance,' he said. 'But I needed to see you.'

'I needed to see you too,' she said with the smile that produced the hidden dimples that made Pierre long to gather her to him and kiss her. He made do with touching the dimples with the tip of his finger and then said, 'There's something we need to discuss. First of all, Monsieur St Clair is here in Paris, so I may not be able to see you for some time. We have to return to Belair after the weekend, so I don't know when I can come to you again.' He took her hand as the joy at seeing him faded from her face. 'Listen, chérie,' he said. 'There's more. We've had a letter – at least you have, but it was addressed to me at Belair.'

'A letter.' Annette was immediately intrigued. 'Who from?'

'Who do you think?'

'I don't know, do I? Just tell me.'

'Sir Rupert Chalfont.'

'Rupert?' Annette was stunned. 'But why would he write to me?'

'Because you wrote to him?'

'But that was ages ago. I was so angry with him that I wrote and told him Hélène was going to marry Simon Barnier. And I said I hoped the idea made him feel as sick as it made me.'

Pierre grinned. 'Did you now?' he said. 'Well, I think you got your wish.'

'Good,' said Annette viciously.

'Anyway, you must read what he says. After all, although it was addressed to me on the envelope, the letter is actually for you, and so I've brought it with me.'

'Have you read it?'

'Yes, because I'd opened it and couldn't not!'

'I wonder why he sent it to you,' mused Annette.

'To make sure you actually got it, I should think,' Pierre said as he handed it over. 'He assumed that you were both living at Gavrineau by now. You'll see why when you read it.'

Annette unfolded it.

Dear Annette

I am sorry I haven't replied to your letter before now. Things have been very difficult here ever since I came home from France. We have had three deaths in the family – my brother's, which you knew about, my father's and my wife's. But these are excuses. I could have replied sooner but I didn't know what to say.

You accuse me of deserting Hélène. I would never have done that had she not cut me out of her life. She did not reply to my letters, or if she did, I didn't receive them... or the one you mention from Pierre, for that matter. That

I find strange... where did they go? To someone else? You say I caused her misery, but you must know that would be the furthest thing from my mind. I fell in love with her the moment I saw her and I love her still. That will never change.

As she is now married, any further contact will be impossible... for both of us.

Yours sincerely

Rupert Chalfont

'Do you believe him?' Annette said, looking up. 'About not receiving the letters?'

'It's possible,' said Pierre, 'but it doesn't explain why he didn't write to her either... at least until he told her he was married.'

'I shan't write to him again,' Annette said, offering the letter back to Pierre. When he shook his head, she put it into her pocket.

'I don't think he's expecting you to,' Pierre was saying. 'But he did say one thing we didn't expect.'

'What was that?'

'He said,' answered Pierre, 'that his wife is dead. He doesn't say how, but don't you see? That means he could marry again... and Hélène is free.'

'Maybe.' Annette looked doubtful. 'But I think it's probably too late, don't you?'

'I don't know,' answered Pierre. 'I don't understand what women think about these things. Might Hélène forgive him, do you think? Does she still love him despite everything?'

Annette shook her head. 'I don't know either, but she swore the other day that she would never, never marry.'

'Because she couldn't marry Rupert, or because the whole idea of marriage is repugnant to her?'

Annette shrugged. 'Either or both. But we don't know that Rupert would want to marry her now anyway.'

'Don't we?' Pierre looked at her quizzically. 'I think we do. I know you will find it hard to forgive him for what you believe he has done, but set that against Hélène's happiness. If he suddenly came back to France looking for her and free to marry her, how do you think she would react? Would she fall into his arms or would she show him the door... or somewhere in between?'

'I don't know,' admitted Annette.

'Nor do I, though I guess probably something in between, but don't you think there's been enough interference in their lives? Don't you think we should give him a chance to make his peace with her if he wants to? I know you'll find it hard to forgive him, but we can be pretty sure it isn't entirely his fault. We can't play God, you know.'

'There isn't a God,' stated Annette flatly.

'Maybe, maybe not, but either way it isn't up to us to make other people's decisions for them. If I were Rupert I'd never forgive anyone who knew that the woman he says he still loves was free to marry him and didn't tell him so.' He looked at Annette, his eyes holding hers. 'If it were you and me, wouldn't you want to know? If you thought I was married and lost to you, wouldn't you want to discover that I was free after all?'

'I suppose.' Annette sounded reluctant.

'You don't seem very sure,' Pierre teased.

'If it was you, of course I would,' she said, her face breaking into a smile, 'but I just think Hélène's had enough to put up with. Suppose he has changed his mind? Or if he's engaged to someone else now.'

'This could be her chance of happiness, you know,' Pierre pointed out. 'Who are we to judge? We should leave it up to him. We should tell him that she hasn't married Simon Barnier and that she's living in Paris and see what happens. If he writes to her, then he'll have made his decision and she can make hers.'

'I'll think about it,' Annette said. 'Even if I do write back to him, he may never get the letter.'

'That's a risk we'll have to take,' Pierre said. 'But if someone has been stealing his post they've probably stopped now, believing there's no further need.'

'I'll think about it,' repeated Annette, 'and in the meantime I shall say absolutely nothing of this to Hélène. And,' she added, 'I shan't tell her that you're all going back to Belair, either, in case she tries to visit her mother again before you go.'

'Certainly she mustn't do that,' Pierre agreed, 'especially as her father is in the house, but if you think about what she did the other day, how much she needed to go home, we have to accept that she can't stay hidden here indefinitely... and nor can you.'

'If Jeannot hadn't been there...'

'He was and kept her safe, but this has to be resolved one way or another. I think you should write back and tell Rupert her situation.'

Later that evening, when Hélène had gone to bed, Annette gave great thought to what Pierre had said about making other people's decisions for them and reluctantly came to the conclusion that he was right. How would she feel if someone willingly kept her away from Pierre? She had never loved or been loved as she was now. Pierre was her rock. Could she stand between Rupert and Hélène? With a sigh she took pen and paper and wrote a short note to Rupert, addressing it to him at Pilgrim's Oak as before. If they heard no more from him, she decided, at least it wouldn't be her fault and Hélène would never know she'd tried. She discarded several efforts before she was happy with what she had written. The letter she put in her pocket, ready to post in the morning; the discards she burned. There should be no trace of any letters to England. Sleep didn't come easily that night as she lay in bed wondering if they would ever hear from him again.

Chapter 46

When Rupert received Annette's letter he could hardly
believe what he was reading. Not only was Hélène not
married to Simon Barnier, but she was in hiding from him.
How could she be so afraid that she couldn't even live with
her own family? Surely they hadn't disowned her because she
had refused to marry him at the last minute? He pictured
Rosalie, a charming and sensible woman who loved all her
children and had seemed particularly protective of Hélène.
He must go to her at once. Annette had not given him an
address but had suggested that, if he wanted to reply, he write
care of Pierre as he had before. The words reminded him yet
again of the mysterious disappearance of letters, both in and
out of Pilgrim's Oak.

Someone must have intercepted them. Looking back with
clear hindsight there was no other conclusion. Once he'd
allowed himself to accept that conclusion, it was equally clear
that there was only one person who could have done it, had
any reason to do it.

None of the servants. They would have no knowledge of
letters from France, nor know the significance of such letters.

Not his mother. As far as he knew, she knew nothing about
Hélène; but even if she had heard of her, she was beyond

doing anything about anything, and had been ever since the shock of Justin's death. Indeed, she seemed unaware of either of the subsequent deaths, of her husband and her daughter-in-law.

His father had been ill long before Rupert had come home, but he had still been head of the family and complete master in his own house. He had been determined that Rupert should take Justin's place and marry Kitty for the benefit of both families, but Rupert knew that his strict moral compass would never have allowed him to do anything underhand. If he wanted something done or not done, he was completely honest about his wishes. He would never have resorted to stealing anyone's mail.

Which left Fran.

Rupert knew it had to be Fran. She, too, had wanted him to marry Kitty. Partly because the idea was so important to her father but also because she wanted everything at Pilgrim's Oak to remain as it always had been. He knew Fran thought it was unlikely she would marry now with her mother to look after, and that Pilgrim's Oak would always be her home. The introduction of some strange young Frenchwoman could have changed everything.

With the news that Hélène was not married as he'd thought and knowing that he was now a widower, it suddenly seemed imperative to Rupert that he should tax Frances with her deception. It must be brought out into the open and dealt with if he were to consider bringing Hélène to Pilgrim's Oak as his bride... if she would have him after all the misery he – and Fran – had caused her. The decision taken, he wasted no time in implementing it. He put Annette's letter into his desk drawer and went to find Fran.

She was in the garden room arranging some early daffodils

in a vase for her mother's parlour. She looked up and smiled as he came into the room.

'Aren't these lovely,' she said. 'Quite a breath of spring, and there are hundreds more coming at the far end of the orchard.'

When Rupert didn't return her smile, she said, 'Rupert? What's wrong? Has something happened? Mama…?'

Rupert didn't answer any of her questions, he simply asked, 'Frances, where are my letters?'

He saw the colour drain from his sister's cheeks, but she looked at him steadily as she replied, 'Letters, Rupert? What letters?'

'You know perfectly well what letters,' he snapped. 'The letters that came to me from France.'

'Letters from France?'

'And the letters I wrote to the woman I love – in France.'

'Rupert, I haven't a clue what you're talking about.'

'Oh yes, Fran. I think you have. Did you destroy them once you'd read them? Burn them, perhaps?'

'I wouldn't destroy someone else's post. What do you think I am?'

'That's what I'm asking myself,' returned Rupert. 'I know that my letters never reached Hélène, and I can only believe that those she wrote never reached me.'

'There's nothing surprising in that,' snapped Frances. 'International post is notoriously unreliable.'

'The thing is, Frances, that since someone stopped monitoring our postbag, I have received two letters from France with very little delay. So' – he fixed her with an unwavering look – 'what's happened to the other letters? I know they were sent, but I never received them. I also know that nothing I sent arrived in France. Only you could have intercepted them, Fran. While my father was ill and my mother indisposed and I was working with Foxton, Mitchell always brought the postbag to you. I'm asking you now for a straight answer. Did you take my mail?'

'What if I did?' Fran tossed her head. 'You, the future *Sir* Rupert Chalfont, couldn't possibly be allowed to marry some French chit of no family or consequence. Papa was totally against it and he was still the head of the family. It should have been completely impossible for you to defy him. I agreed with him. You had to marry a suitable bride, a lady of proper social status. You had to produce an heir so that the family's future would be assured.'

'And who were you to decide who was suitable?' Rupert's voice was icy.

'Rupert!' Fran's tone was challenging. 'If Justin had lived and married Kitty, it wouldn't have mattered who you threw yourself away on. You were not Papa's heir, but once you were, you should have recognised and accepted your duty to your family.' She turned away and, snatching up another daffodil, crammed it into the vase. 'It wasn't even as if you didn't like Kitty. She wasn't some stranger foisted on you, she was a girl you'd known all your life. Someone you used to love. She certainly loved you!'

Ignoring this outburst, Rupert asked, 'So what did you do with my letters, Fran? Did you read them?'

'Certainly not,' replied Fran hotly. 'I am not in the habit of reading other people's letters and I had no interest in what they contained.'

'So you just destroyed them,' Rupert said flatly.

'No, I did not!' Frances's temper was rising. 'I kept them all. You can have them,' she added dismissively, 'if you really want them, but they are of no consequence now, are they?'

'Where are they?'

'In a box in my room.'

Rupert kept a firm hold on his temper as he replied, 'Please go and fetch them.'

'I'll get them when I've finished doing these flowers for Mama.'

'Now, Fran!' Something in his voice made her put down the daffodil she was holding and, without answering, walk out of the room and go upstairs.

Moments later she returned, meeting him in the hall, carrying a wooden box. She thrust it at him and, apparently entirely unrepentant, said, 'I'm going up to sit with Mama. I hope you won't upset her with this nonsense.'

Rupert gave no answer; he simply took the box and, going into his study, closed the door behind him. Frances was left standing in the hall with her heart thumping, her colour high and the knowledge that she had damaged, irreparably, her relationship with her brother.

Seated at the desk in his study; Rupert opened the box and, lifted out the letters it contained. Fran had been telling the truth. They were all sealed and clearly had not been tampered with. One by one he opened them, laying them aside in date order to be read as they had been intended. His own letters were there too, those that had carried his love to Hélène, promising to come back for her as soon as he could. Those he left until last. First he had to read what Hélène had written to him, full of love and interest to start with and then gradually begging him to write. He pictured her face, so beautiful, the way she had looked at him with shining eyes on that last day, and recognised her distress at his imagined desertion.

There was also a letter from Pierre. If only he had received that one, he would have left Pilgrim's Oak and returned to St Etienne immediately. He could have set everything right, but as it was he'd begun to accept that Hélène had had second thoughts, had changed her mind, and finally he had allowed himself to be persuaded into marriage with Kitty.

He stared at the letters laid out before him, and his anger at what Frances had done fuelled his determination. He would write to Pierre as suggested and go at once to Paris. He would stay as usual at the Hotel Montreux and beg Pierre and Annette to keep Hélène safely hidden away until he got there. He told Pierre to leave a message for him at the hotel and he would contact him immediately he arrived.

Having sealed his letter, he addressed it to Pierre, put on his coat and walked to the village to the post office.

Rupert arrived at the Hotel Montreux with his man, Parker, and a quantity of luggage on the same day that his letter reached Pierre at Belair. He was welcomed with even greater enthusiasm than usual by Jacques Rocher when Parker corrected him for addressing Rupert as Monsieur Chalfont and informed him that his master was now Sir Rupert Chalfont, baronet.

'Will you be making a long stay with us, Sir Rupert?'

'I am undecided at present,' replied Rupert cheerfully. 'I trust there will be no problem if I make an extended stay.'

'Certainly not,' responded Rocher. 'The room is yours for as long as you wish to honour us with your presence. The suite on the first floor, with a room across the landing for your man.'

'Have there been any messages for me?' Rupert asked.

'No, sir, I fear not.'

'Well, I'm expecting one in the next day or two, so please let me know as soon as it arrives.'

In her letter Annette had begged him not to go anywhere near Belair, where he might be recognised, and for the moment he was happy enough to accept this, but he knew that should there be no message in the next couple of days he would go to St Etienne and announce his intention there, and said as much in his reply.

Reading this, Pierre was extremely worried. It would be disastrous if Rupert Chalfont turned up at Belair before he had met and talked with Hélène. He took his worry to Agathe, who agreed with him that Rupert must not appear in St Etienne until everything had been resolved.

'If he met with Monsieur Barnier...' Her voice trailed off at the thought of such an awkward encounter.

'We must write to Annette and let her know that he's on his way and where he will be staying,' said Pierre. 'She can go to the hotel and meet him, and between them they can decide the best way forward.'

'A letter may take too long,' Agathe said. 'One of us needs to go.'

'I can't,' said Pierre flatly. 'Monsieur St Clair has told me he needs me to drive him to Versailles tomorrow to visit Captain Georges. I believe he plans to stay overnight.'

'Perhaps I might go,' Agathe said thoughtfully. 'I have not taken my day off yet this month, so perhaps I can ask Madame if I might take it tomorrow.'

Pierre agreed that it was worth a try and Agathe went to see Rosalie in her parlour.

'I'm afraid it is not that convenient, Madame Sauze,' she

said. 'My husband is going to Versailles to see our son and is planning to bring the whole family back here for an extended stay. I shall need you to oversee the preparations for their arrival.'

'I quite understand, madame,' Agathe said, 'but I would only need one day. I hope to attend a funeral in Paris tomorrow, and would be back by tomorrow evening.'

'I see.' Rosalie didn't look best pleased. 'Is it someone close to you?'

'My cousin,' improvised Agathe, 'but we were brought up together as children and so are... were very close.'

'Well, I suppose you must go, but I do expect you to be back tomorrow night.'

'Certainly, madame, that will be no problem. The funeral is at midday. I shall take an early train and be there in plenty of time.'

'Fair enough,' Rosalie agreed. 'I don't think Captain Georges and his family will be arriving until the evening of the day after, but I rely on you to leave instructions before you go and oversee everything when you get back.'

Agathe thanked her and went to tell Pierre that she had leave to go.

The following morning she went to the station. As she walked onto the platform she saw Simon Barnier getting into a first-class compartment. Instinctively she ducked back out of sight, pulling her hat down to shade her face before hurrying across the platform to board the train herself. She could only hope that if he were looking out of the window, he would pay no attention to an elderly lady getting into a third-class carriage further up the train. She was anxious that he should not recognise her. She sat back into her seat and closed her eyes, thinking. Why was he going to Paris? she wondered.

It could of course be for any number of reasons, but she was disconcerted by his presence on the train.

When they finally arrived in Paris, Agathe waited in her carriage until she saw Simon Barnier walk past and greet a young man hovering on the platform. Only then did she step down from the train and make her way out of the station. As she emerged into the street, looking for the omnibus stop, she almost walked straight into him. Simon Barnier was standing at the kerbside while the young man summoned a fiacre. He turned with an angry, 'Look where you're—', only then seeing who it was and saying, 'Madame Sauze. What can bring you to Paris, I wonder?'

'Good morning, Monsieur Barnier,' she replied. 'A funeral, I'm afraid.'

His eyes drilled into her. 'Not in search of your niece?'

'My niece, sir?'

'The maid Annette.'

'No, sir,' replied Agathe. She was tempted to say more, but at the last moment held her peace. Better to say too little rather than too much.

At that minute the young man appeared with a fiacre. 'You've taken your time, Eugène,' snapped Simon. He looked back at Agathe. 'I'm surprised that Madame St Clair can spare you to come to the city with her son and his family arriving so soon.'

'I'm only here for the day, sir. I shall be returning on the evening train.'

Simon climbed into the cab and was driven away, moments later disappearing round a bend in the road.

I wonder how Monsieur Barnier knows so much about what's happening at Belair, mused Agathe. I only heard of Georges's arrival myself yesterday. He must have someone in his pay, keeping watch on the family. She found the idea didn't surprise her; after all, he had tried to suborn Annette while Rupert was there.

Pierre had told her to go to the market, where Annette would be working on Benny's stall.

'It will give you a chance to speak to her without Hélène knowing anything about it. You must tell her to go to the hotel and find Rupert. Warn him not to come here. What they decide to do... well, they'll have to decide themselves, but make sure Rupert understands what has happened and that if he is going to try to see Hélène, he must move softly, or that will be the end of any chance he has.'

Agathe found Annette looking after Benny's stall and the two women greeted each other in delight.

'I've come with a message,' Agathe told her. 'Rupert's had your letter and is coming to Paris. He should arrive any time, but if he's not here yet, you're to leave a message for him at the Hotel Montreux.' She gripped Annette's hands. 'Whatever happens, don't let him go to St Etienne.'

'I don't suppose he'll want to,' Annette said. 'He'll want to see Hélène and she's here.'

'Still, we need to leave him a message as soon as possible. When will you go?'

'As soon as Benny gets back,' replied Annette. 'I can't leave his stall unattended.'

While Annette and Agathe were talking in the marketplace Rupert Chalfont was renewing some of his acquaintances in Paris. It was nearly nine months since he had been there, on his way to Lucas Barrineau's wedding. His hope that there would be a message from Annette or Pierre when he arrived had been disappointed, and rather than wait around in the hotel, he sent Parker with a note to David Bertram, with whom he'd been at school and who was now an attaché in the British Embassy. Parker soon returned with a reply, saying David was delighted to hear Rupert was back in Paris, had immediately suggested that they lunch together and had suggested Le Chien Dansant, a restaurant in a side street close by the embassy and a favourite with them both. It was a bright spring day, the sort of day that clothed the city in sunshine and lifted the spirits with the promise of summer, and Rupert decided that the walk would do him good. He was in no particular hurry as he made his way towards the restaurant in the street off the Rue du Faubourg St Honoré. His thoughts were filled with Hélène. How long before he learned where she was? Before he saw her with his own eyes? As he turned into the side street he was unaware of a well-dressed gentleman coming towards him. He reached the restaurant, seeing the familiar dancing dog sign above the window, and pushed open the door to enter.

Simon Barnier had slowed to a standstill, hardly able to believe his eyes as he saw Rupert Chalfont enter the restaurant a little way ahead.

Surely he must be mistaken. Why would Rupert Chalfont be here in Paris? He should be home in England looking after his new wife, not dining in restaurants in Paris. Perhaps it was not him. Slowly he walked past the window and glanced in. A man was just getting to his feet to shake hands with his guest, and that guest, Simon was quite certain now, was Rupert Chalfont.

'Eugène,' he said, turning to the young man, who was still with him. 'Did you see the tall man who went into Le Chien Dansant?'

Eugène nodded. 'Who is he, monsieur?' he asked.

'Never mind who,' snapped Simon, 'but I need to know

where he is staying. Get André straight away. I want him followed. Tell André to find out where the man is staying and then come and report back to me at the hotel. Go, now.'

Eugène scurried off in search of André, while Simon wandered slowly past Le Chien to the entrance of an apartment building a little further up the street from whose shelter he could watch the restaurant to make sure that his quarry didn't leave before his tail was in place.

Once André had arrived and was installed in the apartment building's porch, Simon left him, not wanting to be seen or recognised by Rupert when he finally emerged.

Due to his unexpected vigil, he had missed both his lunch and his appointment with the young lady whom he visited on his trips to Paris, and he knew she would not be best pleased. Mademoiselle Angélique knew how to please him, her erotic person and ingenious games providing him with the release he needed from time to time. He had assumed that once he was married to Hélène there would be no need of further visits to Mademoiselle Angélique; he would simply use Hélène in the same way – teach her what he liked and expect her to provide it whenever he chose.

Now, he returned to the Pension Marguerite, where he stayed on such visits, and thought about the day. First, there was the housekeeper, Madame Sauze. She was Annette the maid's aunt and she was in Paris for one day. Then he'd seen Rupert, the foppish Englishman who had deserted Hélène last autumn. What were they both doing in Paris on the same day? Surely that couldn't be a coincidence? There had to be something going on, something to do with Hélène. That old woman must know where she's hiding, he thought. Perhaps she'd known all along. Well, once André had done his stuff and discovered where Rupert was staying, Simon could plan his next move. He only hoped that André made a better job of following Rupert than he had when he'd tried to follow Hélène from the Avenue St Anne. Simon had been furious when he'd heard that André had had her in his sights and then had somehow managed to lose her when he had been attacked by some cutpurse and left sprawling in the gutter, clutching his private parts.

Simon still wanted Hélène, to own her and bend her to his will. When she finally came back home she would be ruined, having run away and lived who knew where and with who knew whom. Her reputation would be in the gutter. Her only way back was to allow him to forgive her and marry him after all. He had been patient, and now here was that damned Englishman again.

The damned Englishman and his old friend David had a leisurely luncheon at Le Chien Dansant. The food, Rupert decided, was even better than he remembered. As always he enjoyed the French dishes that passed across the table, and the wine that accompanied them – so much more interesting than the plain English fare offered in restaurants at home – and it was some considerable time later that they left the restaurant and made their way back towards the embassy.

'If you're going to be in Paris for any length of time,' said David as they paused to shake hands, 'you must come and dine with us one evening. Christine would love to see you again, especially now you're *Sir* Rupert.' He saluted him with a mock bow and went into the embassy, leaving Rupert to walk back to the Hotel Montreux to see if any messages had been left for him.

An hour later André was able to report to Eugène that

the man he'd been set to follow was staying at the Hotel Montreux off the Boulevard St Germain. A chat with one of the ostlers and an exchange of five francs had elicited the fact that the man was indeed Sir Rupert Chalfont and that he had come with his man and a quantity of luggage which seemed to indicate that he was not planning to return home in the near future.

Entirely unaware of anyone's interest in his movements, Rupert wandered into the public lounge and sent Parker to ask if there had been any messages for him while he was out.

Moments later Jacques Rocher came in carrying a folded note on a tray.

'A young woman, Sir Rupert,' he said. 'Not the sort of clientele we encourage, but when she said she had a message for you and we knew you were expecting one, we gave her admittance and took charge of her note. She said she has to speak with you, but as you weren't here, we sent her away and told her to come back tomorrow.'

'Pity you sent her away, Rocher. I need to speak to her.'

'I'm sorry, Sir Rupert, but I wasn't to know, and it doesn't do the hotel any good to have the likes of her loitering about outside. Anyone seeing her might think it was a bawdy house.'

Rupert sighed. 'If she comes here again, ask her to wait. If I'm not here and you can't allow her to wait in the hallway to deliver her message, you must take her into the servants' quarters and permit her to wait for me there.'

Chapter 47

Annette's note had not given Rupert the address of the apartment where she and Hélène were living; all she had said was that as he had arrived in Paris he should come to the market at St Eustache the next morning and find her at the poulterer's stall. She might tell him where Hélène was then. Rupert had to accept that his approach to Hélène must be carefully managed and meeting Annette was the first step. He knew he couldn't assume that Hélène would be pleased to see him; indeed, she might refuse to meet him at all. All he did know was that though he was aching to see her, he would have to wait. So that evening he stayed in his suite and played backgammon with Parker, with André keeping a fruitless vigil in the street.

In the morning Rupert was just finishing his breakfast when Rocher announced that he had a visitor. Thinking it must be Annette, he asked Rocher to bring her into the dining room and to bring more coffee. He looked expectantly at the door and was amazed to see, not Annette, but Simon Barnier walking into the room. He paused in the doorway, staring at Rupert with an implacable hostility.

Rupert got to his feet and, speaking amiably, said, 'Monsieur Barnier, what a surprise to see you here. How do you do?'

'None the better for seeing you, Chalfont!'

'Did you know I was staying here,' enquired Rupert, 'or is our meeting here pure coincidence?'

'I heard you were here,' replied Simon, 'and I came to find out why.'

'I wonder whom you heard it from?' He paused to allow Simon to answer, but as no answer was forthcoming, he went on, 'And why I have come, of course, is no business of yours.'

'It is if it has anything to do with Mademoiselle Hélène St Clair, my fiancée.'

'Your fiancée!' echoed Rupert. 'Allow me to congratulate you. When will you be married?'

'The date will be set very soon,' answered Simon, '*if* that is any business of yours.'

'That is surprising news,' responded Rupert. 'I had heard that Miss Hélène was away at present.'

'Indeed! And who told you that?'

'Probably the same person who told you that I was staying here,' replied Rupert smoothly. 'Now, if you'll excuse me, much as I'd like to chat some more about mutual friends, I have business to attend to, which as I mentioned before has nothing to do with you. I'll bid you good day, monsieur.'

Simon remained in the doorway, barring Rupert's path, but as Rupert simply walked towards him he gave way, allowing him to leave the room.

'You haven't heard the last of this, Chalfont,' Simon snarled as he passed. 'You had your chance, but now she's mine. You're a married man and you're in no position to approach her. You sully her reputation by even thinking of speaking to her. I should have known yesterday when I saw that old bag of a housekeeper coming to Paris that she was up to something. Coming to a funeral indeed! What Hélène's parents will say when I tell them that Madame Sauze has known where their daughter has been all this time, I can't imagine. Out on the street if she were my housekeeper.'

Rupert made no reply until he reached the foot of the stairs, when he turned back, smiling enigmatically. 'How fortunate that she isn't,' he said.

When he came downstairs again ready to go and meet Annette in the market, Parker was waiting for him in the hall.

'Just thought you'd like to know, sir, that I saw the man who just left speak to a young man outside. A young man with red hair, which he keeps covered with an old cap. Not a gentleman, dressed in corduroy trousers and a sackcloth jacket. He slipped away to the stable yard, and your gentleman returned to the fiacre he'd arrived in and drove off. The other man is still in the yard.'

'Good work, Parker. I imagine he's been left as a tail. We'd better use the trick we used in Padua.'

'Right-ho, sir. Just give me the word when to start.'

'Oh, I think we might as well get on with it, but don't forget there might be two watching us, so keep your eyes peeled. If you think it's clear, meet me at St Eustache church as soon as you're sure you're not being followed.'

Parker grinned. 'Got us out of a tight spot in Padua,' he said. 'Should work here, too. I'll go round to the stable now. Our friends don't know about me, so shouldn't be any trouble.'

Minutes later, as he waited in the hotel hallway, Rupert heard an altercation in the stable yard. Shouting and the grunts and bellows of a fist fight; a horse was whinnying and there was the crash of hooves on cobbles, followed by more and louder shouts as the hotel's ostlers joined the fray.

Rupert made no effort to go and investigate, but slipped out into the street and vanished into a side alley. Parker would eventually be explaining how he had seen the man with the red hair sliding his hand into the saddlebag of a mare standing ready, waiting for her owner to set out.

Redhead was denying everything, but he had been detained by the ostlers, who wanted no thieves other than themselves in their yard. After more shouting, and threatened fisticuffs, Jacques Rocher made his way outside. Hearing it was Sir Rupert's man who had seen the thief and caught him red-handed, he had him searched. When nothing was found on him, Rocher told his men to throw him out of the yard with a farewell boot in the backside and an instruction never to show his face at the Hotel Montreux again.

'I am so sorry that you should have been involved in such an uproar, Monsieur Parker,' Rocher said as they went back into the hotel. 'You obviously caught the thief just in time, before he actually managed to take anything from the saddlebag. But with nothing in his hands or pockets we had to let him go. I hope Sir Rupert was not incommoded?'

'No, monsieur, I'm sure he wasn't. If you'll excuse me I'll go up to his suite.'

Rocher returned through the old oak door to his quarters, and Parker went up to the empty suite and looked down into the street. There were plenty of people about, but no sign of Redhead, or anyone else idly loitering as if waiting for someone.

Parker went back downstairs and walked away down the road, turning into the Boulevard St Germain and taking a circuitous route to St Eustache. When he was quite sure he had shaken any possible tail, he made his way to the church, where Rupert was waiting.

'I'm going to speak to someone now you're here,' Rupert told him. 'Keep your eyes peeled and if there's any sign we're being watched, simply walk past me whistling and we'll deal with it.'

While he had been waiting for Parker to find him, he had walked through the marketplace and spotted the poulterer's stall, where Annette was dealing with a customer. He would go nowhere near her until Parker returned without a tail.

Now, he wandered casually between the jumble of stalls, pausing at several before approaching Annette.

Although she had been expecting him, she only saw him at the last minute.

'Good morning,' he said with a smile.

Annette looked anxiously about her, but no one seemed to be interested in either of them.

'We can't talk here,' she said and, pointing out the café she and Pierre usually frequented, added, 'I'll meet you there as soon as Benny comes back.'

Twenty minutes later they were sitting in the corner at the back of the café with coffee and pastries in front of them.

'How is she?' Rupert asked. 'Is she safe?'

'She's quite safe,' replied Annette. 'No one knows where we are.'

'Well,' Rupert said, 'I don't want to worry you, but Simon Barnier turned up at my hotel this morning, warning me away. Saying that he and Hélène were about to get married.'

'How did he know where to find you?'

Rupert shrugged. 'I don't know. Just bad luck, I think. He must have seen me yesterday when I arrived. Anyway, he came to the hotel this morning to warn me off.'

Annette stared at him, pale-faced. 'What did you do? What did you say?'

'Well, first of all I didn't say I wasn't married,' Rupert said, 'so he doesn't think I'm a real threat at present. I don't know how he found out I was in Paris, but he set someone to follow me when I left the hotel this morning.'

'You haven't been followed here, have you?'

'No, my man Parker dealt with him. However, now they know where I'm staying, they may well try again and it would certainly be better if you didn't come back to the hotel.'

'Madame Sauze was here in Paris yesterday. She came to tell me that you were on your way and to warn you not to go to St Etienne. She was afraid you might meet up with Simon Barnier and everything would be stirred up again. Anyway, when she was catching the train she saw him. He was catching it too, though he didn't see her at the time. The trouble is he did see her at the station when they arrived. She had waited until he'd disappeared but then almost bumped into him as he was getting into a fiacre.'

'Did he speak to her?'

'Yes, she told him she was going to a funeral. But the thing is, he seemed to know what was happening at Belair, news that Agathe had only heard herself the day before. He must have someone spying for him there.'

'Then Pierre must take extra care,' Rupert said.

'Aunt Agathe was going to warn him. She considered warning Madame St Clair too, but that would have meant revealing that we were all involved in Hélène's disappearance, and perhaps lead them to her.'

'I think we have to leave that end of things to Pierre,' Rupert said. 'As long as he's been warned. I'm more worried about what Simon Barnier is doing here in Paris and how he found me so quickly.'

Silence lapsed about them for several moments as each of

them assessed the new situation. It was Rupert who broke it, his thoughts returning to Hélène.

'Will she see me, do you think?'

'I don't know,' replied Annette. 'She doesn't know you're here, and she doesn't know... well, about your wife. You have to understand she was devastated when you wrote and told her you were married. It was only the second letter she'd had from you since you'd left.'

'I know. My sister Frances was intercepting our letters, both the ones Hélène wrote to me and the ones I wrote her. Frances has admitted that now and I have all the letters she took.'

'She didn't take the one saying you were married,' pointed out Annette. 'Why was that?'

'I didn't know that she was taking them, but I posted that one myself.' He looked at her worried face. 'I had been going to suggest that you bring her to the hotel, where we could meet in private, but clearly we can't do that now. Simon Barnier will suspect I'm up to something and have the hotel watched.'

'Well, you can't come to the apartment for the same reason,' Annette told him firmly. 'I'm not even going to tell you where it is, in case you're tempted to come and bring your shadow with you.'

'That's fair enough for the moment,' Rupert agreed. 'Look, Annette, you've been a good friend to Hélène, and so I'm going to trust you even more than before.' He reached into his pocket and pulled out a bundle tied up in brown paper. 'These are all the letters that Frances stole. She didn't read them, they were still sealed when I got them back. I've opened them and when they are read in order, they tell the whole sorry story. Please will you go home to Hélène and tell her that I'm here in Paris? Tell her that Kitty, the girl I married, died with our child in February. Tell her... no, I'll tell her that myself. Please give her the letters so that she can see I was begging her to write. Ask her to read them all and then ask her if she will let me come to her.'

Annette hesitated and then reached for the bundle and tucked it into her bag. 'I'll tell her what you say,' she promised. 'I have to get back to the stall now, but if you come and find me tomorrow I'll tell you.' She stood up and went on, 'Don't come near me again today – if you're being followed we can't risk them transferring the follower to me.'

'Don't worry, Annette.' Rupert tried to sound reassuring. 'I promise you, no one followed me this morning.'

'Make sure no one does when you come tomorrow,' warned Annette.

When she had gone, the precious bundle of letters in her bag, Rupert ordered more coffee and waited for her to get safely back to the market stall. When he left the café, he found Parker waiting for him outside.

'You saw that girl I was with?' Rupert asked.

'Yes, sir.'

'When she leaves the market later today, I want you to follow her and see where she goes. I want to know where she lives, and make sure no one else is tailing her. I'm going back to the hotel now.'

'What about your shadow, sir?'

'Oh, if he's come back, or I get another, I'll keep them busy. There's lots of Paris to see, after all! Report back to me at the hotel this evening and we'll take it from there.'

Chapter 48

Annette left the market and walked back towards the apartment. Several times she stopped and turned suddenly, and once she went round a corner and ducked into a doorway, watching to see if anyone was following her, but by the time she approached the apartment building she was almost certain there was no one. Even so, she first went into the butcher's shop as if to buy something, and looked out of the window. It was then that she nearly caught sight of Parker, but he, as he saw her looking out of the shop window, continued walking and disappeared round the corner. While the street was still empty, Annette slipped out of the shop and in through the door beside it, and ran up the stairs to the apartment.

Hélène was sitting in the window, finishing collars and cuffs on some blouses. 'They should pay more for these,' she said as Annette came in. 'They're very fiddly!' She looked up as Annette crossed to the window beside her and peered down into the street.

'What are you looking at?' Hélène asked.

'Just checking that I wasn't followed here, but I can't see anyone down there now.'

'Followed?' Hélène was immediately apprehensive. 'Who was following you?'

'No one, but yesterday Aunt Agathe came into Paris and when I saw her she said that Simon Barnier was on the same train, and though she tried to avoid him, he saw her at the station and demanded to know why she'd come in.'

'Madame Sauze? Was she coming to see us?' asked Hélène. 'To bring us news from Belair? What did she say?'

'She told him she was coming for a funeral.'

'And was she?'

'No, she was coming to find me. She wasn't coming here, as she didn't want to risk it, but she was coming to find me at the market, as she did have some news for us.'

'What was it? Is someone ill? Maman or Louise?'

'No, nothing like that, but we do have to talk, Hélène.'

Hélène folded the last blouse and laid it aside. 'Well, what news did she bring?'

Annette didn't answer immediately. On her way home from the market she had been deciding just how she would break the news about Rupert to Hélène. She had thought she would find the words when necessary, but now they failed her.

'Was it bad news? Come on, Annette. Tell me.'

'Not bad news, no,' replied Annette. 'Just something... surprising.'

'Come on, then,' urged Hélène with a smile. 'Surprise me!'

'Pierre has had a letter – well, it was addressed to him on the envelope, but inside it was to me.'

'Who was it from?'

'It was... it was from Rupert Chalfont.'

The colour drained from Hélène's face and she said, 'I don't think that's a very good joke, Annette.'

'I promise you, it isn't a joke. He wrote to me to ask about you.'

'Why?' demanded Hélène angrily. 'Why did he write to

you? No, I don't want to hear. I never want to hear a word about him, ever again.'

Ignoring her outburst and knowing she must go on until she'd told all, Annette said, 'He wrote to me because I wrote to him.'

'You wrote to him?' Hélène was incredulous. 'Why? When? What for?'

'I wrote to him back in January, to tell him you were going to marry Simon Barnier. I said I hoped it made him feel as sick as it made me.'

Hélène managed a weak smile at that. 'Nothing like as sick as it made me,' she said.

'Anyway, he didn't write back,' Annette went on. 'I wasn't surprised, I didn't expect him to. He didn't answer the letter Pierre wrote to him, back in the autumn.'

'Pierre wrote to him? What on earth for?'

'To ask him why he wasn't answering your letters.'

'Well, we know the answer to that now,' said Hélène bitterly. 'It was because he was married.'

'Let me finish,' Annette said firmly. 'Let me explain everything.'

Hélène gave a heavy sigh. 'If you must.'

'I must,' insisted Annette, and quietly she began to explain exactly what had happened, about the letters, about Frances, about Kitty and her baby, and finally about Rupert being in Paris.

'He thought, because of my letter in January, that you were married to Simon now, that you were beyond his reach. He had set my letter aside as he dealt with his father's illness and death and then the death of his wife and baby. It was only when he came across it again very recently that he answered it, mentioning the three deaths his family had suffered, one of them being his wife. It was his final farewell to you. Pierre and I didn't know what to do.' For a moment Annette lapsed into silence.

'So, what did you do?'

'We talked it through and in the end decided to write and tell him you hadn't married Simon, that you'd run away before the wedding and were in hiding.'

'You didn't think to consult me?' Hélène suggested coldly.

'No, not then. At least, we did think of it but decided against it until we knew more.'

'And?'

'I did write and it was in answer to that letter that we received one the other day. It was sent to Pierre at Belair.'

'What did it say?' Hélène's voice was little more than a whisper.

'He said he was on his way, and to make sure we kept you safely hidden until he got here. Well, he's here now, in Paris. I saw him today. He came to the market to find me... and he wants to see you.'

'Well, I don't want to see him.'

'He's given me something for you,' Annette said.

'I don't want it, whatever it is,' asserted Hélène.

In answer, Annette took the parcel from her bag and put it down on the table between them. Hélène didn't pick it up, simply looked at it.

'What is it? Does he think he can buy me with presents? Take it back to him, wherever he is, and tell him it's all too late. I'm not going to marry Simon Barnier, I'm not going to marry anyone and I don't want to see him. I've forgotten him now and there's no point in opening old wounds and so you can tell him.'

'Fine,' said Annette, getting up from her chair. 'I've brought home some chicken legs. I thought I'd fry them for supper. Have we still got onions and garlic?'

Faced with this sudden change of subject, Hélène said, 'Onions? I don't know.'

'Have you finished your sewing?' asked Annette. 'If so, I'll drop it off at the workshop tomorrow on my way to the market.'

Later, when they had eaten their evening meal, taken in almost complete silence, Annette said, 'I'm going to bed. It's been a long day, and Benny wants me all day tomorrow.'

Left alone in the living room, Hélène looked at the brown paper parcel that still lay on the small table by the window. Whatever he had sent her, she didn't want it. But it was there, almost like a magnet, drawing her towards it, and she turned her chair away so that she could no longer see it. She pulled the curtains across the window, shutting out the night, and below in the street someone turned away, as certain as he could be that no one from that apartment was going to go out again that night.

In the apartment Hélène turned down the lamp and went into her bedroom, the one that had belonged to Fleur, Madame Sauze's sister. Madame Sauze. Madame Sauze had seen Simon Barnier yesterday and been seen by him. What was he doing in Paris? Had he simply come up on business or was he really still looking for her? As she got undressed and climbed into bed, she shuddered at the thought of his touch on her face. She was about to blow out the candle when she changed her mind and went back into the living room. The shadows jumped about the flickering candle as she crept over to the table in the window, picked up the brown paper parcel... and carried it back to bed.

When Annette got up in the morning she noticed that the

parcel had disappeared and made no comment. When she left for the market she took with her the blouses complete with their attached collars and cuffs and said she would bring more home that evening.

Once she was alone in the apartment, Hélène retrieved the bundle of letters from under her bed and laid them out on the table. She had read through them last night, squinting at the handwriting by the light of her candle. Now she wanted to study them in closer detail. To the pile she added the ones she had brought with her from Belair. As she read the earliest ones, she found herself listening to Rupert's voice, once again bringing tears to her eyes. She had long ago promised herself she would cry no more tears for him, no more tears for any man, but despite this, she found them slipping down her cheeks. If she closed her eyes she could see his beloved face, and immediately she snapped them open again. Whatever had happened about the letters, he had allowed himself to be persuaded to marry someone else when he was already promised to her.

'You allowed yourself to be persuaded, too,' a little voice inside her whispered.

'But only when I knew he was already married,' she answered aloud.

She read all the letters through again, including the ones sent by Pierre and Annette. She had been angry that they had taken it upon themselves to tell Rupert her heart was breaking. It left her no pride, and it was pride had carried her through the dark days that followed the news of Rupert's desertion.

She thought of Rupert, coming at once to Paris when he heard she was not married. He had spoken to Annette in the marketplace yesterday, given her the letters. Perhaps he would come to the market again today to find out what she had said. Well, she had told Annette to send him away.

She picked up the letters one by one and folded them back into their envelopes. It was too late. Whatever reason there had been, all the misery and misunderstandings, it was too late.

And with that thought in mind she put on her hat and coat and left the apartment. It was too late, she kept telling herself as she walked to the market, but perhaps she could see him, just one more time. See him without him seeing her. When she reached the market square she moved from stall to stall, keeping watch on the poulterer's stand, seeing Annette serving customers, and then suddenly, there he was. Her Rupert. Not her Rupert. Just Rupert. He walked casually to where Annette was selling eggs to a large woman with a basket, waiting for her to be free. Benny was there too, and when he saw Rupert, he nodded to Annette and the two of them drifted away from the stall. Staying well back, Hélène watched them enter the café. It took all her determination not to follow them inside. Annette would be giving him her message now and then it would all be over. Rupert would go back home to England, he'd settle down at Pilgrim's Oak, probably after some time he would remarry and start a family and she would never see him again. She would be able to push him into the recesses of her mind, as she had already begun to do.

Quickly she turned on her heel and, with tears flooding down her cheeks, set off back to the apartment. She had made the complete break and when she got home she would take her courage in her hands and go back to Belair, to the rest of her life. She would become a doting aunt, but she would never have any children of her own. She should never have run away, but should have stood up against the proposed marriage with Simon Barnier as soon as she'd realised his true character. No one could force her into such a marriage, and though she knew her reputation was now in tatters, she had to believe that her family would stand by her and take her back. She climbed the stairs to the apartment. She would pack up her few things and then leave, take the train home and face the music.

As Hélène was walking slowly back to the apartment, Annette was breaking the news to Rupert.

'She says she won't see you,' she told him. 'She says there's no point in opening old wounds.'

'Did you give her the letters?'

'Yes, but she didn't open the parcel, at least not while I was there. I left it on the table when I went to bed, but it had disappeared this morning, so I think she's read them now. I'm hoping to persuade her to see you when I get back later today, but I can't leave the stall till the market closes. Benny has business elsewhere.'

Rupert's hopes took a fall, but they weren't completely dashed. He gave a rueful smile. 'I'll come and find you again tomorrow,' he said, 'and hope you've persuaded her to change her mind. That she'll at least see me.'

Annette went back to the stall and Rupert returned to the Hotel Montreux. Parker was waiting for him in the suite.

'Any luck?' Rupert asked.

'Yes, sir. I was outside that butcher's shop this morning and saw Annette come out of the door beside it. There are three apartments in the building and they must be living in one of those.'

'Good man,' responded Rupert. 'Tell me how to get there.'

Chapter 49

Hélène had packed her bag and was writing a note to explain to Annette that she was going to go back to Belair. She promised that she would not implicate Pierre or Agathe Sauze in her flight, but knew there was nothing she could do to hide Annette's part, as they had both disappeared together.

> *I shan't say where we've been staying, or how we have contrived to live in the weeks since we've been away, but I shall insist that it was you who kept me safe while I was hiding and hope that my family won't blame you for my decision to go. You are the best friend anyone could ever have and whatever happens to me I shan't let you suffer for all the help and affection you've given me.*

She was just reading through what she had written when there was a knock at the door. She froze. Who would be knocking on their door at this time of day? Quietly she crept across the room and listened. The knock came again. Could Simon finally have found her? Had Annette been right about being followed home yesterday evening? Hélène wished she weren't alone in the apartment, but suddenly she realised, if it was Simon Barnier standing on the other side of the door, it would be her chance to deal with him once and for all. She drew a deep breath and turned the key, flinging the door wide, standing with her head high, determined not to be intimidated.

'Hello, my darling girl,' Rupert said. 'May I come in?'

The colour fled her cheeks and for a long moment she simply stared at him, then she stood aside and he walked into the apartment and back into her life.

Rupert made no move to touch her, but followed her into the living room, where she sank into a chair.

'I had your message from Annette,' he said, 'but I couldn't leave without seeing you just once again.' He gave a rueful smile. 'Now I have, would you like me to go?'

'How did you find me?' she asked.

'I'm afraid I had Annette followed last night when she came home. I couldn't bear to be in Paris and not know where you were.'

'I didn't want to see you.'

'I know and I understand, but I couldn't bear not to see you, just one last time.'

'Are you going home again now?' Despite her attempt to be calm and unemotional, Hélène's question sounded wistful.

'Unless you want me to stay,' replied Rupert.

'There's no point,' sighed Hélène. 'I've just decided to go back to Belair and face them out. I won't marry Simon, no matter what they say.'

'Very sensible,' he agreed. 'But will you marry *me*?'

The question caught her off guard. 'Marry you? How can I? Even if I wanted to, my reputation—'

'I don't care a fig about your reputation,' he broke in. 'But will you marry me?'

'Oh, Rupert, how can you ask? After all that's happened, it's far too late.'

'Too late for what?' he said. He took a step towards her. 'You're not married, I'm not married, and I love you. Love you beyond everyone and everything there is in this world. I always have and I always will. What I need to know is if you still love me, just a little, and if you can forgive me for not coming back to find you. At least I should have come back to ask you why you'd changed your mind.' He realised that he was standing over her and lowered himself in to the chair opposite hers.

'I love you, Hélène, I have from the first moment I saw you, and when I left to go back to England, when Justin died, I held you in my arms and I thought you loved me in the same way.' He looked across at her, his eyes intent upon her face. 'Was I wrong, Hélène?'

Unable to speak for fear of weeping, Hélène simply shook her head.

'And do you still?'

'I don't know.' Her words came out on a sob.

'Then I won't say any more for now. If you send me away, I'll go. If you ask me to wait, I'll wait... for as long as it takes.' He pulled a handkerchief from his pocket, handing it to her to mop the tears.

'I've still got the other ones,' she said as she took it and dabbed her cheeks.

Rupert looked confused. 'What other ones?' he asked.

'The hankies you lent me when I was telling you about poor Annette losing her baby.'

'Have you?' Rupert couldn't hide his surprise.

'They're the only things I have of yours,' she said.

'Oh my darling girl,' he said, a break in his voice. 'Everything I have in the world is yours.'

For a long moment neither of them spoke, both too full of emotion, neither knowing what to say. At length Rupert said, 'Well, I'd better go. What will you do now?'

'I don't know,' replied Hélène. 'I was about to go back to Belair, but now I don't know. Do they know you've come back?'

'Who? Your family? I don't know, but I don't think so, unless Simon Barnier has told them.'

'Simon! How does he know?'

Rupert heard the fear in her voice and his lips tightened. 'He saw me yesterday and he told me you were going to be married, very soon.'

'Then he lied to you,' Hélène said sharply. 'He doesn't even know where I am.'

'Darling, I hate to say this, but if I can find you, so can he. Now he knows that I'm here, he's going to be looking even harder. Is there somewhere else you can go?'

'No, only home.'

'Listen, my darling girl, you may not want to marry me, but I'm not going to walk away and leave you here to the mercy of that man.'

'I didn't say I didn't want to,' she said, so softly that for a moment Rupert did not realise what she was saying, 'I just said I thought it was too late.'

For moment he stared at her and then moved swiftly across to kneel beside her chair. He took her hands in his and very gently raised them to his lips. She felt the tenderness in his hands and, looking up into his face, saw such love in his eyes she had to turn away.

'Darling,' he whispered, 'what is it?'

'I... I—' Her voice broke on a sob.

'Tell me.'

'I can't, I'm too ashamed.'

'Hélène, my love. You can tell me anything, anything at all, always and with no shame.'

'I... I couldn't bear Simon to touch me. I hated his hands on my face and his mouth and... and his tongue. And,' she said in a rush before she lost the nerve to say it at all, 'and he said that's what it would be like when we were married, and I knew I couldn't do it. I looked at him and I was afraid and he knew I was afraid... and he liked it.'

'Hélène, I swear to you now, you will never be afraid of me—' Rupert began, but Hélène interrupted him.

'I know that you have to do all that to have children.' Her face flushed red with humiliation. 'So I won't be able to... with you.'

'Hélène, one thing I absolutely promise is that I won't make you do anything you don't like, and I also promise you that nothing between us will be anything like what Simon Barnier wanted to do.'

Encouraged by his gentleness, Hélène took the final plunge and told him about the nightmares that sometimes woke her screaming, and as he listened in silence she told him of the root cause. 'The man who took me... well, Simon was like him. Rupert, I'm afraid of my dreams.'

'If your dreams wake you, I shall be there beside you,' Rupert said softly. 'And the further you get from Simon Barnier, the less they will haunt you. You will always be quite safe with me, I promise you.'

'Will I?' Hélène looked up into his face. 'Annette said that it would be different with someone you love. When I asked her about wanting to marry Pierre, she said it was quite different to what had happened to her before.'

Rupert did not ask what had happened to Annette before,

but he said, 'She was quite right. It is quite different when you love someone as much as I love you.'

'But... but supposing it isn't?'

Rupert got to his feet and said, 'Do you remember that last day, before I went home to England?'

'When we had the picnic? Yes, of course.'

'And when I was leaving, that evening? When I held you in my arms when we said goodbye?'

Hélène nodded. She had held the memory close in the weeks after he'd gone. 'Yes,' she whispered, 'I remember.'

'You didn't mind me holding you close then, did you? Will you let me hold you again, now, before I go?'

Hélène looked up at him as he pulled her gently to her feet, and then as he slipped his arms round her, she buried her face in his shoulder, clinging to him as if her life depended on it. He made no move to kiss her, simply held her close until he felt her relax. Then he let her go and she sank back down into her chair, and he sat on the floor beside her.

'This time,' he said, 'I won't go back to England without you. I can't risk losing you again.'

They sat together as the shafts of dusty sunlight moved slowly across the floor, talking to each other as they had used to.

Hélène told him how they had managed, with the help of Pierre and the generosity of Madame Sauze, to escape from St Etienne and maintain themselves in the little apartment, taking in sewing and working on the stall in the market.

'I had to learn so many things,' she said. 'Things I had never thought about before.'

Rupert told her of all the sadness that had overtaken his family at Pilgrim's Oak, not only the deaths of his father and wife, but of his mother's slide into senility and Fran's perfidy.

He told her everything and she listened to the pain in his voice, holding his hands enfolded in her own.

'Will you be happy to come back there with me?' It was a question he had not dared to ask earlier. She'd said she loved him, she'd said she would marry him, but was he asking too much of her? Could she really be happy living in a house she didn't know, in a country she didn't know, with a family who so far had clearly not wanted her?

'As long as I have you,' she said, 'I will be happy anywhere.'

Sometime later, he said, 'I must go back to the hotel soon and make some plans. I don't like you being here by yourself. I'll wait till Annette comes home, but then I'll have to go.'

At that moment there came a pounding on the door. Rupert got to his feet and, telling Hélène to stay out of sight, went to the front door. He unlocked and opened it to find not Simon Barnier, as he'd half expected, but a young man he'd never seen before.

'Who're you?' demanded the young man.

'I might ask the same of you,' replied Rupert, not moving an inch. Suddenly he heard Hélène's voice.

'Jeannot! Is that you?'

The young man pushed his way past Rupert, who had turned at Hélène's words.

'Yeah. Everything all right, is it? Who's this bloke?'

'Everything's fine, Jeannot. Come in!'

'He already has,' Rupert said drily as he closed and locked the door behind the unexpected visitor and followed him into the apartment.

'Who's this then?' Jeannot jerked his head at Rupert.

'He's the man I'm going to marry,' Hélène replied with glowing eyes.

'Not that Simon bloke what's been looking for you?'

'No, not him. This is Rupert Chalfont. He's English.'

'Oh, him.' Jeannot looked across at Rupert. 'Wasn't you the one what gave her the old heave-ho? Pierre said he was English.'

'Jeannot, why are you here?' Hélène said quickly to deflect any further comments about Rupert.

'I'm here,' he told her, 'because my lad told me that he thought Annette was followed home last night. Silly sod should have told me straight away yesterday an' I'd've come round then, but no, he didn't tell me till just now, did he? So here I am to find out what's going on.'

'I'm afraid it was my man Parker who followed Annette yesterday,' Rupert said. 'I was trying to find Hélène.'

'And now you found her, what you going to do about it? She's supposed to be safe here and not have visitors. That Simon bloke is a nasty bit of work, so I been keeping an eye, know what I mean? I hope *you* wasn't followed!'

'No,' Rupert said, but even as he said it he wondered. When Parker had told him of Annette's address he had come straight here. Had he been followed? He didn't think so – he had seen no one.

'Simon Barnier knows I'm in Paris,' he admitted, 'so we have to be extra careful until I can take Hélène to a place he'll never find her. I've had an idea, but I'll need to set it up.'

'What's this idea then?' demanded Jeannot, and realising that he might need Jeannot's help to carry it through, Rupert told him.

Chapter 50

Rupert left Hélène in the apartment in Jeannot's safe-keeping and made his way back to the hotel, where Parker awaited him.

'I'm going out again,' Rupert told him. 'I need you to watch my back. I can't risk being followed. We'll leave by the rear entrance and you can watch to see if I've picked up a tail.'

Together they went down the iron fire escape at the back of the hotel and Parker waited for a moment in the kitchen yard, watching as Rupert set out, taking the narrow streets that led to the river. Parker lounged along behind him but could see no one paying any attention to him, and when Rupert finally waited before crossing the river, Parker was able to assure him that he had no tail.

As Rupert and Parker left the hotel from the kitchen yard, red-headed André hurried away from the Hotel Montreux to report his day's work to Simon Barnier. André had managed to follow the Englishman unobserved this morning, first to the St Eustache market and then through the streets to Batignolles. He had seen him enter an apartment building, but dared not follow to see which apartment he visited. For a long time he waited, concealed in the tiny alley opposite, ready to follow him when he came out again. Monsieur

Barnier would want to know where else he went. When at last his mark did emerge from the building, André, having taken refuge from the cold in a nearby tabac, nearly missed him, but loitering along behind him was relieved when he realised that the Englishman was returning to the hotel. Now he could report all the Englishman's movements to Monsieur Barnier and collect the promised payment.

When he reached the hotel where Monsieur Barnier lodged, he was told by Eugène that Monsieur was out and was instructed to wait for his return.

It was some hours later that Simon Barnier came back. He had been renewing his acquaintance with Mademoiselle Angélique, and her attentions, costing double the price due to his broken appointment earlier, were so exquisite that he had remained in her care, and that of several of her younger ladies, for the whole afternoon. Could Hélène, even after the training he planned to give her, ever take him to the heights that Mademoiselle Angélique achieved? It would, he decided, be an interesting comparison. As he entered the front door, Eugène told him that André had come back and immediately Simon summoned him to his private parlour.

'I followed the Englishman this morning,' André told him. 'First to the market, where he spoke to some woman working on one of the stalls. Not the one you was looking for, what I followed from Passy.'

Annette? wondered Simon. It would be worth keeping an eye on her in case.

'Anyhow,' continued André, 'he went back to the hotel for a while and then he come out again and went to a street in Batignolles, to an apartment house, with a butcher's shop. I kept watch till he come out, and followed him back to his hotel. Then I come straight here to tell you.'

'You should have come as soon as you discovered where he went this morning,' snapped Simon.

'You told me to follow him wherever he went,' replied André sulkily. 'So I stuck with him, in case he went somewhere else after.'

'Go back to the Montreux tomorrow morning, and stay with him,' said Simon as he paid André. 'I still want to know where he goes and what he does. Understand?'

With promise of more money, André agreed and set off to the nearest bar to drink what he'd been paid so far.

As Simon had hoped, Rupert had led him to Hélène, and by the sound of it to the maid, Annette, as well. Now he had to decide what he was going to do about it. Should he go to the apartment in Batignolles and confront her? Or would that be better coming from her father? Suppose he brought Emile St Clair up to that apartment, a squalid apartment above a butcher's shop in Batignolles – surely he would insist that they married, to avoid a scandal that would affect the prospects of the whole family?

I shall sleep on it, he thought, and make my decision in the morning.

Rupert, once assured that he had no tail, made his way quickly to the British Embassy in the Rue du Faubourg St Honoré, where he gave his name and asked if he might speak with David Bertram. He was shown into a small reception room, where David appeared five minutes later.

'Rupert,' he said as they shook hands. 'Is everything all right?'

'Yes and no,' Rupert said with a smile. 'I'm sorry to come and beard you in your lair, David, but I've got a problem and I thought you might be able to help me sort it out.'

David looked doubtful but said, 'Well, I will if I can, old

friend, but if it's embassy business I haven't much clout here. I'm very much an underling. What's the problem?'

'Well, it's all a bit complicated,' Rupert began, and as briefly as he could he explained the situation. 'She is afraid if she goes back to her family now, she will be forced into marriage against her will, with this man Simon Barnier.'

'I see; a bad business.' David Bertram took out his pocket watch and, glancing at it, continued, 'Look, old chap, I was about to go home. Why don't you come with me and we can discuss all this over dinner? Christine would be delighted to see you and maybe she can think of something to help you.'

Rupert readily agreed. He felt he hadn't made everything as clear as he had wished and perhaps Christine, as a woman, might bring a different perspective to the various problems that needed to be solved.

In this he was not disappointed. Christine listened attentively to his story of their earlier engagement and everything that had happened since Justin's death last year, asking nothing until he fell silent.

'And does she want to renew her engagement to you?' she asked.

'Yes,' replied Rupert. 'She does. I just need somewhere safe for her to stay while I arrange for us to be married.'

'She can't stay at the embassy, if that's what you're after,' said David firmly. 'She's a foreign national.'

'I understand that,' Rupert said, 'but what I wanted to discover was whether it's possible for us to be married in the embassy. Under British law. I assume that we'd be on British soil there.'

'Indeed you would,' agreed David. 'Well,' he went on thoughtfully, 'I suppose it might be possible to bring in an English priest to marry you there. It's not something that would happen very often, but in special circumstances it might be arranged. You'd need a special licence, of course, but you could apply to the ambassador's office for that. But you'd have to find her somewhere else to stay until it can all be arranged.'

'I thought of her staying at one of the large hotels. She will have her maid with her, so it would be quite proper, but she would be easier to find. I'm afraid if he found her Barnier might well put pressure on her to return to him.'

'If that's the case,' Christine Bertram said, 'you're welcome to bring her here, Sir Rupert. It is clear to me that you have to be married before she goes home to her family. She must return as a respectable married woman. That way her reputation will be safe and there could be no question of coercion into marriage with this Monsieur Barnier.'

'It will have to be declared that there is no legal impediment to the marriage,' pointed out David thoughtfully.

'Just bring her here,' his wife said. 'We'll look after her. She will live with us until one way or the other you can be married, at the embassy or at the local Mairie.'

'What about her parents?' asked David. '

'They gave me their consent some months ago,' replied Rupert.

'Hmm,' David grunted. 'I wonder if that still stands!'

'Well, I imagine that they will be only too pleased that she is legally married when she reappears,' Christine Bertram said, 'so that it scotches any scandal, and in the way of these things, the matter of her disappearance will soon be overtaken by some other excitement.'

'When we get back to England it will never be known,' stated Rupert. 'I shall simply be bringing home the bride I married while I was in France.'

They discussed what they were going to do, and when their plans were made, Rupert thanked them for their hospitality and offers of help and returned to his hotel.

There was nothing more he could do until tomorrow, but at least they now had a plan, and if it worked, he and Hélène finally had a future.

Chapter 51

Rupert had an early breakfast and then walked to the market, where he found Annette.

'Is Jeannot still with Hélène?' he asked.

'He said he'd wait till you came for her,' Annette replied.

'I'm going there now,' Rupert told her. 'And you must come with me. We have to maintain the proprieties.'

That made Annette laugh. 'Isn't it a bit late for that?'

'No, it's most important. I've arranged for her to stay with a friend of mine and his wife, and when we get to their home, Hélène must be seen to be accompanied by her maid. And it isn't as if you haven't been living with her in the apartment, is it?'

'Have you told Jeannot what you've got planned?' asked Annette.

'I outlined it to him yesterday, but gave no details. I didn't know then if my idea would work. Now I've got everything arranged, we need to put it into action as soon as we can. We need to get you both to a safe and respectable place while I make arrangements for our wedding.'

'Hélène told me you were going to be married,' Annette said. 'I hope you mean it this time.'

'I meant it last time,' Rupert said ruefully.

'But you got talked out of it.'

'Annette, you know what happened and you know the trouble it's caused, but now I'm going to put it right.' He took her by the shoulders, turning her to look at him. 'You did everything I asked you to before I left. I'm incredibly grateful to both you and Pierre. If you hadn't helped her, she'd be married to that monster now. I'm for ever in your debt, and I shall see that you lose nothing for doing what you did.

'Now I'm asking you to do this one more thing, to stay with Hélène until we can be married and return to Belair as husband and wife.'

Annette looked up at him scornfully. 'And where else would I be?' she demanded, and turning away, she marched ahead of him as they returned towards Batignolles.

When they reached the apartment they found Hélène waiting with Jeannot.

'All set?' asked Jeannot.

'Yes, Hélène and Annette are going to stay in the home of some friends of mine, Monsieur and Madame Bertram. They will stay there until we can be married. I'm hoping that will be in a few days' time, at the British Embassy. Madame Bertram will act as chaperone, and Annette will be with her so that all possible proprieties can be maintained.' He turned back to Jeannot. 'Did you find a fiacre?'

'Yeah, a mate of mine, Joubert, drives one. He'll be here in a while. Very convenient memory he's got. Once he drops you off, he won't have any recollection of where he picked you up or where he's been.'

'Are you coming with us, Jeannot?' Hélène asked.

'Nope!' replied Jeannot. 'You got someone else to look after you now, ain't you? Three's a crowd.'

'But I'll see you again, won't I?'

'Never know your luck,' grinned Jeannot. 'When you're back in the Avenue Ste Anne. I look in on Pierre from time to time.' He added, 'That's if he's allowed callers at the door once he's married?' And he gave her a broad wink as he saw Annette's cheeks flush pink.

Ignoring this interchange, Rupert was watching from the window for the arrival of Joubert in his fiacre. As he stared along the street he suddenly saw a movement in the mouth of an alley a little further along. A young man he'd seen in the Hotel Montreux stable yard, a young man with a halo of red hair. Redhead! No doubt about it. Rupert drew back from the window and murmured to Jeannot, 'Come and have a look.'

Jeannot peered down into the street.

'There, in that alleyway, there's... somebody. I think he was at the Montreux the other day. A bloke with red hair.'

'I see him,' said Jeannot, 'and I know him, too. Caught him following Hélène when she was fool enough to try an' go visiting her ma. Don't worry, I'll deal with him. Look, here comes Joubert. Once you're downstairs, quick as you like into the cab. If Redhead makes any trouble he'll wish he hadn't.'

'Come on,' Rupert said to the two girls as he picked up the two valises. 'Straight out and into the cab. I'm right behind you.'

'I told him to drive on soon as you're all inside,' Jeannot told Rupert. 'Once you're out of sight you can tell him where you want to go.'

'What do I pay him?' asked Rupert.

'Nuthink!' answered Jeannot. 'He owes me!'

'So do I, now,' said Rupert.

"S'all right.' Jeannot grinned. 'I'll remember.'

★

André had known he was in trouble when he woke up that morning with a raging thirst and a sledgehammer pounding his brain. When he opened his eyes, he found himself naked in his own bed, but with little recollection of how he had come to be there. He'd had a drink in a bar, he remembered that, and there'd been a girl. He'd bought her a drink too, but as they passed the evening together, working their way through his wages, things became rather hazy. He was alone now, but he was pretty sure the girl had come back to his room with him. He hauled himself out of bed and crossed to the jug of water standing on the table, and took a long swallow. His head continued to pound, and he sat back down on the bed. His clothes were in a heap on the floor and as he dragged on his trousers, he put his hand into his pocket, feeling for the last of his cash, and found it empty.

Shit! he thought. The bitch has cleaned me out!

As he struggled with his shirt, he heard the church clock at the end of the street strike nine and his heart sank. He should have been back outside the Montreux hours ago, watching for the Englishman to go out again. He'd have missed him by now for sure. Not daring to return to Monsieur Barnier and admit that he'd overslept and awoken with a hangover, he drank another long draught of water. With his money gone, he'd have to go back to the street in Batignolles. He could always tell Barnier that he'd followed the Englishman there again this morning and hope he was believed.

André had hurried as fast as his hangover would let him and had only just arrived and taken his position in the alley when a fiacre turned the corner into the lane. He wondered what a four-wheeled cab was doing in such a shabby little street, and then to his surprise it pulled up outside the butcher's shop, blocking his line of sight to the apartment house door. He scurried out from his hiding place in time to catch sight of two people already settling into the cab before the blinds were drawn and they were hidden from view. They were followed by a man with a valise in each hand, getting in and slamming the door behind him. At once the driver whipped up the horse and the cab moved away, causing André to jump back into the alley. At first the street was so narrow that the fiacre made slow progress and André, setting off after it, managed to keep up, but as it reached a junction, the road widened and the cab picked up speed, leaving him choking in the cloud of dust it left behind. He stood gasping as he watched it round a corner and disappear, with no idea of where it was going, or indeed who was in it. What was he going to tell Barnier? It wasn't his fault that they'd driven away in a fiacre. He had tried to follow, but it was, of course, impossible on foot. Still, he was pretty sure that the man he'd seen climb in was the Englishman he'd been following much of yesterday; but who were the other two? He wasn't even certain that they were women. Was one of them the girl Monsieur Barnier was looking for? If so, she was gone.

He turned back the way he had come, considering what to do next. Should he continue to keep watch on the apartment, just in case there was something further to see, or should he go straight back to Barnier and tell him what he'd seen? He needed something to report or there'd be no more cash.

He was just deciding to go to the Pension Marguerite when a figure emerged from the alley and André suddenly found himself being dragged back out of sight, his arm twisted so high up his back that he screeched in pain.

'Shut it!' said a voice in his left ear. 'And listen to me. I got a few questions for you. Answer them straight and I'll let you go. Right?' There was another sharp jerk on André's arm and he screamed again. 'Right?' repeated the voice.

'Right!' croaked André. 'Right!'

'Who're you working for?' demanded the voice. 'Barnier?'

'Barnier!' agree André.

'And where will I find Monsieur Barnier?'

'Pension Marguerite,' squeaked André. 'Rue des Loups.'

'There we go then.' The pressure went from his arm and he was given a hefty push that sent him staggering into the midden that ran down the middle of the alley. When he'd struggled to his feet, covered in the effluent of the street drain, and looked about him, he was alone. The alley was empty.

Chapter 52

Sir Rupert and Lady Chalfont were married a week later in the embassy chapel by the ambassador's chaplain in the presence of Mr and Mrs David Bertram and Madame Annette Dubois and Mr Peter Parker. The arrangements had been far more straightforward than Rupert had feared. David Bertram had made the necessary enquires and all they were asked for was a declaration that there was no impediment to their marriage. Rupert was declared a widower and Hélène, spinster.

In the few days Hélène lived with the Bertrams, Christine told her a good deal about the British way of life. She also suggested that Hélène should practise her English. Mademoiselle Corbine had done her best, and Hélène had the basics, but when Christine realised how limited Hélène's grasp of the language was, she only spoke to her in English from then on. She also took the question of Hélène's wardrobe in hand and, using her influence with her own dressmaker, managed to ensure that Hélène had a suitable outfit in which to be married and another for travelling. At Hélène's insistence, Annette was also provided with new clothes. Though bought ready-made, the two dresses and the skirt and bodice were far better than anything Annette had ever owned before.

After the short ceremony, they left the embassy hand in hand as husband and wife. Christine had insisted on providing a celebratory meal for when they returned to their apartment.

'It's not going to be much of a wedding day for the poor girl if we don't celebrate together and have a glass of champagne to toast your happiness.'

Rupert agreed. How could he not when the Bertrams had been so kind in looking after Hélène?

As the evening began to draw in, Rupert took his bride to his suite in the Hotel Montreux. He had ordered Jacques Rocher to fill it with flowers and to serve a quiet supper for the two of them. A fire had been lit against a chill in the air and they sat together in front of its warmth as the darkness deepened outside.

'Happy?' asked Rupert as Hélène nestled against him.

'Mmm,' she sighed. 'Very.'

That night they slept in each other's arms. Rupert made no effort to consummate the marriage, simply held Hélène close until, unafraid, she drifted off into sleep.

The following morning, when they had been served breakfast in their suite, they prepared to travel to St Etienne. Rupert had hired a carriage and a coachman to drive them, so that when they arrived at Belair it would be in some style. The journey by road would take two days and they would have to pass a night at an inn on the way, but to Rupert's mind that was no bad thing, enabling Hélène to become less afraid of the marriage bed before arriving at Belair. Annette was travelling with them, happy enough to return to her place as Hélène's maid, and longing to be back with Pierre.

Rupert and Hélène's second night together, though in a rather lumpy bed at the inn, passed as peacefully as the first, with Rupert making no physical demands on her and

Hélène comfortably asleep in his arms. Annette, in a small side room, lay wondering what sort of reception she was going to get when she arrived at Belair. She was sure that even if they welcomed Hélène back with open arms, they would blame her for going with her. Well, she decided, she didn't care; Pierre would be there waiting for her. Would he really marry her and would everything be different with him, as she'd told Hélène?

They arrived in St Etienne early the next afternoon. Rupert stopped the coach at Le Coq d'Argent and bespoke a suite for them for that night. He was aware that their arrival at Belair might not be as welcome as it might once have been. He had noticed Hélène growing increasingly tense the nearer they got to the village and he wanted to be able to remove her from any unpleasantness if necessary.

It was Louise who saw the carriage first. She stared wide-eyed as she realised who was in it.

'Maman,' she shrieked, bursting into her mother's parlour. 'Maman, Hélène's come home. She's in a coach and she's with Rupert!'

Rosalie stared at her in dismay. With Rupert? Surely the silly girl hadn't run all the way to England to find him, a married man who'd deserted her?

'Calm down,' she instructed her daughter. 'Stop shouting while I go and find your father.' She hurried down the stairs and found Emile in his study.

'Hélène's come home,' she told him. 'Rupert Chalfont has brought her home.'

'She shall not enter this house,' Emile stated. 'She has disgraced us all and is no longer a daughter of mine.'

'She will always be your daughter, whether you approve of her or not,' said Rosalie firmly, 'and she will always be a daughter of mine. We lost her once before, I will not turn her away and lose her again.'

'And what's she doing with that man?' Emile demanded as if Rosalie hadn't spoken. 'A married man bringing her here. Has she no shame? I will not see her.'

'They are at the door,' Rosalie told him. 'You may stay in here, Emile, but I shall go and welcome her home. Where's your charity? Haven't you heard of the prodigal son?' And with that she swept out of the room to meet her daughter at the front door.

As soon as the carriage drew up and the steps were lowered, Rupert sprang out and handed down his bride. Annette jumped down behind them and without a moment's hesitation disappeared in search of Pierre.

Rosalie waited for Hélène under the portico, watching as she took Rupert's arm.

'Madame,' he said, pausing at the bottom of the steps, 'may I present my wife, Lady Chalfont?'

'Your wife!' Rosalie's hand flew to her mouth. 'You're married?'

'Indeed, madame, two days ago at the British Embassy, Hélène did me the honour of becoming my wife.'

'But... but I thought you were married,' stammered Rosalie.

'Perhaps we might come inside, madame,' Rupert replied smoothly, 'and we can explain what's happened.'

Rosalie looked down at Hélène. So far she'd said nothing, but there was the bloom of happiness on her cheeks, a brightness in her eyes as she stood, her fingers resting on her husband's arm. Now she said, 'Rupert and I are married, Maman. I have come home to tell you this and to say that we shall be returning to his home in England in the near future. I wanted to see you all before I went. Can we not come indoors and talk?'

At that moment Emile appeared beside his wife at the door and stared down at them.

'Well, miss,' he said. 'What makes you think you're welcome in this house?'

'My husband and I have come to visit you before we leave for England,' Hélène said, apparently unmoved by his anger.

'Your husband!' snorted Emile. 'What nonsense is this?'

'No nonsense at all,' replied Rupert. 'Hélène is now Lady Chalfont of Pilgrim's Oak, Somerset, England.'

'I gave no permission for her to marry.'

'And none was asked for,' answered Rupert, 'but we are indeed married.'

'And what about Monsieur Barnier, may I ask? Hélène is still engaged to be married to him.'

'Hélène made it clear she had changed her mind about her marriage with him some weeks ago,' Rupert said.

'And I thought you'd changed your mind about marrying Hélène,' Emile blustered. 'What do you say to that, young man? You wrote and told her you were married to someone else, so how can you now be married to her? Answer me that!'

'I did indeed marry someone else,' admitted Rupert, 'but unfortunately my wife died. Until the day before yesterday I was a widower; now I am the husband of a woman I've never stopped loving from the first day I saw her.'

'Poof, all this love stuff. What about duty? Eh? What about that?'

'Papa,' Hélène said, her voice clear and strong, 'I think it very undignified to be discussing all this on the doorstep. If you won't allow me to cross your threshold, we shall leave at once and we shall not return. It's your decision.'

'Of course you can come in,' said Rosalie before Emile could overcome his surprise at the way Hélène had addressed him. 'We shall go into the drawing room.' And turning to the butler, who was hovering in the background, she said, 'Didier, please bring us some refreshment. I'm sure Lady Chalfont is tired after her journey.'

Outmanoeuvred, Emile turned on his heel and disappeared indoors. Rosalie held out her hands to Hélène, who ran up the steps and into her mother's embrace.

'My dearest child,' Rosalie murmured. 'Thank God you're safe.'

'I'm sorry I ran away, Maman,' Hélène said softly, 'but I couldn't marry Simon.'

'I know,' replied her mother as she led her indoors. 'We can talk later. Don't worry, your papa will come round to your marriage eventually, but in the meantime the less he knows about your time in Paris, the better. It will be easier for him, for all of us, simply to say that you are now married to Sir Rupert Chalfont and will be moving to his estate in England.' She turned to Rupert and extended her hand. 'I'm glad Hélène has come home a respectable married woman, Sir Rupert. It is something my husband will come to accept in time. For my part, I know she will be far happier with you than she would ever have been with Monsieur Barnier.'

Didier closed the front door behind them and went to the kitchen, where the news of Miss Hélène's return was already the excitement of the day. Annette and Agathe were closeted in the housekeeper's room.

As a tray of refreshments was being prepared for the drawing room, a horseman came galloping up the drive. As he reached the front door he flung himself from the saddle and, running up the steps, pounded on the door. Moments later

Didier, opening in answer to the knock, was pushed aside as Simon Barnier strode into the hall and walked straight through the open drawing room door to confront the family gathered there.

'Well,' he cried, 'I thought at first my eyes must have deceived me when I saw your daughter, my fiancée, driving into St Etienne with that man. Flaunting herself after she ran away to live with him in Paris.'

'Monsieur Barnier,' Rupert interrupted his tirade. 'May I present my wife, Lady Chalfont?'

'You can't have married her, as you're married already,' snapped Simon. 'Living in sin with her, more like, with the pretence of marriage.' He turned on Rosalie. 'I found out where she's been living, in a poky little apartment in Batignolles, above a butcher's shop, of all things, while he' – he jabbed a finger at Rupert – 'he has been staying in the Hotel Montreux, entertaining her and who knows who else there. An adulterous English "milor" whose wife is safely out of the way in England. Well, "milor", you're welcome to her. I wouldn't touch such soiled goods. No one of good character will want her now, when they hear how she's been living. And when you move on she'll be left with her reputation in tatters and it will be too late, far too late, to retrieve it. I wish you joy of her!'

To Rosalie's amazement, Rupert smiled, and though his smile didn't reach his eyes he made Simon a small bow and said, 'Thank you, Monsieur Barnier, we are delighted to have your blessing on our union.' He reached for Hélène's hand and added, 'It means so much to us both!'

Simon glared at him. 'Well, it will be interesting to see how well you're received into society, for you can have no doubt that this whole sordid affair will soon be common knowledge, and I, for one, will never associate with anyone from this family again! Dross from the gutter!' And with that Simon turned and strode out of the room.

Rupert followed him into the hall and stayed him with a hand on his arm. 'A moment, Monsieur Barnier.'

Simon shook his hand away as if it were a wasp. 'I have nothing to say to you, sir.'

'Well, I have something to say to you, monsieur, and I'd be obliged if you would listen. It is to your advantage. I've a message for you from a certain Mademoiselle Angélique.' Simon's eyes widened but he said nothing. 'She says to tell you how much she and her young ladies are looking forward to entertaining you again, next time you're in Paris and staying at the Pension Marguerite. She asks that you recommend her to all your friends when they're visiting the city.'

Simon froze and then gave an awkward laugh. 'I have no idea what you're talking about.'

'Haven't you? Well, never mind, but I'll deliver the second part of her message anyway. She said something about a dead child? She said to tell you she will keep her mouth shut... if you do. That mean anything to you?'

For a moment Simon gave him a look of pure hatred and then he flung open the door and disappeared down the steps.

Rupert watched him go with a faint smile and thought, Well done, Jeannot.

Rupert and Hélène spent that night at Le Coq d'Argent, but the next day they moved into Belair.

'For what will everyone think,' asked Rosalie, 'if you continue to stay there? Let us give the gossips nothing to chew on. And anyway, I'm sure you'd be more comfortable here.'

She was right, and as Emile got used to seeing his daughter and Rupert together every day, he found it more and more difficult to maintain his disapproval.

Once the couple had clearly been accepted at Belair, the Barrineaux, despite some reluctance on the part of Suzanne, followed their example and Hélène was able to be reunited with Clarice and Lucas and meet her brand-new niece, Céleste.

Rupert, remembering his promise to Madame Barrineau senior, took the opportunity to pay her a second visit. When he was shown into her apartment, she was seated by the window. She did not get up, but greeted him with a smile and said, 'Well, now, I hear you got yourself into another scrape, young man.'

Rupert returned her smile and replied, 'And got myself out of it again, madame.'

'So I heard, and a good thing too. Young Hélène St Clair deserved better of you.' She fixed him with an eagle eye for a moment and added, 'Let us hope there will be no more scrapes in the future, monsieur.'

'That I can assure you, madame,' answered Rupert. 'My love and my life are hers from now on.'

Recognising he spoke with complete sincerity, Madame Barrineau nodded and replied, 'Just as it should be. What has gone before will be a nine days' wonder and soon forgotten.'

The old lady was right, and over the next three weeks Hélène was accepted back into society as the respectable wife of an English baronet. There was, of course, speculation, whispers behind hands, nods and winks, but Hélène behaved with the same dignity as before. She walked into receiving rooms, this time on her husband's arm, with a smile on her lips, her chin held high, and together they faced down anyone who might suggest that there had been anything improper in her being away. No one mentioned Simon Barnier, who had returned to Paris and not been home since.

Once they had settled in at Belair, Rosalie invited Hélène into her parlour for a long talk. She accepted that Hélène had fled because she was truly afraid, but when she had heard Simon's description of the apartment where Hélène had lived, she had been horrified.

'How did you come to be living in such a place?' she asked. 'Who looked after you?'

Hélène ignored the first question but answered the second readily enough. 'We looked after ourselves, Maman. Annette taught me to cook and to iron and take care of the place. She found work in the market and brought me sewing from a nearby dressmaker.'

'You took in sewing!' cried Rosalie.

'It's the only thing of any use that I knew how to do,' pointed out Hélène. 'Annette was far more use.'

'But taking in sewing!'

'We had to earn enough to keep us, Maman.'

'But how did you find the apartment?' persisted Rosalie.

'Annette knew of it from a friend,' was all Hélène would answer.

Of the actual escape she would say nothing more than, 'We went to the station and caught the early train.'

It was clear to Rosalie that Hélène was going to tell her nothing more and she decided to leave things at that. Christine Bertram had been right. Rosalie was just grateful that Hélène was safely home, respectably married. The least said about her time in Paris was the soonest forgotten. What she suspected and what she knew were two different things, and she shared neither of them with her husband.

There was a stir in the servants' quarters when Pierre

announced that he and Annette were going to be married. Emile had been for turning Annette out into the street for the part she had played in Hélène's disgrace, but when Rupert gently pointed out that as Hélène's personal maid she worked for him now, there was nothing he could do. Emile had no wish to lose Pierre as his coachman – he had been in their employ for more than ten years – so he had to accept that either Annette remained as Pierre's wife, or he would be looking for a new coachman.

'They could have the empty cottage on the home farm,' suggested Rosalie. 'Pierre could come in daily, as could Annette if she wanted to work here. If they're getting married she won't be going with Hélène and Rupert when they go to England.'

'Hmm,' grunted Emile. He'd been outmanoeuvred again. 'If that's what you think best,' he said and returned to his study.

Hélène also spent some time with Madame Sauze, taking coffee with her in the housekeeper's parlour.

'I wanted to thank you,' Hélène said. 'Without your apartment I could never have gone. I'd be married to Simon Barnier by now.'

'It was nothing,' Agathe told her, 'though it would be better for me if your parents did not know.'

'They'll hear nothing from me,' promised Hélène. 'I owe you so much. It's the second time you've rescued me.'

'You owe me nothing. Your family gave Annette shelter when she needed it and took us both in when we had nowhere else to go. That is something that can never be repaid. And now she and Pierre are going to be married, Annette's future will be a happy one.' She looked at Hélène, sitting comfortably in the armchair on the other side of the fireplace. How will she manage at this place, Pilgrim's Oak? she wondered. 'Will you mind her staying here, rather than going to England with you?' she asked.

'I shall miss her, of course. I couldn't have had a better friend these last months, but her place is here with Pierre. He's her future, not me. I shall see them married before we leave and wish them both every happiness together. They deserve it.'

The day they set out for England at last, the whole family had gathered to bid them farewell. Georges and Sylvie and their children had come from Versailles, Lucas and Clarice from Montmichel with the baby, Céleste. Hélène hugged them each in turn. But when she had done, she climbed, without a backward glance, into the carriage that was waiting to take them back to Paris. As they were driven down the drive, Rupert reached for her hand and Hélène gripped his tightly. It wasn't easy leaving Belair and it wouldn't be easy arriving at Pilgrim's Oak either. Rupert had written of his marriage and his sister Frances had replied to say that she was moving herself and her mother into the Dower House, leaving Pilgrim's Oak for them alone.

Hélène knew she would miss her family. She would miss Annette, who was now married to Pierre and installed in the cottage on the estate. And she would miss Madame Sauze, who for the second time had come to her aid when she was in trouble.

Hélène had unshed tears in her eyes as she left Belair behind, but she knew that whatever the future held for them, Rupert and she had each other and with Rupert she would be safe.

Epilogue

The Times newspaper

Births
Chalfont
On 31st January 1879 to Hélène (née St Clair) and Sir
Rupert Chalfont Bt, a son, Justin Philip.

About the Author

DINEY COSTELOE is the author of twenty-five novels, several short stories, and many articles and poems. She has three children and seven grandchildren, so when she isn't writing, she's busy with family. She and her husband divide their time between Somerset and West Cork.